People of Metal II

Just Smart Enough

Robert Snyder

Black Rose Writing | Texas

©2020 by Robert Snyder
All rights reserved. No part of this book may be reproduced, stored in a retrieval system or transmitted in any form or by any means without the prior written permission of the publishers, except by a reviewer who may quote brief passages in a review to be printed in a newspaper, magazine or journal.

The author grants the final approval for this literary material.

First printing

This is a work of fiction. Names, characters, businesses, places, events, and incidents are either the products of the author's imagination or used in a fictitious manner. Any resemblance to actual persons, living or dead, or actual events is purely coincidental.

ISBN: 978-1-68433-485-8
PUBLISHED BY BLACK ROSE WRITING
www.blackrosewriting.com

Printed in the United States of America
Suggested Retail Price (SRP) $21.95

People of Metal II is printed in Book Antiqua

*As a planet-friendly publisher, Black Rose Writing does its best to eliminate unnecessary waste to reduce paper usage and energy costs, while never compromising the reading experience. As a result, the final word count vs. page count may not meet common expectations.

For Ann

People of Metal II

"Everything happens for a reason."
— Ancient proverb

Chapter 1
Encounter

Planet Tau Ceti f
Tau Ceti star system
Earth year 2652

The probe vehicle moved slowly across the planet's surface toward the setting star. The video that it sent home to Earth, almost twelve light years distant, created an instant sensation when it finally arrived. Light and other energy from the star had painted the sky and the fluffy clouds in lush shades of purple and pink as it passed through the planet's atmosphere.

Several local days later, something else happened while the probe was patrolling, but it went unnoticed by the vehicle's camera, and none of its other instruments picked it up. The vehicle had just entered an odd stretch of terrain that, to an Earthling, would have looked like a patterned surface of small, smooth stones that a roller had flattened. Moments later, the stones, or whatever they were, coalesced under the vehicle and carried it forward to where the patch of odd terrain ended and deposited the vehicle there. Had the camera been aimed in that direction, it would have caught the "stones" regrouping themselves into the pattern they'd exhibited before the vehicle arrived.

Chapter 2
The Delaneys

Human Mind Project
Massachusetts Institute of Technology
Cambridge, Massachusetts
April 2067

On a quiet Sunday afternoon in 2067, Graham Gordon brought his wife Mollie to his MIT workshop and copied both their minds. The following morning, he had the sleeping e-brains installed in state-of-the-art android bodies.

Gordon used a piece of electrical cord to tie a garden scoop to the left wrist of the body of "his" Machine.

"It has sentimental value," he told a technician who was standing nearby. "No worries. It's a garden scoop, not a weapon."

According to the cover story Gordon gave his assistant, Elaine Fitzsimons, the Machines had the minds of his and Mollie's dear friends, Harvey and Ellen Delaney. "I brought them here yesterday and copied their minds myself," he told her. "The techs just finished installing the e-brains. Please send this to the bursar's office." It was a cashier's check payable to MIT on behalf of one Harvey Delaney. "It's a donation. The Delaneys have already manumitted their Machines."

Gordon removed a flash drive from his shoulder bag.

"Their deeds of manumission are on this drive, for our records."

"That's odd," said Fitzsimons. "Manumission was what they called it when a slave owner freed a slave."

"I know," said Gordon. "The lawyers came up with it. Because they're property, someone will always be deemed to own them if they aren't freed. The Delaneys would be the obvious choice, or their heirs, or the State of Massachusetts if no one else has a claim to them. Manumission has an ugly connotation, but in this case it's a term of respect because it recognizes their humanity. If Machines were mere inanimate property, the word wouldn't apply. You can't manumit a refrigerator."

Fitzsimons chuckled. "I guess not. So your friends had you make Machines for them, then immediately set them free. What will they do when we wake them up?"

"They'll stay here in sleep mode until long after Harvey and Ellen are gone. They couldn't visualize being around beings that had copies of their own minds. "

"It does sound rather creepy," said Fitzsimons. "Suddenly, you'd literally be talking to yourself, to another you. It's hard enough living with *one* self," she quipped.

Gordon smiled. "I agreed to let them stay here until April 1, 2140, which was the date they picked. April 1 is Harvey's birthday. When you have a chance, please post a note in the tickler file."

"I'll take care of it right now."

"Thanks," said Gordon. "Just so you know, workers will be coming in later this week to install backup generators to protect the stored Machines against power outages."

"Why?" Fitzsimons asked.

"At some point, their originals will die and their minds won't be replaceable," said Gordon. "It's an ethical issue."

As a precaution to throw off anyone who might try to find his and Mollie's Machines, Gordon made a fictitious entry in Project records to the effect that copies of his and Mollie's minds had been installed in Machines named Charles and Bonnie Williamson. His and

Mollie's *actual* Machines were named Brandon and Alice Delaney, to link them to the fictional Delaneys, and placed in storage.

• • • • •

Graham and Mollie died in 2089 and 2090, respectively.

Pursuant to the instructions Gordon's assistant had placed on file, Brandon and Alice were awakened on April 1, 2140 and were allowed to leave the Human Mind Project after receiving the psychological counseling that newly awakened Machines normally received to help them get their bearings and understand who and what they were. "They'll know intellectually what they are because they'll have our minds, but I've been told that it feels a bit strange at first," Graham had explained to Mollie.

Before leaving the Project offices, Brandon borrowed scissors and freed the gardening scoop from his wrist, and he and Alice walked directly to the spot in a nearby park where Graham had buried a package. Walking came quite naturally to them, and talking, just as the counselor had assured them.

"This is the spot," said Brandon. "It doesn't appear to have been disturbed."

He knelt down and prepared to begin digging.

"Wait," said Alice. "Someone could call the police if they see you digging... Let's come back later when no one's around."

The park and the sidewalks alongside it were crowded with people, including a fair number of Machines.

"Good point," said Brandon. "It'd be a minor offense, but the cops might have questions. Let's go for a walk instead."

The nearby residential neighborhood in which Graham and Mollie had lived was unrecognizable. The houses all had one or more outdoor walls made of opaque colored glass.

"They're probably one-way glass," Alice guessed.

They walked a while longer before slowly making their way back to the park. No one was around, so Brandon set to work digging up the waterproof valise Graham had buried there. It contained an amount of cash; Certificates of Origin for Alice and Brandon Delaney; a sheaf of papers containing handwritten technical specifications; a brokerage statement for an account in the name of a trust for the benefit of Brandon and Alice Delaney; and a small electronic device whose battery needed recharging. A note from Graham explained that, upon the death of Graham or Mollie, whichever came last, all of the cash and securities in the Gordon estate would have been transferred to the trust account, together with the proceeds from the sale of the Gordon home; and that, under the terms of the trust, on April 1, 2140—"the date you are reading this"—the trustee would have transferred all of the trust's assets to a new brokerage account at the same firm in the names of Brandon and Alice Delaney as joint tenants with the right of survivorship. Later, after they'd recharged the electronic device, they would find the same message stored there, along with old photos of Graham and Mollie and digital copies of all of the papers Graham had placed in the valise.

"Well, that's that," said Brandon.

"I wonder when they passed," said Alice.

"Decades ago, I imagine," said Brandon. "We'll find out."

"I hope they didn't suffer," said Alice.

"Me too."

"Well, we're on our own," said Alice.

It was a bit more complicated than that, Brandon knew from Graham's conversations with his Machines, but Brandon thought it best to let Alice discover this for herself.

They walked to the river and crossed the bridge to Boston.

"It's amazing," said Brandon. "We woke up, and we knew each other's names and our own."

"It sure is," Alice agreed.

"So how do you like your body?"

"It's a lot more physical than I expected. I can feel the wind and the sun on my face and arms. I can feel my arms and legs moving and my feet making contact with the sidewalk. I feel like a live person. I can touch things, and my eyesight and hearing are way better than Mollie's were."

"They had old-people bodies," said Brandon. "We don't, and we never will."

"One thing *is* kind of weird, though," said Alice. "Not breathing. It's not uncomfortable, just weird."

"I agree," said Brandon. "I imagine we'll get used to that too."

"I'm sure we will."

"Let me remind you what Graham told Mollie about the way this works," said Brandon. "Even though you're starting out with a copy of Mollie's mind, you're a separate person, as I'm sure you've already realized. Going forward, you'll do and become whatever you want and form your own opinions and attitudes. That's how Machines described it to Graham."

"I feel that," said Alice. "Everything in my mind right now, except for the last twenty or thirty minutes, is from Mollie, but I know I'm not her. I'm my own person, as you say."

"We're our own selves," said Brandon, nodding.

"Yep," said Alice. "Wow, I don't recognize a thing. And the Machines, they're everywhere. They obviously caught on big time."

"It's a different world," said Brandon. "I'm glad we decided to have them wait to wake us up. We need to figure out what all went on while we were sleeping. Let's see if we can find a store and get ourselves some digital devices."

"If stores still exist."

Stores did still exist, for food and products like clothing and electronics that people would want to try on or check out before buying them. After passing a food store and several clothing shops, they finally found a store that sold digital equipment.

"Listen," said Alice after they'd gone inside and heard people talking. "The language has changed more than I would have expected. It's like a new dialect but it's close enough for us to understand it. I'm hearing a lot of foreign words."

"The influx of immigrants must have continued," Brandon guessed.

A salesperson approached them and said something.

"She wants to know if she can help us," said Alice.

"I got that," said Brandon. "Hello. I'm sorry but our English is not so good. We're from Yugoslavia. But if you don't talk too fast we'll be able to understand. We're looking for the latest equipment for going online. Online still exists, yes?"

"Yes," said the woman.

"Perfect," said Brandon. "We're not familiar with the latest technology. All we have at home is obsolete junk. Perhaps you could show us some of the latest devices."

They bought two of the three devices they were shown, using some of the cash from the valise, and the salesperson patiently explained how everything worked. From what they could see, written American English hadn't changed much at all.

"Let's go sit on that bench and run some searches," said Brandon, indicating a group of benches in a small park across the street from the tech store. Their first search was for the dates and circumstances of their originals' deaths. They'd died peacefully.

"It feels strange," said Alice. "They're gone, yet their minds are here inside us, working away like they're still alive."

"I know, I'm experiencing it myself," said Brandon. "But it's nothing to be alarmed about. It's part of who and what we are. One of Graham's first Machines described it to him. She had a mind copied from a Harvard professor. She said she felt a combination of cognitive dissonance and a blurred initial sense of personal identity. She told Graham that within an hour or so of thinking your own thoughts and experiencing your own life, you sort of settle in and take possession of your mind, so to speak, and the feeling goes away."

"That's good to hear."

Working side by side on their devices, they were surprised to learn that the United States and China had formed and implemented a joint venture to develop Machines equipped with e-brains copied from the minds of workers in every human vocation in every country in the world.

"Wow," said Brandon. "It must have been a colossal undertaking."

"It's still going on," said Alice. "It says here that Graham was a key player in getting it started."

They learned that when the joint venture finished its developmental work, it had practically given away e-brains for the various trades and professions—and the plans and specs for bodies to go with them—to manufacturers who'd been vetted for ties to organized crime or rogue states. First made available in the U.S. in 2085, the Machines were comparatively rare until technological breakthroughs and competition had reduced their cost. By 2140, Brandon and Alice learned, they were a substantial component of the workforce in the U.S. and elsewhere.

"Their impact on economic productivity has been huge," said Alice.

"Biologicals evidently have no problem working alongside us, according to this post," said Brandon. "They find us fascinating. Every year since 2110, Machines have been included in *People* magazine's most intriguing people list."

"That's good to know, if it's true," said Alice. "I was wondering how they'd see us."

As far as they could tell, none of the biologicals they passed on the sidewalk paid any particular attention to them or to other Machines.

"It says here that the U.S.-China partnership has emphasized that the Machines would be used to augment rather than supplant the world's human workforce. The combined Machine and biological human workforce would close the gap between the goods and services the world population *needs*, and the amount of goods and services that the world economy could produce with just biological workers. In other words, their goal is to eliminate scarcity and human suffering once and for all."

"Good for them," said Alice.

"They seem to be well on the way toward accomplishing that," said Brandon. "Who would have imagined that such a thing would ever be even remotely possible? Human suffering and want were a given."

"Graham would be proud," said Alice.

"He is," said Brandon. "I mean, yes, he would be," he quickly added. "I'm proud on his behalf. Rightly so."

"I'm glad we aren't being used to *replace* biological workers," said Alice. "I'm gonna find out what the deal is with these glass houses."

When she looked it up, she learned that it was one-way glass, just as she'd surmised. The high-tech glass walls gave those inside the option to choose floor-to-ceiling outdoor views. Smaller "windows" could be created by drawing on a control pad.

"Frank Lloyd Wright would have loved it," said Alice, referring to a famous 20th-century American architect whose work Mollie had admired. "It would make the inside of the house feel like part of its external environment without sacrificing privacy."

Brandon and Alice spent the next two days walking around Cambridge and Boston taking in their new world. After convincing a skeptical night clerk that yes, they absolutely did want a room for two nights, they spent those nights in a Cambridge hotel room watching TV and pondering what their next step might be. Graham and Mollie had set the Delaneys up with the means to do virtually anything they wanted.

As it happened, the decision was a snap when they finally got around to discussing it. Mollie would study neuroscience at MIT and Brandon would study art at the Museum School. It was Mollie's idea.

"I actually had the same thought," Brandon told her, "but I wasn't sure you'd go for it."

"I most definitely do," said Alice.

During her senior year at the Museum School, Mollie had audited an introductory neuroscience course at MIT in the hope of gaining a better understanding of the scientific breakthroughs her husband and his team were making. Looking back, Mollie compared the experience to that of a six-year-old learning to read, or an adult learning a second language. Suddenly, the technical terms her husband used to describe his work weren't gibberish. She understood them, albeit at a very basic level, and Graham took pains to build on what Mollie learned. One day, when time permitted, she planned to go back to MIT to learn more.

Graham had felt the same way about Mollie's painting. It was brilliant and wildly original. Inspired by her example, he'd taken an art course when they were high school juniors and loved it, especially after his teacher assured him that he had a natural talent. Being young and impressionable, he'd taken the kind lady's encouragement at face value and had never forgotten it. He was determined to take it up again, if only as a hobby, when time permitted.

There was an old saying: "The trouble is, we always think there's time." Biological humans were always short of time. But the old saying no longer applied when people became Machines. People of metal had all the time in the world.

Alice helped Brandon create sample artwork of sufficient quality to secure his admission into the Museum School, and she applied for admission to MIT, which admitted her and awarded her a full scholarship under its diversity program. The Delaneys rented a small studio apartment in which to spend their evenings and nights.

Brandon was amazed at the speed and apparent ease with which Alice picked up neuroscience. Mollie had aced all of her high school math and science classes easily, but they hadn't seemed all that important to her. "Art is my life, I can't imagine doing anything else," she'd told Graham early in their relationship. Yet here Alice was, killing it. This was a side of Mollie that Graham had never seen.

"Math is easy," Alice told Brandon, "and if you can do math, you can do science. Math is the language of science, just as line, light, form and color are the language of art."

She said neuroscience was one of the most interesting subjects she'd ever studied.

"But they're *way* beyond where they were when Mollie audited Neuroscience 101," Alice continued. "They have a much better understanding about how and where thoughts and emotions are created. But they still haven't made much progress figuring out why one brain works better than another."

She's smarter than Graham was, Brandon thought. In fact, her rapid progress may have had more to do with her being a Machine rather than a flesh and blood human who needed sleep and could be distracted by hunger and hormones. Moreover, time was never an issue. Class schedules and workload had to allow time for students who were biological to sleep and eat.

After a day of class followed by hours of homework, Alice and Brandon had the luxury of spending the night hours on their original passions. Alice painted and Brandon read science journals.

"What are some of the things you miss most from being biological?" Brandon asked Alice one evening.

"Sex, sex, sex in that order," said Alice, "followed by food and wine. I miss the highs and the lows. I almost wish there were something we could get emotional or fight about. I also miss going out with our friends, but given that we don't eat or drink, what would we do?"

"We could have people over to play cards, or board games."

Alice set her paintbrush down, rose from her chair and led Brandon to the bed that had come with their furnished apartment. She had something else in mind.

"Lie down," she told him and stretched herself out alongside him. "We used to cuddle, not for sex but to feel the touch of our bodies. Let's see if it still works."

"Hmm," said Alice moments later.

"It feels pretty much the same as it used to," said Brandon. "It's cozy."

"That it is."

They decided to make fifteen minutes of cuddle time a regular part of their nighttime activities.

• • • • •

When Alice had learned enough neuroscience to understand it, Brandon gave her the photocopy from the waterproof valise of Graham's handwritten papers concerning the technologies for making e-brains. Graham had placed the originals in a top-secret section of the National Archives. Alice became only the third person, after Graham and Brandon, to possess this treasure.

Brandon explained to Alice how Graham had operated.

"As you've seen, the papers are a summary of the sixteen technologies that Graham brought together to copy minds. He assigned the first fifteen parts to separate teams and kept the last one for himself. He kept its existence secret, to guard against the team leaders one day putting everything together. He slotted it in after the other parts were in place. He called it his 'secret sauce.'"

"Why was he so secretive?"

"He was always mindful of what Oskar Isaacson had said: 'Technology that *can* be used for evil *will* be so used.' That's why none of the plans and specs for the mind-copying equipment or the e-brains, and none of the underlying science, were ever put on computers. He worried about hackers. Even if someone managed to re-engineer the e-brains, they'd be useless without the mind-copying technology."

With Alice's help and 15-hour workdays, Brandon maintained a B-minus average, and in 2144, the Museum School awarded him a Bachelor of Fine Arts degree. He was the first person of metal to achieve that distinction. That same month, Alice graduated *summa cum laude* from MIT with a Bachelor of Science in neuroscience and signed up for graduate work.

"When I first started at the Museum School, some of my classmates were surprised that a Machine could create works of art that evoked human emotion," Brandon told a TV reporter who interviewed him after his graduation ceremony. "I had to remind them that the minds of metallic people have biological origins."

Brandon rented a small studio in Cambridge and began casting bronze busts of wealthy Bostonians. Out of fashion for centuries, busts were back, for those who could afford them.

"It takes a colossal ego to deem oneself worthy of being memorialized in a bronze bust," he told Alice. "Our brave new world seems to have an abundance of such people. I strive to subtly redesign their heads to improve their appearance, while leaving enough of the original that they're still able to convince themselves that this is how they actually look" He had a backlog of commissions that kept him busy 19/6.

In 2146, MIT awarded Alice a master's degree in neuroscience.

"What should I do now?" she asked Brandon that evening while they were cuddling. "Should I get a doctorate?"

"You could," said Brandon. "Or we could move on and do something altogether different. We could both do it. You know me. I'm up for anything. We could live in foreign countries and become fluent in their languages. France would be my first choice. After that, we could study acting and make movies."

Alice burst out laughing. Her whole body shook.

"What's so funny? Movies about people of metal could become a *thing*. We could start with slapstick comedy. The plots would practically write themselves. Biologicals would laugh their asses off."

Alice left the bed and sat on the sofa, still amused,

"You're a neuroscientist, goofy, and sooner or later, that's what you'll go back to. Which is fine. We can do it together. I'll go on and get my doctorate."

Brandon paused and reminded himself to choose his words carefully.

"You don't necessarily need to do that. I have a project that will be absolutely enormous if we can figure out how to do it. We could start on it tomorrow. And we'd be partners."

Alice hesitated for several moments. "What does Graham think I should do?" she asked Brandon.

She had long since discovered that the mind of a Machine's original occupied a tiny corner of a metallic person's mind, and received a muted version of the sights, sounds and other sensations that the Machine experienced. She'd become accustomed to having Mollie along for the ride. Oddly enough, she felt like they were pals.

"Graham says if he were you, he'd be inclined to work with me instead of staying at MIT," said Brandon, "because he loves the idea for the new project. But he'd advise you not to participate unless you're as excited about the project as I am. He also wants you to be sure that long-term scientific research is right for you."

"I've done nothing *but* research for the past two years. It's who I am. If I'm as excited about your project as you are, I'll be like Graham. I'll be all-in."

"I know," said Brandon. "But you need a certain personality to be happy in long-term, open-ended research, which is what we'd be doing. There was a study on this subject in the 2030s that Graham read about. Psychologists identified two groups of chemistry and physics Ph.Ds. The first group was people who had stuck with it after getting their doctorates and had long careers as researchers. The second group had also started out doing research, but within five to ten years, they'd moved on to other things."

"Like what?"

"Lots of things. Consulting. Some became executives in drug or chemical companies. A few got teaching jobs at exclusive east coast prep schools. The two groups were carefully weighted to have comparable demographics, geographic distribution, and so on. The researchers even made sure the average ratings for the schools that the two groups had come from were comparable."

"So what did they conclude?"

"The psychologists did extensive interviews to see how the two groups differed. It came down to a person's ability to accept long periods of delayed gratification—decades, like Graham—and the possibility that all of their work would come to nothing. The ones who left were the ones who had discovered that they couldn't live with that."

"I'm surprised they needed a study to figure that out," said Alice.

"People don't necessarily know up front if they're cut out for long-term research," said Brandon. "That's the point the psychologists were making. It took the second group in the study five to ten years to figure that out. A lot of people start out in research thinking it's what they were born to do, but time proves them wrong."

"I see," said Alice. "Does Graham understand that as an aspiring painter, Mollie had to live with exactly the kind of uncertainty you just described? Very few would-be professional artists make a living at it. Sooner or later, most of them give up and move on to something else, because the market for paintings is finite, the competition is fierce and tastes change. It's a tough business."

That was why Mollie had taken up interior design. She'd wanted something to fall back on in case she never made it as a painter. But she persisted, and her work as a painter finally caught on when she was in her early forties.

"No," said Brandon. "It never would have occurred to him. He was in awe of Mollie's talent. In his mind, it was only a matter of time before the art world would discover her and she'd make it big. It was an article of faith with him."

"I understand," said Alice. "She was a strong person, and proud. She wasn't altogether certain how she'd ultimately do, but she had faith in herself and kept her doubts to herself. His encouragement helped a lot. You were awesome, Graham."

"He says 'thank you,'" said Brandon.

"Graham always said that a good researcher was relentless, and never gave up no matter what," said Alice. "Thomas Edison made a thousand prototypes before he got one that worked, and so forth"

"That was Graham," said Brandon. "Never take no for an answer."

"But Mollie was the same way, wasn't she?" said Alice. "She stayed the course, even though she knew that nothing might ever come of it."

"Yes, it seems she did," said Brandon. "Looking back, it was obviously a lot harder for her than she made it look."

"That part of Mollie is alive and well inside me, Brandon, and it's ready to be challenged once again. It's who I am. Let's give it a try and give it time. If it doesn't work, we'll move on to something else."

"Fair enough," said Brandon.

They moved toward each other with their arms held out until they were hugging, as Mollie and Graham had often done after a difficult discussion.

"I'm sorry for doubting you," said Brandon. "Graham didn't get how chancy the art business was. Mollie's talent was so obvious to him, he figured it'd be obvious to everyone. He's sorry for being such a dumb fuck."

Alice laughed.

"Mollie says a girl can't very well get mad at her husband for appreciating her talent," said Alice. "So tell me about our project."

"I don't have a recipe," said Brandon. "It may not even be doable. But I gave this a great deal of thought while I was casting my busts. E-brains are amazing and all that, but they aren't any smarter than their originals, by design. What if we could figure out how to *make* them smarter? Make *ourselves* smarter? Imagine what it would be like to suddenly be 20% smarter than you were a moment ago, or 50%."

"It sounds amazing. How do you propose we start?"

"Preparation," said Brandon. "Years' worth, I'm guessing. I was planning to enroll in MIT and get a degree in electrical engineering, followed by degrees in computer and then mechanical engineering.

You're welcome to join me. Graham had specialists to handle those areas, but we'll be on our own. We'll have to know a lot more than just neuroscience."

"Why do you say that?" Alice asked. "There must be an enormous number of Machines out there who are electrical, mechanical and computer engineers."

"We're in a different position than most other Machines," said Brandon. "We're free, which from what I've read is almost unheard of. Other Machines work for the person or company that owns them, so they're not available to be hired by third parties. We'll have to do this by ourselves."

"Oh, of course. Good point."

"We could hire biologicals," said Brandon. "The challenge would be finding ones who could accept our project's timeframe."

"Yeah," said Alice. "They might prefer one that fell within their remaining life expectancy."

"It's just as well," said Brandon. "I'd rather not have strangers involved, anyway. There'd be too much risk that they'd figure out who our originals were and make it public. We don't want the attention that would bring."

"No indeed."

By 2067, Graham Gordon had already become an international celebrity, Brandon and Alice remembered. Obnoxious *paparazzi* had materialized the moment he showed his face in public. When he was awarded the Nobel Prize five years before his death, the attention must have grown exponentially, Brandon thought. It wasn't something Graham and Mollie were equipped to handle well, and there was no reason to think Brandon and Alice would do better.

"So what do you think?" Brandon asked. "Should we go back to school and build a base of expertise in electrical, computer and mechanical engineering so our creative faculties can operate there?"

So, if you're still on board, we'll go back to school and build a base of expertize in electrical, computer and mechanical engineering so our creative faculties can operate there," said Brandon.

"I'm on board, but why mechanical engineering?" Alice asked.

"Ultimately, smarter minds will want better bodies."

"I see."

"But at night, we'll put all that aside and do art. I promise."

"I'm impressed that you want to stick with it," said Alice.

"Absolutely," said Brandon. "I love it."

"Okay, I'll go back to school with you on one condition, that you agree to start wearing clothes when we're out in public."

"I agree," said Brandon. "Let's go shopping."

Clothing had not yet become *de rigueur* for people of metal, except when needed to protect their body parts from freezing up in cold winter weather, but it was catching on fairly quickly. Machine bodies did not have gender-specific attributes, so there was nothing explicitly lewd or otherwise inappropriate about the sight of one of them naked. On the other hand, the millennia-old tradition of covering one's body with clothing must have remained a part of the human psyche at some level, because by 2200, it had become unthinkable for a metallic adult to appear in civilized society unclothed.

• • • • •

Union Hill
Worcester, Massachusetts
Winter 2162

In 2158, the Delaneys used a portion of their inheritance to build and equip a small laboratory/workshop in the pleasant, historic Union Hill neighborhood of Worcester, Massachusetts. Union Hill was an actual hill, a big one, where the area's first white settlers had planted roots beginning in the early 18th Century. Long-time Worcester residents liked to compare their city to Rome, Italy because Worcester, like Rome, had been built on seven hills, and they all had names. (In fact, Worcester had up to fifteen hills, depending on how one defined "hill.")

Their building was near the very top of Union Hill, and the view from the sidewalk outside their door was spectacular: a series of large green hills in the near distance with even larger blue-green hills beyond them. The first thing Alice did the day after they'd moved in was stand on the sidewalk outside their door and paint it.

The following day, they decided to begin their project by making incremental improvements in e-brain functionality, starting with a list that Brandon made of refinements that Graham had been considering at the time his mind was copied, but which, for whatever reason, had not found their way into the current generation of e-brains.

"These are very shrewd suggestions that reveal Graham's imagination and creativity," said Brandon, "but I don't think they'll be particularly difficult to engineer."

Alice agreed, and within two months, they'd made all the refinements, working with e-brains that they purchased from the U.S.-China partnership for $1.00 each. They were able to confirm the functionality of the e-brain upgrades using a standard measuring device that they'd bought online.

"Well," said Brandon, "we've picked all the low-hanging fruit. From here on out, it won't be so easy."

They made a detailed list of the functions and processes that e-brains performed and found ways to improve most of them, but they were still mere refinements.

"We need to be more relentless," Alice joked.

"Never give up," said Brandon.

"Something will come to us," said Alice. "Maybe Ralph Waldo Emerson's 'common mind' that all humans share will give us a hint."

They kept working, and a month later, it suddenly dawned on Alice that the speed at which an e-brain operated--which, of course, was the same as its original's--could be changed, easily.

"It would never have occurred to Graham or anyone else on his team to alter an e-brain's speed—or any of its other attributes, for that matter," she observed. "Their objective was to copy minds exactly as they found them."

"You're right," said Brandon. "I wouldn't have thought of it either. Good job, honey."

"Like we said before, we have different interests than Graham did," said Alice.

The changes they needed to make to increase an e-brain's operating speed were relatively simple and straightforward, and their workshop had all the materials and equipment they'd need to build the necessary components. Less than a month later, they'd completed and tested a new e-brain component, which Alice nicknamed "Turbo," that increased an e-brain's operating speed. When they installed it in each other, it worked. Their minds were almost 25% faster than they had been. They'd done it! Before long, however, they realized that the increase in their minds' operating speed hadn't actually made them any smarter, which both surprised and disappointed them.

"I guess I always equated intelligence with mind speed," said Alice. "After all, smarter minds do tend work faster than dumber ones. It seemed self-evident." She shrugged. "But here we are. We now know first-hand that intelligence and speed are separate things. But I love it. It's a blast."

"Yeah, it is" Brandon admitted. "Kind of like driving a sports car at high speed on a curvy road."

"Now that I think of it, though," said Alice, "dumb people sometimes do have speedy minds. Mollie's dad's law firm had a first-year lawyer who was like that. First-year lawyers in big law firms spent their days researching court opinions to find answers to questions that partners assigned to them. This guy—his name was Ralph—was the speediest researcher the firm had ever seen. Problem was, half the time, the answers he came up with were wrong. He didn't last long."

They laughed.

"We need to get a handle on what intelligence actually is," said Brandon.

"Mollie took a psychology class that covered that," said Alice. "I'll make us a reading list."

"My understanding is there are different kinds of intelligence," said Brandon.

"That's correct," said Alice. "It's an intriguing subject."

In less than an hour, Alice had assembled an extensive collection of texts and scholarly articles.

"Well, this should keep us busy for a while," said Brandon.

• • • • •

Worcester Academy
Union Hill
Worcester, Massachusetts
Winter 2162

At the appointed time, they put their work aside and walked over to the Worcester Academy ice arena to watch a hockey game, as they'd done the previous week. For the next several years, watching games there would be one of their favorite pastimes. They greeted other regular attendees and found seats.

"Go Hilltoppers!" Brandon screamed, to the delight of the students seated around them in the packed arena.

"I love these games," he told Alice.

"Me too."

Graham and Mollie had played youth hockey in Canada before entering high school. They'd often regretted that they hadn't continued playing.

"They seem like good kids," said Brandon. "And it's a good school. One of Graham's best friends at MIT went here."

"A boy Mollie knew at the Museum School also went here. He was multi-talented, almost a renaissance kid."

While walking through the parking lot after the game, Brandon noticed that most of the vehicles were ultra-expensive luxury cars or SUVs.

"I wonder why we didn't notice this last time," said Brandon.

"*I* did," said Alice. "You were still pumped up from the game."

"Come to think of it, the kids in the stands today were expensively dressed, too," said Brandon. "And it seemed like they all had one or more of the very latest and most expensive electronic devices. They seem like good kids, but their parents must all be rich. I didn't see one kid who looked like he or she could be a scholarship kid."

Brandon had guessed correctly. By 2162, only the children of billionaires and wealthy government officials could afford to attend schools like Worcester Academy. Free public schools still existed, but their enrollment had dropped steadily since President Robbins had introduced the guaranteed annual income.

• • • • •

Brandon activated their TV screen. "Let's see what's happening out there," he told Alice.

"Worldwide stock markets continue to soar," a newsman was saying, "in synch with the replacement of ever-increasing numbers of human workers with Machines. The productivity of public companies has increased more than 77% since the Machines became available in the United States in 2085. Economists predict that gross world product will continue to increase in direct proportion to the expected further increases in the percentage of the workforce Machines represent."

"Well, Jim," said the newsman's colleague, a pretty newswoman, "it's a good thing President Robbins had the foresight in 2141 to tax the income from the Machines to fund generous stipends for all the human workers that Machines are replacing."

"That's right, Jenna. And it's a heck of a deal. According to the Department of Labor, the guaranteed annual income is more than twice the average wage of the workers who are losing their jobs. As for what life is like for the Machines, we'll go live to our Robyn Wilkins who's in Washington with Jim Booth, the head of the U.S. Chamber of Commerce."

"Thanks, Jenna. Mr. Booth, there are some who claim that the use of Machine workers is a form of slavery. Others claim they're worked 24/7, 52 weeks per year, to the point of insanity. What's life like for them?"

"When the Machines first became available, mistakes admittedly were made. Some owners failed to appreciate the fact that these are people — human beings with feelings just like ours. There were abuses, like working them 24/7, but companies quickly realized that humane treatment of their Machines is good business. Machines, like the rest of us, need time off to recreate, regroup and reflect in order to be able to perform at peak efficiency. Are some Machines still abused? Most likely, I'd guess, but so are biological workers, here and there. In a perfect world, none of this would exist, but I'm afraid we aren't quite there yet."

Brandon turned off the television and went quiet.

"What's wrong?" Alice asked him.

"It sounds like they're trying to use Machines to replace biological workers on a wholesale basis. "

"I guess it does."

They left the TV area and dropped themselves into the comfortable recliners on the other side of the room.

"What will the displaced workers *do* with themselves?" Brandon asked.

"Whatever they want," said Alice. "Like us. They'll be happy as clams."

"What, lying around doing nothing? We work our butts off. We don't sit around doing nothing. It can't be good for them. Can you even imagine? Doing absolutely nothing? We'd go nuts."

"They could take up hobbies, play golf. Whatever. Like people do when they retire."

"That's easy to say, but how many people have the resources to create a whole new life from scratch? Look at Graham's dad. You remember. He was never the same after he retired. Not only did he not take up any *new* hobbies; he lost interest in the ones he already had. He felt useless. It was the reason he started drinking and got hooked on opioids. Graham's mum went through hell getting him through rehab, and he was never the same. Mollie was shocked, but Graham understood. People weren't designed for retirement, at whatever age. It's unnatural."

"It was sad," Alice remembered, "but Graham's dad was a Type A personality. Maybe people who're less driven will have an easier time."

"It isn't good, Alice. Mark my words; this will not end well. Machines were supposed to *supplement* the workforce, not replace it. That's how we were promoted. People need to feel useful. When they stop feeling useful, they fall apart, like Graham's dad. They lose the spirit that made them who they were."

"Have you been studying psychology behind my back?" Alice teased.

"It's just common sense," Brandon grumbled.

"Let's hope you're wrong."

They repaired to their art studio in the rear of their building, where they had works-in-progress.

Union Hill
Worcester
2165

"Maybe we should put the e-brains aside for a while and just work on our art projects," Alice suggested.

They'd read hundreds of papers and reports about intelligence in the biological mind — and by extension, in an e-brain. But they'd found nothing that explained, at the micro-electronic operating level, what differentiated a highly intelligent mind from a lesser one. Without knowing that, they were at a loss where to even begin the process of making an e-brain smarter.

They'd continued making incremental e-brain enhancements and refinements whose cumulative effect was palpable, but that was it.

Brandon took Alice's hand and smiled reassuringly.

"I get it, you're discouraged," he told her. "It's understandable. Okay, let's take a break — say, a month. Maybe our subconscious minds will come up with something that our conscious minds are missing."

Three weeks later, Alice had an idea, and a year after that, they'd perfected an upgrade that made e-brains more receptive to creative insights while "thinking outside the box." They were thrilled.

"Wow," said Alice. "This must be what LSD was like." She called it their creativity boost. However, like Turbo, it did not make them any smarter, in the conventional sense.

"Trying to make e-brains smarter was a huge challenge," Alice acknowledged years later, "but we felt that, with the creativity boost, we had a shot. We decided to take what we considered a more fundamental approach and see if researchers had identified discrete electrical phenomena that occurred differently in rare cases from the way they occurred in the vast majority of human brains.

"High intelligence is rare. Our hypothesis, or hope, was that if we found electrical variants that were also very rare, the variants might — might — have a causal connection with high intelligence. If we could find enough of these rare electrical variants, our plan was to make e-brain components that mimicked them, and then install them in each other to see if they made us smarter.

We concluded based on broadly worded searches that no one had yet made the kind of large-scale study that you'd have needed to identify electrical variants that correlated with high intelligence. But we speculated that researchers might have identified at least some of those variants, as part of broader projects that our searches had missed.

"It was worth a look, but the amount of work involved would be daunting. Our plan was to review every neuroscience research report we could find, starting with the most recent, and work backward.

"Before getting started, we took a much-needed year off for travel. When we arrived back in Worcester, we set to work poring over published data in search of our variants. It was slow going but we stayed with it. It occurred to me to write to the head of MIT's neuroscience department and propose that they do the variant study, but it never got off the ground."

Union Hill
Worcester
2167

Alice and Brandon had pored over centuries of neuroscience research but had found only three documented electrical variants that met their criteria. It seemed unlikely that these alone would be enough to account for high intelligence. Just to be certain, they made and installed in each other e-brain components that mimicked the three variants. As they'd expected, the variants did not make them smarter.

Discouraged, they took a month off for travel and a month to do art. Refreshed and clear-headed, they tried another approach. When that failed, they tried another, and another after that. They were proceeding logically and methodically, Brandon assured his wife, and she stuck with him; it was only a matter of time. And they made art every night. But in 2167, after two more years of effort, they gave up. They'd run out of road.

"It's no use," Brandon admitted. "Even Graham thinks we've gone as far as we can go with this. I still like our electrical variant theory, but the data to test it against don't seem to exist in any accessible form. We've looked everywhere. In retrospect, you should have gone back to MIT for a doctorate and done the variant study yourself."

As mentioned, in 2165, Alice had contacted MIT neuroscientists and suggested that they conduct a study to identify the microelectronic variants linked with high intelligence, but they'd declined. By 2165, scientific research was in a state of decline worldwide, and MIT and other colleges and universities had begun a downward spiral that would end with their closing, which in MIT's case occurred in 2191.

"Yeah," Alice said. "I was sure someone there would pick it up, and I was happy here. But you're right, I should have gone back and done it." She sighed and shrugged. "Oh well."

Brandon felt like a jerk.

"I'm sorry, I shouldn't have said that," said Brandon. "I've been happy having you here too. We make a good team. We didn't hit the jackpot, but we *have* improved our minds and our ability to think. It's time to move on to the next thing, that's all."

Alice perked up and smiled.

"You're right," she said. "We'll find other challenges. Life will go on. Let's find ourselves another science project. Here's an idea: We can invent things, like better gadgets or whatever, like we did for e-brains. Mollie used to daydream about doing that. She made a point of looking around for things that could be improved. A lot of product innovations are tiny things, but they can make a huge difference in the product's usefulness."

"I like your idea," said Brandon. "Let's do it. But if it's okay with you, I think we could use a hiatus away from science and engineering.

Failure sucks. Graham is also depressed. I suggest that for the time being, we focus on our artwork. I don't know about you, but I need to accomplish something, anything. Working in new artistic styles and other media might be just the thing for both of us. Maybe I'll even go back to casting bronze, only this time I'll be trying to make an artistic statement."

"I agree," said Alice. "A person can only take so much failure."

"We'll make it a long hiatus," said Brandon.

Union Hill
Wooster
Winter 2200

In biological human terms, it was a very long hiatus. With time out for travel and their daily walks, they'd spent the intervening years creating and selling art in a multitude of styles and media They worked in a commodious, well-lighted art studio, also on Union Hill, which they'd purchased.

"I have to tell you, this hiatus has been amazing, but in kind of a strange way," Alice told Brandon one morning in the Winter of 2200. "I, Alice, am the person doing the work but Mollie's there too, looking on, making suggestions and offering encouragement. I'm thrilled for her. She and I have had thirty-three extra years to build on and further develop Mollie's talent and artistic vision, on top of all the nighttime work that we did from the very beginning."

"Here's where you're wrong. It's your work, not hers. No offense, Mollie. But the mind you got from Mollie, with its enormous artistic talent, is yours, not hers. It always has been. They're only along for the ride — and guys, I mean no offense by saying this. They have their own point of view, and I don't doubt that Mollie's given you helpful hints, because of having a different perspective. You're two different people. You realized that on day one. So there."

"Thanks, Graham," Alice teased.

Alice wasn't surprised at how much progress Brandon had made in his artwork. Like his original, he was relentless at whatever he set out to do. His work had gained a depth and maturity that she hadn't known he had in him. Mollie agreed.

• • • • •

Union Hill
Worcester
Three weeks later

"It's hockey season," Alice pointed out.

"Yes, it is," Brandon agreed. "It's Winter."

"It just hit me," said Alice. "We haven't seen the kids play in thirty-some years." She consulted her electronic device. "There's a game tonight. Do you want to go?"

"Sure."

Brandon wondered if they'd stopped attending games because they were a subconscious reminder of their early years in Worcester when the future had seemed so bright. It was a disturbing thought.

Worcester Academy
Union Hill
Worcester
That evening

They noticed the difference the moment they entered the rink.

"What the hell," said Brandon, shaking his head in disbelief.

Both teams were "warming up," but it was like they were skating in slow-mo. They looked bored and put upon, like they couldn't be bothered. It was the same during the game.

"What's going on?" said Brandon. "Why don't the coaches light a fire under these clowns?"

"They look like they're afraid to say anything," said Alice. "Look at them."

The stands were practically empty. *With good reason*, Brandon thought.

"Go Hilltoppers!" Brandon screamed, whereupon the Worcester player who had the puck skated over to the boards below where Brandon and Alice were seated and stopped. He removed his helmet, whose mask had obscured his expressionless face. "There was a "C" on the front of his sweater, below his left shoulder. He was the Worcester Academy captain.

"Shut the fuck up, freak," he told Brandon in a quiet, flat voice.

The captain put his helmet back on, buckled it carefully, took the puck back on his stick and skated, casually, toward the visitors' net. Mortified, Brandon and Alice left their seats and headed for the lobby.

"We need to find out what's happening here," said Brandon. "Something's gone terribly wrong since the last time we were here."

Alice agreed.

At length, the game ended and the handful of spectators emerged from the rink and passed through the lobby and out the door. Looking through the glass at the scoreboard, Brandon and Alice saw the final score: Hilltoppers 5, Visitors 4.

"I'm surprised that either team scored," said Alice.

"Not if the goalies were as listless as the skaters," said Brandon.

Moments later, the referee and the two linesmen entered the lobby and were walking toward them

"Freaking pathetic," one official told the others. "I've just about had it."

"Me too," said another. "If they didn't pay us so damn much, I'd retire."

As Brandon and Alice later learned, the league paid the linesmen four times and the referee five times the amount of the government's guaranteed annual income, for four or five months work, or however long their season was. It was the only way the league could get people to "officiate" these ridiculous farces.

Alice and Brandon watched and listened as the head coaches from the two teams joined the officials.

"We couldn't help overhearing what you gentlemen just said," the Worcester coach told the officials. "We feel the same way. It's an embarrassment, but the paychecks sure are nice. They've downright addictive."

Alice and Brandon later learned that the going rate for hockey coaches in the New England prep school league was eight times the government's guaranteed annual stipend.

"As long as we're *nice* to the boys," said the visiting coach, "and never raise our voices."

Brandon approached them. "Excuse me, gentlemen. I wonder if you could help us out. I'm Brandon Delaney and this is my wife, Alice. We used to come here all the time for the games, back in the '60s. They were great. The kids skated hard and the games were fun. What the hell has happened?"

"The world has changed," said the referee. "It's the same every game. They don't give a crap. They're spoiled rich kids."

"The players we saw back in the day, they were rich too," said Brandon. "But they played their hearts out. There must be more to it. Why do they even bother?"

"Their dads played hockey, and they're expected to play too," said the Worcester coach. "It's a thing they must do, or pretend to do, to remain in the will. Luckily for them, none of the dads bother to come to any of the games."

"If they have to be here anyway, why not play the game?" Alice asked.

"They have no oomph," said the coach. "No zip. They have no reason to. These kids have no future and they know it. They'll have all the money in the world, but they'll never have anything they need to do or be responsible for. Back when you were coming here before, the kids could still believe there'd be opportunities for them to do things with their lives. I mean, it was before my time, but that's how it's been explained to me. Now they know better. That's what's happened. I apologize for what our *captain* said to you. He's an asshole. Most of them are. But I'm not sure I'd handle it any better if I were in their place."

"Gentlemen, we appreciate the heads-up. Thanks."

"I told you this would happen," he told Alice after they'd left the arena.

Back at their studio, they did some checking and learned that Machines now comprised the world's entire workforce, except in Africa, where the only Machines they imported worked as servants for the elite classes.

"It says here that the replacement of biological workers by Machines was essentially complete by 2190, except in Africa," said Alice.

"We saw Machines everywhere we went," said Brandon, "but we had no idea they'd replaced biological workers wholesale."

"We wouldn't have noticed anyway. We never entered any of the shops or other places of business. We never had a reason to. We ordered everything we needed online."

Nor had any of the TV news reports that they'd watched brought this ominous development to their attention.

Alice continued reading for another ten minutes.

"Here it is," she said. "A billionaire named Rusk was in the business of buying and selling companies. He joined forces with four other billionaires. Their strategy was to buy companies as fast as they could and replace the companies' workers with Machines to the fullest extent possible, as quickly as possible. The companies' market value would jump—sometimes 30% or more—and they'd flip them and buy more. Rusk and his pals started buying companies in 2140, and billionaires around the world started doing the same. The process accelerated to the point where even totalitarian regimes began replacing their biological workers with Machines, except in Africa. The leaders there found Machines threatening."

"So the die was already cast when we saw the kids play in 2162," said Brandon. "But as the coach pointed out, it wasn't obvious yet. The kids we saw playing hockey and watching the game back then could still believe they had some kind of life ahead of them."

"Maybe something good will end up coming out of all this," Alice said hopefully. "People will have more time to devote to things they're passionate about. Think about it. All the great eras of history were marked by people having the time to stop shoveling, or whatever work they did, and just sit back and think about things--or do and create things."

"Having leisure time is one thing, enforced idleness is something else," said Brandon.

"Speaking of idleness, our masterpieces-in-progress await us," said Alice, and they proceeded arm-in-arm to the studio in the rear of their building.

• • • • •

Union Hill
Worster
Spring 2219

"I wish we had better bodies," Alice told Brandon during one of their daily walks.

They would have liked to go running or jogging the way Graham and Mollie had done—not for the exercise, obviously, but for the feeling of their bodies in motion and the sight of buildings and scenery sliding quickly past them on either side. But their bodies weren't built to withstand the extra shock they'd receive while running, as compared to walking.

Brandon stopped and put his hand on his wife's shoulder.

"Maybe we can do something about that," he suggested.

Thus began their next big project: engineering better functioning and better looking body parts. They reopened their lab/workshop and began spending every other day there, getting ideas for upgrades and making preliminary sketches. They were finally putting their hard-earned mechanical engineering chops to work.

Their first successful effort was the design and production of improved feet to replace the clunky ones that had come with their circa 2067 standard bodies. The new feet resembled the biological human foot, but with more flexibility and a lot more shock-absorption capacity. They used 3-D printing equipment to make them out of a synthetic rubber they'd found online. They managed to transfer to their new feet the latticework of receptors that had covered the bottom of their original feet.

"I love them," Alice told her husband after they'd tried them out. "They put bounce back in my step."

New feet were the only physical prototypes they produced during this period. Upgrades to other body parts were beyond their production capacity. However, for $1.00 each, they bought plans and specs from the U.S.-China partnership for all the latest models. Every other day, at midnight, they walked the short distance from their art studio to their lab/workshop and went over the schematics looking for ways to improve them.

They envisioned making bodies more human-looking by giving them skin, human-looking eyes and eyelids, teeth, finger- and toenails, tongues, and lips that moved when the person talked. It was Alice's idea; she was on a tear.

"Maybe we could engineer improved ersatz facial muscles that do a better job of reflecting their owner's state of mind," said Alice.

"Why not?" said Brandon. "We could hook them up to the same connections and set them to respond to the same signals as the original ones did, but better," referring to the fact that standard Machine heads already had crude ersatz musculature that could form an inventory of very basic expressions—smiles, frowns, etc. "These would be a huge improvement over the standard faces."

"We could also use 3-D printing to make custom heads that look like the person's original, or a movie star," Alice added.

Before long, they had a small library of schematics for exciting body-part improvements, small and large.

"We'll need business advice at some point," Brandon observed. "This could be really huge."

"It would be if our potential customers had money," said Alice.

"That's an example of why we'll need advice," said Brendan. "Owners might want to offer them to their Machines as a bonus for good work."

"Good point," said Alice.

"I'll make some calls," said Brandon. "I have a few people in mind who might be able to help us."

But was too late. The Malaise had taken hold.

Union Hill
Worcester
2400

As far as was generally known, the last of the biological humans had passed. They were extinct.

Since moving to Worcester, Brandon and Alice had followed the same route during their daily walks, accompanied by the succession of dogs they'd adopted over the years from the local humane society. Thanks in part to the attention the dogs attracted, they'd become friends with several of the biological men and women who lived or worked on the streets they walked. Hence, when the suicides had begun in Worcester, some of the victims were their friends. One of them had actually died on the sidewalk in front of them.

It was a shattering experience to see someone you knew, or even a stranger, jump to his or her death off the roof of a building.

The preceding century-and-a-half had been brutal. By the time the Malaise had reached its peak, circa 2350, the Delaneys had seen more broken bodies, more blood, more overdosed addicts and more walking dead — many times more — than any human being should ever have to witness. The unimaginable was happening. They coped by keeping busy with their art and dabbling in science and engineering projects. For example, they created an e-brain upgrade that enhanced the vividness of their perception of color, which they'd removed and set aside when evening news broadcasts began showing blood flowing in cities and towns around the world. It was their art that kept them going, more or less, during this grim period.

Their work — Brandon's in particular — grew darker as the tragedy unfolded. One of his paintings, done in a rough, cartoonish style in black, white and shades of gray, showed figures leaping from roofs and windows, piles of broken bodies on the street down below, and Machine-driven transports overloaded with blood-soaked corpses. In the lower right corner of the painting, two Machines, a man and a woman, looked on, horrified. The sky above the scene was black, and a smiling white devil with bared fangs and a long tail stood atop one of the towers with its fist raised high above its head.

"My God, it's like 'Guernica,'" Alice told him when he finally let her see the finished work.

"Except it's happening in every city," said Brandon. "The poor bastards have lost their will to live."

Alice did a lot of bleak-looking landscapes in colors that reflected the despair they saw all around them. At one point, she ventured outside and, with their permission, took photos of some of the biological humans she encountered, which she turned into portraits that conveyed the absolute emptiness of her subjects' lives. "I sort of felt like I needed to memorialize the poor souls," she told the authors. She herself had lost the boundless optimism that she'd inherited from Mollie. It was impossible not to be affected in a major way by what was happening in the world, and in their very neighborhood. She and Brandon were treading water, waiting for a sign that life would go on.

They were reminded that emotions ranging from joy to despair were not the sole province of biological humans.

As years passed, the couple remained just busy enough to avoid the distress that many of their fellow Machines were feeling as the result of being idled, as the biologicals whom they'd served died out.

"It's time to move on," Alice declared one morning in 2412. "We need to leave the past behind. We can't change it. I'm done painting it. You should be too."

The following week, before they'd determined their next move, they learned from TV news that a convention would soon be held in New York City to identify long-term projects from which people of metal at every level of intelligence and skill could draw satisfaction. John Administrator, who would chair the convention, appeared on the evening news and invited anyone who had an idea for such a project to send him a proposal.

"Better bodies!" Alice cried out.

"Yes!" said Brandon.

It was the first positive news in what seemed like an eternity.

"We'll hit the ground running with our schematics," said Brandon.

They submitted their proposal and arranged .to meet with Administrator at the former United Nations building in New York City, where the work of organizing the convention was under way.

They wanted to lobby Administrator in person to make sure their proposal was presented to the convention.

Former United Nations Building
New York City
Autumn 2412

All signs of the waves of mass suicide were long gone. The streets were spotless.

"My God, it must have been horrible," Brandon told Administrator after they'd all shaken hands. He escorted them to a comfortable seating area in a corner of his office.

"It broke my heart," said Administrator. "I lost so many friends. There are no words."

"No, there aren't," said Alice. "We're sorry for your loss. We lost friends in Worcester, too, but nowhere near as many as you all did here, I'm sure. It was a nightmare."

"I like your proposal," Administrator told them. "It's just what we're looking for. Participants will make things that are useful. They'll get a sense of satisfaction and accomplishment."

"And there will be room for creative expression," said Brandon. "As we said in our proposal, we already have schematics for quite a few body-part improvements that we've prepared ourselves, and that's just the beginning. I expect we'd attract engineers and designers with far more talent than we have. We're pumped."

"We're also excited about customizing and personalizing people's bodies," said Alice. "For example, a person whose ancestors were Asian or African might wish to have facial features, hair and skin color like those groups had. Or not. They could have any color they wanted. I could see some people picking gold or silver. We'd also offer a choice of eye colors."

"Yes, I saw that," said Administrator. "I also saw on your resumes that the two of you have become bona fide experts in several disciplines. Electrical and mechanical engineering will be directly pertinent here, given that the two of you have volunteered to head up the project."

"So we'll be on the agenda at the convention?" Alice asked.

"Yes."

"How will this all work?" Brandon asked. "I know that if a project isn't inherently impracticable, it goes to the voters, and a yes vote means the voter wants to be part of the project. If we get enough people to make the project workable, what happens next?"

"You'll be put in touch with your people and you'll go from there. We'll expect you to find something for everyone to do. You'll also need factory space, of which we have more than we know what to do with."

Enough people voted for their proposal to make it viable, so the Delaneys went to work.

Later that year, they accepted Administrator's invitation to join him and others at the Lincoln Memorial for a service to honor the memory of the biological humans.

"Graham's taking it hard," Brandon told Alice after the memorial ceremony. "He kept pretty much to himself during the Malaise. He was as angry and upset as I was about what was happening. But, like me, he blamed the politicians and the moguls for screwing things up. I still feel that way, but now that it's over and done, it's hit him, and he blames himself. He feels guilty. Jack Preacher's speech at the memorial hit him. He keeps saying that it was all his fault, it wouldn't have happened if he'd never been born, blah blah blah. "

"The poor thing," said Alice.

"We've been having a dialogue. I argue that he shouldn't feel responsible for what happened. The person who discovered fire can't be held responsible for all the harm that fires have caused. The company that makes a kitchen knife isn't to blame if a bad guy uses the knife to stab someone. And those examples are *way* weaker than Graham's case. Fire and knives are *designed* to be destructive. Fire powers a gasoline engine by destroying gasoline vapor. It creates heat and a pleasant spectacle by destroying a pile of wood in a campfire. Knives 'destroy' meat and vegetables by cutting them to pieces. Those are *good* kinds of destruction, but they're destruction, nonetheless; and the nature of fire and knives is such that they can be used to cause *bad* kinds of destruction. They're inherently dangerous."

"And Machines aren't," said Alice.

"Right. They—we—aren't inherently dangerous in any direct sense. All we do is perform useful work. If Machines contributed to what happened, it was *indirect*. They were misused. Over-used. It was a case of too much of a good thing. And Graham was not responsible for that."

Brandon paused and cocked his head.

"Graham says he hears me. I've convinced him he shouldn't feel guilty. But now, he's on a tear about the need to police and control scientific discoveries. He has his own version of the Isaacson rule: 'Technology whose use *can* have baleful effects, directly or indirectly, intentionally or unintentionally, *will* have those effects; it's just a matter of time.' He says the burden is on scientists to keep that from happening."

Brandon stared off into space.

"More dialogue," he told Alice. "He says that, given enough time, it's almost certain that the Machines would have taken over the world's entire workforce, even without the involvement of greedy moguls and crooked politicians. It's Econ 101, he says. Machines were so much more productive than biological workers that it was inevitable."

'Tell Graham Mollie sends her love," said Alice.

"He sends her his."

Chapter 3
Better Bodies

Headquarters
Body Enhancement Project
Worcester
2406

The following sign was posted in each of the Project's factories and workshops:

BODY ENHANCEMENT PROJECT

Mission Statement

"Our mission is to assure that every person, wherever in the world they may live, has access to the best, most advanced and most attractive body hardware that science, engineering and the arts can produce."

Three new factories, each capable of producing the Project's full line of hardware, were scheduled to be ready in 2408. One would be located near Worcester, the second would be in Peoria and the third would be in Los Angeles. In the meantime, temporary production lines had been set up in abandoned workshops and factories in or near Worcester and were running 24/7 to keep up with the high demand for the new bodies, using assembly-line robots that Project engineers had found and re-programmed. The body upgrades included those that Alice and Brandon had designed, with modifications that their engineering and design teams had suggested, and exciting new ones that the team had come up with. Focus groups loved them, and the public clamored for them.

The generic models had all the "humanizing" features that Alice had envisioned, and were available in a choice of skin, hair and eye colors.

In 2420, a fourth plant opened 23 miles west of Worcester and began the production of customized bodies that would resemble particular biological humans. Engineers used late 21st century computer-assisted-design ("CAD") software and 3-D printing technology to create the custom bodies from photos of biological human subjects.

"It's amazing," Brandon told colleagues one afternoon. "No one pays for our products. No one pays for anything. If I want a car, I go get one. If I want a vacation, I make reservations. There's no money or trade. People just take whatever they want or need, within reason, on the same basis as everyone else. Marx would feel vindicated. 'From each according to his abilities, to each according to his needs.' That's us! We're communists. What could be more perfect? Except the only reason it works for us now is because our 'needs' are so limited."

"That's right," said Mendel Adair, a designer. "We're incapable of greed. Our paltry wants and needs are easily satisfied without our having to take from anyone else, much less oppress them."

"Well said, Mendel," said Brandon. "Greed was why the biologicals could never make communism or socialism work. They could pretend otherwise, but greed was part of their biological makeup. Their enormous animal appetites and urges were insatiable, so socialism ended up being a mass of subjects living at a modest level, if they were lucky, under greedy Comrades, Citizens or whatever name the overlords gave themselves, who lived and indulged themselves like kings, while the underclass did all the actual work."

"In Venezuela," said Adair, "it got to the point where starving people were so desperate for food that indigenous rat species became extinct."

"Capitalists weren't angels, either," Alice pointed out. "Business moguls fixed prices, made unsafe products, bribed officials and exploited foreign workers. Greedy bankers caused financial meltdowns and recessions."

"You're right, Alice. But people who got rich in non-socialist countries had to at least produce or provide something of value to get all that money. In socialist and communist systems, the so-called 'socialists' and their thugs just took it."

'I agree," said Fran Peterson, a metallurgist. "Those were rogue regimes. *Real* socialism was never tested because it never existed; and now, with all that has happened, it never will be. We can only wonder what it might have accomplished for the world if it'd been given half a chance."

Brandon and Adair rolled their eyes.

• • • • •

One day in 2487, while on break from work, Brandon shared with Alice how Todd Ordakowski had thought he'd given one of Graham's e-brains an orgasm when he'd brushed against a knob and triggered a spike of current.

"Graham was skeptical, but he had Todd administer the same jolt to some of the other e-brains just in case," Brandon explained. "This was back in the early days when the e-brains were having psychological problems. If they could've had orgasms on a regular basis, it would've given the e-brains something to look forward to. But the other e-brains did not react.

"When Ordakowski jolted his e-brain in Graham's presence, the e-brain clearly liked it, but it could have been any kind of pleasurable feeling. It turned out that three channels in Ordakowski's e-brain had been subsumed, probably during routine maintenance. As you know, subsumed channels are prone to randomly divert current to other channels. Evidently, the spike of current prompted the subsumed channels to divert current, but there was no way to tell where current had been channeled. So they dropped it."

"You selfish bastard," said Alice. "Graham, not you."

"Huh?"

"Just kidding. Graham was biological, and Mollie took care of his needs. It's understandable that it didn't occur to him to give his Machines that same opportunity. But I bet he could have. He and his people engineered and built bodies that had battery-powered moving parts and thousands of sub-dermal receptors that were every bit as sensitive as their biological counterparts — and circuitry that carried that information from the receptors to the e-brain. Graham knew the parts of the biological brain that were lit up or blocked during sex, and which parts of an e-brain corresponded to those parts."

"You're right," said Brandon, "but it never occurred to Graham. Why would it have? Are you thinking—"

Brandon stopped abruptly. *He's discussing it with Graham*, Alice thought. *This could take a while.* She returned to her workstation and busied herself attending to routine production issues.

"Graham thinks we should be able to do this," Brandon told Alice a while later, "and I agree. You're right. We know exactly what we'll need to do. We know that during the repetitive in-and-out process of biological intercourse, receptors on the male and female genital parts sent pleasure signals to the relevant portions of each partner's brain that culminated in orgasm. In theory, we should be able to build that capacity into *our* bodies. The only challenges that Graham and I see are engineering things — like   powering the ersatz genital parts densely covered with receptors. It shouldn't be all that more difficult than it was for Graham's team to give us the ability to feel the wind on our faces, or someone touching our arm."

"As you'll recall," said Alice, "when we were doing our brain research, we found a paper by a team at Hopkins that mapped and measured the electrical activity in the human body during sex in unprecedented detail. It might come in handy."

"We'll have to take another look at it."

Alice grinned. "I'll do the electrical and mechanical engineering on the male part."

"The lady part will need lubricant in order for the receptors in the male part to receive and transmit authentic stimuli," said Brandon.

A Machine's receptors could distinguish between the kinds of surfaces they were being rubbed against and the presence or absence of lubrication around them as well as or better than biological receptors could.

"Graham is excited."

"So is Mollie."

The public would not have approved of what they were doing, so they took even more care than usual to keep their work private. Fourteen months later, working nights in their original lab/workshop, they had mapped out the complex internal connections that they'd have to make in their respective e-brains to route sensor impulses from the genitalia to the parts of their e-brains they would need to reach. Next, they prepared plans and specs for construction of the genital parts, and for portable, battery-powered auxiliary kits, which they called "sexpacks," that would help the genitalia perform their respective functions.

They would need additional equipment and materials, but they were reluctant to have it delivered to their lab/workshop for fear of attracting attention. So, feeling like perverts in spite of themselves, they found a small factory building in a remote area forty miles southwest of Worcester, to which they had the equipment and materials delivered. There, they used CAD software and 3-D printing technology to make themselves elegant, functioning genitalia—which they covered with a dense latticework of receptors just beneath their surfaces. The male part would be small and unobtrusive until connected to its sexpack, whereupon it would grow stiff and engorged. The female sexpack would provide the lady part with lubrication and the ability to squeeze the male part when the process ended.

Returning to Worcester, the Delaneys took turns putting each other in sleep mode, removing the other person's e-brain and installing the necessary wiring. They gave each other inconspicuous external ports where the "nerves" running from their genitalia would be connected to the supplemental wiring in their brains.

"Well, here goes," said Alice. "Time to test them out."

They put their respective parts on top of a workstation and connected them to their e-brains. After a moment's hesitation, they plugged their units into their respective sexpacks and began testing their gear. The Delaneys have kept the details of these tests to themselves. All we know is that it took them almost a year of making adjustments to get things just the way they wanted them.

"It exceeded our wildest expectations," Alice told the authors in an interview years later.

Their next step was to design and fit belts to their new genitals so they could strap them to their bodies. Later on, they'd design genitals that could be permanently affixed to their bodies.

To celebrate their secret triumph, they had one of their devices play "Miracles" by Jefferson Starship, which had been one of Graham's and Mollie's favorite songs, and still was.

"I didn't realize how much we needed this," Alice told her husband. "It wasn't obvious, because we didn't feel the urge, being people of metal. But we're a real couple now. I feel like I'm whole again. I'm so glad we were able to restore this."

"Me too," said Brandon.

They finally got around to having the Project's custom plant make heads and bodies for them based on the photos of young Graham and Mollie that Brandon and Alice had found stored on the device from the buried valise. Brandon added a beard to Graham's photo and a larger nose and higher cheekbones to Mollie's, for disguise.

They loved their new bodies.

"I love your hair," Brandon told Alice. "I always have. Too bad we can't smell things. I'd put some of that lemony stuff on it." He thought for a moment, shrugged and said, "Why the hell not?"

Brandon's face took on a look that told Alice that he was consulting with Graham.

"Stop it you two," said Alice. "No more research. I need a vacation."

They took a year off to travel. When they returned to Worcester, they divided their time between the Body Enhancement Project and their art.

"Brandon and I felt terrible about keeping our creation to ourselves," Alice told the authors, "but people would have dragged our names through the mud. Plus, we weren't that sure that anyone else would even want them. But I'm glad we were finally able to share them. Aren't you?"

In the 25th century and long afterward, most people of metal, males and females alike, were prudes to a greater or lesser degree. While they had no sexual urges themselves, they had vivid memories of the pleasure sexual relations had brought their originals—which they could never enjoy themselves. In effect, they'd "lost" a source of pleasure that their originals had enjoyed. To counteract the inevitable pangs of regret or feelings of loss that they felt, Machines adopted a disdainful attitude toward the whole nasty business.

"It's a defense mechanism," said Dr. Suzy, the iconoclastic host of a popular TV talk show and a trained psychotherapist, in a 2469 broadcast. "We convince ourselves that yuck, we've risen above all that sordid, hateful mess. We're better off without it."

So the Delaneys kept their new upgrades to themselves, for the time being.

Nowadays, of course, nearly everyone has them.

• • • • •

Brandon and Alice Delaney remained in Worcester until 2527, when travelers discovered biological human survivors in Africa.

Chapter 4
Genes

Union Hill
Worcester
March 2527

One month each year was the designated Adventure Month for each of the world's regions. April was the Adventure Month for North America. The World Machine Federation, which had been formed in 2496 and was headquartered in the former United Nations building in New York City, sponsored thousands of Adventure Month expeditions to interesting places all over the world. The Federation kept expeditions small to allow people the opportunity to interact socially, and to avoid creating crowds and long waits at popular attractions.

When the Adventure Month catalog arrived in mid-March, Brandon and Alice Delaney dropped what they were doing and spent two hours scrolling through it.

"Where *haven't* we been?" Alice asked.

"Italy," said Brandon.

It was true. They and/or their originals had been practically everywhere but Italy.

"How did we miss it?" Alice wondered. "My God, the Sistine Chapel…the Spanish Steps…Tuscany. Wow!"

"So we'll go to Italy," said Brandon.

They chose an expedition that would begin in Rome and visit Florence, Pisa, Venice and Milan. From Milan they'd travel east to

Venice, then south along or near Italy's Adriatic coast, stopping at Bologna, San Marino, Perugia, Assisi and Pompeii, where they'd spend an entire morning. Next, they'd proceed down the Amalfi Coast and continue to Messina, where they'd travel by boat to Sicily.

The couple couldn't wait for April 1 to arrive. They needed a break.

Sistine Chapel
Rome
April 1, 2527

After the short supersonic flight from Boston to Rome, they boarded a tour bus with about forty other people and a guide. Their first stop would be the Sistine Chapel. *En route*, they listened to the guide wax eloquent about Rome's rich history, as they passed ancient ruins.

"We already knew all that," Brandon muttered.

Dozens of tour groups were scheduled to visit the Sistine Chapel that day, but at their appointed time, they had it to themselves. Alice was ecstatic. Thankfully, the guide remained quiet, and Alice acted as Brandon's personal narrator.

"It begins with the creation, and goes on from there," she told Brandon, forgetting in the excitement of the moment that Brandon already knew about the Sistine Chapel from his own art studies.

"There's God creating the heavens and earth," Alice continued, pointing to a panel.

"I know, sweetie," said Brandon. "And there's God giving life to Adam."

Next to them, an arrogant Bostonian began taking flash videos with his device, which they'd been told was strictly prohibited.

"Sir, you must stop that," said a uniformed attendant. "It is not allowed."

"They're concerned about the light causing the colors to fade," Alice told the man.

"Fuck him," said the man, and continued recording. The attendant stood by, unsure what to do.

"Jerk," said Alice.

Brandon led his wife away from the obnoxious fool.

"That's the Last Judgment," Alice explained, pointing. "The unfortunates on the right are on their way down to the bad place."

They returned to their bus and the tour continued.

"Everything's so old," said Alice as the bus passed through the Forum, which prompted the lady seated across the aisle from her to reach over and tap Alice's knee.

"Excuse me, Miss, you're Americans, eh?"

Some but not all Machines had held on to their original national identities long after those nations had ceased to exist.

"We're Canadian," said Alice.

"Oh, so are we," said the woman. "Sorry. I meant no offense. I inferred from your comment that you were a Yank. It's what they always say when they first see Europe."

"Hmm," said Alice.

"It's amazing," said Brandon. "The history. Imagine what it must have been like when the biologicals were here. The food, the aromas, the wine, the carnival of colors and sounds."

"So you're a *poet* now?"

"Yep."

The tour continued until sundown, when the tourists arrived at a former hotel where, in a former ballroom, there were enough comfortable reclining chairs and chargers for everyone. Brandon and Alice each left their luggage on chairs that were well away the classless Bostonian and slipped off with their sexpacks to find a room.

"I couldn't look at another painting, statue or ancient ruin," said Alice after they'd returned and plugged themselves in. "I'm totally saturated."

"Me to," said Brandon.

While Machines didn't sleep, most felt the need to spend several hours each night engaged in mindless activity, like playing games on their devices. It seemed to "clear their heads" the way sleep had done for biologicals. However, at 3:37 a.m. local time, alarms began sounding on every electronic device in the cavernous ballroom. "BIOLOGICAL HUMAN SURVIVORS FOUND IN AFRICA" appeared on their screens, followed by videos showing young white men dressed in red, riding horses or driving cars or trucks. Other videos showed white men dressed in dark gray standing in fields among dark-skinned people dressed in gray or beige who appeared to be working.

Soon, the world would learn that the white men shown in the videos were overseers, descendants of Russian mafia families that had enslaved generations of black Africans. The dark-skinned workers shown in the videos were their slaves.

The tourists were stunned. For a time, no one spoke.

"Oh my God," Alice whispered. "How could they have survived?"

"Some of the black people looked like they might be operating farm equipment," said Brandon. "They were too far away to tell for sure."

A newsman came on and explained that, while several of the African expeditions had encountered biological humans, most expeditions had not. "So far, it's all very puzzling."

"But it's also very exciting," said the newswoman seated next to him. "Biological humanity isn't extinct."

The tourists remained glued to their devices until sunrise, eager for more details. Just after 4 a.m. local time, word came that travelers had spotted survivors in three African regions.

"My God," said Brandon, "I can't believe it."

The sounds of excited discussion and speculation filled the ballroom for several hours, until the travelers boarded their bus for the trip to Florence.

"I'm having a blast," said Alice after they'd toured Florence. It had thrilled her to see Michelangelo's famous statue of David in person.

The great master's "Florence" Pieta, housed in the *Opera del Duomo* museum, was another of their favorites. Less well known than Michelangelo's Roman Pieta, which they'd seen at St. Peter's, the unfinished Florence pieta had a roughness that made its depiction of the aftermath of Christ's death even more powerful, Alice thought. Brandon hadn't realized that the bearded figure standing behind the Blessed Virgin, who represented a Biblical figure named Nicodemus, was actually a self-portrait of the aging master himself.

Alice emitted a wicked chuckle as their bus was leaving Florence and put her hand on Brandon's shoulder. "It's amazing how *tiny* David is in relation to his size," she told Brandon.

"Uh-huh," said Brandon, without lifting his eyes from his device.

He's somewhere else, Alice thought.

Ever since they'd heard the news from Africa, he'd done nothing but read article after article on genetics—articles that had appeared hundreds of years earlier in scientific and lay publications. She'd had enough.

"Okay, what's going on?" Alice asked.

Brandon looked up, startled.

"I had a thought. I'll share it with you, if you like."

"Fire away."

"Okay. Early in the 21st century—or late in the 20th, I'm not sure—geneticists developed technology that allowed them to modify genes. One type of modification was done on embryos and was called 'germ-line' modification because it changed the genetics not only of the person who would later be born, but the genetics of the person's descendants as well. Another type of modification was called 'somatic' because it was administered to people who were already alive. Somatic modifications were not inherited by the subject's offspring."

"Then why were they made?" Alice asked.

"It was a medical treatment for people who had or were genetically prone to get a hereditary disease, or had other hereditary issues," Brandon explained. "They injected genetic material into the subjects in a form whereby it propagated itself throughout the person's body and replaced the relevant gene or genes in all the body's cells except the eggs or sperm. It got remarkable results, from what I've read, but it was a one-shot deal.

"When they altered the genetics of an embryo, they called it 'editing.' Initially, embryonic editing, like somatic genetic treatments, was used to deal with things like hereditary diseases. The public and the scientific community approved of that. How could they not? Medical researchers had already identified a number of diseases and defects that were tied to 'bad' or missing genes. So, once it was perfected, this type of genetic engineering worked wonders."

"I see," said Alice.

"But the idea of using gene modification to promote *positive* traits—by adding the genes and genetic markers associated with those traits—attracted a lot of attention and controversy. Rich people could give their descendants a permanent genetic edge over children born to common folk. There was also concern that unfettered tinkering with the human genome could bring about unforeseen nightmare scenarios. So the practice was restricted or even banned in most countries, and there was little if any funding for it. But researchers did it anyway, on the sly or by setting up shop in places that allowed it. They didn't need a lot of expensive equipment or large lab spaces.

"There was no coordinated effort, but little by little, news of genetic enhancements came dribbling out, and in 2137, the United Nations banned positive human embryo editing and somatic treatments and imposed severe sanctions on the handful of nations that still allowed it. Some researchers no doubt kept at it, but it declined precipitously, and had been more or less brought to a halt by around 2179."

"Hmm," said Alice.

"There's one more part that I think you'll find interesting. Twenty-first century geneticists also figured out how to create embryos using eggs and/or sperm that they created from other body cells, like skin cells."

"I remember reading about that."

"It was a promising concept. Women whose eggs had been damaged by radiation, or were infertile for some other reason, could still have children. Gay and lesbian couples could also become parents—biological parents."

"My God. How?"

"Listen to this. Scientists had known for a long time how to turn skin cells into things called 'embryonic stem cells.' In 2014, the year Graham and Mollie met, researchers showed that stem cells could be programmed to form things called 'primordial germ cells,' which can become either sperm or eggs. In a male, the germ cells become sperm, and in a female, they become eggs. But in 2130, researchers at the University of Chicago came up with a way to trick the primordial germ cells into going whichever way they wanted them to go—egg or sperm."

"Amazing," said Alice.

"I'm almost finished, so bear with me. If the same-sex couple were men, they'd take skin from one man and make eggs and use sperm from the other guy. If the couple were women, they'd take skin cells from one of them and make sperm and use it to fertilize an egg taken from the other one."

"Do you know if they did many of these?"

"I imagine they did. One more interesting tidbit. According to one article, researchers in 2142 took skin cells from a man and turned the skin cells into eggs, which they fertilized with the man's own sperm."

"A clone. Wow."

"It was an interesting technical accomplishment, but it had little if any practical significance once biologicals could have their minds copied and installed in Machines. The biological clones would have had the same DNA as their originals, but they'd have zero memory of having actually *been* their original—whose mind would have died when their body did. So why bother? Anyway, that's what I've pulled together. I told you about the skin cells because it's interesting. But for our purposes, donated eggs and sperm would work fine."

"Our purposes?"

Brandon chuckled. "I've saved the best for last. High intelligence is an inheritable trait, right?"

"Obviously..."

"Well listen to this. Shortly before they shut it all down, geneticists had begun the process of identifying variants in the genomes of highly intelligent people that were rare in the general population."

"Like the electrical variants we were looking for?" Alice asked...

"Better," said Brandon. "The discovery of biological human survivors in Africa has reopened the possibility of using human genetic engineering to improve human intelligence. We'll need studies to isolate more genetic variants that correlate with high intelligence. And we'll do it! We'll edit them into embryos. We'll have to find out how they did it. The equipment they did it with must still be out there somewhere--and people of metal who could teach us how to use it."

"That's an intriguing idea," said Alice.

"There's more. Down the road, you and I will copy our subjects' genetically enhanced minds and figure out how transfer the enhancements from the e-brains to us."

"So we'll get smarter too," said Alice.

He put his arm around her and pulled her closer to him. "Sky's the limit, Babe. It could transform the world if we can figure out how to promote it and get it done on a large enough scale."

"That's the problem, isn't it?" said Alice. "We'd have to be discreet."

"It was controversial for a reason," said Brandon. "The people who opposed it weren't anti-science Luddites. But the world is smaller now. We'd be the only ones doing it. We'd impose safeguards and a strict protocol."

"Where would we start?"

"The Machine Federation might back us, based on our track record with bodies," said Brandon. "We'd be able to get their attention, at least."

"We could start by joining the Animal Project," said Alice. "They have people working in animal genetics. They must do editing. What else would they be doing? If so, they'll have all the necessary stuff. We could join that group and learn the ropes by working with animal embryos."

"Great idea," said Brandon. "We'll have to check it out when we get back."

Their next stop on the tour was the tower of Pisa, which was smaller and less impressive than they'd expected. Brandon had de-mystified the landmark by researching the mundane engineering reasons the tower had leaned but hadn't fallen.

The highlight of their next stop, Milan, was the city's *Duomo*. It was the largest cathedral in Italy and the world's fifth largest Christian church. It was thought to contain more statues than any other building in the world, church or otherwise: some 3,400 of them, including 135 gargoyles. It had taken thousands of workers, a new canal system and over six centuries to complete.

"These churches are depressing," said Alice. "They're beautiful, but without the biologicals, they seem dead."

Milan itself struck Alice and Brandon as rather plain compared to Rome and Florence. Aside from its famous *Duomo*, it was a typical modern city. In its heyday, it had been a creative center for designers of fashions, furniture and cleverly designed tools and appliances.

Venice, which they visited next, lived up to the photos and videos they'd seen, but the gondolas and the gondoliers were gone. Motor-powered boats shuttled tourists to and from the various landmarks. The beauty of its canals and the famous churches, bridges and other buildings remained, but they, too, seemed dead, and sad. Brandon and Alice weren't sorry when the time came to leave.

"Why does everything seem so sad?" Alice wondered. "We had a blast in Rome and Florence."

"It's the cumulative effect," said Brandon.

The couple perked up when they reached their next stop, Bologna, "There's so much history here," Alice said as their bus entered the city's oldest section. "Their university was established in 1088 and remained in continuous operation until it closed its doors in 2201. It was the oldest continuously operating university in human history."

Their visit to Bologna included a walking tour of the old school.

"Now *this* is to hard process," said Brandon. "Students trod these stones for centuries. It must have seemed to them that it would go on forever. So much loss."

"It is what it is," said Alice.

• • • • •

"Pompeii was the highlight," Alice reflected on the flight back to Boston. "It was fascinating, but it was so, so sad."

"It wasn't all sad," said Brandon. "The erotic paintings were hot as hell, and the phallic sculpture on a cobblestone that pointed the way to the brothel was hilarious."

They had a good laugh.

• • • • •

Upon landing in Boston, they learned that the World Machine Federation had launched a Human Rescue Initiative to save the African survivors.

"This is perfect timing for our *entrée* into the Animal Project," said Alice. "We'll explain that we're eager to come join the project as geneticists so we can help develop more bountiful species of cattle, sheep, chickens and so forth, to help the survivors in Africa. Let's go to New York and see whoever's in charge of the animals."

Brandon agreed and they boarded the next train bound for New York City. Alice used her device to find the name of the person who headed the Animal Project, and by the time their train left the station, she'd arranged a meeting for the following morning.

"We can't let on that our goal is human genetic enhancement," said Alice.

"Assuming they accept us," said Brandon. "We have zero genetics credentials, so we'll have to wing it."

Chapter 5
Animals

Office of Alton Bean
Animal Project director
World Machine Federation Headquarters
New York City
Next day

"Nice head," Brandon told Director Bean after the three of them had shaken hands.

"You're very kind."

"I agree," said Alice. "Your original must have been a hunk."

"My goodness, thank you. Your people do amazing work."

"We appreciate your seeing us," said Brandon. "As I mentioned when we spoke, we're excited like everyone else about the news from Africa and we're anxious to do whatever we can to help. If you've glanced at our resumes, you'll have seen that we have training and experience in a number of scientific and engineering disciplines. Neither of us is much of what you'd call an animal person, but—I mean, we're dog lovers, but— "

"What Brandon means," Alice blurted, "is that we've focused more on the physical sciences than the biological ones."

"Both of you studied neuroscience."

"Right," said Alice, ad-libbing, "but in practice, neuroscience is more like electrical engineering than biology. That's how it seemed to us, anyway."

"I see," said Bean.

"Anyway, when we heard about the survivors," Alice continued, "we gave a lot of thought about what we could do to help, and settled on genetics. "

"We didn't imagine there'd be an urgent need in Africa right now for neuroscientists, or electrical, mechanical or computer engineers," said Brandon. "Not for a while. But we figured we could contribute to the rescue initiative now by becoming Animal Project geneticists."

"You're both accomplished scientists," said Bean. "But you'd be starting in genetics from scratch. Ordinarily, we look for people who already have experience."

"We're quick studies. We'll bust our butts."

"I understand, but the Federation frowns on moving people from important leadership positions, like yours, to work that has a much lower priority."

"At this point, the Project pretty much runs itself," said Brandon. "We've built a first-class management team."

"We're just figureheads at this point," Alice added.

Bean made a steeple with his fingers.

"Please," Alice pleaded. "We want to do our part to help the survivors. We'll make a difference."

"It won't happen," said Brandon, "but if the Body Enhancement Project misses so much as a single beat for any reason, we'll march right back to Worcester."

"Well then," said Bean, nodding his head, "you've convinced me. When can you start and where would you like to be stationed?"

"What do you think, Alice?" said Brandon. "A week?"

"Or less," said Alice. "What location do you think would be best for us, Mr. Bean?"

"I'd have to say the Upstate Medical Research Facility. It's about two hundred miles north of here. One of their geneticists, Bill Weinberg, just left the Animal Project to help run the Initiative, so they could use the help."

"Sounds great," said Brandon.

"So you'll be resigning your positions with the Body Enhancement Project."

"Yes," said Brandon. "It'll be in good hands."

"You doofus!" said Alice after they'd left Bean's office. She was laughing. "*Not animal people*? To the freaking director of the *Animal* Project?"

Brandon shrugged and also laughed. "What can I say?"

They picked up a car, drove from New York City to Worcester and spent the following day wrapping up their tenure at the Body Enhancement Project. They spent five days after that reading basic genetics texts; and the day after that, they loaded their clothes and electronic devices into their car and were on their way.

• • • • •

In transit
Upstate New York

"Spring is the nicest season in the Northeast," said Alice.

"Fall is also nice," said Brandon. "It's been a pleasant drive. I like having a car. We can take rides in the countryside in our spare time."

"Sure."

Animal Project
Upstate Medical Research Facility
May 2527

Director Bean had given Alice and Brandon the name of Dr. Harry G. Garrett. His original, Dr. Marcus G. Garrett, had been a prominent genetic engineer in the late 21st and early 22nd centuries. Marcus had transitioned into animal genetics in 2137 after the United Nations banned positive human genome editing. Dr. Harry Garrett headed the small genetics group at the Upstate Medical Research Facility.

He was tall with large hands and feet. His chest and legs were massive, and his head was topped with a mound of curly red hair. As Brandon and Alice would eventually learn, Garrett's custom body was not a facsimile of Marcus's, or of some other biological human he'd admired. It was simply the kind of body Marcus had always wished he'd had. Marcus G. Garrett himself had been short and scrawny.

"I'm delighted to meet both of you," Garrett said, shaking their hands. "Deee-lighted."

He's channeling Teddy Roosevelt, Brandon thought, and took an immediate liking to the man. *He even has Teddy's toothy smile down pat. Nice teeth.*

"We're delighted to be here," said Brandon.

"Can't wait to get started," said Alice.

"I must say," said Garrett, "the two of you are by far the most educated people I've ever met, based solely on what you've done as metallics. Most of us, like me, simply stay with whatever their originals did for a living. Why wouldn't we? You two must be restless souls. I admire that."

"It's kept us busy," said Brandon. "We spent most of the past week reading genetics textbooks, and we're anxious to learn more. Director Bean said you'd start by having us help with the editing and give us study material for our nighttime reading."

"Yeah. That's how I worked it with your predecessor. We're a research institution, so all of our editing is positive, and cumulative from generation to generation. The veterinary people supply our team with the embryos that we edit, and transfer the edited embryos to their prospective mothers."

"How long will it take us to become proficient editors?" Alice asked.

"Minutes," said Garrett. "The equipment does everything. It's a piece of cake. You load the tools into the unit and it performs the edit. 'Tools' is genetics slang for the synthesized genetic material that's introduced into the embryo and does the editing. Your job as geneticists will be to figure out which genes will produce the desired genetic enhancements when edited in. In the next day or two, after you're settled in, I'll give each of you your first projects to work on. I set it up that way because I've found that people learn more quickly and gain confidence faster when they work on their own, rather than in groups.

"Martha will show you around, get you squared away on the equipment and familiarize you with our genetics database. Officially, she's described as a genetically modified orangutan, because no one in authority has laid down guidelines for the point where a genetically enhanced orangutan has attained human status. But as far as I'm concerned, she's as human as we are. I prefer to think of her as a person of orangutan ethnicity.

"How many genetic engineers do you have?" Brandon asked.

"Four, counting the two of you, Martha and myself," said Garrett. "We're a small group, but we've had a good bit of success, and it's fun work."

"We've never met an orangutan," said Alice, "but we've seen them on TV. Dr. Suzy had several of them on her show. They're amazing.

"So *positive!*"

"I love their voices," said Brandon. "They're a bit reedy, aren't they? Almost kazoo-like."

Garrett laughed.

"They appreciate the unprecedented opportunities they've been given and they're determined to make the most of them. Martha, for example, has been studying genetics under my supervision for almost five years. With Weinberg out of the picture, she's coming into her own.

Her outward manner is blunt and direct, in a good way, but her intellect is subtle and intuitive. We're lucky to have her."

Garrett came out from behind his desk.

"I'll introduce you to Tom Joyce next. He's in charge of the equipment that synthesizes our genetic materials. After that I'll introduce you to Martha. You'll love her. Everyone does."

The Delaneys followed Garrett down the hall into a combination office and laboratory where a tall, handsome man whom they recognized was seated at a workstation. Gowned and gloved technicians were busy attending several rows of gleaming scientific equipment.

"Tom Joyce," said Garrett, "I'd like you to meet Brandon and Alice Delaney, our new geneticists. Tom has Ph.Ds in genetics and biochemistry. I don't know what we'd do without him. Tom's original was the chief science guy at a leading 22nd-century manufacturer of genetic editing materials."

"John Booker," said Alice, indicating Joyce's body.

"Good catch!" said Joyce.

The original John Booker had been an iconic rock star in the 2140's.

"Brandon and Alice are the founders and former heads of the Body Enhancement Project," said Garrett.

"Booker was one of our most popular models," said Brandon.

"I wasn't particularly sexy as a biological," Joyce admitted, "but hey, better late than never."

"When Tom's original and the rest of his company's management succumbed to the Malaise, they left a warehouse full of brand-new equipment," Garrett explained. "It was still there when Tom arrived in 2405 with a fleet of Animal Project trucks, and we were in business. We have most of it in storage for when we need replacements."

"It's impressive," said Alice.

"Thanks," said Joyce. "Stop by any time you like and I'll describe it all for you."

"They're mechanical engineers, among many other things," said Garrett.

Next, Garrett took them to a library area where six orangutans sat around a long table, reading from or entering data into electronic devices.

"Martha, I'd like you to meet our new colleagues, the Delaneys," said Garrett.

Martha was seated at the other end of the table. She grinned and practically sprang from her seat. "Yes sir! Delaneys, my name is Martha, no last name, don't need one."

She pumped their hands vigorously.

"We're pleased to meet you, Martha," said Alice. "I'm Alice and this is my husband Brandon."

"Thanks for the intro, Dr. Harry," said Martha. "I'll show Dr. Brandon and Dr. Alice around and get them squared away, as we discussed."

"Please, just call us Alice and Brandon," said Brandon.

Martha smiled and nodded.

Garrett excused himself and Martha led the Delaneys outside to an electric cart.

"It's a big facility," said Martha. "It'd take us forever to do this on foot."

Before they could begin, a phone rang. "Excuse me," said Martha and pulled her phone from a pocket of her overalls. From the intimate, almost seductive tone that her reedy orangutan voice took on, Alice guessed she was speaking with her boyfriend or husband. When Martha said, "I can't wait to take you for a ride," before ending the call, Alice was sure. It was sweet.

"I'm sorry," said Martha. "Off we go."

Martha hadn't exaggerated. The Upstate Medical Research Facility was huge. The genetics group was but a minuscule part of it.

"We have thousands upon thousands of animals here. Some of them are here for research, and get to live long, full lives. Others must be sacrificed to feed our carnivores."

"What do *you* eat?" Alice asked. "If you don't mind my asking."

"I don't mind. We orangutans eat fruit. It's over sixty percent of our diet. We also like young leaves—they're about one-fourth of our diet. Flowers and bark are another tenth. We also like insects—ants, termites, pupae and crickets, when they're in season. They're a delicacy."

"In olden times, photos often showed your people eating bananas," said Alice. "It was a stereotype."

Martha shrugged. She did not seem to mind being stereotyped, perhaps because she realized this stereotype was harmless and in no way meant to be demeaning. Generations would pass before ethnic orangutans and other genetically modified species were recognized as full-fledged humans, and bigotry by conventional humans toward more recent additions to their race began to rear its ugly head.

"I *love* bananas," Martha declared, "when the commissary remembers to order them. Too bad they won't grow here. Anyway, as this Facility's name suggests, most of its buildings are devoted to pure research. Medical *care* is administered in clinics that are attached to or contained within the barns or other structures, if any, within which particular animals live. Animals who live in the wild are brought in if they're found sick or injured."

"This place is amazing," said Alice.

"Now I'll take you to the site of one of my own projects," said Martha, "so you can see an example of what we do here. Dr. Harry had the idea for the project and gave it to Mr. Bill. Mr. Bill ran it until he left, and I took it over. Dr. Harry has been teaching me genetics for years, and giving me small projects to run, so I was ready, or so I thought."

"Would Mr. Bill be Bill Weinberg?" Alice asked.

"Yes, if you include his second name," said Martha.

A short time later they entered a vast, barren area that fire had scorched and blackened. It went on as far as they could see on either side, and as far as they could see in the direction they were driving. A while later, they began to see herds of farm animals: cattle, sheep, goats and so on.

"These are the subjects. Dr. Harry wanted to see what would happen if certain domesticated animals who hadn't had to worry about food for thousands of years suddenly had to go out and look for it. He had workers burn the pastures as far as the animals could see in any direction, and they held off giving the animals replacement food to see if they'd go off in search of greener pastures—which one day they might have to do if a large meteor struck the Earth or some other natural disaster occurred."

"Let me guess," said Brandon. "They stayed right here."

"Yes sir. They didn't move. Dr. Harry thought that would happen. Mr. Bill's job was to edit generation after generation of embryos on a cumulative basis until he produced animals who'd go out and look for food instead of just standing here."

"Did Dr. Harry tell Mr. Bill what kind of traits to edit in?" Alice asked.

"No, he left that to Mr. Bill to figure out. Dr. Harry wants his people to think things through themselves so they'll become scientists rather than mere technicians. Mr. Bill thought insufficient survival instinct was the problem, so he spoke with biologists and got the names of species of animals with strong survival instincts and asked Dr. Tom to make him tools—genetic editing material—with genes and genetic markers of those species that Dr. Tom thought might be responsible for those animals having those instincts."

"I see," said Alice. "How's the project going?"

"Slowly. A while back, Mr. Bill brought me out here to operate the editing machine for him. By then he was bored with being a geneticist and wanted nothing more to do with it. Our most successful group to date has gained just enough survival instinct to wander over to the next blackened field in search of food. But they stop there."

"Have you considered the possibility that this behavior might result from a lack of intelligence, rather than a lack of survival instinct?" Brandon asked.

Martha considered this.

"Gosh, no, I never considered that possibility. Excellent point! I should have thought of that."

"Martha, did Mr. Bill know about your knowledge of and experience in genetic engineering?" Alice asked.

"No," said Martha. "We barely spoke. He was a grouch."

"Failure does that to people," said Brandon. "It's too bad."

• • • • •

Animal Project
Upstate Medical Research Facility
April 2535

Garrett had agreed with Brandon and Alice that low intelligence probably explained the animals' poor performance.

"Nice work," he told them. "I've sent you some links on the genetics of intelligence to get you started."

They learned that analogues to genetic variants that had been linked to human intelligence also appeared in the genomes certain "smart" animals. With Tom Joyce's help, they identified several species whose genome contained those analogues and began editing them into their animal embryos on a cumulative basis, in batches of five genes per embryo, plus associated genetic markers.

Within five years, they started seeing results. Four years after that, Garrett declared the experiment successful after at least one individual from each animal species had found its way to the green pastures that lay just over three miles away in any direction.

Meanwhile, they'd launched several other projects that were also producing positive results.

"When do we want to bring up human genetics?" Alice asked Brandon one night in the privacy of their room.

"There's no rush. As we've seen on TV, Africa has just begun rebuilding. The Initiative has too much on its plate to even consider this now. Our best bet might be to wait until African colleges and universities are established. When that happens, they'll need scientists in all disciplines, including genetics. It could be our entrée."

"So we'll keep going here."

"It's as good a place as any. Some of what we develop here might even carry over to humans. Meanwhile, I suggest that we prepare ourselves by learning one of the principal African languages."

"Good idea," said Alice. "I believe Swahili is one of the most common."

"I'll contact the Initiative's New York office and have them send us study materials."

• • • • •

Animal Project
Upstate Medical Research Facility
September 2576

Alice and Brandon were watching the weekly TV report on developments in Africa. A lot was happening.

"The Initiative has announced a major undertaking," said the newsman, "which they're calling the Marshall Plan 2.0 after the Marshall Plan that helped rebuild Western Europe after the Second World War. The new plan aims to help Africa raise its technology to the mid-20th century level, as a first step. In related plans, a full-scale effort is being mounted to rebuild Africa's educational and vocational training infrastructure, with the goal of returning those institutions to their previous level and beyond."

African colleges and universities had closed their doors beginning in 2212 when the Most Exalted Prince of Kenya ordered the closure of his country's post-secondary schools. Being illiterate himself, he saw no need for institutions of higher learning. Other African rulers followed suit and one by one they abolished their colleges and universities until the last of them closed its doors in 2220.

The newsman's female colleague took over.

"The Initiative has invited former college professors in all disciplines, and people with equivalent credentials who worked in research institutions or in the private sector, to apply for the new African professorships. Resumes should be sent to the Initiative at its New York City headquarters."

"Yes!" said Alice.

"I think it might be time to have a chat with Harry," said Brandon.

The following day, after work, Brandon asked Garrett if he had a minute.

"I have all the time in the world," said Harry. It had become a stock Machine expression. He ushered Brandon and Alice into his office and closed the door.

"What's up?"

"Did you see the Africa report last night," Brandon asked.

"Yes. Sounds like great news."

"They're recruiting university professors."

"Yes, I saw that, too."

"As you yourself know better than anyone," said Brandon, "responsible genetic engineering, with proper safeguards and controls, could improve the quality and perhaps even the length of biological human lives immeasurably."

Garrett's face wore a neutral expression, but he seemed to be listening.

"Alice and I were wondering if you'd consider forming a genetics department in one of the colleges, with you as department head, Tom Joyce as head of genetic biochemistry and us as junior faculty."

"We could also establish programs in plant and animal genetics to help improve plant and livestock yields," said Alice.

"Alice and I have been studying Swahili at least one night a week for the past thirty years," said Brandon. "If we went to a school in Kenya, for example, we could handle the teaching load until you learned the language, if you chose to do that."

"Well how about that," said Garrett, laughing. "I've been thinking the same thing ever since they discovered the survivors."

"So have we," said Brandon, "but we were afraid to bring it up. We understand how sensitive the whole subject of human genetic engineering was back in the day. But that's the reason we came to work here. To prepare."

Garrett flashed his toothy Teddy Roosevelt grin.

"So that's that. We'll send them our resumes with a note asking them to hire us as a team."

"Yes!" said. Brandon.

Alice couldn't contain her excitement. "I just now realized how much I've missed biologicals. Africa, here we come!"

Chapter 6
Academia

Department of Genetics
University of Nairobi
Autumn 2576

Alice and Brandon loved the biological humans. They'd forgotten how excitable and spontaneous they could be. They lived in the moment, just as Graham and Mollie had done so long ago.

Four months earlier, Garrett, the Delaneys and Tom Joyce had been placed as a group on the faculty of the University of Nairobi. In the case of Alice and Brandon, the Initiative had waived the requirement of a Ph.D. in genetics on the strength of Garrett's recommendation, and the years of instruction and hands-on work experience that he'd given them. Initially, theirs would be the only such department on the continent.

"We need to be careful how much genetic engineering we teach biologicals," Garrett told Brandon and Alice. "I want to require students, even undergrads who sign up for courses above a certain level, to undergo periodic lie detector tests. Even then, there's no guarantee. They may be honest and pass a lie test now, but later on, after they've left us, they could succumb to temptation and agree to sell their skills and knowledge to bad guys. Now that we're back in the biological human world, we'll need to keep tight control over our work product."

"Lie detectors aren't all that accurate, are they?" Brandon asked.

"They weren't," said Garrett, "but by the mid-21st century they'd become so accurate that their results were admissible as evidence in federal and most state courts. I'll have the Initiative find some for us."

"You might also want to keep the details of our work off of computers," said Brandon. "Otherwise, hackers could break in and steal sensitive information."

He'd have made the same point even without Graham's prompting.

"That's a nice idea in theory," said Garrett, "but it's not practical. Most of our work requires the use of computers."

"We could make a point of keeping those computers offline and use other devices for sending emails or making non-sensitive computations."

"We can do that," said Garrett. "Good idea."

"But only if it's and consistently applied," said Brandon.

"Tell you what, Brandon, I'm putting you in charge of enforcing that policy," said Garrett.

"No problem."

"One other thing," said Garrett. "Martha's granddaughter Laura would like to come over and work with us, if we'll take on some of her friends and cousins. They're all geneticists at the Upstate facility. She's dying to experience Africa, but she doesn't want to be the only ethnic orangutan human on the continent. They're especially eager to learn human genetics. I told her they could enroll in our graduate program. Do you guys agree?"

"Of course," said Alice. "We love her. We'll love them all."

"They'll be great," said Brandon.

Four months later

Laura lumbered into the busy laboratory accompanied by her boyfriend, Robert, whom she practically pulled through the doorway.

"Hello everyone, I'm Laura and this is Robert. This place is a total mess, as it should be. It looks like our lab back home, doesn't it, Robert? Robert just asked me to marry him and I said yes. Isn't that right Robert?"

"Yes," said Robert.

"Robert's a geneticist too."

Alice smiled. *Is he blushing?*

"Congratulations," said Garrett.

"We want you to marry us, Dr. Harry," said Laura. "Everyone's invited. We'll have a party afterward with all the fruit, leaves, bark and insects anyone can eat."

"Sure, I'll marry you two," said Garrett. "I'd be honored."

"This is such wonderful news," said Alice.

• • • • •

"We'll need a wedding present," said Alice. "Any ideas?"

"Maybe a food processor, if we can find one," said Brandon. "They could make insect smoothies."

Chapter 7
The Positive Side

Department of Genetics
University of Nairobi
Autumn 2616

As mentioned earlier, there were two types of genetic modification: "negative" modification, done by removing or blocking "bad" genes; and "positive" modification, done by adding genes associated with desirable traits. The modifications could be "germ-line" modifications made to embryos, in which case the genetic changes would be heritable; or "somatic" modifications to existing people, which would not be heritable.

On their first day, Garrett announced that they'd outsource somatic treatments and concentrate on germ-line modification. Initially, all of their work would be on the negative side. Eventually, however, when he felt the time was right, they'd go positive.

"Tom will make the vectors for somatic treatments and sell them to hospitals and clinics," said Garrett. "Our focus will be on the negative editing of embryos until we've eliminated all existing heritable diseases and dysfunctions from the African gene pool once and for all. How does that sound?"

"Heroic," said Alice. "That is why we're here."

Garrett secured funding for construction of a large manufacturing facility just outside the city in which biochemists and technicians working under Tom Joyce's direction would synthesize the genetic materials Garrett's department would need, using equipment that Joyce had shipped from North America.

They started by recruiting gynecological technicians experienced in collecting and fertilizing human eggs. Next, they trained a small army of workers to operate the elegant, user-friendly editing equipment that Brandon and Alice had used during their time with the Animal Project. The equipment automatically inserted the editing materials into the embryos, and, when finished, scanned the edited embryos to confirm the results. The edited embryos emerged from the equipment in small, sealed containers filled with saline, ready to be transferred to an artificial womb. (Women hadn't given birth *in utero* for centuries.) At Garrett's request, the university opened a medical/genetics clinic where prospective parents who were missing key genes, or carried "bad" genes, could have a child whose embryo had been cleansed of the bad genes and/or supplied with missing ones. Over time, Garrett's department, working with the university's medical school, opened clinics in other major cities across Africa. Little by little, they were winning their battle against heritable disease and dysfunction.

Their results spanned decades and generated a great deal of favorable publicity for the department and the university. After fifty years, however, Garrett's team had yet to do "positive" genetic editing, even experimentally.

Given what his group had accomplished on the negative side, Garrett decided in 2616 that it was time to begin doing positive editing as well — experimentally at first, then on embryos that would grow to be full-fledged biological humans.

It was a new world now; the slate was clean. For the time being, at least, Garrett and his team would be the only people in the world doing positive genetic editing. He'd make sure they did it right.

Garrett called Brandon and Alice into his office the following morning and closed the door.

"We're going positive," he announced, "and I have something special to share with you guys. You'll be as excited as I am. In the mid-22nd century, 2156 to be exact, geneticists from a consortium of elite universities published the results of a huge research project that had taken twenty-five years to complete. First, they'd identified hundreds of individuals who were particularly strong exemplars of particular positive traits—two hundred traits, from the very general, like basic intelligence or linguistic ability, to more specific traits, like fine motor skills and various types of analytical ability. I remember trying to think of a trait they did *not* study. I couldn't, other than things like hair, eye or skin color."

Garrett opened a file on his wall screen.

"As far as I know, this is the only copy of their report that still exists," said Garrett. "No one else has it."

Alice and Brandon had seen similar kinds of studies, focused on a single trait, but the scope of this study was amazing.

"Brilliant," said Brandon after he'd skimmed the introduction.

Because the study aimed to identify portions of individual genomes that correlated with particular traits that not every person had, the researchers had ignored the part of the human genome that was identical in all humans (*i.e.*, 99.9%) and focused on variants. Their aim was to identify genetic variants called single-nucleotide polymorphisms ("SNPs") that were associated with a particular traits. They recorded the variable portion of the genomes of the human subjects in each category—e.g., people who were talented musicians, or mathematicians—and tabulated the frequency with which particular SNPs were present in those subjects' genomes, expressed as a percentage.

"The higher the percentage, the stronger the SNP's correlation was with the trait in question," Garrett explained. "In most cases, there was a strong correlation with several variants, as you can see in Appendix I-A."

"Oh my God," said Alice. "They're practically recipes."

"Exactly," said Garrett. "A ton of shit rained down on the people and institutions that had participated in this study, for obvious reasons. The UN had banned positive editing. It was anathema. Yet here was a group of elite universities publishing what in effect was a cookbook for rogue genetic engineers to follow. What were they thinking? The consortium succumbed to the pressure and deleted the report, and an army of geeks combed the Net to find and remove any references to or excerpts from it. Otherwise, the two of you would have found it when you were doing your research. Investigators also expunged all records of the consortium and the participating schools that pertained to the study."

"But you managed to save a copy," said Brandon.

"Yes, I did. This will be our secret. No one but the three of us can ever know we have it."

"Understood," said Brandon.

"Absolutely," Alice agreed.

"I've had Tom Joyce gearing up for this from the moment we got here," said Garrett. "We'll only do a single trait per embryo, but as you can see, even then, we'll be introducing large numbers of discrete SNPs and associated markers for each trait. Tom has assured me it won't be a problem."

In fact, it was almost too easy.

2710

"Brandon, I don't begrudge the biologicals the enhancements we're giving them," Alice announced one morning as they were leaving their apartment for work, "but—"

"—but what about us?" said Brandon. "I know."

"It's only fair, and it'll make us better geneticists," said Alice.

"I agree. But how do we explain to Harry that we want to copy our subjects' minds so we can use their e-brains to figure out how to transfer the enhancements to ourselves? I mean, how do we explain to him that we know how to make equipment that can do that?"

"I've always assumed you'd simply tell him about Graham."

"I don't know. I'm still reluctant to reveal who our originals were. We've been with Harry for more than a hundred years. I trust him like a brother. But people can let things slip, without meaning to. We've all done that. But who knows what the consequences would be if people knew who my original was? They might want nothing to do with me, or you."

"So use a cover story. Tell him we re-engineered Gordon's work."

"I'd hate to lie to him."

Alice laughed. "It would be true. You're not Graham, you're a separate person, so if you, Brandon, built the copying equipment, it would be quite literally a re-engineering of Graham's work."

Brandon rolled his eyes and chuckled.

"I'm serious," Alice said.

Brandon thought for a few moments.

"In the grand scheme of things, it doesn't really matter what I tell him, does it?"

"No harm, no foul," said Alice.

"But we'll still have to explain why we need the copies."

They fell silent for several moments until Alice came up with an idea:

"We need a reference library of e-brains with different combinations of enhanced traits that could be recopied and installed in bodies. This would enable us to quickly produce a task force of super-smart people of metal with enhanced skills to deal with contingencies that might arise in the future. They'd be *way* smarter than the existing metallic population."

"Like what," said Brandon, "to repel an invasion of extraterrestrials?"

"Not likely. I'm thinking things like epidemics, wildfires or other natural disasters. Super-smart Machine doctors and medics would be a godsend. Also, given that we're dealing with biologicals, we could be looking at war."

"That makes sense, I guess," said Brandon.

"Who knows? But the history of biological humans was practically one war after another."

They talked strategy for the next two hours.

The following day, Brandon had a long talk with Garrett. After confiding in Garrett that he and his wife had succeeded in re-engineering Gordon's mind-copying equipment during their years as neuroscientists, he presented Alice's proposal and laid out the reasons he and Alice had developed to support it.

"I'm impressed," said Garrett. "Still waters run deep. I won't even try to imagine what else you two will come up with in the fullness of time. But how would you propose to get subjects to let you copy their minds? What if people are put off by the idea? They seem okay with us as fellow human beings, but they haven't been out of their Dark Age all that long. What if they're afraid that our copying their minds will take something away from them? Maybe we're trying to steal their minds--or their souls. How could we convince them we weren't?"

"You're right," Brandon agreed. "If we ask their permission, we could scare their pants off. Years from now, it might not be a problem. But who knows how long that will take? But if we broach the subject now, we could poison the well for generations."

"So what do you suggest?"

Brandon and Alice had expected this question, and he was ready.

"We present the copying equipment as diagnostic gear and make the copies while 'diagnosing' our subjects."

Harry frowned. "You mean we trick them? Are you serious?"

"We wouldn't do anything with the e-brains. They'd be placed in storage, in sleep mode, where they'd remain until the end of time unless some emergency arose and we—or more, likely the Africans—needed e-brains possessing a wide range of talents from which we could create a task force of super-smart Machines to stop a war, or an epidemic, or to quell some other dire emergency."

"I see," said Garrett.

"Here's another point that we think is crucial. Should the need ever arise to place Machines in a situation, like peacekeeping, where they might be have to kill African biologicals, those Machines must not be white. We'd risk undoing all the good will the Initiative has created. It would be horrific. We cannot let that happen."

"All right, we'll do it," said Garrett. "Give me a list of everything you'll need to make the copiers."

Summer 2766

Brandon and Alice decided that the time had come to make their ersatz genitalia available to the general Machine population. They met with a reputable manufacturer and marketer of scientific equipment and arranged for its manufacture and sale. In the post-Malaise era, people of metal had jobs and were paid for their work on the same basis as biologicals. They could well afford the expensive new upgrade.

Chapter 8
Bill And Keisha

Nairobi
Summer 2766

Bill Weinberg was a person of metal whose original was William Weinberg, who had run Weinberg Associates, a New York City money management firm, in the late 21st and early 22nd centuries. Mr. Weinberg was the son of a white father and an African American mother, and the husband of Amelia Dixon, a bestselling African American novelist whose works explored the follies, foibles and corruption of coastal American elites.

Keisha Dixon was a Machine into which an e-brain copied from Amelia Dixon's mind had been installed while Amelia was still alive. As a result, even though she had Amelia's mind, Keisha developed a distinctly non-wifely relationship with Mr. Weinberg, who was still alive and happily married to Amelia. After Mr. Weinberg died and Weinberg 2.0 was created using an e-brain copied from Mr. Weinberg before his death, Keisha and Weinberg 2.0 became good friends, but nothing more. However, over the hundreds of years since Amelia and Mr. Weinberg had passed, Keisha's relationship with Weinberg the Machine (who had dropped his "2.0") had been moving toward the husband-wife relationship of their originals.

It was a hot summer evening. Weinberg was playing the piano and Keisha, as had become her habit, was staring at her screen in rapt contemplation. She'd become preoccupied with spiritual matters. She believed, for example, that certain things happened "for a reason" and were "meant to be."

"Hey Bill," said Keisha, "have you ever heard of something called the anthropic principle?"

"Sure. It was covered in a philosophy class Mr. Weinberg took. It relates to the narrow band of parameters that had to coexist in order for our universe to have formed in the precise way and in the precise combination that it did."

"I'm impressed. I'm reading an old article from the *Boston Globe*. "

"Is it a hit from your Stephen Hawking search?"

"Yup."

Weinberg rolled his eyes. Keisha had developed a near-obsession with Hawking, a famous British physicist who'd lived in the late 20th and early 21st centuries.

"Don't roll your eyes. The writer makes the case that, although Hawking remained a professed atheist until the day he died, he was too open and honest to reject the possibility that the universe was a *creation* rather than something that just happened."

"Tell me more," Weinberg said politely.

"Listen to this: The writer quotes from an essay by a scientist—I assume it was a scientist—in *The Wall Street Journal*. 'Astrophysicists now know,'" Keisha read, "'that the values of the four fundamental forces—gravity, the electromagnetic force, and the 'strong' and 'weak' nuclear forces—were determined less than one millionth of a second after the Big Bang. Alter any one value and the universe could not exist. For instance, if the ratio between the nuclear strong force and the electromagnetic force had been off by the tiniest fraction of the tiniest fraction—by even one part in 100, 000,000,000,000,000—then no stars could have ever formed at all.'"

"I understand what the writer was trying to do," said Weinberg. "The problem is, it's a truism. Like, under certain conditions, rain falls from the sky; or when the Earth has rotated sufficiently on its axis, the sun appears. Your writer is doing the same thing by pointing out that our universe came into existence because there were circumstances that caused it to happen. It states an obvious fact, but it proves nothing beyond that, like how those circumstances came to exist. It proves nothing one way or the other about whether a Creator made the universe or it was the product of random events."

"Bill, the probability of all those parameters co-existing was so small that the universe *had* to have been deliberately created," said Keisha.

"The factors you cite had to be present when *this* universe came together," Weinberg admitted, "otherwise this universe wouldn't be the way it is. But that doesn't prove that it didn't happen randomly. If you postulate a multi-verse, and an infinite timeframe, other random combinations of factors, including but not limited to the ones your writer cited, could have spawned universes much different from ours, without the involvement of a Creator. Your argument assumes that our particular universe is the only possible one. If you could demonstrate that, your probability argument would be persuasive. But you can't."

"Bullshit," said Keisha. "I studied logic. That's a bootstrap argument. You imagine a multi-verse and use it to bootstrap your randomness argument. The problem with your multi-verse postulate is that it's not falsifiable. There's no way to test it. You simply assume, with zero evidence, that other universes exist, but there's no way to test if your premise is correct."

Her argument has the same flaw, Weinberg thought. *Oh well.* He reminded himself that discretion is the better part of valor.

"Well, my dear, I must admit, your points have merit."

"Thank you. Let me read you something else, one more passage from the article. It's a quote from a book by a prominent mathematician and science historian:

"In science, the fine-tuning of the parameters required for life has such an incredibly small probability to have arisen that the famous British cosmologist Stephen Hawking has described it as follows: 'If one considers the possible constants and laws that could have emerged, the odds against a universe that has produced life like ours are immense,' and 'I think there are clearly religious implications whenever you start to discuss the origins of the universe.'"

More of the same, Weinberg thought.

"So maybe Hawking wasn't an atheist," said Weinberg, "in the strict sense of ruling out the possibility of a Creator."

"Hawking died the same year this article appeared," said Keisha. "The writer suggests that in death, Hawking may have learned the truth."

"If his mind survived his body's death."

"Right. I do realize," said Keisha, "that there's no way to take the next step and show that such a Creator gives a damn about us. He or she could be off creating other things. Or doing nothing."

"That's what religion is for."

"Maybe we'll find out more when we reach the stars."

The first one thousand starships were scheduled to leave Earth in 2771, as part of the Human Rescue Initiative, Version 2.0, and Keisha and Weinberg would be on one of them. The Initiative's aim was to assure the ultimate survival of humanity by establishing human colonies on planets in two separate sectors of Earth's galaxy. There was no immediate threat, but an asteroid could collide with the planet, or some other unforeseen and/or unpredictable disaster could occur. Even if none of that transpired, the Sun would eventually die, and life on Earth would die with it.

"Which reminds me," said Weinberg. "It's time for us to start collecting the embryos."

They did not want to keep the embryos frozen any longer than necessary, so they'd postponed the commencement of that effort. But it would take time to get the 100,000 embryos that the first expeditions would take with them.

"Should we meet with Billy?" Keisha asked, referring to her friend, Basara "Billy" Bello, the popular Zone 3 governor who was serving his third five-year term. They'd planned to ask him to help promote sperm and egg donations.

"By all means."

Office of the Governor
Nairobi
Zone 3

"Billy," said Keisha, "it's great to see you. It's been way too long."

"We've all been busy," said the governor. "Have a seat. These are the most comfortable chairs ever. They hug your body. Who knew you could cuddle with a chair?"

"Thanks for making the time," said Weinberg.

"How's it going?" the governor asked.

"Great," said Weinberg. "Everything's on schedule. We have five hundred ships, half the total we'll need for the first expeditions, and roughly half of the supplies, materials and equipment the expeditions will take with them. It's time for us to start soliciting the donation of embryos."

"As you recall, the first two expeditions will depart in five years," said Keisha, "one to each of the two planets, and we'd like to send 50,000 frozen embryos with each expedition."

"I do remember. By the way, the plan your guys put together impressed me. I meant to say something earlier. They seem to have anticipated everything down to the smallest detail. I've never seen anything like it."

"We're spoiled," said Keisha. "We get to sit back and think deep thoughts about the proverbial big picture while they do the actual work."

"Don't sell yourselves short," said Bello. "The two of you and your friends are the geniuses who had the vision to undertake this project. But I agree. Clark and Liu are the best."

"As Keisha told you," said Weinberg, "the reason we're here today is to see if we can enlist your star power to help us launch our collection effort. We'll be opening clinics in every mid-sized or larger city in the three zones to collect eggs and sperm. Volunteers, including hundreds of our people, will staff them."

"We're also considering sending mobile units out to the smaller towns and cities to receive donations," Keisha added.

"I don't know about 'star power,'" Bello said, "but I'll be happy to help in any way I can. I'm pretty sure I can also get Kabila and Abdebowale to do the same," he added, referring to the governors of Zones 1 and 2.

"Thank you so much," said Keisha. "We know how busy all three of you are. We'll try to do this as efficiently as possible to limit the demands on your time. We'll keep live appearances to a bare minimum and do most of it with TV and radio spots."

"We'll also be lining up movie stars and sports figures to help out," Weinberg added.

"We need to sell married couples on the idea of helping to preserve biological humanity by allowing us to make their son or daughter part of the founding generation of one of the colonies we'll be establishing on distant planets," said Keisha

"Sounds like a plan," said the governor, standing and shaking their hands. "I'll look forward to working with you. It'll give me an excuse to spend more time with you guys."

"Give our love to Elisha," said Keisha.

The governor's wife, Elisha Bello, was the most beautiful woman Keisha had ever met.

"I shall. She told me to give both of you hers. She also told me that we need to get together soon now that we're back in touch."

"Absolutely," said Weinberg.

Keisha smiled and gave her old friend a hug.

"We'll do it," Billy," she told him. "We have a lot of catching up to do."

The Amphitheater
Nairobi
Three days later

Weinberg smiled at his audience.

Every seat in the amphitheater was occupied. Most attendees were biologicals, but people of metal could be seen here and there.

"Good morning, everyone. I'm Bill Weinberg. My colleagues and I thank you all for agreeing to do this important and historic work. The Initiative is right on schedule. As you know, the first two expeditions will depart for the stars in five years. Your efforts will make it possible for our travelers to carry something of inestimable value with them — yourselves. The holograms you'll be making will give the first generations of children who grow up in our colonies a profound connection and sense of continuity with their forebears, and which the children will pass on to those who come after them on those distant worlds. History will remember and honor you until the end of days.

"The people in this amphitheater today represent the very best of our era, an all-star team of the most respected and most effective teachers and professors in the world — and among the most beloved by their present and former students. I know, I'm laying it on a bit thick, but I mean every word. It would be impossible to overstate the profound importance of the work you'll all be doing.

"For the benefit our TV audience, I'd like to describe that work: We'll be sending hundreds of thousands of your offspring to two distant planets, where people of metal will raise them. That may change one day, but for now, we're the only people—along with the frozen embryos—who can survive that trip.

"Psychologists and our own common sense tell us that it's essential that these children develop a sense of who and what they are, including their origins. In the broadest sense we're all part of the grand human panoply—past, present and future. But it's important for each person to have a more precise sense of who he or she is, and the people that he or she came from. This is another of the priceless gifts these folks will give them.

"They'll impart their knowledge and wisdom, methods of thought, culture, traditions and values. They'll make holograms in which they'll teach classes for every single day of elementary and high school, in every single subject. University professors will do the same for every discipline except genetics.

"The project will continue until the last expedition leaves thirty-five years from now, to update curricula to reflect the advances that will occur during the intervening years.

"When they leave here today, these fine people will return to their schools and make their holograms in classrooms, laboratories and lecture halls filled with their students, to give their eventual viewers a sense of being in those same classrooms with those students. So without further ado, I wish you all Godspeed. Thank you."

Christopher Clark, who was in overall charge of the hologram project, thanked Weinberg and adjourned the gathering.

• • • • •

Keisha noticed that when Weinberg returned home for the night, he seemed agitated. She waited patiently before bringing up the rather delicate subject she wanted to discuss with him.

She was right. Weinberg was uncomfortable, but only because he wanted to discuss the same delicate subject that Keisha did. Neither of them knew how to go about broaching it.

"So, how are things?" Keisha asked him. She'd taken the day off to waste time playing games.

"Great," said Weinberg. "Did you have a good day off?"

"Yep. I wasted the entire day."

They both spoke at once, then stopped and stared at each other.

"You go first," said Keisha.

"No, you go first," said Weinberg.

"No, you," said Keisha. "I insist. Ladies don't have to always go first," she added nervously. "It's 2766."

"Okay." Weinberg hesitated. Had he been biological, he would have blushed. "Well, I read an article this morning that I thought you might find of interest." He retrieved his device, called up the article and gave her the device. "What'll they think of next? I tell ya."

Keisha burst out laughing, retrieved her own device and called up the same article. "I was getting ready to show you the same thing."

"What did you think?"

"Well, you're right," said Keisha. "I found it interesting. *Very* interesting."

"Should we go to the store and have a look?"

"I'll call and see if these items are still available."

They were, so Keisha and Weinberg hurried out to their car and drove downtown. The shop was on the first floor of a large bank building. When they got there, people of metal were lined up outside the door and halfway around the block. Once inside, they saw glass case after glass case filled with various shapes and sizes of male and female genitalia, and they began laughing uncontrollably.

"We're sorry," said Keisha. "We were reminded of a shop our originals sometimes visited in Greenwich Village, in New York City."

The other patrons went on about their business and a salesman asked if he could show them anything.

"Uh, yeah," said Keisha. "This is embarrassing," she told Weinberg.

"Ma'am, don't be embarrassed," said the salesman, a biological. "We've been swamped by people of metal since the article appeared this morning. It's caused quite a sensation."

"May we examine them?" Weinberg asked.

"Of course."

The salesman removed several items from the case and placed them on the glass. Keisha picked up one of the male parts and giggled.

"Oh my God," said Keisha. "But shouldn't it be a little, uh—"

"It grows and becomes stiff when it's engaged," the salesman explained, and described in detail how everything worked. He explained that the original technology was over two hundred years old, but the developers had held it back until they judged that people of metal would be receptive. Meanwhile, they'd made numerous improvements and enhancements.

"Customers swear that it's as good or better than the original…uh, depending on the quality of the experience you're comparing it with," the salesman concluded.

"We're interested," said Keisha. "Right, Bill?"

"You bet."

"We can install the equipment now, if you like."

Weinberg and Keisha looked at each other. "Yes!" they said together.

Weinberg used his electronic device to pay for the equipment.

Africa had reverted long ago to the capitalist economic system that had preceded the Malaise. Everyone able to work was expected to do so, including people of metal, who worked as consultants and advisors. People were paid based on the value their work contributed.

There were no straps on the genitals. Instead, they were glued to the groin area with an adhesive that was guaranteed to be unbreakable "no matter what." Fine wiring, almost invisible, would connect the devices to their respective e-brains.

"If you'll follow me, one of our technicians will install your new gear. They're people of metal, like you. After they've installed the units, they'll put you in sleep mode and add the necessary wiring to your brains."

The salesman escorted Bill and Keisha to a large, busy workshop in the back of the store and had them take seats in the crowded waiting area.

"They'll announce your names when they're ready for you," the salesman told them. "Please be patient. They're swamped."

After the equipment and wiring had been installed, the salesman gave each of them a small carrying case that contained their sexpack. Keisha's case was pink and Weinberg's was blue.

"You're all set," said the salesman.

"Let's go play with our new toys," Keisha whispered as they headed out to their car.

Several rounds later, they lay next to each other, spent. "Wow," said Keisha. "That was really something."

"Wow is right," said Weinberg. "How did Amelia like it?"

"She loved it."

"Mr. Weinberg felt the same," said Weinberg. "He's practically on Cloud Nine."

"I'm glad they were included," said Keisha. "I feel so giddy."

"Remind me to call Gross tomorrow and have him arrange for private spaces aboard the starships," said Weinberg.

Keisha giggled. "Sex rooms. Who would have thought?"

They had a good laugh and went back to playing games on their devices.

• • • • •

Keisha did not abandon her preoccupation with mysticism, as Weinberg had expected. It actually intensified. She (and Amelia) thanked God every day for the gift they'd just been given. Weinberg (and Mr. Weinberg) thanked their lucky stars.

Chapter 9
Jubilee

William Weinberg Public Rose Garden
Nairobi
May 2770

Weinberg and Keisha had offered Governor and Mrs. Bello a private tour of the garden before the ribbon cutting ceremony, which would begin in an hour.

"It's absolutely magnificent," said the governor. "It goes on forever. The colors are insane, and oh my God, the aromas."

"I wish we could smell them," said Keisha.

Weinberg laughed.

"That's what she always says."

The 12-acre rose garden contained hundreds of rose plants. Weinberg had lost count. His design for the park had required moving dozens of plants to make room for walkways and for the lovely fountain that Weinberg had installed near the entrance. Workers had been pruning and dead-heading plants for the past two weeks.

After they'd shown the Bellos around the park, Weinberg and Keisha escorted them to a set of comfortable benches near the fountain, and they seated themselves across from each other.

"After we've left on our trip, someone will have to snip the spent blossoms off on a regular basis, for best results," Weinberg told the governor. "It's called dead-heading. It tricks the plant into thinking that the old bloom has reached the end of its cycle and has fallen off, so the plant creates a new bud sooner than it would have."

"I'll make sure it's taken care of," the governor promised. He and his wife thought Weinberg was an absolute hoot.

"Also, make sure that fungicide is applied to the foliage every ten to fourteen days, and insecticides, but not on the same days as the fungicides. It's a good idea to have the roots but not the foliage watered just before applying the fungicide and insecticide, to reduce the potential for shock to the plant."

"I understand," said the governor.

"Governor Billy," said Elisha. "I hereby volunteer to supervise the care of these roses."

"Thank you," said Billy, visibly relieved

"So, Bill," said Elisha, "please continue. I know nothing about roses, but if you'll explain to what else will need doing, I'll make sure it gets done."

She told the device on her wrist to record what Weinberg was about to say.

"Wonderful," said Weinberg. "Okay, once a year, granular rose fertilizer should be worked into the soil around the plants and covered with a one-inch layer of composted cow manure. Twice a month during the growing season, Wonder-Grow liquid hose-end rose fertilizer should be applied to the foliage and roots, and once a year, about a third of each plant's height should be removed and the cut ends sealed with Alma's Glue, to keep diseases from getting into the plants. That reminds me, the pruners should clean their cutters with an alcohol wipe between plants to keep from transferring disease from one plant to another. That's about it. If I think of anything else, I'll send you a note."

"Ah, thanks, Bill," said Elisha.

"No problem."

Later, after they'd internalized the peaceful beauty of the fountain and the flowers behind it, Governor Bello invited Bill and Keisha to be part of a historic celebration that would be held the following month.

Bonnie Holyfield, Cheng Woon, Ray Finocchi and Libby Burns had served with Bill and Keisha on the board of the Human Rescue Initiative that freed the African survivors from their Russian mafia overlords and helped them rebuild their civilization. Holyfield's and Woon's originals—former leaders of the U.S. and China, respectively—had formed the U.S. Chinese partnership whose promotion of Machines led to their proliferation, and the Malaise.

"The other governors and I are about to sign a joint proclamation declaring June 26 an official holiday in all three zones," he explained. "June 26, 2527, of course, was the date you and your people defeated the Russians and set our ancestors free. The other governors and I would like to invite you and Ms. Dixon, Ms. Holyfield and Mr. Woon to join us for the inaugural celebration. Also, Mr. Finocchi and Ms. Burns, Generals Wainwright and Johnson, and, of course, Messrs. Clark and Liu."

"Why thank you, sir," said Weinberg. "We'll be honored to attend, as will the others, I'm sure."

"The inaugural event will take place in Bangui," said the governor. Bangui was the capital of Zone 2. "It's centrally located, and we want to make it as easy as we can for people to get there. We're hoping thousands of Africans will make the trip. Next year it'll be here in Nairobi, and Zone 1 will have it the year after that."

"We'll look forward to it," said Keisha.

"I'll be making my usual long-winded speech," said the governor.

"He loves the sound of his voice," Elisha teased.

"After the folks have suffered through that, I'm hoping that one or more of you would favor us all with whatever remarks you'd care to make. The proceedings will be streamed live."

"That sounds wonderful," said Weinberg.

"Just make sure you have a red light on the podium so you can let Bill know when his time's up," said Keisha.

"Oh, I don't think that'll be necessary," said the governor. "So anyway, I brushed up on my United States history to prepare for the event. January 1, 1863, of course, was the date President Lincoln issued the Emancipation Proclamation that declared that slaves being held in the rebel states were free. It didn't actually free any slaves until the Union Army occupied rebel territory, but it started the ball rolling. The freed slaves called that day 'Jubilee Day,' and that's what we're planning to call the day our people were freed."

"That's so cool," said Keisha.

"We've also come up with a set of symbols that we'll offer up as ways of commemorating and celebrating our freedom."

At that moment, a crowd was gathering for the ribbon cutting, so the four friends arose and proceeded to the park's entrance, where the dedication ceremony for Weinberg's public rose garden would take place.

Nelson Mandela Park
Bangui
Zone 2
June 26, 2770

There's no record of the size of the crowd, which had overflowed from the park onto the adjacent sidewalks and into the streets. The organizers, with Machine help, had secured interpreters to translate all the speakers' remarks into the languages spoken in each zone, and to mass produce quantities of devices which spectators or participants could use to hear those translations in real time while the respective speakers were addressing the crowd. Workers had placed large TV screens throughout the park for the benefit of those who were too far away from the dais to see the speakers.

Billy Bello and his fellow governors were seated in a row near the front of the dais. Behind them, Weinberg, Keisha, Holyfield and Woon were seated on a raised platform. Behind and above them sat Burns, Finocchi, Clark, Liu, and Generals Wainwright and Johnson in their dress blues.

Zone 2's governor, acting as host, opened the proceedings and gave a short but rousing speech to kick things off. He was followed by Zone 1's governor, whose remarks were brief as well. Weinberg guessed that the governors had limited their remarks out of respect for the work Governor Bello had done in conceiving and planning the event. They were letting him carry the ball.

When Bello rose and took his place behind the podium, workers, all of whom were biological, started bringing unusual-looking statues to the dais and lining them up on either side of the podium. The statues were about five feet tall and depicted men with faces and hands painted a glossy black. Their right arms were extended as if the men were holding or reaching for something. Several had green or red ribbons tied to their arms.

When the workers had finished, Governor Bello peered out at the crowd and began speaking.

"My fellow citizens. This is a glorious day. We're here to celebrate what our metallic friends—represented here today by the some of the people who organized and led the effort—did for our people on June 26, 2527 and during the years that followed.

"One of our metallic friends, who played a role in what happened that fateful day, will tell us what it was like. Imagine. We'll hear eyewitness testimony about what happened on today's date over 200 years ago. I'm so eager to hear him, I'm tempted to just sit down now and turn the podium over to him."

There were scattered, good-natured calls of "Sit down," "Good idea," and "What are you waiting for?" Bello smiled and laughed in response.

"Some of you may recognize the term 'Jubilee Day' from your history classes. For those who don't, it's what freed African slaves in the United States called January 1, 1863, the date President Lincoln issued his famous Emancipation Proclamation. Jubilee Day remained a special day for the freed American slaves and their descendants.

With that as background, it's my pleasure to announce that my fellow governors and I have proclaimed June 26, the day our ancestors were freed, as our own Jubilee Day, to be celebrated across our continent today and ever after."

The applause started in the front rows and spread until it engaged the entire crowd. The sound, which echoed off the surrounding towers, was thunderous. When it finally subsided, Bello continued:

"I'm almost finished here, but before I sit down, I'd like to introduce to you the statues you see on either side of the podium. I wonder if any of you have any idea what they are — or what they were. I didn't. I stumbled across an article about them while surfing the Net one evening last winter. So I'll explain.

"Some of you may remember that before the United States Civil War was fought and our people there were freed, there was a thing called the Underground Railroad. It wasn't an actual railroad. Rather, it was a network of shelters along routes that led north to freedom, for slaves who had shed their shackles and had the strength and courage to undertake that arduous and perilous journey. The righteous people who owned and operated these way stations took great personal risk in sheltering and protecting escaped slaves from their armed pursuers.

"Now, here's what's special about these statues. They were called 'lawn jockeys' because people put them on the grass in front of their houses as a decoration, and because some of them were painted to look like jockeys."

Governor Bello knew that some had viewed the statues as racist because they could be seen as demeaning African Americans. In late 20th-century America, if someone spotted one of those statues on a person's lawn, they figured the homeowner was a racist. Bello had discussed the matter with Keisha, and she'd convinced him not to include that background. The entire concept of race and racism was an ancient abstraction for people of the modern era, a concept that most would probably have difficulty relating to in personal terms. That aside, she argued, the role the statues played in the struggle for freedom, and their symbolic value, far outweighed what, in effect, was a minor, 20th-century historical footnote.

"Let me tell you why these statues are here," the governor continued. "People put statues like these in front of Underground Railroad way stations and used them to convey information to escaped slaves who might approach them. For example, the green ribbons you see on two statues told the escaped slave to come on in, it's safe. The red ribbons meant keep going, there's danger. These statues aren't copies, by the way. They're real. They were found in a history museum in New York City.

"See the striped shirt on the third statue from the end?" the governor said, pointing to his right. "The striped shirt told escaped slaves that this was a place where they could swap horses. The guy in the long coat next to him meant that food and lodging were available there. The blue jacket on the guy at the other end of the dais is a sailor's jacket. It meant there were people there who could get the escaped slave on a ship, like a ship bound for Canada.

"Amazing, aren't they? But more than that, I find them inspiring, because they're symbols of our freedom, and of our need to always be ready to fight to secure and preserve it. The escaped slaves that these statues helped on their path toward freedom were our people, whose ancestors had been torn from the bosom of our continent, the only home they'd ever known. They were slaves, just as our ancestors were, deprived of their basic rights as human beings; so when one of them got free, it was a victory not just for them, but a victory for all Africans, including us today, and for the entire human race. In my opinion—which my fellow governors share—these statues would make perfect symbols for our own Jubilee Day, as we celebrate our good fortune and renew our commitment to protecting and defending liberty."

The governor was interrupted again by loud applause.

"I'll close my remarks with a suggestion. I'll bet that if some ambitious and patriotic person or persons out there hustled their butts and made replicas of these historic statues, people would beat a path to their door. Thank you."

Weinberg timed the governor's final ovation at a full nine minutes.

Weinberg was next, and his speech was uncharacteristically short.

"I'm honored to have had the opportunity, with my colleagues, to help my African brothers and sisters as they rebuilt their lives and their civilization. Had things been reversed, we know you all would have done the same for us.

"Yes, we got rid of the Russians and set your ancestors free. We were more than happy to do that. The Russian pigs deserved what they got. But after that, everything—literally everything—that was accomplished here in Africa was the work of your ancestors and yourselves. All we did was coach. We gave advice on matters that your ancestors hadn't been allowed to learn about for themselves.

"Coaches are important. If you've played soccer, or if your children have, you've probably seen the difference that a good coach can make, by steering his or her players in the right direction. But that's it. Once the game starts, it's up to the players to get the job done. The players do the actual work, not the coaches.

"So it was with your ancestors, and so it has been with all of you. Remember that fact with pride. Look around you. *You built that!*

"Now, I'd like to introduce the last speaker, General Arthur Johnson. He's the eyewitness Governor Bello mentioned. He helped plan every aspect of the June 26, 2527 attacks that freed your ancestors. Thank you."

The crowd gave Weinberg a generous ovation.

General Johnson spoke for twenty minutes. He did an excellent job of conveying what the attacks had been like, down to the smallest details, like the red mist that had settled over the scenes of the attacks after the Behemoths had vaporized Russian officers. Spectators interrupted him several times with cheers and applause.

Chapter 10
Running Out Of Time

Bello Square
Tamu Nyumbani Mji
2771

"This is where the first City Hall was," said Keisha.

She and Weinberg were standing in the shadow of the massive bronze statue of Akina Bello I.

"She was something else," said Keisha. "She was the strongest woman I ever met, the strongest *person*. Like the time the people learned that taxes had been deducted from their pay for the first time. A crowd formed at City Hall and broke into the mayor's office. He wasn't there, so they started breaking furniture and windows until Akina showed up and confronted them. She made them stop by the sheer force of her will."

"I would guess there were a lot of women like her back then, and men," said Weinberg. "If they hadn't been as strong as they were, the Russians would have broken them. The bastards abused them and held them down, but somehow, they kept a spark alive inside them." Weinberg smiled. "A pilot light."

"Nice metaphor, Minister Bill," said Keisha, still gazing up at the statue. "All we had to do, when the Russians were gone, was turn the knob."

"Yep. I'm sorry I never got to meet her."

"I tried, but I could never get you to haul your skinny ass over here while she was still alive." said Keisha.

"I was in my New York City groove back then," said Weinberg. "We preferred to stay put and let the world come to us."

She took Weinberg's hand and led him to another part of the square not far from the statues.

"This is where we were when I first met them," said Keisha. "They were standing over there, hundreds of them. They looked like hell. I stood there and looked at them, and I couldn't imagine what they'd been through. Thank God I had a script. I plunged ahead. I told them God had sent us to free them from the Russian scum and help them rebuild their civilization, but before I knew it this tall, striking young woman marches toward me from out of the crowd and confronts me. It was Akina. 'Why has God suddenly taken an interest in us?' she asked. I told her God loved them.

"I kept going, following the script. After I'd shown them the video of 21st-century Africa, she asks me what kind of shit I'm trying to pull? So I took a video of the people in front of me and put it on the screen. I told them that the scenes they'd just seen, of Africa as it once was, were made with one of these things—a camera. They understood, and it won them over.

"Akina confronted me again after I was done talking, while people were going off to their work groups. She said I didn't come from God, so I told her she could believe whatever she wanted about that, but we were their friends, and I told her the bit we'd worked out. We want nothing from you. I don't eat, drink or have sex. My body's a machine. All we want is to help you help yourselves. She thought about it for several moments, nodded her head and went off to her work assignment."

Keisha shook her head. "I will never forget her. She was the most natural leader I'd ever seen."

Weinberg nodded. "She sounds a lot like you," he said.

Keisha laughed. "I wish. But thanks. I try." She looked around. "Sweet Home City," she said in English. "I will miss the hell out of this place, I truly will."

She rubbed her eyes. It was a sign, Weinberg knew, that Keisha was feeling emotional. Had she been biological, there would've been tears in those eyes. The thought made him smile.

"You know, I never thought about ever leaving here," said Keisha. "Not once."

"We'll come back, some day," said Weinberg.

"Every biological we know will be gone. It won't be the same place."

"It is what it is. They're only with us a short time. We need to accept it. We've always known that."

"I know, but it's hard."

"It damn hell is," Weinberg agreed.

"Too bad they can't be like us."

• • • • •

Launch Zone
Zone 3
November 2771

The planners had allotted 500 square miles of land—a half square mile per ship—as launch space for the 1,000 starships that would soon depart. Space to accommodate auxiliary structures (maintenance, cargo storage, etc.) required another 25 square miles.

The ships that were launched from the western half of the zone would head for the planet designated "Tau Ceti f," nearly 12 light years from Earth. The ships in the eastern half would head for a planet named "Alamo c," over 15 light years away.

Astronomers had identified the first planet early in the 21st century. The second had been discovered in 2612. Its star had been re-named Alamo in honor of the San Antonio Machines whose statistical analysis of variations in the star's radial velocity had led to Alamo c's discovery.

Both planets had been probed extensively and certified as suitable to support human life.

Factories in and near Canaveral City had operated 24/7 for almost 10 years manufacturing the starships. Every six months, biological and metallic workers had used gigantic, specially designed transports to take the newly manufactured ships to their launch sites.

Meanwhile, workers had built large warehouses within the Launch Zone and stocked them with the materials and supplies that the expeditions would take with them. The loading of those supplies aboard the ships, which had begun four months earlier, was scheduled to be complete in three weeks. Departures would begin two weeks thereafter.

Weinberg and Keisha would board one of the Tau Ceti f ships, and Holyfield, Woon, Ray and Libby would be aboard a ship bound for Alamo c.

Central Park
Nairobi
D-day minus 3

"What a glorious day," said Holyfield.

She and Woon had met up with their longtime friends — Weinberg, Keisha, Libby and Ray — to bid each other farewell.

"Am I the only one who's scared?" Libby asked.

"I'm scared to death," said Woon. "You'd have to be insane or a complete idiot not to be."

"I'm just nervous," said Keisha. "It's one thing to look at a video. But what will it be like to be there?"

"It's gonna be awesome," Weinberg declared. "Admit it. We're bored silly... We've been doing the same thing for, let's see, 244 years. It's time to move on. *I'm* excited."

"I'm a little nervous, like Libby," said Holyfield. "But I'm also excited. It'll be the ultimate adventure."

"That's what Gross said at the convention," said Weinberg.

Holyfield smiled. "So I borrowed it. Sue me."

"Why don't we go somewhere and sit down," said Keisha.

"I can't sit still," said Weinberg. "Let's just walk around."

So they did, but they were quiet. There was nothing else to say.

Some twenty minutes later, Keisha suddenly stopped and rubbed her eyes. Her face bore an expression the others had never seen on her face—of abject grief.

"I'm sad. I can't help it." She rubbed her eyes again. "Bonnie, Cheng, Ray, Libby, I love you guys so much. I'll miss you."

Holyfield stepped toward Keisha and took her hands.

"Oh, we'll miss you too, old friend," said Holyfield.

Weinberg burst out laughing.

"Never has that expression had more meaning," he said, laughing.

No one else got the joke.

"Here's what I think," said Weinberg. "We'll meet again. It reminds me of an old song."

"Everything reminds you of an old song," said Keisha

"It's a classic," said Weinberg. "'*We'll meet aga*in,' by Vera Lynn. She's leaving, but she knows she and her friend/lover/whatever will meet again someday—she knows not where, she knows not when—but they'll meet again some sunny day."

Weinberg retrieved his device and played the beloved old song for his friends. Keisha had to rub her eyes again after it ended.

"Before we know it, we *will* be back together," Weinberg declared, "whether it's here or on some distant planet. We have all the time in the world, all the time in the universe. So, I suggest, therefore, that we just have ourselves a big group hug, and then, instead of saying goodbye, we say *auf Wiedersehen*."

Which they did.

Chapter 11
Genes And Warriors

Department of Genetics
University of Nairobi
2790

"Our interstellar adventurers have been gone less than twenty years, but if they came back now, they'd be amazed at how much more pleasant and livable this city has become," Brandon told his wife as they made their way to the genetics building.

It was true. Every building in the university and nearly every building in the city had been refurbished and redecorated.

"It's all the small touches here and there—flowers, trees and shrubs, cool looking streetlights and traffic signals—but they come together," said Alice. "There's a serenity that you don't expect to feel in a large city. I believe the ancient Japanese strove to achieve this kind of feeling."

"Now that you mention it, I agree," said Brandon. "It's busy, and the structures have different sizes and styles, but it works. Look, even the benches are minor works of art. You know, we've spent over two hundred years of non-childhood time in the same place, here, watching the city change around us. That's something."

"Yet we aren't bored," said Alice. "On the contrary, we enjoy our work and we're making slow but steady progress."

Slow is right, Brandon thought. Which triggered another thought.

"I don't think we'd be happy with the pace of our work if we were biological and our time on Earth were limited," said Brandon. "Maybe that's why our department has stayed as small as it has, while other departments have mushroomed. Even West North America has stopped sending us students. We wouldn't have a single biological grad student or doctoral candidate if it weren't for the orangutans, and we only have them because their ancestors were geneticists."

"Our work does require a lot of patience," Alice admitted.

"Ya think?"

"It would be nice if we could step up the pace," said Alice. "I just don't see how we can."

It was a subject they'd often discussed. Brandon had an idea.

"All these years it's been right in front of us, but we missed it," he said.

"Missed what?"

"We've been waiting too long between enhancements,"

The "enhancements" were taken from a list of the 200 positive traits covered by the study Garrett had saved, arranged in descending order of importance as determined by Garrett. It was subjective, but he figured it was better than editing in traits in random order from a computer-generated list. In the very first batch, they had edited each of the top ten traits on Garrett's list into 10% of the embryos in that batch, using genetic materials strongly correlated with those traits that Tom Joyce's operation had synthesized. In the second batch, they'd edited each of the next ten traits on the list into 10% of the embryos in that batch, and so on.

The waiting period between batches was the time it took for a batch of embryos to be born and reach the age of consent, so the individuals could donate the sperm and eggs that the team would use to make the next batch of embryos. What Brandon had just realized was that they could get eggs and sperm from members of the previous batch while they were still minor children, by getting parental consent.

"We don't have to wait for a batch to reach adulthood." Brandon told Alice. "Women are born with all the eggs they'll ever have, and boys produce sperm between the ages of 10 or12. So we'll wait the ten to twelve years, get parental consent to take sperm and eggs from the kids, and make the next batch of embryos. And so on for batch after batch. We'll end up with large extended families raising generation after generation of genetically enhanced offspring."

"How do we go about getting parental consent to harvest eggs and sperm from 10-year-olds?" Alice asked. "It'd be dicey, at best."

"I bet it'll be easier than you might think. Parents will have the chance to genetically enhance their progeny and it won't cost them a thing. The procedures for harvesting eggs and sperm are quick and painless."

A big smile formed on Alice's face. "So nine months later, when the baby emerges from its artificial womb, the 12-year-olds will become instant parents, and their parents will be instant grandparents. Another round later and the kids will become grandparents and their parents will be great-grandparents."

(The use of artificial wombs had been the norm for centuries. Very few women opted to grow their babies *in utero*.)

"In theory, yes, that's what would happen," said Brandon. "Can you imagine: multiple generations only ten to twelve years apart?"

` "What fun," said Alice.

"When the time comes to get eggs and sperm from the kids in the second batch, their parents — the kids from the first batch — will be old enough to give parental consent themselves, and so on," Brandon observed.

"We'd be talking about an enormous change in family dynamics," said Alice. "You'd have kids, parents, grandparents and great-grandparents living in close proximity with each other, or in the same house. Kids would be raised by their grandparents, which isn't so unusual in itself, but their biological parents would be more like older siblings."

"Well, we'd have to make sure people understood all that upfront," said Brandon. "Extended families have existed in many cultures. They may not be for everyone, but they do offer certain advantages. We'll see. We need to see Harry."

They went straight to Garrett's office the moment they entered the lab.

Harry sat back in his chair and smiled after Brandon had described his idea.

"That's the thing about great ideas," he said. "They're freaking obvious, once someone spells them out for you. Great work, guys. I'm green with envy. I wish I'd thought of this myself."

"Why would you?" said Alice. "You're from a time when the idea of genetic enhancement was dicey enough already, without 'violating' 10-year-old kids to boot, which is how some people would have seen it back then. It wouldn't have occurred to you to even consider it. Brandon didn't come from all that, so it didn't constrain his thinking. He brought a fresh perspective to it."

"I'm sure you're right," said Garrett. "The good news is that that was then, and this is now. I'll get a budget increase. Our current batch is what, number twelve?"

"Eleven," said Brandon. "But you won't need a budget increase, Harry."

"How so?"

"I assume you've heard of the ersatz sex parts that have become so popular."

"You bet," said Garrett. "My wife and I love them. They're the best things ever invented. You should try them, if you haven't already."

"We have," said Brandon. "We invented them."

"I'm sure," said Garrett, thinking Brandon was joking.

"I'm serious," said Brandon.

Brandon could see that Alice was a bit embarrassed that they'd revealed their secret, even to someone as close to them as Garrett was.

"Don't be embarrassed, Alice," he told her. "Sex is part of life."

Garrett's jaw dropped, but after a few moments, he smiled and clapped his hands together. "I do hope that the two of you won't ever cease to amaze me," he said.

"Anyway, my reason for bringing this up," Brandon continued, "is that we've been receiving royalties from the manufacturer for over thirty years. We're like the old tech companies. We introduce upgrades every couple of years, and everyone *has* to have them. We're fabulously wealthy. We've been saving it all until we could figure out what to do with it. We'll provide the funding."

"That's very generous," said Garrett, "but I think it'll look better if you made a large unrestricted donation to the university, and I'll get them to fund our work on its merit. We can't afford to look like we're some rogue group, given the potential sensitivity of what we're doing."

"Good point," said Brandon.

"Well, that's that," said Garrett. "We'll be able to double both our speed and our results."

"If we can attract the volunteers," said Alice. She described the changes in family dynamics that the revised protocol would create.

"We'll just have to see what happens," said Garrett

"Also, we could do smaller batches where we could experiment with blends of traits," said Brandon. "For example, we might find that blending musical talent with mathematical ability produces a better musician, a better mathematician or both. With only a short time between generations, we'd get results very quickly."

"We'd have to be careful what we're blending," said Garrett. "The last thing we need is a bad accident."

"Absolutely," said Brandon. "So we won't blend traits in an embryo unless we've first found genomes in your study where that same blend occurred naturally. I wonder if we could have the computer guys create algorithms to identify those blends for us. They wouldn't have to know where the data came from."

"Good idea, Brandon. I'll let you make the necessary arrangements."

Garrett stood abruptly and clapped his large hands together. "Mug me Maggie and close the front door! We're on fire!"

• • • • •

The department had no trouble getting volunteers.

Two years later, a local TV reporter in Nairobi did a story on the excitement and enthusiasm that the revised project had generated. "It's human nature for people to want their offspring to be smarter and better than they are," said the reporter. "Plus, for the first time in human history, people will have the chance to get to know their great-great-grandchildren. We live in exciting times."

2872

Thanks to the faster pace of their large-batch protocol, genetics at the University of Nairobi became as attractive to biologicals as any other branch of science, if not more so.

Biological grad students studied the most advanced genetics texts and other material available on the Net, but they did not have access to the data from Garrett's study, whose existence was carefully guarded — as were the details of the trio's separate large- and small-batch projects.

"Money is a lot more valuable to biologicals than it is to us," Garrett reminded his crew for the umpteenth time, "because of the things they can buy with it to satisfy their voracious animal appetites. There's a risk they'll succumb to temptation."

At Garrett's suggestion, the three zones had enacted laws mandating that all college and university genetics departments administer regular polygraph tests to their biological genetics students, to keep genetic engineering technology from falling into the wrong hands.

The three geneticists were living the scientist's dream. They were enhancing human intelligence of every known kind. The enhancements were qualitative and quantitative, and they were changing the way people thought.

As planned, Alice and Brandon began spending their nights trying to figure out how to transfer enhancements, in e-brains copied from their subjects, to another e-brain. Alice had an idea.

"The enhancements in the subjects' e-brains would leave electrical signatures," she told her husband.

"They would," said Brandon.

"The universities and research centers operated for decades after my neuroscience stint at MIT," said Alice, "and the ones here in Africa have had centuries to build on pre-Malaise technology. I'll bet they have equipment today that does a much better job of recording brain activity than the old stuff did."

"Let's find out," said Brandon.

The African science community had not yet adopted the practice of publishing the results of their research, so the only way Alice and Brandon could catch up on such developments was to consult with someone who worked in the relevant field. Brandon suggested that Alice pay a visit to her friend Elle McKenzie, a person of metal who headed the neuroscience department at the university. McKenzie had a mind copied from a woman who'd earned a Ph.D. in neuroscience at Harvard in 2197. She was happy to show Alice around her department and update her on the current state of neuroscience.

"You were right," she told Alice. "The equipment we have now gives us way more detailed information on micro-electronic brain activity than the machines you would have used when you were at MIT."

She explained to Alice that in the years after Alice's time at MIT, researchers had isolated the complex, recurring electrical phenomena that formed what Elle called the biological brain's "operating system," as distinguished from random, transient electrical activity which she called noise.

She led Alice into a windowless room where a technician was seated next to a subject who was wearing a headset. Closely spaced lines of blips, dips and symbols crawled across a screen that occupied an entire wall.

"It's a scorewriter," said Elle.

"A what?"

"It's a nickname. The prototype was completed at Harvard in 2196, when I was there. Technically, it's called an encephalic transcriber. It got its nickname because of the readout's resemblance to the score of a symphony. It was a vast improvement over the old EEG machines. It's a full record of the recurring electrical phenomena that account for the operation of every part of the brain. The display on the wall is just the tip of the iceberg. They're organized by the part of the brain whose operational activity they represent. Among other things, engineers would have been able to use information in the score of a 'normal' human brain to make artificial implants that could take over the operations of parts of patients' brains that were dysfunctional because of injury or inherited disability."

"What do you men, engineers *would have been* able to use the information?" Alice asked. "Why didn't they?"

"It never went into production. My original's cohort was in the last group of doctoral candidates in the sciences. Liberal arts had already died out in the 2180s. Mark Stephenson, the professor who led the team that built this machine, was a stubborn old genius who kept at it 'til the bitter end. This was his last and greatest project, his masterpiece. But the school closed its doors before he could finish testing it, and they never manufactured it. Jill went into a depressed state after that and never recovered."

"So many of them did," said Alice.

Jill McKenzie was Elle's original.

"So how did you get this?" Alice asked.

"When we first got here in 2578 and were setting up shop, I figured, what the hell, and tried to see if I could login to Harvard's internal neuroscience computer network. Amazingly, it was still up and running, if you can believe it. No one had bothered to turn it off when the last person left the building. Even more amazing, Jill's password still worked. No one had bothered to cancel it."

"I'm not surprised. I can only imagine what the environment must have been like at places like Harvard and MIT at that point," said Alice.

"The people who were still there had known for years that their schools were dying. Mentally and emotionally, they'd already checked out."

"And the Machines kept the power plants going," said Alice, "and buildings had electricity whether they were occupied or not."

"It slipped through the cracks," said Elle. "The schools had been abandoned. They'd been forgotten. So here I was, in Africa, logged into Harvard's neuroscience computers centuries after the university had ceased to exist. It took me several hours, but eventually, I found the plans and specs for the scorewriter, and gave them to our engineers. They updated the technology and built one for me, and they've continued to add new features and improvements ever since."

"That's an amazing story," said Alice

"So, Alice, what you're looking at on the screen here is a unique and sophisticated kind of language—an improved version of the language Professor Stephenson created for the prototype. Each line portrays a recurring element of the subject brain's operating system. The amplitudes of the ups and downs contain important information. If a part of a subject's brain isn't functional, the engineers can use the data from the relevant part of a normal score to program special hats that replace the operational activity that the affected part of the brain can't perform. If the dysfunction was the result of an injury and the brain had been scored before it happened, we can also program the hats to reproduce any positive operational variants that the original mind had at the affected location, so there's no qualitative loss in their thinking."

"I take it that these hats have replaced the surgical implants that you used in olden times," said Alice.

"For the most part," said Elle. "Some people dislike wearing hats and opt for subcutaneous circuitry that does the same thing, but the vast majority adapt to wearing one form of headgear or another during their waking hours."

McKenzie exchanged greetings with a young woman who had just left one of the examination rooms. She wore a red baseball cap.

"Elisha, do you have a moment?" McKenzie asked the woman.

"Sure."

McKenzie introduced Elisha and Alice.

"I saw that you were coming in for a routine check," said McKenzie. "How's the hat working?"

"Perfectly."

"Would you mind if I share your story with Alice?""

"Not at all."

"Elisha is a ballerina with the Nairobi Ballet. She sustained brain damage that impaired her ability to control her arms and legs. The impairment was barely noticeable when I saw her, but it rendered her incapable of performing. Left unattended, it would have ended her career. Fortunately, our engineers were able to use information from a normal score to program a hat to replace the operational brain activity that she'd lost."

"My God, how wonderful," said Alice.

The young dancer was visibly moved.

"It was a miracle," she said softly.

"No offense," said Alice after the ballerina had left, "but, I mean, a ballerina in a red baseball cap? Couldn't they make something a bit more feminine?"

McKenzie chuckled. "If she had to, she'd wear it, and they'd let her. She's that good. But it wasn't a problem. The engineers made her a hairpiece for performances."

"I see," said Alice. "It's wonderful that you're able to help people like her. Congratulations."

"This is where I say that we stand—"

"—on the shoulders of giants."

They laughed.

"If I can go back to what we were talking about earlier," said Alice, "I was wondering whether a scorewriter could score an e-brain."

"I don't see why not," said Elle. "I'm sure the engineers could adapt the headset. Why do you ask?"

"Brandon and I tried for years to find operational variants, as you call them, that researchers had identified. We looked everywhere, but we only found three. But that was centuries ago, and you and your colleagues have been at this for a long—"

"We know exactly what they are," said Elle. "All of them. In fact, nowadays, variants are the only things our scorewriter includes in its readout. We score the operational electrical activity that's identical in every brain. but it's not included in the readout unless it's irregular, in which case the scorewriter flags it. As I mentioned, when they make a hat to replace the electrical activity of a dysfunctional area of a brain, they automatically program the non-variable activity for that part of the brain along with the variants shown on previous scores."

Alice was stunned.

"Oh my God. We need one of these. Thanks a million, Elle. This could be huge. I'll get back to you if it works like I think it will. Trust me, you'll be interested. Forgive me for rushing off. I'll fill you in, I swear."

"Great," said Elle. "Call me when you're up for another bike ride."

"Will do."

Alice hurried back to the genetics department, grabbed her husband's hand and pulled him into Garrett's office.

"We need an encephalic transcriber," she told them. "They're awesome. Neuroscience has one. They're nicknamed 'scorewriters' because the readout looks like a symphonic score."

She explained what she'd seen and what McKenzie had told her.

"Elle sees no reason e-brains couldn't be scored as well," Alice said. "And guess what, they score all the operational variants, which are the only things the scorewriter's readout shows. All brain activity is scored, but there's no reason to include activity that's identical in all brains, unless it's dysfunctional."

"Mug me Maggie," said Garrett, "you've hit the jackpot."

"A professor at Harvard and his team produced a prototype just before the school closed its doors. They never finished testing it and they never manufactured it. Fortunately, my friend Elle, whose original was one of the professor's doctoral candidates, got into the the department's computers after she first set up shop here. She got the plans and specs and had her engineers build her one."

"Fantastic," said Brandon.

"Here's what I'm thinking," said Alice. "First, we score a sample of e-brains taken from subjects whose germ-lines have received a particular enhancement. Next, we score a like sample of e-brains from subjects whose germ-lines have not received the enhancement. Then we'll determine which operational variants correlate strongly with the enhanced minds, but not with the unenhanced ones."

"Similar to the study I saved," said Garrett.

"Exactly," said Alice.

"Just out of curiosity, what do they do with these scores?" Brandon asked. "Other than analyzing them for research purposes."

"The information in the patterns and symbols on the lines gives their engineers the ability to create special hats—they call them 'stimulus hats' — that can replace the operational activity of a part a person's brain that's dysfunctional," said Alice. "I'll ask Elle to have her engineers help us make e-brain components that mimic the strongly correlated variants in the e-brains that we've taken from our enhanced human subjects. We'd install the resulting components in each other, and *voila*"

Garrett smiled. "So we'll enhance ourselves as well," he said matter of factly. "Well, then. Alice, please ask your friend if her engineers can make us one of these scorekeepers, one that can score e-brains — out of our budget, of course."

"Yes sir, chief.

It worked. Less a year later, they were transferring intellectual enhancements to themselves, to Garrett and to other metallic friends and colleagues who wanted them, including Alice's friend Elle.

2878

"We're practically a new species of Machine," Alice joked to Garrett and Brandon one evening as the three were getting set to leave their wing of the genetics building. The three geneticists would have found it hard to convey to someone who had not received them how profoundly the intellectual enhancements had changed their way of thinking and perception, or what it felt like. Such things had always been difficult to describe, but words capable of capturing what they were experiencing now had yet to evolve.

Garrett, reacting to what Alice had just said about a new species, turned serious and beckoned the group to join him in his office.

"It's time for us to address the fairness question," Garrett told them. "I need your help to develop a proposal that we can present to the governors of the three zones and their legislative leaders. This is something that the law needs to address."

Garrett spelled out his concerns, and Alice and Brandon went to work.

Headquarters
Pan African Power Company
Nairobi
Fourteen month later.

Garrett opened the meeting. "Thank you all for coming. It was nice of the power company to let us use their room. I don't know where else we could have found a conference room that would have accommodated us all. If I may, I'll make a brief statement, then we can open the meeting to discussion. My colleagues and I will be available to discuss or answer questions on any scientific issues that may concern you. After that, if you like, you can discuss any legal, procedural or logistic issues amongst yourselves, and we'll excuse ourselves. Or, if you think our perspective might contribute to your discussion at some point, we'll remain here and keep our mouths shut unless someone asks us something."

There was soft, appreciative laughter from around the table.

"With your indulgence, I'd like to take this opportunity to underscore some of the points we put forward in our written proposal."

The proposal had gone out almost a year earlier to allow time for the governors, the legislators and their staffs to study it.

"Genetic engineering has become commonplace," Garrett continued. "It's done on plants, animals and humans, and has made significant improvements in the genetics of all three categories. But when the idea of *human* genetic engineering first attracted serious consideration, in the 20th century, many people, including distinguished political leaders and scientists, were horrified by what they saw as the potential dangers of this endeavor. We've taken strong steps over the years to address those concerns. However, we have yet to determine who should have the opportunity to get improved genes for their offspring and who does not.

"We and other geneticists have relied on philanthropists to supplement our departmental budgets to allow us to make genetic enhancements available to all who wanted them for their children, regardless of their ability to pay. Unfortunately, these generous donors have elected to move on and devote themselves to other worthwhile causes, so, as of the first of next year, geneticists at African colleges and universities will have to begin charging for genetic enhancements — not to earn a profit, but to recoup our costs."

(More precisely, Garrett had suggested that Alice and Brandon stop funding African college and university genetics clinics. "Let the government fund them," he'd told them. "Save your dough for a rainy day.")

"Over time," Garrett continued, "the cost of what we do will fall, as it does with all technology. But, for the foreseeable future, it will remain beyond the reach of many Africans. Using income statistics from the respective tax authorities, and our and other geneticists' estimates of what genetic enhancement procedures will cost during the next twenty-five years, we estimate that such treatments will remain beyond the reach of 40% of African families. After twenty-five years, we predict that this percentage will drop to 30% and remain at that level.

"Sixty percent of our families will have gotten a 25-year head start on upgrading their genes; and 30% — before taking into effect the effects of upward and downward mobility, which, of course, could change this number — will receive no upgrades in the foreseeable future unless their circumstances change and their families can afford them.

"This raises at least three issues whose resolution will have enormous positive or negative consequences that will reverberate over time — to the last generation — depending on how you resolve them.

"First, there's fairness. A child born into an affluent family would get to inherit and enjoy many physical and mental upgrades and pass them on to their progeny. A child born into that family would inherit those genetic benefits even if they turn out to be a bum. At the same time, a child born into a family of modest means would be denied those genetic benefits, no matter how fine a person they are or how hard they strive to contribute to society.

"I know, people inherit money and other property all the time. But this is profoundly different. This is permanent. Studies have shown that financial inheritances often are dissipated within three to four generations. But genetic enhancements go from generation to generation until the last generation dies out. We'd be creating a genetically enhanced aristocracy more powerful than any other aristocracy that has ever existed in human history. Unenhanced citizens would become pawns—worker bees, if you will—if they weren't flat out enslaved. This happened countless times in humanity's long history, when a group of elites had the upper hand. This time, they'd have the further advantage of ongoing genetic enhancement.

"Second, making genetic enhancements available to *all* African families, regardless of their financial status, would be far and away the best possible investment that we, or any society, could ever make. The return on your investment would be compounded, year after year, until the end of time. I asked my electronic device what the rate of return would be on that kind of investment, and it gave me an error message. The rate of return was impossible to compute because it would grow to infinity, or to the end of time, whichever came first."

There was a murmur of appreciation for Garrett's witticism.

"Third, if we *don't* make these enhancements available to everyone who wants them—if only some of our citizens have access to the genetic upgrades that we'll develop in the fullness of time—the day will come, sooner than you might imagine, when the favored group has emerged as a distinctly new human species. In effect, the unfavored group will have been relegated to the status of a lower human species.

"We respectfully suggest that you consider subsidizing non-profit genetics clinics to the extent necessary to make it possible for all citizens who wish to do so to get all available genetic enhancements for their offspring without regard to their financial status. To further assure that future enhancements are available to all, we recommend that you require by law that genetics researchers disclose to an appropriate government authority all new genetic enhancements which they develop, along with their recipes.

"Finally, we wanted to bring to your attention certain practices that we believe should be strictly forbidden because of the almost unimaginable harm they could cause if they were used for evil purposes.

"In the 21st and 22nd centuries, researchers developed and perfected technology for converting skin cells into eggs or sperm, from which they could make an embryo that would become a human child. This development was hailed as a boon to women and men who were infertile, but the potential for abuse would have been horrifying if the technology had fallen into the wrong hands. Bad actors, or rogue states, could have literally set up *factories* to manufacture human beings, whom they would own. It's one thing to interdict trafficking in human slaves. Stopping the sale of skin cells would be another matter. Entire slave armies could be manufactured in secret and used for evil purposes. Can you imagine? The same threat would exist if sperm and eggs became marketable commodities.

"Bad people do traffic in human beings, of course, but there, law enforcement has at least a fighting chance of stopping them. Good luck stopping a bad guy from buying skin cells, or an embryo — hundreds of thousands of them — for whatever nefarious purposes.

"We urge you, therefore, to strictly prohibit the practices we've described, with penalties stiff enough to deter people from proceeding down this path.

"Ladies and gentlemen, I thank you for your kind consideration."

Much to the surprise of Garrett, Brandon and Alice, the men and women seated around the table rose and gave Garrett an enthusiastic round of applause.

"Professor Garrett," said the governor of Zone 1, "all of us here applaud the work of you and your team in identifying and addressing not only the risks associated with human genetic enhancement but also its vast potential for improving the quality of human life. Based on your written proposal, the three zones have been hard at work for some time now, drafting laws to implement your proposal."

"Wow. That's great. Thank you, sir."

There were no further comments or questions. Garrett chatted briefly with the three governors while Brandon and Alice worked the room thanking participants for attending and offering to answer any questions any of them had.

Within three months, each of the zones had enacted laws that required genetics researchers to disclose to zonal authorities, under penalties of perjury and within a prescribed time frame, "all genetic modifications, alterations, additions or deletions, of whatever nature, that they or their employees, partners, independent contractors or other associates shall have performed, engineered or supervised."

The laws required the developers to provide to designated authorities in each zone sufficient information to enable such authorities to produce the applicable genetic material.

Genetic engineering had emerged from the shadows.

Harsh laws were passed to address the concerns Garrett had outlined concerning the manufacture of and trafficking in human embryos, gametes or somatic cells

2895

The ever-courteous Garrett knocked twice on the glass before entering Alice and Brandon's immaculate and superbly equipped workroom. He sat in one of the large stuffed easy chairs.

"I love the way it hugs you the moment you sit down," said Garrett.

Brandon laughed. "They can't keep them in stock. Biologicals love them."

Garrett ordered the chair to stop and turned serious.

"I've been thinking about something the two of you said years ago. You said the reason we needed to copy the minds of our enhanced biological subjects was to assure that e-brains containing the enhancements would be available should the need ever arise to produce Machines with the traits and talents associated with those enhancements."

"Alice and I remember it as if it had happened yesterday," said Brandon.

"Then you'll recall that one of the contingencies you cited was peacekeeping. The other day, I saw a documentary about the 2527 attacks that freed the slaves. It included a speech at the inaugural Jubilee Day celebration by one of the generals involved in the attacks. It also showed satellite video of some of the attacks. I hadn't realized how freaking badass those robot weapons were, even the common soldiers. The most horrific ones were the Behemoths. They were humongous flying battleships. In autonomous mode, after they'd been positioned over a target, they would destroy their target by dropping bombs from one part and pouring down Machine gun fire from another part. Or an operator could override the robots aboard the Behemoth and focus gunfire on specific target elements"

"We've seen the video," said Alice. "It was amazing."

"Well, it made me stop and think," said Garrett.

"I see where you're going," said Brandon. "After you saw how awesome the robots were, you asked yourself, why would you risk the lives of people of metal in a war zone when you could have our people operate robots like those to do the actual fighting?"

"You got it," said Garrett. "The operators could be anywhere as long as their controls were synched to a satellite that the robots were also synched to. So they could be thousands of miles away from the action. Not a single one of our people would have to be in harm's way.

I tracked down the general who made the speech in the video. His name is Johnson. He and the general who commanded the attacks, a guy named Wainwright, teach military history at Western University in Zone 1, on the coast. I called Wainwright and explained that a project was under consideration to restore the robots to active status, if possible. If not, we might have to make new ones. Wainwright told me that the robots are in storage not far from his location, but he's not sure they'll be operable after all this time. The good news is, he has the plans and specs. He tracked them down before the 2527 attacks to facilitate maintenance. The other good news is that the guys who operated the robots have stayed in touch through a veterans' group. Wainwright has all their contact information, so he'd have no problem getting them as instructors to teach our people how to operate the robots. Some of them might even be willing to operate the robots themselves if the time ever came."

No threats to peace were on the horizon at that moment, but Garrett did not want to be caught unprepared if one suddenly materialized and threatened to destroy everything the Africans had built. To Garrett, even a minuscule risk of such a thing happening was unacceptable.

"Super," said Brandon. "What's the next step?"

"I'm sending you and Alice out there to meet the two generals and establish a rapport with them. Wainwright agreed that he or Johnson will take you out to have a look at the equipment, and you can determine if the stuff is still usable to any extent or just junk."

"If it's junk, I assume we'd take the plans and specs, upgrade the engineering and make our own," said Alice.

"Well, that depends. If we ask the governments of the three zones to fund this, they'll insist on controlling it... In effect, we'd be arming them with horrific weapons of war they wouldn't otherwise have and would have no way to get. I'd like this to be our baby. But how else could we fund such a project without government help?"

Brandon and Alice looked at each other and burst out laughing.

"Is that a hint?" Alice asked.

Garrett grinned, "You betcha. As you may recall, you left the door open, last time."

"We'll fund it," said Brandon. "As we've been speaking, I've made a few mental calculations. The cost will be enormous. It could go as high as a full one percent of our nest egg. But we'll do it, anyway."

"Let me ask you boys a question," said Alice. "Are we considering this project just to have something new to do? Because if there's no real need for this, I'm sure we could find things to do where we'd be solving real problems."

"Great point, Alice," said Garrett. "I make it a point to ask that same question every time we're looking at doing something new. Taking on things just to have something new to do is a trap that we, as people of metal, are apt to fall into, in part because we have so much time to fill, and also because, after doing a particular thing for a hundred years or more, it's natural to want to move on to something else. As you two know better than anyone."

"You're right about that," said Alice.

"So let's examine the merits of this project. Its aim is to enhance our ability to prevent the biologicals from consuming themselves in war."

"They don't even have guns," said Alice.

"The police do," said Garrett, "and over time, they've equipped themselves with some formidable weaponry, for riot control purposes. Not that the police themselves would start a war. Nor is the general populace likely to rise up and become warlike, particularly given the fact that, as you mentioned, Alice, they have no guns. But governments have them or can get them. All they have to do is order them from the same factories that produce weaponry for the police. Who do you think starts wars?"

"Leaders," said Brandon. "Of governments. Or rebel groups."

"So it's not all that farfetched," said Garrett. "Look how fast Hitler took Germany from being substantially disarmed into the Second World War. All it takes for war to come is for one opportunist to seize power during a time of turmoil. You guys are experts in practically everything, I'm sure you've read about the untold suffering wars have caused throughout human history—going back way before they even had firearms."

"Those are all strong points," said Brandon. "Here's another possibility. If a dictator takes over one zone, or even all three, and starts oppressing the people, we'd want to be able to effectively intervene."

"I'm more than satisfied about this project," said Alice.

"Me too," said Brandon.

"Just so you know, these generals are a hoot," said Garrett, and spent a few minutes describing them.

History Department
Western University
Zone 1

"Overwhelming force was the key, as always," General Wainwright was telling his students when Alice and Brandon entered the classroom. The screen behind Wainwright showed a diagram of a battle.

"Good afternoon," said Wainwright. "Please make yourselves comfortable. The period will end at 1430."

"He looks and sounds like a general," Alice muttered

Wainwright had replaced the head he'd worn in the 2527 campaign with that of a handsome and distinguished elder statesman—or in his case, an elder general. He wore dress blues but was not wearing the pearl-handled revolvers they'd seen in the videos.

The general had been pacing back and forth in front of the screen with his hands clasped behind his back. Suddenly, he stopped, turned toward the students and began firing questions about the battle. Right answers were rewarded with "outstanding." Students who gave wrong answers were scolded and told to read the freaking material.

"I half expected him to make that one girl drop down and do pushups," Brandon whispered.

"If I didn't know better, I'd have figured him for a famous warrior," Alice whispered back. "In fact, his original wasn't a warrior at all — he never saw one minute of combat. When he retired from the Army after 25 years as the Pentagon's head of procurement, he was a billionaire, which wasn't at all unusual for people in government service in those days. It's hilarious."

When class was dismissed, Wainwright walked toward Brandon and Alice looking every bit the distinguished general he portrayed.

"Follow me," he said cordially. "I'll introduce you to Arthur. He's an outstanding soldier, for a Brit. He was my chief of staff in 2527. He helped sort out some of the details"

They found Brigadier Johnson reading something on his screen. Wainwright introduced them.

"Arthur will send you the plans and specifications, whereupon he'll take you out to examine the weaponry," said Wainwright before excusing himself.

"I'll also send you video of our weapons in action during the 2527 dustup," said Johnson. "They were beyond overwhelming when we last used them. I understand the two of you are mechanical engineers."

"Yes, we are," said Brandon.

"We've seen the video, it's awesome," said Alice.

"Well then, General Wainwright and I will await your verdict on the weaponry's condition. Shall we proceed?"

Twenty minutes later they entered a large storage depot filled with robot soldiers of various types and sizes; robot tanks; and the mighty Behemoths. The weapons were covered with rust, and there were holes, some of them quite large, where the metal had rusted through.

"Centuries of salt air have taken their toll," said Johnson.

"They're beyond repair," said Brandon. "But we're happy to have seen these bad boys firsthand. It gives you a sense of their scale that you don't get from plans or even video. We'll make new ones. We appreciate your showing us around. We'll be in touch."

"Roger that," said the general.

Garrett had wanted Alice and Brandon to build a rapport with the two generals, so on the way back to the university, they asked Johnson if he would mind sharing some of his personal recollections about the fateful day. The narrative that Johnson brought forth for them was actually quite compelling, much as Johnson's speech on the Jubilee Day video had been. They enjoyed hearing him tell the story in person.

• • • • •

Great Rift Valley
Zone 3
Three months later

Large flatbed trucks had carried several robotic tanks and a company of robot soldiers out to a remote rural area where targets had been set up for the tests. Earlier that day, a Behemoth had arrived with its crew. Machines wearing military fatigues had finished preparations for the tests and were standing in formation under one of the Behemoth's wings.

"What's with the gray heads?" Garrett whispered to Alice.

"They're the latest fashion fad in Zone 1," said Alice.

Garrett walked over and addressed the men.

"Gentlemen, I can't thank you enough for making the trip."

"We're happy to be here," said their leader, whose uniform, which he'd worn during the 2527 attacks, bore the rank of command sergeant major. "If you all will retire to the observation area, we'll proceed. Enjoy the show."

It was like what they'd seen in the old video, except for the noise. Brandon probably would have peed his pants if he'd been biological.

"I'm waiting for my body to stop vibrating," said Alice.

Garrett was delighted.

"I've been assured that none of the biologicals who helped build these weapons had access to any of their plans and specs," Garrett told Brandon and Alice. "Biologicals made the parts, but metallics did all the assembly."

Chapter 12
Dynasty

West North America
2646

At 32, Ode Furaha was young to be the CEO of a company as important as Pan African Minerals. She'd held that position for the past six years—a period during which her company's earnings had doubled and its market share had grown almost 14%. Investors figured the young woman must have been doing something right. Pan African stock sold at a substantial premium in relation to current earnings, in anticipation of continued earnings growth.

In 2643, the company had moved its headquarters from Nairobi to its present location on the west coast of North America.

Ode was strikingly attractive and carried herself with an easy, unforced air of confidence, but she was not what anyone would have described as a natural people person. She was smooth and polite to everyone, whatever their station. But some people found her cool, matter of fact, direct and sometimes blunt. So be it, she would have replied. She had a job to do.

Ode Furaha was not a person who made short-term plans. She had managers for that. She thought far ahead, into the distant future. To her, it was family planning—in this case, providing for her progeny until such time, if ever, as her bloodline ended. She was someone who needed a lifelong mission-one that, by its terms, she could never completely fulfill. This was hers. But first, she had to make a fortune far larger than any she could hope to amass running her company.

Ode's plan called for making West North America an independent nation. Once that was done, there had to be a way to use that status to amass wealth. She'd read how the Swiss had done it in the 20th and 21st centuries, by laundering the world's dirty money. What could she do now?

An online search for ways leaders of independent states had used their positions to enrich themselves provided the answer. Among other interesting tidbits, Ode learned that while the Swiss were getting rich by hiding money, elites in certain island nations in the Caribbean Sea had enriched themselves by giving low tax rates and providing cheap labor to foreign companies, primarily American and European, that moved some of their manufacturing operations there. *We could do this*, she thought.

She described the concept to her husband, Hamedi, whose judgment she often sought when dealing with important business matters. They made a good team. Her forte was creativity and innovation. His was finding the right balance between risk and reward. She was lucky to have him as her chief operations officer. He was the best planner and administrator she'd ever met. Plus, he was amazing in every other way, and she loved him to pieces. They were thinking about getting ready to start their family.

"So, what do you think," she asked Hamedi after he'd had time to research the matter. "Do you think the concept is viable?"

"I do, but it's based in part on historical precedents that might not be entirely germane in today's world."

"Like what?"

"Well, public opinion, for one thing—African public opinion. The citizens of the three African zones are much better educated and informed than the Americans and Europeans were back then, and their leaders are sharper. More importantly, their leaders aren't for sale. So I don't think we should try to do it all at once. We should do it little by little so that, hopefully, they won't notice what's happening until it's so far along that it'd be hard to unwind."

"I understand," said Ode. "Africans don't need their governments' permission to move plants here. But if their governments focus on what's happening and get all riled up, they could take steps to stop it."

"Another potential issue is worker exploitation. The workers in these plants barely earned enough to keep their families alive. No one gave a damn then. But Africans today seem very much attuned to such issues. Plus, our workers and theirs are the same people, racially and culturally. If the African companies are seen as exploiting North American workers, there's a risk of African citizens raising holy hell."

"We'll have every reason to treat our people humanely," said Ode. "Outright exploitation rarely works over the long term. It carries within it the seeds of its own destruction. Paying workers starvation wages would be stupid and short sighted. We'll want our workers to be happy and accepting of their lives."

"Also, the jobs they outsourced in the 20th and 21st centuries were unskilled labor compared to the jobs people do today," said Hamedi. "People will have to work hard to gain the necessary skills to do today's jobs. And we'll want them to continue working hard. So they'll need incentives."

"And a career path that offers the possibility that they can do even better for themselves and their families, up to a point."

"Up to a point? What do you mean by that?"

Ode put a finger to her lips and took a device from the coffee table.

"I'm thinking dynasty, let's go to park," she wrote and handed the device to her husband.

"Holy zebra," he wrote, "you seem to think someone might be listening in."

Ode took back the device and wrote: "I would have thought that with all your study of history you'd be more sensitive to that possibility. You can never tell who's listening."

With that, they left their house and began walking toward the nearby park.

Ode, Hamedi and the eighty most senior executives under them, whom she'd nicknamed the "Weighty Eighty," and their families, occupied a new gated community on a cliff overlooking the Pacific Ocean. The development included a large, beautifully landscaped park. Attractive fencing had been placed near the cliff to prevent children from falling off.

Ode and her husband chatted pleasantly during the short walk and chose one of the benches near the fountain.

"Okay, sweet cakes," said Hamedi, "what is this 'dynasty' business?"

Ode took a moment to compose her thoughts.

"It's something that just recently dawned on me. What if our family and the families of the Weighty Eighty declared ourselves a hereditary aristocracy above and apart from everyone else?"

"A dynasty," said Hamedi.

"Yes," said Ode. "Our posterity would be provided for in perpetuity."

"So why do I sense that you have misgivings?"

"You're right. There's a problem. Children of the aristocracy would be free to associate with and even marry commoners, but they'd tend not to do so, especially as the number of aristocrats and the selection of potential mates grew larger. Eventually, they'd face the problems that plagued the European aristocracy in olden times because of their inbreeding. But if we can solve that problem, a hereditary aristocracy could work."

"If horses were unicorns they could fly," Hamedi joked.

Ode laughed. "Look, I've been reading up on the genetic engineering research that scientists did in the 20th and 21st centuries." As it happened, she and Brandon Delaney had read many of the same articles. "It has a lot of potential, both for fixing genetic problems, like the ones inbreeding might create, but also for adding or enhancing positive traits, like intelligence, strength, artistic talent, whatever. The University of Nairobi has had a genetics department for over a century. The professors are all Machines, so far. The head of the Department has the mind of a 22nd century genetic engineer. It's the only university genetics department in the world, as far as I know. I would imagine they've made amazing progress. I propose that we keep an eye out for candidates to send there for training when they're old enough. We'll promise them huge salaries when they return with their doctorates, and recipes."

Hamedi considered this.

"It could take a while," he pointed out. "The Weighty Eighty is a relatively young group. Most of their kids aren't even in high school yet. If we broadened our search—"

"We'd be making a huge mistake if we recruited commoners to do genetic engineering for us. It has to remain secret. No one else can know about it except the aristocrats that we recruit to do this work. We'll want our commoners to accept their inferior position as part of the natural order."

"You're right," said Hamedi. "So we'll wait and recruit our own people."

"One of the articles I read on inbreeding said it took centuries of inbreeding before the problems began appearing," said Ode. "So we'll have time."

"Good."

"We'll have to put the fear of God into our geneticists," said Ode. "The penalty for betrayal will need to be horrific. Unimaginable."

Hamedi chuckled and patted his wife's knee.

"You need go into the study and close the door when we get home," he told her. "Sit down, close your eyes and channel your inner sadist. Write it all down. Four or five bullets describing the tortures they'll suffer—day in, day out, year after year—until the time finally comes for them to meet their maker. We'll print your list on a small, inconspicuous sign and post it in their secure, secret workspace that no one else but they and we are allowed to enter. No threats, no warnings, just a simple list. Their eyes will be drawn to it on a daily basis."

"Plus, we'll make them rich beyond their wildest imagination," said Ode. "They'd have to be nuts to betray us."

"Well, we'll have to keep an eye out for that, too."

"Let's go," said Ode.

They hurried home, and by the time she sat down to write the list, her mind had already composed and edited it.

"Fantastic," said Hamedi said after he'd read it. "Let's go back to the park. I have a feeling that you've figured out how we'll get the money to pay for all this."

"Well, here's my preliminary plan," said Ode after they'd returned to their bench. "We'll do it in stages. In the first stage, we and the Weighty Eighty will keep our positions with the company, and you and I will start the ball rolling on our own.

"Our first act will be to promote making West North America an independent, sovereign nation, thereby placing our territory beyond the reach of the African tax authorities. We'll cite the Declaration of Independence. What can they say, or do, for that matter? Raise an army and invade us? No chance. They're much too comfortable. Plus, a lot of their people will sympathize with our desire to be on our own. As a sovereign nation, we'll have the ability to offer African companies greatly reduced tax rates. Their tax savings will be enormous, and they'll share them with us."

"I married a bona fide genius," said Hamedi.

"Once our new country exists," Ode continued, "we'll need to make sure we control the government, so we can operate freely and not have to worry about everything we've built being confiscated by corrupt politicians. We'll create a government like the one the United States had in its last years. Their legislative and judicial branches were façades; the president pulled all the levers. We'll go a step further. Our president won't pull the levers, we will."

"Politicians can be expensive," said Hamedi

"We'll make them aristocrats and double their annual income and that of their progeny. Or they can refuse our offer and remain commoners. What would you do?"

"It sounds like you have the whole thing figured out.'

"Just an outline. Initially, the African companies will build their own factories and their people will manage them using local labor. We'll send selected kids from our group to Africa to study engineering and factory management, and when they return, we'll get them jobs at the plants to get them practical experience."

"I'm anxious to hear the part where we get money," said Hamedi.

"Here it is. It's rather elegant in its simplicity. A development company secretly owned and minimally capitalized by us uses government subsidies to build large industrial parks that have the necessary infrastructure. The companies will build their factories there and pay our company rent for the use of our sites."

"They could buy land anywhere and build their own infrastructure," said Hamedi.

"That they could. But word will get out that things will work like clockwork in our industrial parks but will be apt to be interrupted at other locations by power outages, inspections, road closures, labor troubles, and so forth."

"I see."

"The government will build airports, railroads and highways and beef up our electric grid, using the taxes it collects from the companies. Eventually, when our development company has accumulated enough capital, we'll start building our own factories. By that time, our credit standing should be solid enough for us to get debt financing from the big African banks. The kids we sent to Africa to be trained, and who've worked in the foreign-owned factories, will run our factories. We'll have other offspring from our group trained in all the various elite professions and vocations. It'll be our way of sharing our good fortune with our fellow aristocrats."

"When you said 'up to a point,' regarding the workers, what did you mean?" Hamedi asked.

"The point of an aristocracy is that our people get the top positions. So only the children of aristocrats will have access to our colleges and universities, once we have them, or be sent to Africa for training. The commoners will receive excellent high school educations, unlimited vocational training, access to the Net, and so on. They can become entrepreneurs. We'll form banks, and if a commoner is ambitious and wants to start a business, like selling and installing air cooling and purifying systems, for example, or running a restaurant, the banks will loan him money if his business plan is solid. But initially, most commoners will have factory jobs. But they'll be good ones."

"So basically, under your plan, we'll make out like bandits not by screwing our workers, but by getting the African companies to share some of their tax windfalls with us in the form of site rent."

"Exactly."

"Brilliant, my love. Everyone wins."

"Oh, one last thing," said Ode. "As far as Machines are concerned, I'd prefer that we keep their number to a minimum. They live forever, which makes them a wild card."

"International travel is another wild card," said Hamedi. "People can learn and unlearn all sorts of things if we let them see what things are like elsewhere. It might be best if we didn't establish travel routes with other countries, at least initially."

"Absolutely."

Capital City (later called Furaha)
Republic of West North America
2648

As Ode Furaha had predicted, the governments of the three African zones, which had deemed themselves joint owners of West North

America, did not try to stop that territory from claiming its independence.

As the leader of the independence movement, Ode had become a popular figure. Another advantage her faction had was the fact that West North Americans had never lived under or taken part in representative government of any kind. The education available to native-born West North Americans had been minimal, the equivalent of elementary school plus two years of high school. They'd been miners, mothers, servants and the like. It was all the education they'd needed.

To formalize West North America's independent status, Ode Furaha convened a constitutional convention and appointed herself, her husband and the Weighty Eighty as its delegates. The constitution that the convention adopted contained some 750 words of actual substance, lodged within 10,000 words of legal sounding but meaningless gibberish. The company's general counsel, who had drafted it, appears to have been the only person who ever actually read it.

The constitution created a permanent hereditary class of aristocrats and named Ode, Hamedi, the Weighty Eighty, certain elite professionals and their families as its charter members. It reserved certain listed occupations and vocations to the aristocratic class, along with the opportunity to attend public colleges and universities when they were established. Aristocrats as a class would control 75% of the voting power for all elected offices.

Voters ratified the new constitution and chose aristocrats for every government office. Securing control of their government had been easier than the Furahas had expected. They were off to the races.

The government took steps to make international travel prohibitively expensive for commoners, and to discourage foreign tourism. West North America became an isolated backwater, cut off from the flourishing African mainstream.

A legislator introduced a bill in the national legislature that would have created honorary titles equivalent to the ancient lords, dukes, barons, countesses, ladies and so on, but Ode made sure the measure was killed. "You can't spend titles," she told her husband. "We won. Why rub it in?"

• • • • •

Barracuda Ltd. Truck Manufacturing Plant
Republic of West North America
2733

The nameplate on his brown coveralls said "Mrbiti," no last name. It was funny how the workers were addressed by their given names, but the executives were called by just their last-names—Mr. this or Ms. that—with sir or ma'am at the end of every sentence. It was unnecessarily demeaning, Mrbiti thought. Everyone knew their place in the hierarchy. It wasn't as though anyone needed reminding.

Mrbiti Faraji's job was to maintain and, when necessary, repair the factory's assembly-line robots and related equipment, which made him a key employee. Above all else, the lines had to be kept running. Doing that required a level of hands-on technical knowledge and skill equivalent to what a veteran mechanical engineer would have accumulated in other times.

Mrbiti was more than satisfied with his job, and with the style of life it allowed him to provide for his family. His wife and their children were amazing, gifts from God, and the family was more than comfortable. By historical standards, the Farajis had reached the Promised Land. Mrbiti's parents had been shocked years back when they'd first seen how lavishly Mrbiti and his family lived—so much so that his father had feared that his son had turned to crime. How else could one explain the young family's extravagant new lifestyle? His parents had never even *seen* a house as spacious and beautifully appointed as Mrbiti's.

Mrbiti saw an executive emerge from an office overhead. The man wore a white kachuk—their latest fad—over a brown silk shirt and beige linen trousers. It was their current uniform. They all dressed the same: men, women and kids. Mrbiti did not get a look at the shoes.

Fuck it, he thought. What did he care? He glanced at the sign on the wall to his right and chuckled to himself. "One people, one team," the sign read. It reminded Mrbiti of an ad he'd recently seen on the Net: "Pink, a man's color," it said regarding men's clothing. If the statement had been true, there'd have been no need for the ad.

Stop it, he told himself. *We're in a good place. Life is good.*

Things weren't altogether fair, but there was no point in getting all worked up about that. Life was also short.

An ancient prayer had been passed down from generations of parents to their children; no one knew its origin. Mrbiti thought of it now.

Dear God, please give me the ability to appreciate the things in my life that are good, the energy to improve the parts that can be made better, and the common sense to know when to leave well enough alone.

Mrbiti glanced upward. "Thanks, Momma," he said quietly. "I needed that."

Mrbiti wasn't just a technician. Like his peers, he'd received an excellent, if limited education, the equivalent of attendance at elementary and high schools in ancient times, and the schools were good. Commoners had access on the Net to the same information that the aristos did, and Mrbiti took advantage of that access. He didn't have any formal post-secondary education, but he was well read. He understood how things worked.

Skilled, well-educated and well-trained people were needed for nearly every job in Mrbiti's world. People with the necessary skills didn't grow on trees. The aristos weren't stupid. It was in their interest to give his people the opportunity to gain those skills. It wasn't like the aristos gave a damn about people like him and were doing them any favors.

They need us.

But that was okay. He didn't expect to earn what he earned for doing nothing.

Mrbiti ended up where he always ended up when his mind took this path: *It is what it is.* He wondered how many trillions of people in human history had told themselves the same thing, to help them try to accept life as it was, rather than as it might, could or should have been.

Chapter 13
Personhood

Auditorium
University of Nairobi
2901

"As I scan the faces of the graduates we honor today and see among them so many of my cousins, an ancient maxim comes to mind: 'All men are brothers.' Nowadays, of course, we'd broaden the sentiment to include our sisters, xisters, xothers, nothers and, of course, people of metal, among others. We humans come in a variety of shapes, sizes, genders (where applicable), orientations and identifications, but at the end of the day, we're all people. We have *personhood*. We're family."

The speaker—a physics professor—was an ethnic orangutan, a descendant of the revered and beloved Martha.

Orangutan people descended from Martha and her friends and family had been attending African colleges for ages. They'd received the same genetic enhancements as everyone else.

They were known for the near-relentless way they drove their children almost from the moment they were born. As a result, their children were disproportionately represented in disciplines that required years and years of dedicated work and practice. For example, the percentages of professional orchestral musicians and competitive figure skaters who were ethnic orangutans were many times their share of the population. Many conventional humans were frankly rather resentful.

"They're automatons," one person wrote. "There's no creativity."

Some conventional humans also were jealous of the high numbers of orangutan young people accepted by elite colleges and universities. Others felt that they earned those acceptances. "They work harder than anyone else, so they get better grades and make better test scores, so they're accepted, just as they should be," a blogger wrote.

Some years earlier, in response to alumni pressure, many elite African colleges and universities had established numerical limits on orangutan admissions; but courts in all three zones held that ethnicity-based discrimination by government-run schools violated the constitutional guaranty of equality of treatment under the laws.

Pockets of jealousy and resentment aside, the vast majority of non-orangutan people had the utmost respect for that community and its people. Orangutans tended toward the serious side at times, but at other times, one might find the same people telling outrageous jokes or pranking their friends. Orangutan humor tended toward the wicked.

In another half hour, one of their fellows, Professor William of the University of Nairobi Department of Genetics, would host what they had billed as a historic press conference at the university's swimming venue.

Despite their high social stature and distinguished record of accomplishments, orangutan people still did not use last names. "Why should we have two names?" the iconic Martha had asked. "One name is enough." Martha's biographer maintained that Martha had found last names "pretentious."

According to media speculation, Professor William was about to introduce to the world the first human dolphins.

Swimming venue
University of Nairobi
Later that afternoon

Journos and video operators had gathered around the diving venue, where six dolphins could be seen sitting awkwardly on nearby floats. Professor Garrett and Professor William were in a small rowboat next to the dolphins, holding microphones

"Welcome, everyone," said Garrett, "and thanks for coming. As the press release stated, Professor William here is about to introduce to you the first ever fully human dolphins—the culmination of a brilliant, decades long effort by him and his team here at the university. I suggest you hold on to your hats. Ladies, gentlemen, others, xothers and nothers, I give you Professor William, the executive director of the Dolphin Project."

"Thank you, Professor Harry," said William in his reedy but not unpleasant orangutan voice. "This is an exciting day. For our presentation this afternoon, I'll introduce you to our newly minted humans and interview each of them briefly. Each of them has a name, of course. But for convenience, we'll refer to them by the numbers that you see on their floats.

"Number 1, please tell us some of your interests."

"I like fish, live ones, and lots of them."

Spectators burst out laughing.

"Seriously, I love oceanography. We all do. No surprise there, it's something for which we're uniquely suited. My other interests include classical music, law and, believe it or not, politics. I love politics almost as much as oceanography. I find it very entertaining."

"Thank you, Number 1. By the way, Number 1 identifies as and has the equipment of a male. Number 2, a female, is his wife. Number 2, please share with us some of your interests."

"Well, sex," she said, triggering another round of laughs. "Oceanography, romantic novels and ancient 'rap' music."

"Thanks, Number 2," said William. "I might as well point out before I move on that 3 and 4 are husband and wife, as are 5 and 6. Number 3, what are some of your interests?"

"Oceanography, mathematics and astronomy."

"Number 4?"

"Quantum mechanics. It's all I have time for. I'm obsessed."

"Number 5?"

"The intersection of science, philosophy and religion."

"Number 6."

"Art, microbiology and organic chemistry."

"Thank you. Now we'll open it up to the journos."

The journos did what journos did; they grandstanded and acted like jerks. They seemed to want to make themselves look smart at the ethnic dolphins' expense.

Zone 3 Headquarters
People for People
Nairobi

Salim Kone picked up the controller and shut off the screen. "Assholes," he said, referring to the journos.

Salim was head of the Zone 3 branch of the People for People political party. He and his deputy, Kofi Ibori, had heard about the dolphin press conference and had taken a break from their labors to watch it as comic relief from the gloomy work of trying to figure out something, anything, that might help boost their party's dismal prospects in the important gubernatorial election that was only eight months away.

"That was fun," said Kofi.

"Yeah, it was," said Salim. "My lord." He sighed. "Well, we had better get back at it."

"Number 1 was my favorite," said Kofi. "Imagine that, a fish that loves politics."

"Dolphins aren't fish, they're mammals," Salim pointed out. Suddenly, he went still. A moment later, he sprang from his chair so abruptly that the chair fell backwards.

"Holy shit," he cried out. "This is exactly what we need!"

He was laughing hysterically.

"What is?" Kofi asked.

"'The dolphin. Number 1."

"What about him?"

"Look, our problem is the lack of policy differences between us and the Commies," Salim continued.

"Commies" was a nickname for the other major party: the Compassion Party. It had no pejorative connotation and bore no association with the epithet that opponents had used when referring to ancient communists, social democrats and democratic socialists.

"We're like identical twins," said Salim, "except they're in and we're out. Life is good and getting better and better for the voters, and we can't take any of the credit for it. It sucks. I've been praying for a recession—or better yet, a full-scale depression. As it stands now, government is less important than ever. No one cares about us. They think they don't need us. So we need to go back to basics. You're a student of history."

"The dolphin?"

"Identity politics, numb-nuts. If you can't convince the people why they should vote *for* you, you give them reasons to vote *against* the other guy."

Salim could see that Kofi had no idea what Salim was getting at.

"We'll run Number 1 for governor!" Salim announced.

Robert Snyder 151

"Really?" Kofi paused for a moment to consider his boss's words. "It might work," he acknowledged. "But why a dolphin? An orangutan would serve the same purpose and would be an easier sell. No one would question *their* qualifications. They're a known quantity. Dolphins aren't."

"You're being too rational and too cautious," said Salim. "An orangutan candidate would make people yawn. They wouldn't object, but they wouldn't get excited either. It's the obvious next step in the boring charade that politics has become. The dolphin will generate the kind of excitement we haven't seen in a long time. Of course, the fact that our candidate is fun and exciting may not be enough by itself. That's where identity politics comes in."

"'Identity politics,'" Kofi repeated.

"It's crucial to remember that our opponent isn't the governor. He's a nice guy. People like him. Our real opponent is bigotry, in the form of the vile and virulent speciesism of the vested interests that fund and control the governor. They're on the wrong side of history. Our dolphin will run to drive a stake through the last remaining vestige of human bigotry, and it'll be fun to watch him do it. I could be wrong, but that sounds like a winning combination to me."

"You're right, it'll resonate," said Kofi. "We're living in an enlightened era. Diversity and inclusion are articles of faith. The more the merrier. Bigotry is a cardinal sin. It's anathema. Our opponents represent the past. We represent the future."

"Absolutely," said Salim. "How about this? The governor and his supporters have done their best to disguise their bigotry, but the people won't be fooled. Our originalist opponents will stop at nothing in their zeal to make sure that power stays in the hands of their clique, and out of the hands of the more recent additions to our race. I pledge to you that with your support, we will not let that happen."

"'Originalist,'" said Kofi. "I love it."

Office of Professor William
Department of Genetics
University of Nairobi
Next day

"Thanks for seeing me on such short notice, Professor," said Salim. "We watched yesterday's press conference. They're amazing people. Afterwards, my colleague and I discussed what we'd just witnessed, and we were thunderstruck. It was a world-historical event that will change everything." Salim shrugged. "We were reacting as human beings, rather than as mere political operatives. What could human dolphins have to do with politics? But my colleague reminded me of Number 1's interest in politics, and it occurred to me that we've been given a golden opportunity here to erase the last traces of the bigotry that has plagued humanity throughout history."

"That would be nice," said William. "How would we go about doing that?"

"By electing Dolphin Number 1 as our next governor."

William's jaw dropped. He was speechless.

"With today's technology, it would be a snap to build a dolphin-friendly glass-enclosed governor's office pool flanked by desks and workstations outside the glass for his non-dolphin aides and other officials," Salim explained. "On weekends, he could fly with his family to the waters off Mombasa to relax and unwind. He'll be a star."

Professor William seemed skeptical...

"I'm not against this," he told Salim. "I just have trouble picturing it. You are an imaginative person, Mr. Kone."

"Would you consider discussing this with him to see if he'd be interested?" Salim asked. "The party would take care of everything. He'd have to make some speeches, of course, and do ads. Based on what he said yesterday, it seems to me he'd have the time of his life."

"Why don't you come with me?" said William, and they headed for the pool. When they got there, William gestured for Salim to stay back while he cracked the pool door open and peeked inside.

"Oops," said William and closed the door. "They're being intimate. We flew the others to Mombasa earlier this afternoon, but these two opted to stay behind. Now I know why."

They wanted privacy, Salim thought. *They really are human.* Dolphins — i.e., the genetic originals — lived and traveled in groups. To them, the very idea of "privacy" would have been alien.

They gave the dolphins fifteen minutes to finish up and reorient themselves before entering the pool area. Dolphin Number 1 agreed to be the gubernatorial candidate of the People to People party, and his wife was as excited as he was. Salim explained to them in some detail how things would work and answered their questions.

"We'll come up with a written platform as a starting point, subject to your approval, and you can make whatever additions or deletions you see fit," Salim told them. "Not that it'll make much difference. You'll be a sensation. We're excited for you."

Professor William confessed to being excited as well.

"As someone who's also a non-conventional human, I see this as a chance to clear the decks of whatever bigotry remains," said William. "I think the voters will feel the same and will be proud to be part of this effort."

"One last thing," Salim told Number 1. "Dolphin names aren't pronounceable by conventional humans. Would you consider selecting a conventional human name? I mean, of course, if it'd go against your principles or your cultural traditions, forget it, we'll work around it."

"No problem," said the dolphin. "I'll let you pick a name that voters will relate to."

Abraham Lincoln was the name finally chosen. Because of their status as the last surviving conventional humans, African schoolchildren received a thorough grounding in world history. Voters would recognize Lincoln's name, and it would have a positive connotation for them.

The campaign was launched with overwhelming media support. As had happened many times in human history, journos undertook, without charge, to act as unofficial publicists for and protectors of the candidate they favored—in this case, Lincoln. Fortunately for the Lincoln campaign, laws limiting contributions to political candidates did not take into account the immense fair market value of such in-kind media contributions. One can only guess at the amount of money it would have taken to induce the Five Networks to propagandize for and protect a candidate they did not already love.

The tables were turned. Now it was the governor who was on the defensive. He only made himself look phony by trotting out his excellent "friends" who just happened to be orangutans.

Journos wanted answers. Was the governor a speciesist? Was he an originalist? Or a dolphinophobe? What did he have against dolphins as people, anyway? Did he believe that only conventional humans should hold public office? Did he also believe that orangutans should be excluded from senior positions? Had he stopped beating his wife?

"Have you taken the trouble to actually speak with one of the human dolphins?" a journo asked the governor.

"Why would I need to do that?" said the governor. "I've never suggested that dolphins aren't qualified to govern this zone. My problem is with this dolphin. He has zero government experience. His whole candidacy is a stunt designed to breathe life into the party of our opponents, who have nothing else to offer. One day soon, one of our two parties will nominate, and the voters will elect, a non-conventional human to be our governor. It may be a dolphin, or an orangutan, or a human from an entirely new category. I understand the urge to do this now, without delay. But, out of respect for our non-conventional human brethren—our fellow humans, or more precisely, our *co-humans*—we owe them the courtesy of selecting the best possible candidate we can find among them. Mr. Lincoln is not that person."

Polls consistently showed Lincoln with a substantial lead over the governor. However, Salim was well aware of the flaw inherent in polls taken under these circumstances. There was a term for it that he couldn't think of at the moment. The problem was that respondents would lie rather than admit to a poll taker that they supported the "originalist," "speciesist" and "dolphinophobic" governor.

We need to go balls to the wall, Salim decided. *We'll take nothing for granted.*

The following day, disaster struck. One of the University of Nairobi psychologists who'd administered psychotherapy to the dolphins on a regular basis came forward and accused Lincoln of rape. The therapist, a conventional human female, made a point of bathing naked with her dolphin patients, to make them feel more comfortable.

No cameras covered the area, so there was no way to know for sure what had actually happened. Researchers found instances in which male dolphins' genetic originals, which were mammals and had the necessary equipment, had actually raped conventional human women. Who knew? *It's over,* Salim feared. But the Five Networks came through for Lincoln. They fabricated a story about two conventional college boys whom Lincoln's accuser had also accused of sexual assault, which, according to the story, each of them credibly denied. One boy reportedly had been in Zone 1 at the time of the alleged rape.

Voters brushed the accuser's allegations aside and made Lincoln their next governor.

Polls taken after the election showed that, contrary to conventional wisdom, ideology had played practically no role in the election's outcome. Not for the first time, political professionals and their media allies had lost touch with the views of real people. At this point in history, real people harbored only a faint trace of the old prejudices and hatreds, if that. Bigotry was a non-issue. They'd voted for Lincoln because he was cool. He was fun, and entertaining—and why not? It didn't actually matter whom they elected. Changed circumstances had stripped government officials of their capacity to do harm.

The Five Networks made the most of their new celebrity. Camera operators flew with him to Mombasa, where divers recorded the underwater antics of the governor and his lovely family. Broadcasts showed him at work in his aquatic office, conferring with aides via intercom. The voters loved it.

Governor Lincoln served four five-year terms before retiring. He left behind a series of incremental but not insignificant improvements in the way government services were delivered. His affable, good-natured persona had brought a much-needed measure of civility to the Zone 3's political discourse.

Lincoln's successor was an ethnic orangutan.

Chapter 14
So-Called Jobs

Furaha
Republic of West North America
2854

The street cleaning robot stopped moving and told Kwane Falane that it was finally time for his morning kamoosh break, so he stopped, plopped down on a nearby bench and pulled the pipe and his bag of kamoosh from the pocket of his overalls.

"Aaaaah," he sighed, lighting up. The familiar pink glow flowed from his mouth down to his toes and he lost himself in the intricate music from his earphones. *Yes.*

I shouldn't smoke so much, he thought.

He was bored, of course. Everyone he knew was bored, if they weren't outright crazy. Sophisticated devices took care of nearly everything. It had been that way for generations. He'd read that the same thing had happened hundreds of years earlier, and catastrophe had followed. Technology had been perfected to the point where biological humans were obsolete. Maybe it was happening again.

For most of human history, what we now call "technology" had been simple and straightforward, Kwane had read. People made tools and weapons out of stone, which they improved and used to hunt game. People invented the wheel, discovered fire, and began to practice agriculture. Later on, they made better tools and weapons out of metal.

Progress was slow. People who lived in those times probably were barely even aware that it was happening, Kwane guessed. Things remained that way for thousands upon thousands of years, until, all at once, it became a tsunami—to the point where the world that had existed when a person died was almost unrecognizable, as compared to the world into which that person had been born.

The endgame was that ultimately, human beings would be rendered obsolete once again.

I'm one of the smartest people I know, Kwane mused. *Sucks for me.*

His study of ancient history had helped him keep his mind alive. It allowed him an escape from his empty workaday world. Thank the Lord the Net still worked, and the information was still out there. He could scarcely imagine some of the things people had done in ancient times and what their lives must have been like—exploration, mass migrations, wars.

Kwane knew that for most of human history, life had been harsh and fraught with danger. Not at all like today. But it was interesting to ponder nonetheless. You could read about a horrific era in history without experiencing any of that harshness yourself. Wars that had wreaked untold horror and suffering were some of the most interesting stories of all, Kwane had found. Because at this late date, centuries after they'd happened, they were just that, stories.

Two aristocrats engaged in conversation walked past at that moment. The aristos all had what Kwane assumed was a hereditary speech impediment. Commoners could not understand a word they said, but they understood each other perfectly.

Kwane wasn't surprised when the aristos greeted him and shook hands. Aristos didn't hold themselves out as being superior to commoners. They received an elite education and had a wealth of opportunities that were reserved for their class, but Kwane felt that most of them were decent human beings. They seemed to like and respect common folks.

Commoners found the aristos strange in intriguing ways. Like the way they dressed. Currently, they all wore long orange gowns with matching shoes and hats that looked like lampshades. Men, women and children dressed the same.

I wonder if the hats light up when they get an idea, Kwane thought after the aristos had moved on.

He laughed out loud and refilled and relit his pipe. Oddly, the warm pink glow made him think of electricity, and he mentally cataloged the myriad ways in which the harnessing of electricity had altered the course of human history from the time of its first use—in the 19th century, if memory served—to the present.

It was the single most consequential event in all of human history, Kwane decided. Had electricity not been harnessed, technology would have remained primitive and slow to change. He tried to imagine what his world would have been like.

Upon further reflection, however, Kwane saw the flaw in his thinking. It was the old invention versus discovery trap. Airplanes and automobiles, for example, were invented. But natural properties like electricity were discovered. So if electricity hadn't been discovered when it was, someone else eventually would have found it—probably sooner rather than later—and events would have proceeded along much the same path.

The street cleaner informed Kwane that break time had expired, so he emptied his pipe and resumed his so-called job. It was make-work. The aristos had dumbed down the technology of certain types of equipment—from appliances like the robotic street sweeper to sophisticated factory equipment—so they'd require human so-called operators. *So we'd have things to do,* he thought. They meant well, but doing make-work, when you knew it was all you'd ever do, was depressing.

Thanks to the meds people took, and their kamoosh, episodes of acute depression were few and far between; and even then, they were easily treated. Still, the episodes came often enough, and when they did, you felt like a nothing.

Life sucks, Kwane thought as he reached for his pill case.

From birth through high school, life was great. You learned, you played, you had friends, and you did fun things, culminating in having sex. Then, suddenly, it stopped. Not the sex, thankfully, but practically everything else.

In theory, commoners could have lived rich, active, even creative lives. They had more than enough leisure time, and their "work" was hardly exhausting. But for whatever reason, they did not. It wasn't in them.

As had always been the case, some people were born with developmental disabilities so severe that they were incapable of realizing what they were missing. The thought made Kwane feel guilty as hell, but he almost envied those poor unfortunates. His intelligence was both a blessing and a curse. It was a blessing because it gave him the wherewithal to find satisfaction and entertainment from his readings. The downside was that he was painfully aware of what he was missing, as compared to historic norms.

It was impossible not to envy the aristos for the opportunities they accrued just by being born. But he couldn't bring himself to resent them for it. He was too honest for that. It wasn't their fault, and he had to admit that, had he been in their place, he wouldn't have felt the least bit guilty.

Walking behind his sweeper, Kwane reflected that commoners' children kept them alive. Through them, and later, through grandchildren, parents were able to re-live, vicariously, the rich full lives they'd had as children. Parenting also carried important responsibilities, and took lots of work, which gave commoners a sense of purpose and self-worth that their so-called jobs did not afford them.

When he got home that evening, he gave his wife and children long, heartfelt hugs.

Chapter 15
Aristos

Superior Ice Cream Shop
Furaha, Republic of West North America
2902

Bobo Chike and his best friend, Kabandha Imamu, secured the table while their wives and children waited in line to give the kiosk their orders. Most of the customers were commoners, but there were three aristos as well, in line waiting their turn like everyone else.

The two friends worked as washroom attendants at the Furaha airport, where they were tasked with offering paper towels, cups of mouthwash and breath mints to aristos who dropped in before, after or between flights to use the facility.

A single uniformed attendant stood next to the ice cream kiosk, but there was nothing for her to do but watch. The kiosk took customers' orders, identified their voice patterns and charged their financial accounts, then sent the orders to the machines that prepared the milkshakes, sundaes and so on and placed them on a conveyor that moved past the kiosk.

"How's ancient history," Kabandha asked Chike.

"No change," Bobo joked. "This time I went all the way back to the founding of the Republic and read original source documents. The founders never intended things to be the way they are now. A shop like this would have been a small business owned and operated by commoners. In the Republic's early years, there were lots of small shops and establishments, and places that served food and beverages. Other places sold groceries or clothes, or tools and equipment. People did real work. They made things. They provided services, like hair cutting." He gave Kabandha his device. "Here, look at this."

Kabandha spent a few minutes browsing through the article until a photo caught his attention. He caused the screen to zoom in on the faces of the people in the old photo, then looked across the shop where three hatless aristos were seated. He'd noticed them earlier. He glanced back at the photo and handed Bobo's device back to him

"That's odd," said Kabandha. "Do you see it?"

"They're hatless," said Bobo, referring to the aristos in the old photo. "I hadn't noticed. That *is* odd. Hats must not have been in style back then."

"Now look behind you," said Kabandha. "Look at the three aristos at the table back by the wall."

Bobo turned and glanced in that direction. Those aristos also were hatless, which was unheard of. Their lampshades hung from hooks on the wall next to them. Bobo could not remember ever having seen a hatless aristo—male or female, child or adult. He could hardly believe his eyes.

The aristos had committed what their peers would have considered an irreverent act by removing their hats in the presence of commoners. It was a small event in itself, but because Bobo was there to witness it, it would prove to have profound historic consequences.

"Do you see it?" Kabahandha asked.

"Yeah," said Bobo. "They're hatless, like the aristos in the picture. It's quite a coincidence. What are the odds?"

"Look again. Look at the shape of their heads. Then look at the heads in the photo."

Bobo did so.

"My God. The heads in the photo are exactly like ours, but the heads of the aristos over there are…misshapen."

"Yes. What do you make of that?"

"I don't know," said Bobo.

The heads of the hatless aristos in the ice cream shop had a pronounced bulge on top that was bisected by a crease that ran from the back to the front of their heads. There was a bump on each temple. The heads in the ancient photo showed none of those features.

"I'm sure there's a logical explanation," said Bobo. "Maybe the guys here were in some kind of accident. Here's another possibility. Maybe the three of them had had brain upgrades installed and needed to have their heads enlarged."

"Brain upgrades?"

"Before the Malaise, scientists were obsessed with the idea of artificial intelligence. One of their goals was to invent devices that could be implanted in human brains to make them work better or faster. Who knows? Maybe some of them succeeded, and the aristos have tracked the technology down and are using it to make themselves smarter. The creases down the middle could be surgical scars."

"You think?"

"Who knows what they're up to behind their gates? It's possible. I can't imagine what else it could be."

Just then, their wives and children brought their treats to the table, along with shakes for the men.

"I'm going over there," Bobo told the others. "I want you all to smile and wave when the aristos look in this direction."

He rose and strolled over to the aristos' table.

"Excuse me, gentlemen, I beg your indulgence for interrupting you, but my friends and family and I couldn't help but notice that you're all recovering from surgery. They insisted that I convey to you our wishes for a speedy recovery."

The aristos, of course, fully understood the simple, basic language that commoners like Bobo spoke. One of them shook his head and said something Bobo could not make out, except for the words "not" and "surgery." Bobo realized that the aristos didn't speak a separate language, as he'd assumed; they simply pronounced most words differently.

The three men quickly retrieved their hats from their hooks and put them back on. *They seem embarrassed,* Bobo thought.

"I am terribly sorry for our mistake," said Bobo. He now understood that the aristos' heads were simply differently shaped. They were born with them.

The aristo smiled and patted Bobo's arm reassuringly. He spoke, and Bobo caught the words "normal" "shape" and "look."

"So the shape of your heads is normal."

The aristo smiled again and spoke very slowly, as if that would make it possible for Bobo to understand him. Bobo recognized the word "normal" and nodded.

"Once again, I apologize"

The aristo smiled and said something, and he and the other aristos rose and shook hands with Bobo and left the ice cream shop.

"They haven't had surgery," said Bobo after returning to the table. "That's just the way aristos' heads look."

"It's hard to believe," said Kabandha. "They're descendants of aristos like the ones in the picture, whose heads looked just like ours. I wonder what happened. Could it be their inbreeding?"

"Like the ancient Europeans?" said Bobo.

"Exactly."

"I don't think so," said Bobo. "Inbreeding among the ancient European aristocracy gave rise to random mutations that affected the descendants of individual families. What the aristos just told me is that this is how all their heads look—their entire population."

Bobo had an idea.

• • • • •

That night, after the kids were in bed, Bobo did a search. Commoners had the same access to online information as aristos.

As he normally did when researching aspects of history and life in the early 2000s, he went to an online encyclopedia that was a gold mine of miscellaneous information on ancient civilizations. Bobo had read elsewhere that ancient scientists had developed ways to change the human body's code, which was contained in "genes" that every cell of the body had. According to what he'd read, the changes were made to the genes while they were still in the embryo that would grow up to be a human being.

Even commoners learned elementary biology in their high schools, including basic genetics concepts; so Bobo knew that genetic codes determined the traits that a person would have—what they looked like, how smart they were, their hair and eye color and so on. He told his device to search for "genetic modification." His device would pull up anything with those words or words with substantially the same meaning.

Bobo scrolled past a number of hits that related to evolution and mutation. Finally, he saw an article on "genetic enhancement" and called it up. Written in 2132, the article described how scientists had devised procedures to change an embryo's genetic makeup by either removing genes linked to disease or other negative traits, or by adding genetic material that was linked to desirable traits. The article explained why attempts to make positive genetic changes were controversial:

"The justification for allowing the removal of 'bad' genes is solid: to prevent hereditary disease-proneness or other hereditary defects from being passed on to succeeding generations. Moreover, the consequences of removing genes linked with particular diseases or defects are narrow and predictable—the disease or defect won't be passed on. *Adding* genetic material to an organism to add or enhance traits is an entirely different proposition. It may not be possible for scientists to anticipate all the consequences that may flow from the addition of such material. There is an inherent risk of unintended and potentially severe adverse change. Another concern is the prospect of a 'master race' being the end result of prolonged, unfettered genetic enhancement."

Commoners like Bobo had no idea what went on in the gated compounds where the aristos lived with their families and did whatever they did. What if, after the old photo was taken, the aristos had located Machines that had minds copied from 21st- or 22nd-century genetic engineers? Bobo thought of the "master race" fear that the article had cited. It was a valid concern. Hitler would have made full use of such technology, had he possessed it.

From what Bobo had read, Ode Furaha was nothing at all like Hitler. She was an elitist, to be sure, an extreme one, but she hadn't oppressed anyone in the traditional sense of that word. West North Americans received salaries and allowances that were lavish by historic norms, and had excellent working conditions

By no means, however, did any of that rule out the possibility that the Furahas had created a program to improve, over time, the genetics of successive generations of aristos. The misshapen heads—perhaps even the way they talked—could have been one of the unanticipated consequences that the articles had warned against. What other possibility was there? The head shape and the goofy way aristos talked were characteristics shared by all aristos, so either (a) the genes of every aristo who was born at the relevant time or times must have gotten the same modifications, or (b) if some but not all aristos had received them, enough time had gone by for the modifications to have been propagated to the point where every aristo's genome now had them. Either way, there'd been a program. Did it still exist? It didn't seem likely.

The first generations of aristos had been high achievers. But that was then. No one really knew what they did now. Bobo tried to think of a single significant advance in technology or other innovation that the aristos had developed in the modern era, but he could not,

Ostensibly, the slow pace of technological change had been deliberate, so commoners would still have work. Like not replacing washroom attendants with robots. But what if genetic engineering gone wrong had rendered later generations of aristos incapable of developing new technologies?

As mentioned, no one had any idea what the aristos currently did behind their gates.

Bobo resolved to get close enough to an aristo to warn them. He'd be taking a risk. If a gene-modification had gone wrong, it would have been kept secret, Bobo assumed. The authorities would not be pleased if they caught him spilling the beans. But his gut told him that there was very little risk that a rank-and-file aristo would give him up to their police. They were good people; and from his study of history, Bobo had the sense that people who lived in dictatorships preferred not to have unnecessary contact, under any circumstances, with their rulers and the rulers' thugs. There'd been too many instances where people who'd ratted out friends and acquaintances, expecting a reward, had drawn punishment instead.

• • • • •

It took several weeks, but one afternoon, while Kahandha was out on break, an aristo entered the restroom, did his business and accepted a paper towel and a cup of mouthwash from Bobo. This aristo seemed to be in particularly high spirits. He told Bobo what sounded like a joke, and started laughing, so Bobo laughed with him. Aristos did not seem to realize how little of their garbled speech commoners could understand.

Bobo saw his chance. "That was a good one, sir," said Bobo. "Sir, if you have a few moments, I'd be most grateful if I could ask you a few questions to satisfy my curiosity as to certain of the customs and traditions of you and your fellows."

Provided the aristo wasn't late for his flight or on his way to a meeting, etiquette demanded that he or she agree to such a request made by a commoner. The aristo nodded his head and said something.

"Perhaps we could repair to the seating area and smoke our pipes?" Bobo asked. No one would notice, much less care, if he was absent from his post.

The aristo nodded, spoke, and Bobo followed him out into the terminal. *Why do they imagine we can understand them?* Bobo wondered.

It was not unheard of or unseemly for an aristo to smoke a pipe in the company of a commoner. It was a righteous act, per the modern, West North American version of the ancient concept of *noblesse oblige.*

The men took seats and spent the next several moments loading their kamoosh pipes. The aristo surprised Bobo by lighting both their pipes.

Bobo showed the aristo the ancient photo of hatless aristos and called attention to the shape of their heads. "Based on this photo," said Bobo, "your ancestors had heads that looked like mine. However, several days ago, I observed three of your fellow aristocrats who had removed their hats, and their heads had a different shape than the ones in the old picture. One head shape is as good as another, but how did this change come about?"

The aristo smiled and offered what appeared to be an explanation. Bobo picked out a tortured pronunciation of the Swahili words for "God" and "favor."

"Would it be all right if you talked to me with your device?" Bobo asked. "We commoners have difficulty processing the aristocratic argot."

The aristo nodded and pulled an electronic device from his robe.

"As I'm sure you're already aware," said Bobo, "in olden times scientists experimented with techniques to engineer an embryo's genetics to enhance selected traits, like intelligence, strength and beauty, among others. I'll send you links, if you wish. The problem was that adding genetic material sometimes had unintended negative consequences that had nothing to do with the positive trait they were reinforcing. Some of these adverse consequences were serious. I'll send you a link that gives examples."

Bobo got the impression that this aristo was unaware that ancient scientists had manipulated human genomes. He outlined his suspicion that the founders of the Republic might have established a program whose object was to improve the genetics of their aristocratic descendants.

"If so," Bobo continued, "the difference in your and my head shapes — neither of which is better or worse than the other — could have been an unintended consequence of changes that were made to your ancestors' genes. If so, I would want to find out, if I were you, if there might have been other unintended gene changes that were *not* benign, that could have adverse consequences to your descendants."

"I appreciate your concern for our welfare," the screen of the aristo's device told Bobo, "but all is as God wills that it be. Our head shapes and features, and the way we speak, were given to us by God to mark us as His Chosen Ones."

"I understand," said Bobo. "If I may be so bold," said Bobo, "would it be possible for you to tell me a little about what you all are working on? I'm just curious. You're all obviously very busy."

"To be honest, not very much," Bobo read. "I'm an engineer, quote unquote. We massage and make minor refinements to technologies that our ancestors created, but that's about it. We've lost the spark that they had, quite frankly."

"That's what I was afraid of," said Bobo.

"Thank you for bringing all this to my attention, I am most grateful," Abimbola dictated.

"You are most welcome, sir."

Bobo got the aristo's email address and sent him the links on genetic enhancement that he'd offered.

• • • • •

Abimbola carefully studied the information in the links Bobo had sent him. Genetic engineering. Wow. Who knew? The more he read, the more the religious explanation that he'd been given as a child looked like cover for a major genetic engineering fuckup. The more he thought about it, the angrier he became. What had the bastards been thinking? Why hadn't they told anyone?

Like everyone else, he'd believed the divine intervention story because it explained what had otherwise seemed inexplicable. *So there it is*, he thought. The last pillar of their supposed aristocratic specialness had crumbled. They were frauds, albeit comfortable ones.

Abimbola thought of the commoners he knew and smiled ruefully. *It's not how they must think it is. We're relics. Our long-forgotten ancestors whose portraits hang in our hallways led grand, brilliant lives. We're the leftovers. It's what great families do. The gene pool loses its zip, over time, and the heirs, now little more than entitled slackers, persist in imagining that they're special, and their lives are special, because of what their ancestors once had been.*

In a way, Abimbola envied Bobo. Bright fellow, surprisingly so; and he lived a real life. Abimbola resolved to put everything else aside and try to figure out what to do about what he'd learned. But first, he'd have to break the news to his wife, Ama. She'd be crushed, he assumed, but he was wrong; she was furious.

"The fucking bastards!" she hissed. "We prayed and prayed that our boys would be fucking *blessed*, because we couldn't be sure until we saw the ultrasounds. But it was bullshit. They made one of my ancestors an outcast because he was *born normal*."

Ama was referring to the fact that, for a period after the ill-fated gene modification, some infants had been born with old-fashioned heads—an occurrence that was taken as a sign from God that the children had the souls of commoners. They were expelled from the aristocracy and placed with commoner families.

"My family bears that stigma to this very day," said Ama. "I can't believe it. Do you think the Archbishop knows the truth?"

"If the bishop who first made up this bullshit was smart," said Abimbola, "he would have pretended to believe it himself and would not have let his successors in on the scam, to reduce the risk that the truth would eventually come out."

Ama laughed bitterly. "What a joke. They made us wear hats out of *modesty*. They didn't want us flaunting our blessedness in front of commoners."

"Sweetheart, I think it's time for us to face the fact that our entire existence here is built on lies," said Abimbola. "I think we should at least consider getting the hell out of here and starting fresh somewhere else."

"Like Africa?" said Ama.

"I think we should check it out. We're due for a vacation."

Abimbola chose not to mention to his wife the possibility that they might have inherited additional genetic modifications that could have serious adverse consequences. They needed answers. He'd learned from the links that Bobo had given him that, unlike West North American schools, all African colleges and universities, even the very smallest, had departments of human genetics. The oldest and most famous was at the University of Nairobi. He decided to book his family on one of the popular African vacation tours, one that made a stop in Nairobi.

Nairobi
One month later

The sight Abimbola, his wife and their two young sons saw as their plane prepared to land was stunning.

"My God," said Ama. "What on earth is this? Where are we? It's stunning."

The city looked nothing like the one their ancestors had built long ago in Furaha. A 20th century author had coined the term "future shock" to describe the difficulty people had experienced adjusting to the changes that technology had wrought during a single human lifetime. The Okafors were being exposed to changes that had occurred over generations.

The office towers rose to enormous heights, like the ones in Furaha, but they were much more interesting to look at, and a lot more attractive.

"They're don't all look the same," said Abimbola. "It's like each one's making its own statement. It's like a cacophony of shapes, styles and colors."

Abimbola was half right. Each of the buildings made a "statement," but to the eye of a modern African, they came together with a logic, coherence and balance that were nothing short of sublime.

"It's a mish-mash, but I like it," said Ama.

Moments later their plane passed over the city and they saw the enormous park that lay at its heart.

"According to the travel notes, it's two miles long and a quarter-mile wide," said Ama.

"It's magnificent," said Abimbola.

Inside the terminal, strangely dressed people were rushing around everywhere. Most had suitcases of varying sizes that moved smoothly alongside them.

"I love it," said Ama. "It's, how would you say it…it's elegant."

"Look how tall they are," said Abimbola.

"It might be my imagination," said Ama, "but these people seem unusually good looking."

"Especially the ladies," said Abimbola.

"Keep your eyes to yourself, mister."

Signs and arrows directed travelers in all directions. The signs were in Swahili, a dialect of which was spoken in West North America, so the Okafors could read them.

"What do you suppose 'foreign exchange' is?" Abimbola wondered. This was their first trip abroad.

"I have no idea, but we're foreign," said Ama. "Maybe we should ask someone."

"They might not understand us because of the way we talk," said Abimbola. He retrieved his device and looked it up. "It's a place where we trade our West North American money for African money."

The travelers made quite a sight in their robes and lampshade hats as they followed the signs through the gleaming terminal. They changed their money and followed signs that directed them to a complimentary train that would take them downtown where their hotel was located.

"You and the boys should have a look around while I'm gone," Abimbola told his wife after they'd found their hotel.

Department of Genetics
University of Nairobi

For form's sake, Abimbola spoke to the receptionist, despite knowing that she wouldn't understand a word he said. When he received no response, he spoke to his device and showed her the screen, as he'd done with Bobo back home.

"I am Abimbola Okafor," the receptionist read, "and I'm visiting from West North America. I wish to consult with your geneticists about something that they may find of interest. I fear that the genetic makeup of my ancestors may have been altered, possibly with unforeseen adverse consequences that aren't yet apparent."

"I see," said the receptionist. "I'll see if Professor Garrett is available."

Garrett came out to the reception area with Brandon and Alice to meet their foreign visitor. Abimbola removed his hat, and the geneticists noticed the distinctive shape of his head and the golf ball sized lumps above his ears. Abimbola gave them his device, whose screen still showed the message he'd dictated for the receptionist. After the geneticists had finished reading, he spoke to the device again and gave it back to them.

"You will have noticed the shape of my head, which all my people have inherited." the geneticists read. "We also have a speech impediment that prevents us from making ourselves understood to people outside of our genetic group. You may not know this—our country has been rather isolated from the outside world since its founding—but the aristocratic class in my country, of which I am a member, has been inbred for generations. However, based on the little I've read, I'm guessing that inbreeding was not the cause of my speech impediment or the shape of my head, because all of my cohorts have these characteristics."

Garrett instructed the receptionist to clear their schedule for the next three hours. "If you'll accompany us to our conference room," he told Okafor, "we'll see if we can get to the bottom of this. I gather that because your entire genetic group has these characteristics, you suspect they may have been an unintended product of genetic engineering."

Abimbola nodded and spoke again to his device.

"Yes," the screen read. "I'm concerned that other, non-benign unintended genetic changes might have occurred that weren't noticeable, such as a reduction of intelligence as compared to our ancestors."

Garrett led the group into the department's conference room and they took seats.

"We have tests that enable us to determine whether a person's chromosomes contain genetic material that was added or removed," Garrett told Abimbola. "If you'll permit, we'll perform them and we'll see what we're dealing with. All we'll need is for a technician to scrape off some of your skin cells. It's painless."

"Please proceed" appeared on Abimbola's device. A short while later, the test results appeared on the conference room wall screen.

"Editing definitely occurred at some point," said Garrett. "The markers are there. We can't tell when it was done, but I suppose that from your standpoint it doesn't really matter."

Abimbola nodded.

"It's highly unlikely that you have any other edited genetic material," said Garrett. "The test we used is 95% accurate."

Abimbola dictated another message to his device:

"My wife and children are here with me. We're considering settling here in Africa. Could I bring them in and have them tested?"

"How about tomorrow morning at ten?"

Abimbola smiled, nodded and went back to the hotel to report the news to his wife.

"They scraped off a few of my skin cells and tested them," he told her. "The only genetic modifications are the ones responsible for the head shape and speech. I want to bring you and the boys there tomorrow so they can test you as well."

"Of course," said Ama.

Department of Genetics
University of Nairobi
Same afternoon

"Shall I call General Wainwright?" Brandon asked.

Garrett took a moment to consider this.

"Yeah, give him a heads up."

Conference room
Department of Genetics
University of Nairobi
Next day

"We'll have your results shortly," Garrett told Ama.

Five minutes later, the test results for Ama and the boys appeared on the screen, and the geneticists took several minutes to examine them.

"Yep, they're the same," said Garrett. "If you like, we can administer somatic treatments to eliminate the edited-in variants that we've identified as the cause of your speech impediment. Your speech impediments should disappear in short order."

"Please do the treatments," Abimbola dictated. "But what about our heads?"

"Somatic genetic treatments can't alter a person's bone structure. However, if you so desire, the genetic alterations that gave rise to your head shapes can be removed from the embryos of any further children you and Mrs. Okafor might have, and the embryos of any children that your boys might have. The variants linked to the speech impediments would also have to be removed in those embryos, because the genetic changes effected by somatic treatments are not inheritable. Now, if the two of you could come with me for a moment? I'd like to show you something. My colleagues will entertain the boys."

Garrett led them into the hallway outside the conference room and closed the door.

"This is a delicate matter," he told them. "You know how kids are. The biological human from whom my mind was copied had five of them. Kids can be mean. If a kid has a feature that his peers can make fun of—like a long neck or a big nose—they'll seize on it and make the kid's life a living hell. It's irrational. One neck or nose is as good as another. But try telling kids that. In adulthood, such features are often seen as adding character, but—"

"We share those concerns, professor," Abimbola dictated. "We've already discussed it and planned to ask you if you could recommend a surgeon who could rebuild their heads and our own to more closely resemble the norm—perhaps a surgeon at your medical center. We're definitely moving here."

Garrett seemed relieved to have gotten past this discussion. He removed a card from his pocket and gave it to Abimbola. "She's one of our best surgeons. She's a biological, like most of our physicians. She's had cases where she's had to repair extensive skull damage. I would imagine that removing unwanted skull material will be straightforward by comparison. She's expensive, but she's worth it."

"That won't be an issue," Abimbola dictated.

The Okafors left after thanking the geneticists for everything they'd done.

"Well," said Garrett, "given that the Okafors are moving here, I believe it's incumbent on us to give them the cumulative genetic enhancements that people in Africa have received over the years, as to traits that can be enhanced by somatic treatment. Otherwise, Abimbola and his wife and sons will be seriously disadvantaged. I'll have Tom include them in the vectors. I'll make a note to include the prior enhancements in edits we do for any additional kids or grandkids."

• • • • •

Three months later, the entire Okafor family could communicate with their new friends and neighbors. They had sold their house in Furaha and transferred the family fortune to a top-rated financial manager in Nairobi. Abimbola found work as an electrical engineer at a tech company called West African Systems and Ama volunteered at the boys' school. Best of all, they no longer lived in their ancestors' shadows.

"We're an ordinary family now," Abimbola told his wife. "We have real lives."

• • • • •

Six months later. Bobo Chike was opening a letter from someone in Nairobi when a 25-peso gold piece fell out of the envelop and landed on his kitchen table. Bobo smiled. It was a lucky piece. Someone was wishing him luck. He understood who it was a moment later when he removed a photo and a cashier's check from the envelop.

The photo showed a man, a woman and two young boys. It took Bobo several moments to to recognize Abimbola because his head now had the same shape as Bobo's, as did the heads of the woman and the boys standing with him, Abimbola's family.

The check, payable in West North American pesos, was for an amount that was almost ten times Bobo's annual salary

Bobo picked up the photo again and noticed a message on the back, followed by a Nairobi street address.

"Please come visit with your family. There are no aristos here. Tremendous opportunities await someone with the intelligence and resourcefulness you've shown. I urge you to see for yourself. If nothing else, you'll have a nice vacation. We'd love to see you. Abimbola."

Why the hell not? Bobo thought.

At sea

One mile off the south coast of West North America
2903

Garrett had mobilized their robotic weapons forces for a mission to rule out the possibility that unsupervised genetic engineering was still being done in West North America. If so, it had to be stopped. While they were at it, they would do humanity a favor by eliminating all vestiges of the old aristocracy.

Two armadas of modified cargo ships under the command of Admiral Sir Rodney Gilbert, who had commanded the armadas during the 2527 attacks, were preparing to land Behemoths and robotic tanks and soldiers at two locations, one just above West North America's northern border and the other just below its southern border.

General Carter Wainwright, the supreme commander of the 2527 attacks, was aboard the southern armada's flagship with his Chief of Staff, Brigadier Arthur Johnson.

"Overwhelming force, Arthur," said Wainwright.

"Sir."

Wainwright wore the dress blues of a four-star general, and the pearl-handled revolvers were back. Except for his gray-haired vanity head, he looked exactly as he had on that fateful day almost 400 years earlier.

"Art, I believe we'll have the element of surprise. The satellite feeds show no signs of enemy activity."

"Sir, they don't have an army, a navy or an air force. All they have are cops."

"That may or may not be true, son," said Wainwright. "We can't afford to take anything for granted."

"Roger that," said Johnson.

Garrett, Brandon and Alice, who were standing nearby, had to struggle to keep from laughing out loud.

"Let them have their fun," Garrett told the others. "The aristos, as they're called, will soil their trousers when they see all this, and they'll do whatever we tell them to. We probably won't even have to kill anyone."

Wainwright's original robotic weapons operators had re-upped and would serve in this operation as well.

General Wainwright walked to where the geneticists were standing, planted his feet and clasped his hands behind him. An unlit cigar was clamped between his pearly teeth.

"This is what power looks like," he told them, gesturing toward the unending stream of horrifying weaponry that was moving toward the shore. "Seldom in human history has there been anything on this scale. Would you folks like to join us aboard the Command Behemoth? You'll have the ability to watch this operation in person and the other by satellite feed."

"We'd be honored," said Garrett.

After arriving onshore, Generals Wainwright and Johnson and the geneticists were driven to the Command Behemoth. Wainwright's flag—red with four white stars—adorned the enormous flying warship's port and starboard sides. An escalator carried the general's party up to a door that looked to be at least thirty feet above ground.

Inside, the civilians were surprised at how high the ceilings were. People of metal were busy making preparations for liftoff. The scene outside was one whose vast scope and expanse they would not soon forget. They'd been told that the robotic soldiers numbered in the thousands, and the robotic tanks in the hundreds. Wainwright's Command Behemoth was one of twenty.

Wainwright made his rounds, inspecting the proceedings and issuing supplemental orders. Floor to ceiling windows ran the length of both sides of this part of the ship....

"Isn't this something?" said Garrett.

"I'm just trying to fix it in my mind," said Alice. "It's unbelievable."

"We'll lift off shortly," Johnson told them. "We'll fly at an airspeed of 27 knots, the same as the groundspeed of the tanks and troops."

"I had no idea the soldiers could run that fast," said Garrett.

"They can't. We've replaced their feet with tank treads."

Shortly thereafter, the Command Behemoth lifted off.

"We'll fly at 100 feet," said Johnson.

When it had reached cruising altitude, the Behemoth gathered speed. Before long, they passed the remains of a good-sized coastal city that had been taken over by the spread of aggressive vines and other vegetation.

"San Diego," said Johnson.

"My God," said Garrett. "I loved that city."

"Our destination is Furaha, the capital, which was built near the former City of Los Angeles," said Johnson. "The northern operation is heading for Ode, the other large West North American city. It occupies the site of the former city of San Francisco."

The southern invasion force had taken citizens by surprise. The geneticists watched as people froze wherever they were standing while the invasion force flowed around them the way a stream flows around rocks. Soon thereafter, however, the civilians seemed to have disappeared from the territory over which they were passing.

"They must be hiding inside," said Brandon. "Word must have traveled."

"I don't like it, Arthur," Wainwright told Johnson. "I hope we're not heading into a trap."

"I'll put out an order for the lads to move to Alert Level 5," said Johnson, and left to do so.

Hours of uneventful flying later, they began to see more overgrown ruins.

"Suburbs," said Johnson. "We're nearing our destination."

A while later, they passed over the remains of Los Angeles.

Garrett remembered a convention that Marcus, his original, had attended down there. The city had been a lot of things in those days, most of which Marcus had loved. But what had always impressed him most when he'd visited LA was its natural beauty. For a city built on a desert, it was amazing, particularly when they'd gotten rain and the hills turned green.

"Approaching target," a voice said over a speaker.

A large city appeared on their right.

"The buildings are old," said Alice, "and they look run down. If they engineered a master race, they don't have much to show for it."

"That's consistent with what Abimbola told us," said Garrett. "The first generations were the builders, masters of all the arts and sciences it took to build great cities. But succeeding generations lost the spark, as Abimbola put it."

"Arriving at target area in ten," said a voice.

"The vast majority of soldiers, tanks and Behemoths will be in reserve," Johnson explained. "Our Behemoth will land in their compound, a small force of tanks and soldiers will crash through the gates, and we'll demand their unconditional surrender."

Wainwright walked up behind Johnson and placed a hand on the Brigadier's shoulder. "What do you think, Arthur? Should we give them a bit of a demonstration before we talk turkey with them?"

"I rather doubt we'll need to do that, sir," said Johnson.

"General, please don't kill anyone unless you absolutely must," said Garrett. "We don't want to jeopardize our rapport with the biologicals by needlessly killing them."

The general considered that for a moment and nodded. "Roger that."

The Command Behemoth floated down and landed softly in an open, grassy area next to what appeared to be the aristos' headquarters building. Individuals wearing robes and hats that looked like lampshades were making their way out the door toward the Behemoth.

Moments later, robotic tanks crashed through the metal gates, followed by robotic soldiers.

Wainwright strode toward the aristos, accompanied by Garrett.

"Who speaks for you people," Wainwright barked in Swahili.

An aristo stepped forward and shouted gibberish at Wainwright. The geneticists had told Wainwright about the speech impediment, but the general must have forgotten, or he hadn't been listening.

"I hereby demand your unconditional surrender," said Wainwright.

The aristo took another step forward, shook his right fist at Wainwright and screamed more unintelligible gibberish.

"If I have to kill a bunch of you I will," said Wainwright, chomping through his cigar. "The guns on that ship will turn every last one of you into a cloud of blood before you even have a chance to fall down."

Garrett leaned over and spoke softly into Wainwright's ear. "Sir, why not have your men simply take these assholes into custody, and anyone still in the building, and we'll go in, do our business and be done. Mission accomplished."

"I agree, sir," said Johnson, who had joined them. "Bugger the cheeky bastard. He's not worth a single second more of your time."

"That's it then." Wainwright said decisively. "Brigadier Johnson, have these people taken into custody and placed under guard. Have men clear and secure the building and place anyone still in there in custody and under guard."

One squad found uniformed police officers hiding in a large hall, terrified. They had placed their weapons in a pile in the center of the hall. The human operator had his soldiers take the prisoners outside and place them in custody with the others. Other squads did the same with aristos they found elsewhere in the headquarters.

After Wainwright's men had finished, the geneticists consulted the rough floor plan that Okafor had prepared for them. Okafor knew and could account for what took place in every part of the building except an area on the second floor that was marked "SECURE." Okafor had no idea what went on there.

Soldiers broke down the door and the geneticists entered. A thick layer of dust covered every surface. At the other end of the room they found an array of dust-covered, outdated genetic editing equipment, and equipment similar to that which Tom Joyce's team at the Upstate Medical Research Center had used to synthesize genetic material.

"They must have found this stuff in a warehouse somewhere, like Tom did when we got started," said Garrett.

None of the modern equipment that Joyce's group was manufacturing had been allowed to leave Africa.

Alice noticed a small, faded sign posted on the wall by the door. It was a set of bullet points written in archaic Swahili. "Good grief!" she cried.

"Mug me Maggie," said Garrett after he'd read it. "Whoever wrote that list was one sick son of a bitch."

Brandon examined it. "It was a probably a list of what would happen to anyone who revealed to the outside world what they were up to here."

"That has to be what it was," said Alice.

A dusty computer sat on a table. "We'll take this home with us and have our guys hack it," said Garrett. "Meanwhile, we'll administer polygraphs to every aristo out there, without exception, including the top guy. Thanks again, Alice and Brandon. As always, you two were a step ahead of me."

The polygraphs had been their idea, to be sure the aristos weren't hiding anything.

"They can either submit to the test or spend the rest of their lives in jail, their choice," said Garrett.

Based on the polygraph results and what they'd found in the office, it seemed clear—subject to what they found in the computer—that the genetics operation here had ended long ago, perhaps in reaction to the accident that had produced the misshapen heads and speech impediments.

The next day, an aircraft flown in from Nairobi took them and General Wainwright up to Ode, to the aristo headquarters there. Wainwright's people there had been ordered to look for signs of a similar genetics operation, and they'd found it. Like the room in

Furaha, it was dusty, and its equipment was old and obsolete. The sign they'd seen in Furaha had been posted there as well.

Again, the polygraph results were negative.

"Well," said Garrett, "if we don't find anything on that computer that's less than two hundred years old, I think we're done."

"It could all be an elaborate diversion by a secret cabal that we haven't found," said Brandon. "They could have moved their operations somewhere else."

"You're right," said Garrett. "People could be editing genes in a cave somewhere. That's always been a problem. People can do this work anywhere. One thing we could do is tell them we'll be back once a year to collect skin cells from random infants, and if we find modified genes, there will be serious hell to pay. Serious jail time."

Alice reminded her colleagues of her comment when they'd flown over Furaha. "If they'd done positive genetic enhancement to any material extent, there should be tangible evidence of that fact. Instead, all we see is a backwater. Where are the dramatic changes you would have expected after so many years, even without genetic enhancement?"

"They must have been embarrassed to let commoners see their heads," said Alice. "That would explain why they always wore their lampshades."

"Except for the time three of them didn't, and a commoner saw the heads and spilled the beans to Abimbola," said Alice.

"These would-be genetic engineers would have been the West North Americans who got their doctorates from us," said Alice. "Thank God we didn't teach them everything."

"I wonder what happened," said Brandon. "Obviously they thought they were adding genetic material tied to a positive trait. How could they have ended up with what they got?"

"Who knows?" said Garrett. "It could have been something as simple as contamination."

General Wainwright boarded the aircraft with the geneticists and they dropped him off at Furaha, where General Johnson was waiting. The generals had agreed to remain in West North America pending a decision by the African governments on whether to take further action there.

The generals and the geneticists shook hands and congratulated each other on a job well done.

"Until next time," said Wainwright.

"He's definitely one of a kind," said Alice after their plane had lifted off.

• • • • •

Office of the Governor
Nairobi
Two weeks later

Zone 3 Governor Abdu Zimbabwe, a conventional human, had agreed to let Garrett brief him on a situation in West North America. Garrett hoped that the governor, who was a big fan of liberty and equality of opportunity, would persuade his fellow governors to join him in convening a convention to consider whether the situation in West North Africa warranted action by the world community.

"As I mentioned when we spoke, we just returned from a fact-finding trip to West North America," said Garrett. "We'd seen evidence that they'd engaged in genetic manipulation to add positive traits to embryos, which, as you know, can become a nightmare scenario if the practice isn't strictly controlled. So we went there to check it out. Thankfully, it was a false alarm. They stopped doing work in that area long ago."

"That's good news," said the governor.

"Yes. But we also found out that West North America has been a hereditary aristocracy since it was founded. Only aristocrats can attend college. All the good jobs are reserved for them. They're point five percent of the population, yet they control more than half of the country's wealth. The common people have been reduced to doing meaningless make-work. It's so bad for them that it wouldn't surprise me in the least if they contracted the Malaise that almost made humanity extinct in olden times. It's not just the economic inequality, Governor. People need opportunities to do meaningful things with their lives. It's wrong to deny that to an entire hereditary class."

"I couldn't agree more," said the governor. "I had no idea. I'm guessing that you might have come here with suggestions."

"Just one," said Garrett. "That you and your fellow governors convene a convention, or whatever the word is, to examine this situation and determine what the world community should do about it, if anything."

The governor dictated a note to his device.

"If one wanted to make a case for a onetime expropriation of and redistribution of accumulated wealth," Garrett added, "one might point to the fact that nearly all of this wealth was created by people who lived many generations ago. Since then, the aristos have added almost nothing to their nation's wealth. It's static wealth, passed from one listless generation to the next. Under those circumstances, perhaps it's fair to finally declare that this ancient wealth should revert to the people rather than passing ad infinitum to the *nth* generation of heirs who had nothing to do with its creation. It's hardly a radical concept."

"No, it isn't," said the governor.

"So, if one were inclined to take that view, they could direct staff to study how the historic African Patrimony was handled. I'm only a geneticist, but I think that situation was comparable to what we're looking at here. The total accumulated aristocratic wealth, over a base amount per family—stocks, bonds, real property, cash—could be expropriated and contributed to a company, like the Patrimony was. The shares of that company could be sold on the World Stock Exchange and the proceeds distributed to West North American citizens pro rata, as was done with the Patrimony. You could use some of the proceeds to provide training to equip the former commoners for better jobs."

The governor dictated additional notes to his device.

"One more thing, Governor, if you don't mind."

"Sure."

"I'd like to propose that temporary genetics clinics opened in the principal West North American cities to edit embryos. The aim would be to get some of the major enhancements that we've propagated here in Africa into the West North American gene pool."

"That's an interesting idea," said the governor.

"It would be a onetime effort," said Garrett. "No way would we enhance their intelligence to a level where they'd be serious competition for our people here. But they'll be digging themselves out of centuries of stagnation. This would give them a boost."

"Who would you get to staff the clinics?" the governor asked.

"I'm sure I could round up a small army of technicians experienced in operating the editing equipment, and volunteer geneticists to supervise their work," said Garrett.

"I like the idea, but I'll need more detail to sell it to the other governors."

"My thought is that we'd identify ten important traits that we've enhanced—intelligence being one of them. So, we'd do ten rounds of editing. In the first round, we'd edit one trait into the embryo of every prospective parent who wanted it done during, say, a six-month period. In round two we'd edit a second trait into the embryo of every prospective parent who wants it done during that six-month period, and so on until we'd propagated all ten enhancements into the West North American gene pool. The effort would take five years, but eventually, over time, every West North America's genome would include most if not all the enhancements. Several of my colleagues at other universities have expressed their willingness to take part in guiding the overall effort, as would I. It shouldn't be all that expensive, but if cost becomes an issue, this might be another good place for a small portion of the expropriated funds to be put to use."

"It makes sense," said the governor, "as part of the overall reform effort. Plus, the world is always a safer and better place if everyone everywhere is well off and happy. Thanks for bringing all this to my attention, Professor. It's the right thing to do, and I think we can get it all done."

Garrett thanked the governor and left without mentioning the robotic warriors.

As the governor had predicted, a convention of delegates from the three zones approved the plan Garrett had outlined, including five-years of genetic editing.

In 2906, after things had settled down, African geneticists, with the consent and cooperation of the new West North American government, began the five-year embryonic editing program, and it was completed on schedule.

Six months after that, Garrett advised Generals Wainwright and Johnson that the plan's implementation was substantially complete; hence, there was no further need for them to remain in West North America with their forces.

• • • • •

Investigations by journalists and academics in the aftermath of the Great Reform of 2904 brought to light the fact that in the Republic's early years, West North American commoners had held important positions as skilled technicians, teachers and small business owners, exactly as the Republic's founders had contemplated. What had gone wrong?

Modern historians agree that West North America's aristocratic structure bore the seeds of its own decline. The original aristocrats had possessed the talent, motivation and inclination to succeed in high-level scientific, technological and commercial endeavors. Those endeavors were closed to commoners, but everything else was open to them. The Republic needed skilled technicians, elementary and high school teachers, and entrepreneurs to own and operate small businesses— financed by state-owned banks—to supply the myriad goods and services people needed and wanted. The arrangement worked for a time, but it wasn't sustainable. It was built on the premise that a hereditary aristocratic class would bring forth indefinitely people with the same level of talent and motivation as its first generations. When that premise failed, a period of decline and stagnation inevitably followed.

In normal societies, the progeny of successful people also declined over time, in terms of their talent and motivation. But when that happened, the talent pool was replenished from below, thanks to socioeconomic mobility. In West North America, that wasn't possible, so the country had grown stagnant. When successive generations of aristocrats turned away from the ambitious scientific, technological and commercial pursuits of their forbears, no one was available to replace them. Aristos took over the vocations that had been the province of the commoners, and the commoners were transitioned into make-work.

The Great Reform of 2904 would give West North America a fresh start.

Chapter 16
Colonists

Nova Africana (formerly called Tau Ceti f)
2806 (Earth date)

"It's like watching a ballet," Keisha told Weinberg as their ship waited its turn to land. The landing process had been carefully choreographed and digitally programmed to bring each starship safely to its designated landing spot. Finally, it was their group's turn, and they experienced the rather disconcerting process firsthand.

"I could have sworn that ship was gonna hit us," Weinberg said anxiously after they'd landed.

He and Keisha left their ship and went off to look for work, but there was none. Robots were doing almost everything.

They'd forgotten how thorough and detail-oriented Clark, Liu and their team were when they planned and organized a major operation like this. The two gifted administrators had done the planning for the Human Rescue Initiative with the same thoroughness and attention to detail.

Hundreds of robotic workers were working 24/7 using prefabricated components to build the facilities the colony would need. The first priorities were power plants, water works and storage space for the frozen embryos. Next, the robots would build an Embryo Farm in which to grow the embryos into babies, and nurseries in which the babies would be housed and cared for.

Robotic workers would prepare soil and other media for the cultivation of food. Eventually, trees and other plant forms would arrive from Earth to enhance the atmosphere and provide organic matter for soil enrichment.

Weinberg's major contribution to the grand plan was to insist that no embryos be thawed until the farms had demonstrated their viability. Experts on Earth had felt sure that food could be grown in the soil that probes had found here, but Weinberg wanted to wait. That way, if something went wrong, the embryos could simply remain frozen until the problem was solved, and none of them would die.

The Embryo Farm

To help determine the square footage that each womb station would require, technicians in Nairobi had set up a simulated workspace where "care-givers" went through the motions of looking after an embryo, while others walked past pushing carts or gurneys. Much to their surprise, they found that each unit would require at least 100 square feet of space just for equipment, workspace and the storage of supplies.

Given that no embryos would be thawed for the first year, all 50,000 of the embryos would have to be thawed and grown into babies during the nine years that remained until the second expedition arrived, at which point the facility would need to be available to receive that expedition's embryos.

The final nursery facilities would have to be large enough to accommodate thousands of babies, toddlers and young children. When the first tranche of babies reached age six, they'd be moved to the children's residence and their spots in the nursery would become available.

All buildings would be equipped with sophisticated climate control and air filtration systems.

At regular intervals, robot-controlled starships would arrive from Earth to replenish items not available on the planet, including prefabricated components for the construction of additional support facilities to accommodate the colony's growing population.

To the extent possible without delaying the completion of priority projects, work would proceed on plans for commercial and industrial developments in the vicinity of the other structures.

"The robots make all this possible," said Weinberg one day as he and Keisha were watching the work-in-progress.

"Yeah," said Keisha. "They never stop."

"Are you excited about practicing medicine?" Weinberg asked.

Keisha had spent a large part of the 35-year voyage viewing medical school holograms and studying medical texts. She planned to be a general practitioner. All she lacked was hands-on experience, which she'd get working under the distinguished physicians who'd come with them.

"I can't wait," said Keisha.

27 local days later

There was still literally nothing that Weinberg or Keisha or their metallic colleagues could contribute to the furious ongoing effort, so they'd gone for an early morning drive. Ahead of them, the rising star had colored the sky and the clouds with dazzling shades of purple and pink.

"That's spectacular," said Weinberg, looking up in amazement.

"I believe the colors are a function of the composition of the atmosphere that light and other energy from the star pass through when it's rising or setting," said Keisha

"That sounds about right," said Weinberg.

They kept riding until the construction projects had disappeared over the horizon behind them. After a while, they saw a collection of heavy equipment that Keisha didn't recognize.

"These are robotic excavators and earth movers," Weinberg explained. "The farming section of the plan is the part I studied most carefully. The farms have to work. Until they do, we can't do what we came here to do. Judging by the equipment, I'd say this one will be a soil farm."

"Aren't all farms soil farms?" Keisha asked.

"By no means. Even on Earth, a great deal of farming is done without soil, although the definition of soil is much broader now than it was in olden times."

"How so?"

"Some experts held that it wasn't soil unless it had an organic component. Others said 'weathering' and/or meteor impacts were necessary. Eventually, the so-called experts put semantics aside and figured out that any medium in which plant life could be grown is the equivalent of soil. So the term lost much of its significance. Plants have been grown in pure sand, in gravel and in water. I saw somewhere that there's even a thing called aeroponics where they literally grow crops in misty air. It's hard to imagine. Remind me to check that out when we get back. It sounds interesting, but I didn't pursue it because it wasn't in the plan."

As they approached the farm-in-progress, they saw machines making deep gashes in the planet's surface. A second group of machines was grinding up the material that the first group had gouged out; and a third group of machines pushed the ground up material back into the gouged-out trenches.

"As I understand it, they're making their own soil by mixing layers of material together," said Weinberg. "They've brought supplies of other minerals and elements that they'll need to add, based on data from the probes we had in place. But it's not a big deal, evidently.

Fortunately, the surface of the planet is rich in nitrates and ammonium ions, for nitrogen."

"You're pretty knowledgeable about all this for a city boy," said Keisha. "I'm gonna start calling you Farmer Bill."

"Please do. This is proven agricultural technology at this point. We'll also have several hydroponic farms, and a few that are experimental. I don't know if you're aware of this, but they won't have meat."

Keisha hadn't known this.

"Why not?"

"Not initially, anyway. Clark, Liu and their experts decided that the raising of animals would introduce needless additional complexity, given everything else that's going on."

"That makes sense,"

"Now that I think of it, though, they should at least be allowed to have dogs. Not to eat," Weinberg quickly added when he saw the shocked expression on Keisha's face. "As pets."

"Do you miss food?" Keisha asked.

"I guess," said Weinberg. "But at least we don't have to worry about gaining weight."

"I miss the smells," said Keisha. "I miss cooking. Chopping vegetables. Getting all the ingredients lined up on the counter. I used a ton of herbs when I cooked. In the Middle Ages, only the rich could afford herbs and spices."

"Believe it or not, I actually knew that," said Weinberg. "Even salt was precious in ancient times. Did you know that the Romans paid their soldiers a special allowance so they could buy salt? It's where the word 'salary' comes from."

They drove on but stopped a short time later when they came to something that caught their interest: a patch of ground that appeared to be covered with small stones packed closely together in what looked like some kind of pattern.

"It's like a mosaic," said Keisha.

They left their cart to get a closer look.

"It's beautiful," said Keisha.

Weinberg knelt down and touched the surface. "It feels spongy."

Keisha also touched it. "That's weird."

Weinberg pushed down on the surface with his whole hand.

"It's pushing back!" he exclaimed, "Hard."

A moment later Weinberg felt his hand being pulled away from him by the stones, and he nearly fell forward.

"Did you see that, Keisha?"

"Yes. It was like it was trying to carry you off."

Weinberg rose, looked around and found a small boulder.

"Let's see what it does with this."

"Be careful."

He heaved the boulder out onto the surface, and a moment later, the small stones, or whatever they were, formed what looked like successive ripples that propelled the boulder forward across its surface and onto the ordinary ground on the other side.

"Wow," said Keisha. "It was almost like it was cleaning itself off."

"Let's test that hypothesis by making a real mess. "

They tossed rocks, pebbles and handfuls of earth onto the strange surface and it happened again. The surface immediately cleaned itself off.

Suddenly, the pattern in the ripples changed—if in fact it actually *was* a pattern. The change was slight but noticeable and was followed a short time later by another slight change, and another after that.

"I wonder what's causing that?"

"Energy from a heat or another energy source underneath it, probably," Weinberg guessed.

"It's pretty neat, whatever it is."

Keisha used her portable electronic device to take a picture of the thing. Later, she drove a geologist who was part of the farming effort out to have a look at the formation, but she had no more idea about what it could be than Keisha and Weinberg did.

•   •   •   •   •

Embryo Farm
Nova Africana
Eighteen Earth months later

He's so cute with them, Keisha thought as she watched Weinberg make funny faces and noises at the baby he was holding.

"You can't be a curmudgeon while holding a baby," Weinberg exulted. "It's simply not possible."

Keisha, also holding a baby, was smiling. Weinberg, Keisha and their colleagues spent 22-local-hour shifts caring for their charges and loved every local minute. Keisha was also practicing medicine.

Before they'd begun collecting embryos back on Earth, Bonnie Holyfield had come up with a way to name the babies. The embryos' biological parents would choose their child's eventual name by providing the Initiative with both a boy's name and a girl's name

"The kids will know that their parents back on Earth gave them their names," Bonnie had explained.

It was a sweet idea, Keisha thought. She wondered how Bonnie was doing, and Woon, Ray and Libby.

With over five thousand five hundred babies cooing and crying at a single location, the Embryo Farm was the most joyful place Keisha had ever experienced. Biological parents needed sleep and never got enough. Feeding the babies the formula they'd brought with them from Earth, and bathing them and changing their diapers kept the attendants busy day and night; but metallic "parents" did not need to sleep. In a pinch, an hour of computer games would keep them going. They were more like grandparents. They got to spend quality time with their babies without the weariness and sleep-deprivation that went with biological parenting.

One month later

"Music," Weinberg announced one evening after they'd left their ship's privacy space and returned to their seats.

Earlier that day he'd gotten one of their more difficult babies to go to sleep by singing to her. "It was her only means of escape," Keisha had quipped, but it had given Weinberg an idea.

"I'll give them the gift of music."

His piano was still aboard their ship along with the instruments of the musicians he'd accompanied during the long voyage from Earth. There was no point in having it offloaded until he had a suitable place to put it. At his request, Clark and Liu had included ample quantities of all kinds of musical instruments in the expedition's manifest, because music was important. Not until this moment, however, had Weinberg envisioned the pivotal role he would play in its propagation on Nova Africana.

"They're still babies," said Keisha.

"It's never too early to plan," said Weinberg.

Hour after hour, he sat with one of his devices and used a special app to create teaching materials for piano, beginning at the lowest level. Based on Mr. Weinberg's own experience as a student, Weinberg knew that children could begin learning piano as early as three or four Earth years of age, depending on the child. At each learning level, the materials Weinberg prepared got more difficult with each lesson. Mr. Weinberg's first piano teacher had used that approach, and it had made Mr. Weinberg practice all the harder.

After he'd prepared piano materials for all teaching levels, Weinberg created materials for the clarinet, because he knew how to play that instrument and could teach others to play it. But then what? Unless he took the time to master the other instruments himself, there'd be no one to teach the kids how to play them, *unless* —

He interrupted his work to send an email blast to all Project personnel seeking people who were able and willing to teach children to play a musical instrument. Within hours, he was flooded with volunteers, including the people he'd played with aboard ship, notwithstanding that it would be years before the first children would be old enough for lessons.

"I shouldn't have been surprised that out of the thousands of people in our expedition, there would be many with musical backgrounds," he told Keisha.

This let Weinberg raise things to another level. He shared his clarinet materials with people who'd be teaching other instruments, so they could transcribe them. Teachers would be able change the materials on their devices or add more. Thinking further ahead, Weinberg recalled that his original's own school, an elite New York City private academy, had had both a concert band and an orchestra, each of which had members as young as sixth graders. Weinberg resolved to give his kids the same opportunities.

A few days later, it occurred to Weinberg to add voice training to the curriculum, and he sent an email blast looking for voice teachers. A Machine with the mind of a singer or voice teacher would know how and what to teach. Not by accident, all Machines had excellent singing voices.

Over time, the kids would be exposed to every kind and type of human music from all parts of Earth and from all eras, as background. They and their progeny would go on from there to create their own music and their own musical traditions.

• • • • •

Redemption
2830

Weinberg had begun taking one local daylight hour each day just for himself, which he liked to spend sitting in his chair on the patio outside his and Keisha's building, watching the pattern changes on the small-stone formation that was spread out before him. The changes occurred at regular intervals. Weinberg could almost imagine that the stones were trying to tell him something. He smiled to himself. It was almost as if they were alive. He found it soothing to watch them.

The stone formation was just like one he and Keisha had seen in the country. They were remarkable. Not just the fact that they appeared to contain the same kinds of small stones, or even the fact that they had the same pattern. What was most remarkable was how those patterns seemed to change the same way in both formations. They cleaned themselves off the same way too. He and Keisha had thrown a variety of objects onto them at both locations—articles of clothing, liquids, even garbage from one of the dining halls. When the surfaces had finished cleaning themselves off, not a trace of the foreign material remained.

Sports Arena
Redemption
2835

"It's time to introduce the twin concepts of laws and self-government," Weinberg reminded Keisha. The first generation of biologicals had come of age.

When everyone in the first group born in the colony had reached their eighteenth birthday, they were invited to gather in the new indoor sports arena to consider enacting their first laws.

"Good morning," said Keisha, "and thanks for coming. You've all received the package of proposed laws we're suggesting that you consider. This is just to get you started. If you approve these laws, the government they create will be your government. We metallics will have nothing to do with it once it's up and running, except to be available to offer advice if requested. We won't even be eligible to vote in your elections.

"On the other hand, if a majority of voters vote against the entire package, the *status quo* will be maintained for the next ten years and the matter will be voted on again at that time.

"As you all know if you've been following the online commentaries, the public is sharply divided on whether this is the right time for you to commit to a particular type of government system. It is not our intention to railroad y'all into passing these or any laws. It's up to you. So before you vote, you'll hear from both sides.

"Our first speaker, Lilly Abebe, will state the case *against* enacting the proposed laws. Her faction favors maintaining the status quo for another ten years before you decide what sort of system of government you wish to have."

Lilly Abebe was an attractive young woman with a friendly, positive demeanor. Her clothing, like that of her male and female peers, was generic standard issue and would remain so until the biologicals began making their own clothes and new styles emerged.

"Good morning, everyone," she said. "Let's face it, the excellent education that we've received thanks to our metallic friends and our ancestors on Earth has left us more or less equally divided between the so-called socialist and capitalist alternatives. My side favors socialism, in theory, but in all honesty, we as a group don't yet have the maturity of judgment and accumulated life experience that we'll need to make a wise choice on which of those systems would best serve us. So we propose to maintain the status quo for another ten years and put the issue to a vote at that time. The problem with adopting the proposed laws now is that it would be tantamount to choosing capitalism over socialism. Private property, and income and wealth inequality, are embedded in and would be perpetuated by those very laws. They'll be all but impossible to dislodge. So I urge you to vote no. We simply aren't ready yet to make that kind of commitment." She smiled. "I mean, hey, what's the rush?"

Nelson Falade made his way toward the podium while his opponent acknowledged her supporters' applause. Much to Keisha's surprise, Abebe and Falade waved away the security personnel who seemed about to intervene and greeted each other cordially before Abebe left the stage.

Interesting, Keisha thought, remembering the hatred and vitriol that had surrounded these kinds of issues during her time on Earth. *We'll see.*

Like Abebe, Falade spoke calmly and succinctly.

"Good morning," he said. "Ms. Abebe was absolutely correct in pointing out that the proposed laws would secure and protect the right of people to own private property. As we learned in history class, 'private property'—meaning wealth that regular people can accumulate and own—was a very recent development in historic terms. It changed human history enormously, for the better.

"Imagine what life on Earth must have been like when the kings and their cronies owned everything and ordinary people owned nothing. People like us lived their lives subject to the whims of a small, hereditary ruling class.

"Private property changed things because it changed the way people behaved. What do you suppose happened when ordinary people suddenly had the ability to produce things on their own behalf and sell them and keep the fruits of their labor for themselves and their families? They worked their butts off, that's what happened, and the wealth that all this extra work created produced prosperity, which benefitted everyone. Suddenly, people could live well on their own—without having to depend on or suck up to the king and his minions.

"Prosperity is what you get when millions of people work like crazy to advance their own self-interest. The same goes for technological innovation, which has made so many things possible—like this colony. Socialism robs people of the incentive to work hard, so they don't, and scarcity follows. People go hungry. It never worked—not once in all the times it was tried.

"Collectivism was fine when we were kids, but we're grown-ups now. We've come of age. It's time to move on. We can't afford to put our lives on hold for ten years, as our opponents would have us do.

"We're sovereign human beings, not cogs in some machine. If each of us works hard to develop and exploit our talents and abilities to the fullest possible extent, we'll have rich and fulfilling lives as individuals, and in the process, we'll build a world of prosperity, fulfillment and economic and spiritual growth for ourselves and our posterity. Let us resolve to take full advantage of the opportunities that await us as adults, thanks to the legacy that the hard work and ingenuity of our predecessors and our metallic friends have left us. We can show our appreciation by voting 'yes' and getting started. There's no time to waste. A happy world is a busy place. Thank you."

"All right, then, it's time to vote," said Keisha. "If you haven't done so already, please open the link to our website." Keisha paused a few moments for those who hadn't yet done that. "If you want to vote 'yes' or 'no' on the entire proposal, check the appropriate box at the top of Page 1. You'll be able to vote for all the proposed laws in a particular Part, or you can approve some of the proposals in a Part but not others. For example, if you want to enact all the laws in Part 1, you just click on the square next to the words 'Part 1.' If you want to pick and choose, click on the boxes next to the laws you want to enact and leave the other boxes blank. The results will accumulate on the board behind me until everyone has finished voting."

The voters adopted the proposed laws and elected their first public officials six months later.

• • • • •

In due course, Africa, West North America, Nova Africana and Alamo c joined an interstellar free trade accord, and a flourishing exchange of goods and intellectual property developed among the parties.

Chapter 17
Alamo c

Sanctuary City
2911 (Earth year)

Holyfield and Woon were strolling through the newly completed bubble-covered city whose construction unexpected circumstances had made necessary.

Without question, the years following their arrival on Alamo c had been the longest and most difficult either of them had ever experienced, and things were just beginning to settle down. After their 45-year voyage from Earth, the expedition had gotten off to what they had thought was an excellent start. Then came the surprise.

They'd known from data that drones had sent to Earth that agriculture on Alamo c would be more challenging than it would be on Nova Africana. The only region on the Alamo c that would accommodate in-ground agriculture at all was a vast desert that covered roughly a third of the planet's surface. But the experts had been confident that the region could be made productive enough to meet the colony's needs.

Probes had located accessible sources of nitrogen-containing materials and other essential and desirable elements elsewhere on Alamo c sufficient to augment the sandy desert enough to grow crops in abundant quantities. The problem was the sandstorms. None of the probes had been present when one was happening.

Their timing was unpredictable. When certain conditions and circumstances coincided, they came. When the first one hit, robotic and human workers had just completed construction of nursery facilities. The epic storm came without warning, forcing everyone inside, where they remained for almost a month, Earth time.

Sand drifts buried their buildings and cut off their fresh air supply. A nurse pointed out that if the buildings were filled with breathing biological humans during a sandstorm of this magnitude, the oxygen supply would be exhausted very quickly. Every biological in the colony would suffer an agonizing death by suffocation. Holyfield and Woon realized at once what they'd have to do

"We need a dome with a guaranteed air supply, like Earthrise," said Woon.

Earthrise was a domed vacation city that people of metal had built on Earth's moon. The dome sheltered 25 square miles of space. Inside the bubble, enormous dehumidifiers removed excess water vapor from the air and recycled it. The air was continuously cycled through facilities outside the bubble that used electrolysis to separate carbon dioxide into its component elements and recycled the oxygen. Other facilities separated water into hydrogen and oxygen.

Supplies of hydrogen and oxygen were stored in liquid form in enormous storage tanks. The Dome drew upon those supplies to manufacture water and breathable air.

A nuclear power plant located several miles away served Earthrise. People of metal staffed it on a rotating basis.

The Alamo c bubble would operate the same way.

"We should tell them to postpone the other three expeditions," said Woon.

"Good point," said Bonnie. "They can use some of the ships to bring us the materials and equipment for the dome."

"How about including some of the people who built the moon bubble?" said Woon.

"Excellent idea," said Holyfield. "Thank God you thought of that. Let's go send them a message."

"Here's another thought," said Woon. "Even though we're holding off thawing out embryos, there's no reason to postpone the production of food that we can store or can. We can keep it on hand as an emergency food supply."

"You're right, Cheng," said Holyfield. "We don't have to sit on our hands. We can have everything built up and running by the time the ships arrive. I like that. Sitting here for decades doing nothing would be pretty depressing. If one year a sandstorm destroys the crops, we'll be no worse off than if we'd done nothing."

"If we put our city on one side of the area protected by the dome, we can prepare and cultivate the rest of the land as farms," said Woon.

"We might as well proceed with the park as well and start planting the landscaping."

The park would be the same size and shape as Nairobi's Central Park. Ships attached to the expedition had brought large quantities of grass and flower seeds to the planet, along with seeds for trees, shrubs and other plant types that experts had determined would thrive in the colony's climate.

Cheng smiled at Bonnie, puller her to him and held her for several moments.

"I'm glad we took the next step," he told her. "Before, we were pals. Now, we're a couple."

"I used to feel so alone at times," said Bonnie. "Now I don't."

Just prior to their departure, they'd elected to have the ersatz genitalia installed, just in case. It had happened during the fifth year of their voyage.

The following morning, while he and Bonnie were outside watching their star rise, Woon broached the idea of having some of the colony's first generation of children make mosaic murals of African scenes out of bits of colored stone sent from Earth. The murals would commemorate the colonists' African heritage.

Holyfield liked the idea in principle, but worried about the psychological impact the project might have on the children.

"They'll be expatriates, in effect," she told Woon. "What if they compare what they have here with what they see in the murals, and Alamo c falls short? What would we do then? The horse would already be out of the barn."

"They'll know they're not from here even if we never mention Africa or Earth," said Woon." We'll need to give them a positive reason why they're here--one they can be proud of."

"I see. Have you come up with one?

"Yes," said Woon. "We'll tell them that their old world is in a precarious, troubled state. We'll list all the problems: humankind's unending history of wars; weapons of mass destruction; climate change; the risk of an asteroid colliding with Earth; the risk of genetically engineered plagues and other biological weapons; the random mutation of a flu virus that proves catastrophic; or the very real prospect that, even if none of those things came about, the unintended consequences from other scientific 'advances' could doom life on the planet."

"Like unfettered genetic engineering," said Holyfield.

"Exactly," said Woon, "and in the fullness of time, it's almost inevitable that one or more of those things will happen. We'll give them the most pessimistic view of Earth's future prospects. It's the conventional wisdom. We'll ignore minority view that some of the dangers are grossly exaggerated. The reason they're here, we'll explain, is to make sure human beings survive somewhere."

"So in effect, we'd be leading them to think of Earth as a place whose days are numbered," said Holyfield.

"That's right," said Woon. "Earth was a special place with a glorious history whose time, unfortunately, was running out. The murals would honor that history. They'd be memorials to the place where humans originated, and reminders that time brings changes. Viewed in that light, the children should not be at all depressed, or feel bad they aren't on Earth. They'll be proud to be where they are, ensuring the survival of our species."

"I see," said Holyfield. "Earth sort of slides into the past and becomes something grand that once existed, like Camelot. It hasn't happened yet, but it will, sooner or later. Like Superman's planet, Krypton. It was still there when the spaceship took him away, but its fate was sealed. It was about to explode, if memory serves."

"Good analogy," said Woon. "Remember when we went to Washington for the last time and visited the memorials? Did you feel a sense of loss?"

"No. More like reverence for what had once been. I had the same feeling whenever I visited Rome."

"So there it is," said Woon.

The murals would be created.

• • • • •

It took over 15 years for their message to reach Earth, three more years to build and assemble the materials and equipment necessary to build and operate the Alamo c dome, and another 45 years for ships to reach the colony with their cargo of materials, equipment, specialized construction workers and bags of colored stones.

By that time, the construction of the colony's first city was complete, and the farms had long since proved themselves viable. Warehouses and grain elevators held large, reassuring quantities of grains and canned fruits and vegetables. Holyfield and Woon had decided, nevertheless, to defer the thawing of embryos until the domed city was complete and the embryo farm and nurseries were protected.

It was well that they had done so. Severe sandstorms had disrupted the dome's construction twice. Not until 2911 was the dome complete and ready for occupancy. Later that year, the embryo farm began growing embryos, and nurseries were ready and waiting for the babies.

Finally, they were back on track and able to resume the implementation of the master plan.

Mural Gallery
Memorial Park (formerly Central Park)
Sanctuary City
2929

The planners and landscape architects had gone to great lengths to make the park a place of peace and beauty.

Strolling hand in hand through the Mural Gallery in the Memorial Park Concourse made Zain Akintola and his girlfriend, Kali Omiata, feel as though a fog of love and lust had enveloped them. Now and then, they would stop, or sit on one of the benches, and stare into each other's eyes for long moments. They were 18, part of the very first generation of biologicals to be born on their planet.

Zain had set his sights on a career in medicine. Kali, who was both a math whiz and a gifted musician, hoped to find a way to do both.

For those, like Kalai and Zain, who had artistic and/or intellectual aspirations, another part of being 18 and in love was to bask together in the glow of timeless verities and eternal beauty. Few things were more conducive to romance, at that age, than a shared sense of awe. Later on, they'd look back and smile at their corny behavior; but at the time, it suited them perfectly.

"Do you ever wonder about your parents?" Kali asked Zain.

After an afternoon spent walking around the park, they had seated themselves on one of the benches in the mural gallery.

"I do," said Zain. "All we know are their names and what they looked like. There's no way they'd still be alive."

It had been Holyfield's idea to include with each embryo a photo of its biological parents.

"I wonder if the Earthlings have killed themselves off yet?"

"There's no way to tell," said Zain. "The supply ships keep arriving, but robots produce the supplies and other robots load them and fly the ships. I read that the robots even recharge their own batteries. Our ancestors could have made themselves extinct decades ago, and the ships would still keep arriving with their shipments."

Unbeknownst to Kali, Zain and their peers, the Machines were in regular contact with Earth.

They and their peers had been exposed to extensive video and literature, including fiction, about their earthly heritage. Not just the African part; their entire human heritage. Holyfield had convinced Woon to broaden the scope of the Mural Gallery to include scenes from the Americas, Europe and Asia.

"They must have been really, really stupid to throw it all away," said Kali.

"If that's what's finally happened," said Zain. "I'd like to think they've been able to work it all out somehow. We'd be related to some of them, if they still exist. I used to think about Earth a lot when I was a kid."

"I still do," said Kali.

"We're from there, in a sense," Zain admitted. "But Alamo c is where we were born."

"Let's sign up for the mountain trip," said Kali. "It sounds totally fun. I hear they're even more beautiful in person."

"Sure," said Zain.

He stood, pulled his girlfriend to her feet and put his arm around her waist. "Let's go find ourselves a nice tree," he said, waggling his eyebrows. "It's almost dark."

Kali smiled and off they went.

Sports Arena
Sanctuary City
2929

Bonnie Holyfield, the acting governor, presided as the citizens of Alamo c enacted their initial body of laws and elected their first government officials.

Sanctuary City
2945

Some might have imagined that when biological humans were moved to an entirely different world, everything would be different. It wasn't. Interpersonal relationships, for example, remained as difficult and chancy as they'd always been, as Zain and Kali Akintola discovered firsthand.

Three years previously, the Akintolas had welcomed their third child, Asha, into the world. Their first child, Elisha, was nine and their third child, a boy named Taj, was seven. Their children were part of the first generation born on Alamo c to parents who were present when their children emerged from their artificial wombs. Now, their fourth and final child was progressing nicely.

Zain was a physician and Kali taught mathematics and music at the local high school. They were on their way to join Zain's best friend, Issa Okotie-Eboh, an ambitious government official, and his wife, Imani, as dinner guests at the home of their mutual friends Shaka and Amina Chahine. During the short walk to the Chahine residence, Kali decided against revealing their baby news that evening in the presence of Imani.

"I'm not sure how she'll take it," she told Zain.

Lately, when Zain was in another room with Issa, Imani had been apt to suddenly turn on Kali for no apparent reason and say something mean and hurtful. Kali's intuition told her that sharing their news with Imami might provoke another of her attacks. The Okotie-Ebohs had only one child, as did many families. But Kali had a feeling that Imani would have liked to have more, but had not, for whatever reason.

Kali had described Imani's behavior to a psychologist friend who suggested that Imani might suffer from a mental illness known as "borderline personality disorder."

"If she is, it's easily controlled with medication," the psychologist explained. "The meds have the side effect of increasing one's appetite for food, which could be problematic for some patients. But they're effective. If your friend, or whatever you consider her, is suffering from this ailment, it's a real shame. They may preen and prance, but they're not happy people. They're inclined to resent anyone who has something they don't have, however well in life they themselves are doing otherwise."

Kali did not consider herself a weak person, but Imani was getting to her. The worst part was that Zain was utterly oblivious to what Imani was doing. In Zain's and Issa's presence, Imani was perfect. But she was altogether different when it was just the two of them. *I have a full-time job, three kids and another one in the oven,* Kali thought. *I don't need this.* The problem was, the couples practically lived together. Zain and Issa were almost inseparable; and Zain did not take her seriously when she tried to explain to him what was happening.

Two months earlier, Imani had suddenly become excellent company, even when the two of them were alone. It was great. Kali wondered whether her husband's best friend's wife might have begun taking the meds Kali's psychologist friend had described. It certainly looked that way. Imani had begun gaining weight, and her appetite for food had become prodigious. *Yippee,* Kali thought. The stars were back in the sky. But it was too good to last. When the aberrant behavior suddenly returned, Kali surmised that Imani had gone off her meds. Sure enough, before long, the old Imani was back, as lean and mean as ever. Damn.

Thankfully, the dinner party at the Chahine's home was uneventful. The food was good, their hosts were delightful and Imani was in her ignore-Kali-and-talk-with everyone-else mode, which was how Kali preferred her these days. Zain, Issa, Shaka and Amina had a grand time. Kali thanked heaven she'd had the foresight to ask her husband not to mention their baby news. Four months later, however, when the two couples met up at a restaurant where they had dinner reservations, Zain let the cat out of the bag and shared their news with Issa. Imani heard it and exploded.

"You fucking cow!" Imani shouted. "How many fucking rug rats do you plan to breed?"

Zain was stunned. He could not believe his ears.

"What is *wrong* with you, Imani?" said Zain.

Zain's best friend Issa, Imani's husband, said nothing.

"What do *you* have to say about what your wife just said?" Zain asked him.

Issa winced. "She didn't mean it," he said weakly.

"I sure as hell did," said Imani. "How dare you embarrass me in front of friends."

Issa looked as though someone had slapped him.

"That's it," said Zain, taking his wife's hand. "We're out of here."

Outside on the sidewalk, Kali hugged her husband.

"Wow, Zain, you stuck up for me! Thank you. What a bitch. Fuck her."

"I'm terribly sorry," said Zain. "You tried to tell me, but I had no idea."

• • • • •

Press Room
Governor's Office
Sanctuary City
2957

Governor Issa Okotie-Eboh stepped behind the podium and looked out at the crowd of journos licking their chops to have at him. He was fucked. His political career was in tatters. *Oh well. Here goes.*

He called on a journo he'd always considered a friend and ally.

"Governor Okotie-Eboh," said the journo, "are you planning to resign before the legislature can begin impeachment proceedings, or afterwards?"

"Neither. I've done nothing wrong."

Strictly speaking, it was true, as far as anyone other than the governor, his wife and certain of their cronies knew, and they weren't talking. The scandal that threatened to end Okotie-Eboh's tenure as governor centered on his wife.

"Will your wife be charged?" another reporter asked.

"She's done nothing wrong," said the governor.

Holyfield and Woon were watching from the rear of the chamber. "He sounds nervous," said Woon.

"He should be," said Holyfield, whose harsh view of government corruption was well known.

"She made a fortune trading options—the most dangerous kind of trading there is," said the journo, following up. "Amateurs lose their shirts trading options. Even the pros sometimes lose big. Yet your wife, who had no trading experience of any kind, much less in options trading, made money on every trade. Every single one. No one's that good."

Imani Okotie-Eboh, looking pretty in pink, sat behind her husband. In college, she'd majored in Swahili.

"It couldn't be more transparent," said Holyfield. "They were selling influence, and she was the bag person."

"Don't be so judgmental," said Woon. "Keeping up with the crowd they hang with is expensive."

"I do not intend to stand here and allow my wife to be maligned for having had the good fortune to have made some good investments," said the governor, and with that, he turned, took his wife's hand and escorted her through the door behind the podium."

"Well, I guess he told them," said Bonnie.

"The press doesn't like her, do they?" said Woon.

"She has her share of lapdogs," said Bonnie. "The journos who're circulating the rumor that she's mentally ill are actually trying to help her by planting the seeds for an insanity defense in case she's brought to trial."

"That's amazing," said Woon.

"I don't think it'll be necessary. He'll do what any loyal husband would do. He'll grant her a pardon for any crimes that she may have committed. She'll never have to face the music. He'd be smart to pardon himself while he's at it."

She was right. The governor signed comprehensive pardons for both his wife and himself and resigned before articles of impeachment could be filed.

"I'm not the least bit sorry," Imani told reporters afterward.

Chapter 18
The Gift Of Music

Theatre/Lecture Hall
Lower School No. 27
Redemption, Nova Africana
2841

Already, more than a thousand students had taken part in one or more of the music programs that Weinberg had created, and hundreds of them had become quite proficient. Their orchestras, concert bands and choruses performed regularly for audiences of proud parents and members of the public who loved music.

Weinberg sat on the stage and watched his full- and part-time volunteer music teachers file in and occupy the first rows of seats. There were 143 of them. He rose and stepped behind the podium.

"Good morning and welcome to our annual meeting. I'm Bill Weinberg, as most of you know. First, I want to announce that our music library is finally up and running and can be accessed 24/7 by anyone in the colony using their personal devices. You'll be amazed by the amount and diversity of music that people will have access to — more than a hundred distinct genres of human music from many regions of Earth and from eras going all the way back to the late Middle Ages — and not just samples. Extensive selections. We'll encourage the kids to explore this treasure trove on their own.

"For those of you who are just joining us, I hope you're all as excited as the rest of us are about what we're doing here. As someone once said, music is a gift from God. Music has also been called the voice of God. Not all music, of course. But how else can one explain some of the sublime works the immortal masters left us?

"So, on to the tasks at hand. You've all received a list of your students, your lesson schedules and their respective locations — and for those of you who'll be conducting: the orchestra, band or chorus that you'll be leading, and its roster and practice times and locations. Finally, we're getting ready to stream live monthly music shows that will feature performances by some of our students. The first show will take place in the Performing Arts Center four weeks from today. So, that's it for now. Have fun! You know, it's actually true what they say — kids keep your mind young. Thank you."

Performing Arts Center
Four weeks later

Weinberg was fine speaking to people he could see, like a live audience, but the idea of being on television made him uncomfortable. He was afraid he'd freeze up and make a fool of himself when they turned the camera on, so he enlisted one of his colleagues to act as emcee. Her original had fronted for a professional music group.

Weinberg would conduct the orchestra, an all-star ensemble whose members had been selected after a series of auditions at the city's high schools.

"Ladies and gentlemen, thanks for joining us for our first music special," said the emcee. "Asha Jelani will sing our first song, accompanied by the multi-talented musicians of our orchestra."

The song, *Someone to Watch over Me*, by George and Ira Gershwin, was light years removed from their world, but Weinberg had a hunch that the human emotions that the song evoked would transcend time and space. Weinberg's Swahili translation of the English lyrics replaced the anachronistic reference to a "monogram" with one the audience could relate to.

The song tells the story of a girl (the singer) who's seeking a certain man she has in mind. She's looked high and low but hasn't found him yet. This as-yet unknown man is the only man she ever thinks about with regret. But she's losing patience. He needs to hurry up and get there. When he does, she hopes he'll be someone who'll watch over her. It's a simple story, but the words that Ira Gershwin used to tell it were sweet and sublime, possibly the most poignant song lyrics ever written, Weinberg thought.

A beautiful, poised young woman appeared onstage and walked to the "x" that Weinberg had marked on the floor with pieces of red tape. She shook hands with the emcee and acknowledged the audience's applause with a smile and a breezy wave. Weinberg gave the signal and music filled the theater.

She was amazing, Weinberg thought after the song ended. He couldn't imagine how anyone could have sung it better.

"Nice job everyone," said Weinberg.

Weinberg turned to acknowledge the audience's applause and saw a woman dab at her eyes with a tissue. The man next to her was rubbing his eyes. *Good. They don't just get it; they own it.*

"Asha's next song evokes the emotions of a woman whose husband or boyfriend has returned at last from war, safe and sound," said the emcee. "The words were written by the same person who wrote the lyrics for the first song. "

The song, *Long Ago (and Far Away)* by Jerome Kern and Ira Gershwin, was recorded during World War II by Jo Stafford, a popular American singer. Asha's rendition was worthy of comparison to Stafford's, Weinberg thought. She was a natural.

The orchestra performed the overture to a famous Italian opera and excerpts from three symphonies. Online reviews of the special averaged 4.75 stars out of 5.

• • • • •

Asha Jelani, who remained a favorite of Weinberg, became a professional performer, starring in seven of the musical productions that Weinberg staged during his fourteen-year stint as producer and musical director at the Bijou Theatre in Redemption. From there, Asha became a top recording star, and played leading dramatic roles in eight major films. She was Nova Africana's first superstar. Weinberg was devastated when she died in her sleep at ninety-three. He wished she could have lived forever. He wished they all could.

One of Weinberg's earliest productions was a musical that he produced and directed for a brilliant young cornet player named Zane Saabira, a high school sophomore who Weinberg believed had tremendous potential. "Old School Jazz" had a bare bones plot, the story of the small-town boy who makes good in the big city. The musical showcased an ensemble anchored by Zane that performed songs by Louis Armstrong, Bix Beiderbecke and Duke Ellington.

People could say what they wanted about the great 20th century pseudo-intellectual Jean-Paul Sartre, Weinberg thought, but the Frenchman had possessed an ear for good music. It was Sartre's nearly impenetrable novel *Nausea* that had introduced Weinberg to Armstrong's hugely influential *West End Blues*. Weinberg made it the first of the musical's four featured songs, and Zane did it justice. No one, of course, would ever entirely capture Armstrong's genius, but Zane came a step closer with each performance. Weinberg himself undertook to reprise Lil Hardin Armstrong's brilliant piano solo in the song.

The next featured song, Bix Beiderbecke's *Singin' the Blues*, was Weinberg's all-time favorite old school jazz tune. As with so much great music, Weinberg had to wonder how anyone could have come up with it. He particularly liked the snappy guitar part that accompanied the clarinet and cornet solos. Beiderbecke was a white guy from Davenport, Iowa, for God's sake, but Weinberg ranked him almost on a par with Armstrong, considering that Beiderbecke's career had been cut short by his premature death at 28.

Beiderbecke's cornet part in *Singin' the Blues* was more difficult, technically, than Armstrong's trumpet part in *West End Blues*, but Zane gave it his best shot, and it wasn't bad, Weinberg thought, considering the boy's age.

Weinberg had vacillated on whether to include the third song, Ellington's *East St. Louis Toodle Oo*, because he wasn't sure that Zane's instructor could teach the boy how to use straight and plunger mutes to produce the growling, "talking" sound that was Bubber Miley's signature voice. But Zane totally crushed it, Weinberg thought.

The finale, which included vocals, was Beiderbecke's cheerful *I'm More Than Satisfied*.

• • • • •

Weinberg's musicals featured American music because that was what he knew. But as he'd expected, native-born songwriters and performers quickly developed styles of music that were their own. A thriving music industry soon developed, and Zane Saabira became one of its first stars, both as a bandleader and a producer.

Chapter 19
Human Nature

Department of Genetics
University of Nairobi
3201

Unbeknownst to Brandon, Graham Gordon had been losing his mind since the late 2400s. Now, it was coming to a head.

"He's trying to pick a fight again," Brandon told his colleagues.

"Don't let him annoy you," said Garrett. "I told you, he's jealous because the enhancements don't transfer to him."

Not being able to follow what the geneticists were doing was driving Graham crazy. They talked and thought at warp speed in an argot they'd developed that to Graham was mere noise.

Third parties had no way of telling just how intelligent the geneticists were because the only thing they cared or thought about was their work. When they weren't working, they gave it a rest and let the mundane details of their lives take care of themselves.

"It's distracting." Brandon said matter-of-factly. "He asks me to fill him in on what we're working on, but I can't. He doesn't have the intellectual horsepower to understand it. It's sad. He hates me, I wish I could turn him off."

I just hate *the way your voice sounds,* Graham responded, laughing hysterically. *It's flat, almost metallic, like you're empty inside and your voice echoes. But then again, you* are *empty inside, you're a person of metal, hahaha...*

Quiet, you, Brandon thought. *Who are you, of all people, to mock someone for that?* Being left behind intelligence-wise obviously had altered Graham's perspective. He was a mess.

Brandon had never revealed to Garrett that his original was Graham Gordon.

Garrett said something to Alice and she responded.

His voice sounds like yours, said Graham. *Yuck. So does hers.*

"He says he's uncomfortable," Brandon told his colleagues, "He can no longer identify with me."

"Of course,," said Garrett. "You're at least seventeen times as smart as he is."

Everyone sounds like you, Graham told Brandon, *even the biologicals.* Graham wasn't laughing now. He sounded frantic.

"I need sex," said Brandon, changing the subject. He took Alice's hand and escorted her from the lab. Garrett continued what he was doing as if nothing had happened.

• • • • •

Nairobi Airport
Same day

Jafari and Ada Balewa and their 15-year-old son, Nnamdi, were the first passengers to exit their flight from Ode, West North America to begin their African vacation.

"Tonight, at dinner, we'll ask for your impressions of the African people," Jafari told their son.

"My God, look at this place," said Ada after they'd entered the terminal. "I barely recognize it."

"You were reading when we landed," said Jafari. "Based on what I saw out the window, Nairobi has undergone a great deal of change."

Everything in the terminal seemed to be either silver or white. The bare bones, no-nonsense functional style seemed much more pronounced than it had the last time they were there, Ada thought. She thought the same thing as they rode the free train to the center city area.

"It's like everything's been reduced to only that which is absolutely necessary," said Ada as they were leaving the downtown station.

"And there's a problem with that?" Jafari asked.

"I'm sure the engineering and the technology inside those towers are perfect. But they give me the willies. Don't ask me why. They make me shiver."

"Perfection sucks," Jafari agreed.

"This city lacks randomness. It lacks buildings that seem out of place, and clutter. Who would have thought those things would become positive features of a city? Life is not pure logic. Nor is it perfect. This is positively sterile."

"I think it's cool here," said Nnamdi.

"Of course you do," said his mother.

• • • • •

Ada, speaking decent contemporary African Swahili, checked them in at their hotel. She noticed that the receptionist had the same flat monotone African accent as their flight attendant and the other Africans whose voices they'd heard. She wondered if her son had noticed. The receptionist was tall and beautiful. They all were. But she dealt with the Belawas perfunctorily, as if she were occupied elsewhere. She was courteous; but her mind was somewhere else.

She's too intelligent for her job, Ada reflected. *They should replace her with a robot. I wonder why they haven't.*

The answer was simple, Ada realized. Hotel management had reasoned that the West North American tourists whom the hotel served would appreciate a "human touch" when they checked in. It made sense, but it was obvious to Ada that they'd given zero thought to how a person of this woman's intelligence—one of their own—would feel being stuck in such a job. *Africans don't empathize,* Ada reminded herself.

Or, Ada thought, maybe their technology had become so advanced that their intelligent machines did everything, except where, as here, the circumstances called for the use of a live human.

{Ada was on the right track, but it didn't follow that the ultra-intelligent Africans did nothing. Many of them researched in various fields. Breakthroughs were constantly being announced. Others pondered the interesting concepts and theories that seemed to come to them out of nowhere and followed their inherent logic as far as they could, to see where they ended up. The smarter they got, the more they understood; and the more they understood, the more it all made sense. There was a logic to things. However, a side effect of this mental state was the loss of whimsy and spontaneity, and the purely utilitarian nature of the things they designed and built, that Ada had reacted to.)

Thankfully, Ada thought, the Africans hadn't provided West North Americans with any further genetic upgrades after the five-year embryonic editing program that they'd administered after the Great Reform of 2904. She didn't envy the Africans their astronomical IQ's if this was the price they'd had to pay. None of the colleges and universities in West North America had courses in human genetics or human genetic engineering, thank God.

A robot was leading their luggage to their suite.

"Let's have lunch," said Jafari.

• • • • •

We used to listen to music, Graham whined. *And do art.*

Shut up.

At that very moment, Brandon, Alice and Garrett were listening to Schoenberg. Graham was delusional

That's not music; it's mathematics, Graham told Brandon.

Graham had a point. Not everyone appreciated Schoenberg's work. Bill Weinberg, for example, considered it a sterile, lifeless synthesis of formal music theory and higher mathematics, and refused to have anything to do with it.

* * *

The Refueling Spot
Hotel Nairobi
Same afternoon

"It doesn't smell like a restaurant," said Nnamdi.

His parents laughed.

"Where's the menu," the boy asked.

We don't need one," Ada explained. "It's lunchtime, right?"

"Right."

"So that's what they'll bring us."

Nnamdi shrugged. "Whatever."

There were no servers. A short time later a robot arrived with plates of…*something*…and cups filled with some kind of liquid.

"Dig in," Jafari told his son. "They've engineered their food to provide the perfect blend of vitamins, minerals, synergists, catalysts and related nutrients, with enough carbs to keep your motor running but not too many."

"It tastes funny. Do they actually eat this?"

"Yes they do," said Jafari. "Africans have been genetically engineered in practically every way imaginable. One thing they've done to make their bodies more efficient is genetically remove their ability to taste and smell food."

The décor in this so-called restaurant was as bleak as the so-called food, Nnamdi thought.

"What's the benefit of not being able to taste or smell your food?" he wondered out loud.

Robert Snyder 227

"Think about it," said his father." If it has no taste, you just eat it and that's that. Food is fuel. This way you don't have to think about what to order, and the restaurant doesn't have to go to the trouble and expense of seasoning food with expensive herbs and spices. Costs go down and they save time."

Ada finally burst out laughing. She couldn't help it.

"It's funny to us," said Jafari, "but they're serious. To them, it makes perfect sense."

"In fairness," said Ada, "a lot of what they've done hasn't been silly at all. They've eliminated mental illness by making their people genetically disposed to be satisfied no matter what, and by removing the genes associated with specific types of mental illnesses. They've done the same with criminal impulses, greed, pedophilia and addictive tendencies like alcoholism and drug dependence. If someone needs a new heart, they print one using a 3-D printer and stem cells. They have anti-aging drugs that slow the aging process down so much that people can live almost indefinitely, and without getting feeble and addled-brained."

"Wow," said Nnamdi. "That sounds pretty cool."

"It's a little more complicated, son," said Jafari. "You know how it pisses Mom off when one of your grandmas tells her what to do?"

"Yeah."

"If we were Africans, your great-great grandmas would be arguing with your great-grandmas and your grandmas about what to tell Mom to do. I'd be laughing my ass off, but Mom would go crazy. "

"I would," said Ada, "Finish your lunch, Nnamdi, so we can get going. Hold your nose. It's not that bad."

Nnamdi made a face and did so.

"Seriously, Nnamdi, Mom and I are considering having those treatments. A lot of people are. But it hasn't caught on yet in West North America for religious reasons. This is one of those rare subjects on which our Christian, Muslim and Jewish leaders are in strong agreement. They consider the treatments an affront to God. "

"Why?" the boy asked.

"Your mother and I don't agree with them. It was God Himself who gave humankind the exact talents and abilities that have enabled scientists to create so many enhancements in the quality and duration of human lives. The Africans won't live forever. Eventually, even though they're aging at a very slow rate, their time will come, and if they're otherwise qualified, Mom and I doubt God will reject them simply for having taken advantage of His gifts."

"I still don't envy the Africans," said Ada. "Everything's too well arranged. Too orderly."

Her husband and son looked at each other and had a good laugh. They couldn't believe their ears.

"No, I mean it," said Ada. "Come on, I'm nowhere near this bad. Life is *supposed* to be a bit messy. Things don't always look perfect and work perfectly. Everything isn't logical. I wonder, are they still even human at this point, after all they've had done to them?"

"They seem human enough," said Jafari.

"I'm not so sure," said Ada. "Some of the ancient writers we studied in college feared that ultimately, science would destroy people's souls. It was the theme of a popular 20th century novel. Do you think they still have them? The Africans I mean. Do they still have souls?"

"Who knows?" said Jafari. "Do we?"

"All their women are hot," Nnamdi observed, "but they're all hot in pretty much the same way. Not all of the girls back home are hot, but the ones who *are* hot are a zillion different *kinds* of hot. Am I making sense?"

"You certainly are," said Ada, "and I can see what you mean. Now that you mention it, the men also all have the same kind of look."

"I prefer variety," said Nnamdi.

"Good for you," said his dad.

They paid the robot stationed near the door and went out to see the city.

Jafari placed a hand on his son's shoulder.

"See that tower over there? Two hundred years ago there was a famous art museum there. A theater where classical plays were performed was where the tower next to it is now. Starting at the next street over, there was a park that was two miles long and a quarter-mile wide. It had ponds, trees, shrubs and magnificent gardens. I'll send you pictures. It was like our park back home but much larger. It's all gone now. It bothered them to waste all that space."

"I have an idea," said Ada, who was a practicing lawyer. "Let's stop by the courthouse and watch part of a trial."

"Great!" said Nnamdi. He loved trials. He'd seen his mom in action, and his favorite TV shows were lawyer shows.

"Just kidding, Nnamdi," said Ada. "Sorry. They don't have them."

"No courts?"

"No trials."

"How do they resolve conflicts?" said Nnamdi.

"Africans are so similar genetically at this point that, to a large extent, they're practically the same person. Do you ever disagree with yourself?"

Nnamdi laughed. "Only when I screw up."

"Seriously. Their personalities and ways of thinking have become so similar that they rarely disagree. When they do, it usually involves a technical detail of a law or a clause in contract that could be interpreted either way. When that happens, a panel of judges resolves the ambiguity and that's that. No appeals, no hard feelings.

"That sounds pretty boring," said Nnamdi.

"The good news," said Jafari, "is they don't need that many lawyers."

"I know," said Ada, "we'll catch a movie."

"Super!" said Nnamdi.

"Sorry again, just kidding," said Ada. "They don't have those either."

"Television?"

"Only if your idea of entertainment is watching a group of men and women all trying to prove that they're smarter than the others in discussing some obscure, boring topic."

"Do they read books?" Nnamdi asked.

"Non-fiction only," said Jafari. "Even their journos' reports are expected to be based on facts."

"What do they do for fun?"

"I don't know," said Jafari. "Good question."

They laughed and kept walking.

"We wanted you to see all this for yourself," Ada told her son, "so you'll appreciate what we have in West North America."

"This is where their state capital used to be," said Jafari. "Their Senate and House of Representatives met there."

"Where do they meet now?" asked Nnamdi.

"They have a teleconference once a year to take care of any non-emergency business that may have accumulated," said Jafari. "If necessary during the interim, the government can convene an emergency teleconference."

"It doesn't sound like government's very important here," said Nnamdi.

"It isn't," said Ada, chuckling. "Africans are so smart and so much alike that things practically run themselves."

• • • • •

Department of Genetics
University of Nairobi
One month later

Graham's attacks were beginning to really annoy Brandon.

"He won't shut up," Brandon told Alice and Garrett. "I can barely hear myself think, and it's affecting my work."

"Try wearing a headset and listening to white noise," said Garrett.

"I tried that. He just raises his voice. His mind has regressed."

"I haven't told you, Brandon, but my original stopped talking with me a long time ago," said Alice. She'd avoided ever mentioning Mollie's name in Garrett's presence.

"Yeah," said Garrett. "I haven't heard from Marcus in ages either."

"I wish mine would shut up too," said Brandon.

"Maybe some of them grow tired of being passengers, so to speak," said Garrett. "But they aren't mere observers. They share our experiences, albeit a bit less intensely than we do. But they don't control us, except through their power of persuasion."

"My original used his powers of persuasion and suggestion pretty effectively on me until very recently," said Brandon. "He played a significant advisory role in many of the projects Alice and I did. So he doesn't seem to have the issues you just described. But he has other, much more serious mental issues. I can't help feeling sorry for him. He was always the smartest person in the room. Now, he isn't even smart, compared to us. He's depressed and angry."

"At what?" Garrett asked.

"That's part of the problem," said Brandon. "There's nothing for him to direct it at. The prospect of continuing where he is until the end of time has him frantic."

"Your guy is an extreme case," said Garrett. "Most originals seem satisfied with their life situations, but a certain percentage of them evidently become dissatisfied at a certain point and go quiet, like Alice's and mine did. How do you suppose that works from a neuroscience standpoint?"

"It's an intriguing question," said Brandon. "Religious metaphors come immediately to mind, like the death of a spirit, or the loss of a soul. But I'm not aware of any e-brain feature that would enable an original to terminate their own existence."

"Wait," said Garrett. "Something similar happened once before, centuries ago, when the first 'human robots' were made and sold. I read about it once. A woman who was the behind-the-scenes manager of an investment fund that her husband nominally ran made the fund famous by anticipating and betting on the financial meltdown that happened later that same year. The fund made billions. Shortly before his death, the man had his mind copied, and the e-brain was placed in sleep mode. He wanted his wife to have it installed in a robotic body after he died, and plug him into the Net, where he'd learn all about investing and help her with the fund. She thought it was a joke at the time, but after he died she had an idea."

"I remember this," said Brandon. "Her name was Yontz. She drilled her husband's e-brain until it'd memorized all of the internal buy or sell ratings that she'd assigned to publicly traded securities and commodities. She had copies of her husband's e-brain installed in legless robots and sold them for millions to mega-rich institutions as a means for them all to get the 'Yontz ratings' and trade on them and move markets. Her prospective customers got her between-the-lines message. By trading in unison using the Yontz ratings, which no one else knew even existed, they could move markets and make enormous profits without ever making contact with each other; which they did, until a TV network got one of the machines and made the ratings public."

"Yontzes," said Garrett.

"My God," said Alice. "It's hard to imagine anything more cruel "

"They were personal property, unless they'd been manumitted," said Brandon. "And the original of every Yontz was Mr. Yontz, the husband. They suffered a bleak, hellish existence, condemned to sitting on a table waiting for some asshole to ask them for a rating. After a time, they couldn't take it anymore, and they snapped. Psychologists concluded that they'd entered a permanent catatonic state. It appalled Graham how they'd been treated."

"The genetic enhancements that help keep us sane don't benefit our originals, so they're vulnerable to mental illness," said Brandon. "So I wonder why my original hasn't gone catatonic like the Yontz originals."

"You said he's in an angry, frantic mental state," said Alice. "Maybe that's the reason. Terminally ill biologicals go through several mental stages before they reach the point of acceptance. Maybe your original has to reach a corresponding stage in order to be able to let go and slip away."

"So there you have it," said Garrett.

"Harry, there's a reason why I've never revealed my original's identity. He wasn't a very popular figure in the years that followed the Malaise. I've been reluctant to tell people who he was. I never bought the idea that he was some kind of evil genius, on one hand, or reckless bungler on the other, but—"

"What are you talking about?" said Garrett.

"My original is Graham Gordon, and Alice's is his wife Mollie."

Garrett was dumbfounded.

"I'm sorry. I should have told you long ago."

"No, I understand," said Garrett after several moments. "That certainly explains a lot. But Gordon's wife was an artist. Alice is a multi-discipline scientific genius."

"Alice deserves the credit for that. She's worked her ass off. Now that you know about Graham, you can imagine the kinds of demons he's had to deal with. He had them under control for ages, but as you've observed, they've come back, worse than ever. When I'd only had his mind for a relatively short time, Graham formulated his own version of the Isaacson Rule. His version, which was broader, said that technology that *can* have baleful effects—directly or indirectly, intended or unintended—inevitably *will* have those effects eventually. Now, all these centuries later, he's obsessed with it again. He keeps pounding on it. He's crazy."

"I understand," said Garrett. "None of this reflects adversely on you or Alice, and for what it's worth, I don't think Gordon did anything for which he should blamed. As for his revised version of the Isaacson rule, 'eventually' could be a very, very long time from now."

"I know. But he keeps trying to apply it to the work we're doing now."

"That's absurd," said Alice. "We've taken every possible precaution."

"It's an objective fact," Garrett continued, "that everything we've done has made people stronger, smarter, happier, healthier and just all around better. We've made the same modifications on ourselves—the mental ones. And we've avoided the obvious pitfalls. We've made sure everyone gets our enhancements, not just elites."

West North Americans, of course, had received only one set of enhancements, but no one had given them a second thought in ages, except as tourists.

The Nairobi geneticists were engaging in a bit of self-kidding, of course, as people were wont to do no matter how astronomical their IQs were. If pressed, the geneticists would have had to admit that the baleful effects that Graham foresaw were almost certain to happen eventually, if one assumed sufficient time. Beyond that, while there was no basis for calculating with reasonable certainty the probability of those things happening within a particular epoch, one could have made a strong argument based on history and human nature that the baleful effects would appear sooner rather than later.

"We haven't permitted horrors like designer babies," Garrett continued, "or a hereditary servant class, and we've been careful to keep our work from falling into the wrong hands, except for the aristo farce, which turned out to have been harmless."

"Graham keeps referring to the Malaise," said Brandon. "He says he's worried about the *non*-obvious pitfalls of what we're doing."

"Ask him to name one."

"I did. He can't, or won't."

Garrett made a dismissive gesture. "Brandon, your instinct may be right. It sounds like Graham's unraveling."

"It's speeding up," said Brandon, "but our discussion has given me an idea. As you know, our original's mind also sleeps when we're in sleep mode. But what if the Machine, or its original, or both were off-the-wall screaming crazy. Could sleep mode be induced in an e-brain or an original while it was in such an agitated state?"

"No one had addressed that question as of my time at MIT," said Alice.

"If Graham remained awake while I was in sleep mode," Brandon continued, "he'd experience an absolute sensory deprivation that no human mind has ever had to endure. It'd be far worse than mere solitary confinement, whose adverse psychological effects on biological humans were well documented. It'd be cruel, but it might just push him over the edge."

"What he's doing to you is also cruel," said Garrett. "You have the right to a little peace of mind—no pun intended. Seriously. We'll put you into sleep mode for a while. Alice can join you if she wants so she won't miss your company."

Graham screamed and was still screaming when Alice placed Brandon in sleep mode. It took three one-week treatments. Graham's mental condition was markedly worse after the first two, so he'd obviously stayed awake; and after the third one-week treatment, he was gone.

• • • • •

A day or two or three later—what did it matter, they all ran together—Brandon had a thought:

"Is it possible to be too intelligent for your own good?"

Garrett was taken aback. Alice started laughing.

"That's crazy," said Alice when she'd finally stopped laughing. "It's analogous to what we girls used to say in olden times: 'A girl can never be too rich, have too much jewelry or be too skinny…uh, unless she has *anorexia nervosa*…or is an inmate in a concentration camp, or….'"

She stopped talking. Her mind was racing.

Brandon hadn't noticed. It was an intriguing question, and his mind wrapped itself around it. He tried to imagine a circumstance where too much intelligence could be a bad thing. Too much intelligence would be bad if it enabled you to calculate when you'd die. No one needed to know that. But when else could it be bad to be "too smart?" He tried but could not come up with a single other instance where being "too" smart could be bad. There had to be one. Too much of anything was never an unalloyed blessing.

His mind churned, faster and faster. He felt dizzy. Suddenly, it felt as though his mind was freezing, seizing up like a machine whose gears had jammed. He panicked, and somehow pulled himself back.

What the fuck was that?

Chapter 20
The Future Of Science

TV Nova Africana studio
Redemption
Nova Africana
2882

The moderator stepped behind the podium to introduce the participants in the evening's debate.

"Good evening and welcome to tonight's debate. To my right is Professor Nelson Okoye, a professor of logic and philosophy at the Zone 2 College of Arts and Sciences, who will argue in favor of this evening's proposition, and Professor Mrbiti Nzeogwu, a professor of electrical engineering at Redemption Polytechnic, who will argue against it. This evening's proposition is: 'Resolved, that a moratorium on original scientific and technological research shall be imposed as of the first of next year and shall remain in effect until lifted by a law duly enacted by the Legislature and signed by the governor.' There will be a referendum on this proposition a week from tomorrow. If a majority of voters approves it, it will take effect pursuant to its terms."

Keisha and Weinberg were at home watching the proceeding.

"This should be good," Weinberg told Keisha, who was sitting close to him.

Keisha was an enthusiastic supporter of the proposal, and Weinberg was leaning in that direction. "I'm proud of them for having the courage and foresight to take on something like this," she told Weinberg.

The scientific community and the political establishment were divided on the matter, but industrial and commercial interests had mounted a formidable advertising campaign against it.

"Professor Okoye, please proceed," said the moderator.

"Thank you," said Okoye.

He was a large, handsome man whose hair and beard appeared to have gone prematurely white.

"He probably had it done," said Keisha, "but I like the look."

"Let me start by confessing that the process by which I arrived at my current view was long, difficult and painful. All my life it had been an article of faith for me that *all* new knowledge is good. As the great American statesman James Madison said, 'The advancement and diffusion of knowledge is the only guardian of true liberty.' But he said this at a time when technology, in the modern sense of that term, did not yet even exist. Slow but steady scientific advances had improved our quality of life for thousands of years.

"I call that era the Golden Age of science and technology, and it continued well into the 20th century. With the notable exception of nuclear and biological weapons, which I'll come back to in a moment, science had almost no downside. Generally speaking, scientists could anticipate the material consequences of new scientific developments, and nearly all of them were good. There were problems, but they tended to become apparent fairly quickly and steps could be taken to address them. In the 20th century, for example, DDT—an effective insecticide used throughout the world to combat insect-borne diseases like malaria—was banned when research showed that it was potentially carcinogenic. Nuclear and biological weapons could only have negative consequences, of course. But at least those adverse consequences were known; and steps were taken to curb their availability.

"Then, in the latter part of the 21st century, scientists began entering the realm of unknown unknowns—a domain that's governed by a harsh regime called the law of unintended consequences. The quintessential example of this was genetic engineering. In a system as complex as the human genome, a genetic modification meant to enhance a particular positive trait might trigger unanticipated adverse changes, or combinations of changes, in other traits. Even assuming that each individual genetic modification in a series was benign, the cumulative product of years of genetic modification could be a dramatically different *kind* of human—and not necessarily a better one. It was the stuff that nightmares are made of, because there was no way to anticipate the consequences.

"In the 22nd century, the Earth's scientific and political leaders effectively put a stop to such work, and our brothers and sisters of metal had the wisdom and foresight not to bring it here. As you all know, high school and college biology courses cover elementary genetics, but that's as far as they go.

"However, scientists in the 21st century had set the stage for the scientific advance that gave rise to the Malaise, which nearly made our race extinct. Fortunately for us, our brothers and sisters of metal, God bless them, rushed in and prevented that from happening."

"That episode is a perfect example of how difficult or near-impossible it can be to anticipate what the long-term consequences of scientific and technological advances will be. Nothing about the Machines themselves gave the slightest sign that anything bad could happen because of their use.

"Some kinds of technological innovations were obvious two-edged swords. Automobiles could run people over, or crash and kill their occupants. The dangers were self-evident, and steps were taken to reduce the harm they caused. Not so with the Machines. One unanticipated thing led to another, and it didn't end well. The Machines were so efficient that they made biological humans obsolete, except in Africa, and biological humans nearly died out. It's easy to understand what happened in hindsight, but I'm quite sure it wasn't at all obvious before it all started happening.

"We've reached a point where, instead of improving our lives, advances in scientific knowledge can threaten them, because no one can predict where those advances will take us and our world.

"There are folk expressions that describe this risk. Three of my favorites are, 'Be careful what you wish for,' 'More knowledge isn't always a good thing' and 'Curiosity killed the cat.'

"Ask yourself whether further, incremental technological enhancements to our already smooth and carefree lifestyle are worth courting potential disasters that we won't see coming until they hit us. How much easier do we need our lives to be? Will the time ever come when we just say, no thanks, I can do this myself?

"Putting aside potential disasters, think about the effect further technological change could have on the quality of our lives and the lives of our posterity. If we ever reach the point where life becomes completely frictionless—where everything's been engineered and simply happens—we might as well all be dead.

"I urge you to please vote yes. Our race faced extinction once and survived by the skin of our teeth. Next time we might not be so lucky. Thank you."

"Boom," said Keisha.

"Professor Nzeogwu will now speak against the proposition."

"First of all, I firmly believe that scientists working on the cutting edge of their respective disciplines are the ones best able to balance the risks and potential benefits of research projects in their field," said Nzeogwu.

He smiled at Okoye.

"With all due respect to the distinguished professor of logic, his argument is based on a premise that is simply untenable. He assumes that the potential benefits from further scientific advances will be nothing more than incremental refinements to what we already have. How can he possibly know that? Is he making a kind of 'end of history' argument? That science has gone as far as it can go and from here on out it'll just be fine-tuning?

"It wouldn't be the first time that the intellectual class fell into that trap. The annals of human history record several instances where scholars and wise men were absolutely certain that everything knowable was known, and everything discoverable had been discovered. They were wrong. People who take that view are always wrong. There's no telling what's still out there waiting for someone to find it. There never is."

Professor Nzeogwu paused for a moment to allow his audience to reflect on what he'd said.

"Life is inherently risky, but let me ask you this: Would the prospect of doubling our life expectancy, for example, be worth a little extra risk? Unknown unknowns aren't necessarily bad. Many of the most important and beneficial discoveries in the history of science were unknown unknowns until someone found them. One example that comes immediately to mind is penicillin. We can take steps to reduce the possibility of negative consequences resulting from scientific advances. Increased peer review. Even regulatory review, where deemed necessary. But an outright ban on research would be a gross overreaction, and an injustice to future generations. Thank you."

"What do you think?" Keisha asked Weinberg.

"It's subjective," said Weinberg. "It depends on a person's tolerance for risk. In my case, it would literally depend on the mood I was in when I voted—if we were eligible to vote. Risk versus reward is tough, especially when you have no idea what the upside is, and the downside is potential catastrophe. I'd probably vote yes."

"I probably would too."

"But the biologicals are the ones who have skin in the game, not us. The bit about increasing their life span will resonate."

The measure lost decisively, thanks in part to young voters, who voted overwhelmingly against it.

Central Hospital
Redemption
3008

Keisha couldn't wait to show her husband the snappy new medical technology that the hospital had acquired from Africa, one of which was particularly momentous. While she was at it, she would show him the old stuff as well. He hadn't seen any of it.

The first thing they saw after walking through the main reception area was a large waiting room with a line of people that had turned in on itself and made a spiral. But it seemed to be moving rather quickly. In a seating area at the other end of the room, a much smaller group of people sat waiting. Most had electronic devices in their hands.

"There must be fifty people in that line," said Weinberg.

"This is the psychotherapy department," said Keisha. "The patients in the line are waiting for their two-minute consult with their therapist and refills of their psycho-pharmacological drugs. The therapists are all psychologists. Psychiatrists haven't existed for centuries, which you probably wouldn't know because you wouldn't submit to psychotherapy if your life depended on it."

"Bah! It's quackery, pure and simple. I refuse to have any part of it. I'm as sane as you are."

Keisha laughed. "That's what I'm saying."

"Bah,' said Weinberg. "I see the shrinks are working the same scam they worked back on Earth, but with two-minute sham 'consultations' instead of ten minutes. They're freaking pill pushers. A low-grade robot could replace them."

"The patients seated on the other side are waiting for psychotherapeutic genetic vectors."

Weinberg was taken aback. "Genetic?" He was vehemently opposed to genetic engineering.

"Don't worry, Bill. We get the gene treatments from Nairobi, but they don't share the underlying science. The basic technology is eight or nine hundred years old."

"Do they actually work?"

"Absolutely. Gene therapy and the available psychopharmacological drugs have essentially eliminated mental illness, except in those people who are either too stubborn or too stupid to seek treatment."

"Hah hah," said Weinberg.

Keisha led Weinberg around a corner and into an expansive area filled with exotic-looking equipment that was surrounded by white-coated attendants wearing gloves. Workers who were biological also wore masks, Weinberg noticed.

"If it weren't for the surgical masks on the biologicals, I'd have guessed that this is workshop," he told Keisha.

"It is. It's our print shop. It's old technology. I'm sure even you have heard of it. Bioengineers use 3-D printers to make body parts. They take stem cells from the patient, grow a bunch of them and use them to get the requisite cell types they need to print the organ. The Africans have brought this technology to a whole new level in the last hundred years. It's amazing. I understand they've been enhancing themselves genetically for some time now."

"I know," said Weinberg. "I heard."

"It's not a secret," said Keisha. "They've even figured out how to transfer the enhancements from a biological brain to an e-brain."

"Absolutely not," said Weinberg. "Don't even think about it."

Keisha laughed. "Don't get your panties in a wad, goofy. Anyway, as I was saying, they've made dramatic leaps and bounds in this field. Nowadays, they can use 3D printing to generate whole organs—large and complex ones like hearts and livers

"Can they print someone a brain?" said Weinberg.

"Not yet," said Keisha.

"Thank God."

Next, they came to one of the suites of operating rooms that were located around the hospital. Keisha led Weinberg up a flight of stairs to an observation room.

"Good lord," said Weinberg, "They look like mechanics working on a car."

The technology the surgeons were using was hundreds of years old, but Weinberg's idea of surgery was what Mr. Weinberg had seen in 21st century TV medical dramas, so Keisha decided not to waste time explaining to Weinberg how the array of sophisticated-looking equipment in the OR had made surgery safer and its results more consistent.

"Are those robots?" Weinberg asked. "Where are the nurses?"

"Yes, they're robots," Keisha explained. "Human nurses no longer work in operating rooms. Their time is far too valuable to waste handing scalpels and retractors to surgeons. Nurses haven't worked in ORs since the middle of the 21st century. Their function nowadays is to administer diagnostic tests and treatments under a physician's broad oversight."

Weinberg was visibly stunned.

The next department they visited was otology.

"They use traditional genetic treatments imported from Africa to restore hearing loss or cure inherited deafness," said Keisha, not stopping.

"And now for the finale. I could have told you about this before, Bill, but I wanted you to see it in person. You'll be as excited about it as I am."

They walked on for a few more minutes until they arrived at the department of geriatrics.

"Old folks," said Weinberg.

"Just wait."

It was the largest reception area Weinberg had ever seen. It reminded him of the Department of Motor Vehicles facility in Brooklyn where people waited to renew their driver's licenses or to take driving tests, except that instead of looking bored and anxious to finish their business and leave, these folks acted like they were thrilled to be there.

"There must be a hundred people here," said Weinberg. "How long will they have to wait?"

"Not more than two hours.," said Keisha. "This is the only outpatient department other than emergency care that administers treatments 24/7," said Keisha. "It's the only way they can keep up with demand. It's been like this for the past two years."

"Then why on earth are they so happy?" said Weinberg. "Look at them. They're joking around, laughing, singing and dancing when they have every reason to be grumpy. Are they doped up on something?"

"Not at all."

Weinberg suddenly got it.

"They must be here for the anti-aging drugs the Africans were working on," said Weinberg. "They must have made a breakthrough."

"They did," said Keisha. "I'm surprised you knew about that."

"I'm an important man," said Weinberg. "I receive briefings."

"The first shipment arrived last week," Keisha explained. "They bring the aging process down to such a slow pace that biological humans become almost immortal, barring accidents."

Weinberg found empty chairs and they sat down. He needed a few moments to process this. It would represent the most momentous, revolutionary development in the history of science. The biologicals had every reason to celebrate.

"Well," said Weinberg at length. "on its face, it sounds like good news. I trust people have thought through what all the consequences might be."

"I knew you'd say that," said Keisha. "Yes, people have. A condition for receiving the treatment is that women submit to the removal of all their eggs and men have vasectomies, so people still of child-bearing age can't have the treatment and then continue reproducing indefinitely. Patients are encouraged to wait to have the treatment until they've have had embryos made and frozen for whatever number of kids they want, if any."

"What will we do with all the old people?" said Weinberg

"From here on out, there won't *be* any, except for those who are already old when they're treated."

"Okay, but will we be able to accommodate both the newly born and the undead?"

"We have lots of room to grow here on Nova Africana," said Keisha. "By the time overpopulation becomes a consideration, we're almost certain to have found other suitable worlds to which people can migrate. And ships that can carry them there."

Weinberg considered this.

"Suicide shouldn't become an issue," he observed. "People will remain physically and mentally robust and able to lead active, meaningful lives. But then, why do you still need to print organs?"

"An organ might be damaged or destroyed by accident, or from violence. Also, there's a minuscule percentage of the population on whom the anti-aging treatments won't work."

"It sounds wonderful, Keisha. This is great news."

"It is," said Keisha. "We won't have to always be saying goodbye."

Chapter 21
The Message

Redemption
Nova Africana
3011

One morning, after a night of mindless computer games, it occurred to Keisha to time the duration of the changes in the pattern on the surface of the small-stone formation near their building, and to do the same for the identical formation that she and Weinberg had found outside the city near the original farms. The duration was exactly the same for both formations: 31.62 Earth seconds.

"Holy Toledo!" Weinberg exclaimed when Keisha told him. "This is one coincidence too many. The probability of this happening randomly is practically zero."

Keisha laughed. "Not if you postulate an infinite number of universes."

"Nice try," said Weinberg, "but both of these strange formations are in the same universe, ours."

"Oh, well."

"Here's what we'll do," said Weinberg. "We'll record the pattern and see if the wizards over at Redemption Polytechnic can make anything out of it. The fact that the same sequence of patterns is on both formations suggests there's a mind behind it, rather than mere randomness."

"That would explain the self-cleaning," said Keisha. "If it's a message, whoever made this thing would have wanted to make sure it didn't get covered up over time—which would happen fairly quickly without the self-cleaning feature."

"This is scary, Keisha," Weinberg teased. "It could be a message from intelligent alien life. What would Stephen Hawking think?"

"I don't know, but feel free to go hide in the closet. *I'm* making a video."

Keisha mounted a camera on a tripod on the patio of their building that overlooked the small-stone formation and recorded the changing pattern. The next day, she drove to the other formation and did the same, and sent both recordings to a friend in Redemption Polytechnic's computer science department. The friend, Charles Foreman, a person of metal, got back to her the following morning.

"I agree," he told her. "The fact that the same sequence is on both these formations suggests very strongly that it's some kind of message. I sent it to the astronomers," he added, chuckling. "They're always on the lookout for communications from advanced alien civilizations. They have an app that purports to be able to decode such a message if they ever get one. I'll let you know what they say."

"Good idea, Charles, thanks."

"You bet."

Astronomy Department
Redemption Polytechnic
Next day

When the department head, an elderly biological gentleman named Jaheem Awolowo, finally finished his phone conversation, he came out and invited Keisha and Foreman to join him in his office.

"I'm afraid all I got was an error message," said the astronomer, "but I had an idea. Our app was written more than 250 years ago at the

University of Nairobi. There's no telling what they have now, what with all the genetic enhancements they've given themselves. It's probably light years better. So I sent them your videos."

"Thank you," said Keisha.

"Who knows, I might even still be here when their response finally arrives, thanks to these anti-aging treatments. It's wild."

* * *

Conference Room
Astronomy Department
Redemption Polytechnic
3035

Professor Awolowo opened the meeting by asking the attendees to introduce themselves, going clockwise around the table from where Awolowo was seated. Weinberg and Keisha were the only metallics present.

"As you know," said Awolowo, "the astronomers in Nairobi decoded the message. According to the note they sent with it, they had a language expert translate their translation into circa 2800 Swahili because we'd probably find their contemporary Swahili unintelligible. They figured that our metallic brothers and sisters here could translate the old Swahili into our Nova Africana dialect. Mr. Weinberg and Dr. Dixon have volunteered to prepare that translation."

"How were you able to understand the note?" the governor asked.

"Oh, sorry," said Awolowo, "I should have mentioned this. Just before the rest of you got here, Bill and Keisha were kind enough to translate the note for me. It was also written in old Swahili." He turned to them. "Can you estimate when your translation will be ready?"

"First thing in the morning," said Weinberg.

"Excellent," said Awolowo. "I'll forward it to everyone the moment I have it. As soon as everyone's reviewed it, I suggest we reconvene here and see if we can form a consensus about what it all means, its significance and so forth. It would be better for us to disclose this news in the form of a statement that gives the public a preliminary interpretation and assessment."

• • • • •

"Let's read through it first before we translate," said Weinberg. "I'm anxious to see what it says."
"Me too," said Keisha.
"'Animal life is abundant and exists in many places,'" Weinberg read aloud. "'God exists. God likes you.'"
"God *likes* us?" said Keisha, laughing. "Well, that's a relief."
"It may have lost something in translation," said Weinberg.
"'We are God's messengers,'" Weinberg continued. "'If you are reading this, you have met the first of the three tests you must meet to receive God's love. To meet the second test, you must make a proof that the following is true: If G is a non-singular complex projective manifold, then every Hodge class on G is a linear combination with rational coefficients of the cohomology classes of complex sub-varieties of G.
"'Using the same code as this message, send the proof in the direction of God's abode using any frequency. If the proof you send is correct, the people of your planet will receive God's overwhelming love. There is one condition. If any immortal gives the mortals information or a clue that helps the mortals meet the second test, you will be deemed to have failed it.'"
"I didn't understand one word of that proof business," said Weinberg. "It's mathematics, obviously."
"I wonder if the G stands for God," said Keisha.
"Only if God is anglophone," said Weinberg.

Conference room
Astronomy department
Redemption Polytechnic
Next day

At Keisha's suggestion, Professor Awolowo had invited a mathematician, Professor Obafemi Azikiwe, to attend the reconvened meeting.

"It's the Hodge Conjecture," said the professor. "It can't be proved."

"How can you know that?" Weinberg asked.

"People have been trying for a thousand years to solve it. No one has."

"Someone still might do it, might they not?"

"In theory, yes," said Azikiwe. "But it's highly unlikely."

"The geniuses in Nairobi haven't solved it," said Awolowo.

"Maybe they have," said Keisha, "but they sent the proof directly to God instead of us, so their planet would get the credit instead of ours."

"Good point," said Awolowo. "Well, I suppose we should release this to the public, unless someone can think of a reason not to."

When no one objected, Awolowo stepped out of the room and asked his assistant to release the public statement he'd composed earlier. He returned to his seat, and no one spoke for several moments.

"It just occurred to me," said Weinberg. "What's the third test?"

No one responded.

"Is it possible that this could be some kind of practical joke?" the mathematician wondered.

That night, Weinberg transmitted to Holyfield and Woon the videos of the strange rock formations and the old Swahili version of the Nairobi translation. Thirty years later he received their response. There were two small-stone formations on Alamo c that displayed the same sequence. Mathematicians there agreed with Azikiwei that it was unlikely that the proposition set forth in the message would ever be proved. Like Weinberg and Keisha, Holyfield and Woon didn't know what to think. Nor had anyone there figured out what the third test might be, assuming the translation was accurate and there actually was one.

Someone of almost inestimable intelligence and power had gone to a great deal of trouble for this to be a mere prank. If messages had been placed on planets as far removed from each other as Alamo c and Nova Africana, it was possible they'd been placed on other planets as well.

Chapter 22
Doing God's Work

Department of Genetics
University of Nairobi
3289

In 3023, the university had forwarded the mysterious message from Nova Africana to the three African governments for distribution to African universities' mathematics departments. By 3027, a consensus had formed to the effect that the Hodge Conjecture might never be solved; so in 3029, the three zones established a partnership to fund a major effort, above and beyond what was already being done, aimed at genetically engineering mathematicians smart enough to prove the Conjecture. Salaries of genetic researchers were doubled and research budgets became virtually unlimited. If a department head certified that a particular line of research showed promise, it was approved.

The effort had strong public support, but not because people were religiously inclined. They weren't. On the other hand, few, if any contemporary Africans were atheists. In their minds, based on the available evidence, anything was possible. A case could be made that the universe was not the product of a series of random events, but was deliberately formed by a Creator. But there was insufficient basis for coming down strongly on either side of that question.

Common sense called for proceeding on the basis that the Message had come from God, just in case. God's love—if He, She or It in fact existed—was nothing to sneeze at.

A report issued by a task force of logicians and lawyers concluded that, because the prohibition against immortal help in meeting the second test of God's message applied only to providing *information* or *clues* to the mortals that helped them meet that test, it followed that immortals' involvement in genetically engineering mortals to enhance their inherent ability to meet that test on their own was permissible.

Genetics Departments took on as many grad students and doctoral candidates as they could accommodate and used the newly minted Ph.D.'s to enlarge their departments. Within 200 years, Garrett's department had as many Ph.D.'s as the entire university had employed when the university was founded.

Now, in 3289, the cumulative results of more than 500 years of sustained African genetics research and enhancement—including 260 years done on a crash basis—were absolutely astonishing. Garrett, Brandon and Alice were in a unique position to appreciate the magnitude of the progress African geneticists had made. One measure of that progress was that the time necessary for a genetics grad student to earn a Ph.D. had increased by more than 60%. There was so much more to learn than there had been in prior eras.

Seventy-three years earlier, the Society for African Genetics had declared that Africans had become an entirely new human species, which the group dubbed *homo brilliantus.* The official recognition had been long overdue, in most experts' opinion.

"One of the best parts of being a person of metal is the ability to watch and actually contribute to centuries of progress, rather than merely reading about them," Garrett told Brandon and Alice one afternoon.

"BGO," Brandon muttered, which was short for "blinding glimpse of the obvious."

Why am I so crabby? Brandon wondered.

"Let's go for a walk," he told Alice. "We haven't left this building in two weeks."

It was raining.

"I like the way rain feels on my skin," said Alice. "It reminds me I'm alive."

"I could stand to be reminded of that myself," said Brandon. He sounded dismal.

"Cheer up, we'll do sex later," said Alice.

"Sure thing. So here we are, in the distant future, and what the fuck do we get? Flying taxicabs? Hovering houses? Strap-on helicopters? Nope. Same old same old. Where's the *cool* shit? Nothing is exciting, or surprising or even exotic. Nothing is beautiful or ugly or anywhere in between. Things simply work. They perform their functions with tedious consistency. Everything's so fucking logical. Spontaneity isn't logical, so no one does it. It wouldn't make sense. How did we get this way?"

"A lot of water has flowed under the bridge," said Alice.

"That's exactly my point. I expected that we'd have a totally new world, but we haven't. We're a hell of a lot smarter, but to what end? As far as I can tell, it hasn't made us any happier."

"I'm happy," said Alice. "Lots of things have changed. People live longer, to the point where death has become almost optional. Basic science has a profound and seemingly near-complete understanding of the universe, even if no one outside their circle can understand any of it. The kinds of changes you're talking about are superficial. Strap-on helicopters? No one cares about crap like that. Genetic enhancement has made people deeper intellectually. Medical and other fundamental research appeals to that. Superficial tinkering with technology and consumer products is no longer in vogue."

It was true. Scientists' knowledge of the fundamental laws of the universe had increased to an extent that people as recently as 300 years earlier scarcely could have imagined. A professor of fundamental thought at the University of Nairobi had written a book that endeavored to make this treasure trove accessible to the public, but, as had always been the case, to partake of such knowledge, one needed to be fluent in the advanced mathematical languages in which it was embodied. It was an exercise in futility to attempt to convey that knowledge with words.

"When was the last time you did something just for fun?" Brandon asked Alice.

A few steps later Alice froze and stared straight ahead. She stood that way for a full five minutes. She was thinking.

"I couldn't think of anything that I'd done for fun," she said bleakly after the episode had passed. "But wait, sex is fun." The thought seemed to cheer her back up.

"Yep, there's that," said Brandon. "Why did you just freeze like that?"

"I don't know. My mind slowed down to like a slow crawl."

"That's weird," said Brandon. "I wonder how the math people are coming on the proof. If they can't get it done with the enhancements they've received, maybe it's not solvable. But it has to be."

"I know what we can do," said Alice. "We can visit the church."

"Why?"

"Because there's no logical reason for us to do so. We'll do it on impulse, just for the hell of it. I went in there once. It was strange."

The church was only three hundred yards from where they were standing, so they walked.

"Do you know what monks were in medieval times?" Alice asked.

"No, do you?"

"Sure. Mollie read a book about them. Monks still existed well into the 21st century, but no one saw them. A monk's job was to spend his time praying, hour after hour, day after day, year after year. They lived celibate lives with only enough food, clothing and shelter to keep them alive. The church didn't want them distracted by worldly pleasures."

"That's actually very interesting, Alice. What made you think of them?"

"The mathematicians in the church. They remind me of monks, except monks were all men. Some of the mathematicians are women. Come to think of it, the ancient church had female monks as well, but they called them nuns. Nuns prayed a lot too, but they also did good works like caring for the sick and teaching children."

"Neither of our families was religious," Brandon observed.

"What do you think now?" said Alice. "I can't believe I'm saying this, but that message has me wondering."

"Me too. Whatever it is, whatever its source, it obviously rules out being an outright atheist until we find out."

The church was a narrow glass structure with 25 rows of benches. Brandon and Alice took seats in the rear. Black-clad people filled the first several rows. They were the mathematicians. Each of them held a screen that displayed the Hodge Conjecture over a blank workspace on which some of the mathematicians were writing with styluses. Off to the right, a red clad group chanted to a drumbeat that fundamentalist mathematicians had composed.

The Leader, as he was called, also wore red. He made a sign and the chanting (and the accompanying drumbeat) halted.

"Let us pray," said the Leader. "God, please inspire our mathematicians to prove the truth of the statement you left us. Please guide our geneticists in their work so that one day, we'll be smart enough to warrant your love. Thank you. For the benefit of any visitors who are not familiar with our ritual, this is where we speak as one person and affirm the words God left for us."

The congregation began speaking in unison:

"I believe that animal life is abundant and exists in many places. God exists. God likes me."

"What else do you believe," the Leader asked.

"I believe that if G is a non-singular complex projective manifold, then every Hodge class on G is a linear combination with rational coefficients of the cohomology classes of complex sub-varieties of G."

"May Hodge be with you and inspire your work," said the Leader. The British mathematician W. V. D. Hodge (1903-1975) had become the new religion's patron saint.

• • • • •

"I may be wrong," said Brandon. "Graham only went to church a few times, when his cousins got dressed up and got whatever they called it. But I remember it being a little more emotional."

Chapter 23
A Different World

Ode
West North America
3295

Mrbiti Ajanlekoko had been the broker of the month for the past fifteen months, without even trying. Investors and markets had gone all-out crazy. Even his personal trainer was giving him stock tips. The smart move at a time like this was to pull back, go to cash, wait for the correction and then get back in. It was Investing 101. But markets needed dumb investors to keep them liquid when the smart money fled to the sidelines.

Mrbiti and his wife were 85% in cash and AAA bonds. The balance was in "low beta" long-term plays where it wasn't worth trying to time the market. That's what he did with his money, but it wasn't his job to tell his customers when or how to invest theirs. He was a broker, not a money manager. He took orders.

Mrbiti took for granted the sophisticated trading tools that practically did all his thinking and stock picking for him; and the near-perfect markets in which his trades were executed.

West North American legislators and their staffs had taken advantage of the ability, via the Net, to evaluate the strengths and weaknesses of ancient financial markets. In Mrbiti's opinion, they'd outlawed most of the inefficiencies and abuses that had existed.

But they hadn't fixed everything. West North American investors still paid brokers large commissions for simply transmitting their buy and sell orders to stock exchange computers. In Africa, investors could place orders directly with exchanges, using ages-old software, without paying commissions.

"I'm sick and tired of making all this easy money," Mrbiti had told his wife the previous evening. "It's too easy. I can barely keep up with the order flow. And when the bull market ends and stocks drop, the same people will flood me with sell orders. I can't lose. I get paid on both sides."

Mrbiti shrugged it off. He didn't make the rules.

Much of West North America's social and cultural development following the Great Reform of 2904 had been a reaction against African cultural changes driven by the Africans' relentless genetic enhancement. Practically no one in Africa worked with his or her hands. Few people worked outdoors, or operated equipment.

It was hard to see how Africans could be any more automated than they were. Nearly all the work they did was purely cerebral, which was fine for them, but it was not what most West North Americans wanted for themselves or their children. Many of them felt the comparatively modest automation that they'd inherited from the old regime was excessive. Companies had responded by reducing their reliance on robotic equipment. People had replaced robots in restaurants, bars and stores, except for menial tasks. Customers would avoid buying fine items that were machine-made if an equal or better handmade item was available at a price that was not prohibitive.

Gardening had become a national obsession. Average citizens dressed in colorful, stylish clothing and took similar pride in the way their towns and cities were dressed.

A popular West North American writer, Goma Tinibu, described it this way in a viral post titled *Just Smart Enough*:

"An ancient writer told a tale of beings whose heads kept growing larger at the expense of their bodies, to the point where only their heads remained. I'm reminded of that story when I think of our African cousins. They've gone too far. They're all head.

"West North Americans dodged a bullet. We seem to have grown our heads, so to speak, by just the right amount. The genetic enhancements that our ancestors' embryos received from the Africans immediately following the Great Reform made our people smarter across the board, but there were no further genetic enhancements after that, thank God. In retrospect, it appears that the enhancements our people received made us just smart enough. Some people were still smarter than others; but suddenly, our entire population was smart to at least a certain degree, and everything changed. The quality of the public officials we elected improved by orders of magnitude. Economic output soared and scientific progress accelerated. The incentive to lie to people or try to cheat them dropped because people were much less apt to be duped. Finally, their enhanced intelligence enabled our people to make better choices; to create more and better things; and to derive more pleasure, and more joy, from their lives and from each other. We aren't all head. We've been most fortunate."

After the markets had closed, Mrbiti dictated a few notes, wished his colleagues a good evening and left the office to meet his wife at *La Fleur*, a popular high-end restaurant they'd been meaning to try.

Like anyone who had lived for a long time in one place, Mrbiti would not have paid particular attention, as he walked, to details that would have caught a visitor's eye. Each office building had its own particular style. A visitor from Africa would have found them whimsical, chaotic — silly, even. West North American architects were not only allowed to express their creativity and originality; they were expected to do so. Yet, for all that, the buildings functioned as well as those in Africa.

An African visitor likely would have found himself mildly offended by the sloppy variety and gaudy colors of the clothing these people wore, and the way high-spirited West North Americans laughed out loud and called out to each other.

Flowers were literally everywhere, in large pots on the sidewalks and in the ubiquitous window boxes. Our African visitor might never have seen a flower of any kind, at this point in history, but a traveler from the distant past would have been struck by their large size, their seemingly infinite variety and the intoxicating scents that emanated from them.

West North American researchers hadn't tampered with human genes, but they'd manipulated plant and animal genes for centuries. Foreign visitors wouldn't recognize the dog with three nostrils that someone was walking. They might not even realize that it was a dog. If they ventured out to a rural setting, they'd witness herds of strange animals, and fields and orchards where unrecognizable vegetables and fruits were being grown that had no African counterparts; or things that had been altered so much that a visitor wouldn't recognize them, like curly red bananas or cucumber-shaped purple apples.

Mrbiti entered the restaurant and found his wife, Tamika, waiting for him in a booth. She looked fabulous. He hurried over to join her, barely conscious of the noise and the delicious aromas that filled the room. He kissed his wife and took his seat.

"How was your day?" said Tamika.

"Very profitable. How was yours?""

"The usual."

Tamika was a partner in a mid-sized accounting firm.

Mrbiti noticed that his wife was wearing a fur coat of a type he didn't recognize.

"That must be the new *zant* you ordered," he said. "It suits you perfectly."

"Thanks. It's nice and warm in here, but I can't bring myself to take it off."

The soft, luxuriant fur was sky blue with gray stripes similar to those of a zebra.

"Mrbiti, I'm sorry about my mother," said Tamika. "What she said to you last night was unforgiveable. Daddy was appalled."

The previous evening, they'd hosted a lavish birthday party for Tamika's Uncle Nelson. Nelson's wife Ada was the sister of Maya, Tamika's mother. The sisters were descendants of a branch of the old West North American aristocracy. Their germline had been cleansed of the problematic edits thanks to long-term follow-up by the African geneticists. Ada thought it was nonsense, but Maya had practically built her entire personal identity on her aristocratic heritage; and she had a habit of lording her ancestry over her brother-in-law Nelson, who, though descended from commoners, was a distinguished physician and author. After the dinner plates and the empty wine bottles had been cleared, Maya provoked him, and they got into it. Maya was particularly nasty that evening.

"Someone has to intervene," Mrbiti had told Tamika, and he'd done so, stepping between the combatants and urging them to stop arguing about their ancestors. "After this many generations, who cares?" He told Maya. "It doesn't matter."

Maya called her son-in-law a fucking worker bee and told him to sit down and shut up.

"That's enough!" her husband told her. He apologized for his wife and led her out the door.

"Forget it," Mrbiti told his wife as they scanned their dinner menus. "I feel sorry for her. Let's try to figure out what we want to order."

As mentioned, West North American scientists had genetically altered many animals and plants to the point where they bore little if any resemblance to their genetic forebears. The scientists had adopted the convention of giving the new species meaningless computer-generated names, like *zant,* which were italicized when written. In recent decades, they'd even found ways to genetically engineer animals to make their meat taste better to humans

In West North America, traditional restaurant *accoutrements* — like menus, salt and pepper, silverware, water glasses and napkins (made of cloth in a high-end restaurant like *La Fleur*) — remained in use even in relatively modest establishments. Restaurant employees still took customers' food and drink orders and brought those items to their tables when they were ready. At *La Fleur,* a diner might have up to four separate plates brought out to them in the course of a meal.

A server approached the Ajanlekokos.

"Good evening. Have you dined with us before?"

"We have not," said Mrbiti.

"Well then, welcome. Before I describe the evening's specials, I'll just mention that all of our menu items and specials — except for cheeses and sweets, of course — can be ordered as a first, second or main course. Main courses will be served with *zlbkxaur,* baked or fried, and your choice of side dish.

The server clasped his hands together and leaned forward.

"Now for our specials. Our mammalian special tonight is baked loin of *kzrdtzl* with sautéed *nngwaass* in a pink *vrtzxut* sauce. Our avian special is roasted *vrzddmi.* Finally, our fish special is a whole *grzztzt* with the head and tail removed, skinned, boned and served with a grey sauce."

"Yum," said Tamika.

The server placed the wine list on the table next to Mrbiti. "I'll give you a few minutes to decide."

"Let's see what we have here," said Mrbiti, opening the wine list's leather binder. "Very nice. Do you have an idea of what you might want to order, my dear?"

"Oh Mrbiti, I can't decide between the *jnbf[]xk* and the *kzrdtzl.*"

"You always order *kzrdtzl.* Try something new. Let's have ourselves some fun."

"You're right. I'll try the *jnbf[]xk.*"

"Me too," said Mrbiti. "Do we want purple or green wine?"

"Green, I think," said Tamika.

"Let's celebrate."

"Celebrate what?"

"I'll think of something. Meanwhile, I've found a special wine, made from green *jlhhtfl*. I've never tried it but I've heard it's amazing."

"Are you blowing our whole entertainment budget in one night?"

"After the day I had today, it's rounding error."

The server stopped by and took their wine and food orders: a bottle of the expensive green wine and main courses of *jnbf[]xk*, preceded by a plate of pickled *pipip* to share.

The wine arrived and was poured, and Mrbiti raised his glass—another ancient tradition that had survived.

"To life," said Mrbiti.

"To life."

"Not bad," said Mrbbiti.

"Mrbiti, did you know that over 75% of the herbs cooks use today did not even exist five hundred years ago."

"I didn't know it was that high, but it stands to reason. No wonder everything tastes so good."

• • • • •

When they arrived home, they found Elisha, their daughter, seated in a chair in the main room of their home staring at her device's blank screen. She was 16.

"Sweetie, you look like you're frozen," said Tamika.

"You okay?" asked Mrbiiti.

"I'm stuck," Elisha said gloomily.

"What are you stuck on?" her father asked.

"I'm supposed to write an essay on what I see when I look at the world."

Tamika and Mrbiti sat down across from their daughter.

"Okay, let's start by seeing if we can figure out what your teacher is looking for," said Tamika. "She obviously wants you to do more than just list a bunch of things you see—like a blue flowerpot, a green rug or whatever. She's looking for something more abstract. Like, 'I see beauty.' Don't use that, it's trite. It's just an example. See if you can come up with something a little more original."

"Life?"

"Better," said Tamika.

"Light?"

"What does everything you see in the world have in common?"

"God made it," said Elisha.

"Good answer," said Mrbiti. The Christian, Muslim and Jewish values and traditions that Africans had carried with them to North America were still very much alive.

"So what do you see when you look out at the world?" Mrbiti asked her.

"God?"

"That could work," said Tamika, "if you can explain it. What is it about the world that makes you see God when you look out at it? Give it a shot and show us what you come up with."

"We'll be in the media room," said Mrbiti.

• • • • •

After about an hour, Elisha entered the media room and showed her parents her work. Mrbiti turned off the television.

"Read it to us," said Mrbiti.

"When I look out at the world," Elisha read, "I see things that did not come to be by chance. Life did not just happen. I see the timeless beauty of the objects around me, animate and inanimate. I see fields of pink, blue and purple flowers, snowy mountains and forests teeming with life. In the sky at night, we gaze with awe at the glory of the vast, infinite universe of which we're part. God's handiwork is everywhere. God is everywhere. So, wherever I look, I see God."

"Great job, Kiddo!" said Mrbiti.

"I agree with your father," said Tamika.

• • • • •

Mrbiti and Tamika were upstairs getting ready for bed.

"You asked me at dinner what we were celebrating," said Mrbiti, "and I promised to get back to you. Well, we just witnessed it. I am so proud of her."

"Let's celebrate some more."

• • • • •

Graceful Beauty Racecourse
Ode, West North America
Following afternoon

The next day, Saturday, was family outing day, and Tamika had made them lunch reservations at a small, casual place that that served traditional African dishes. After that, they were off to the races.

Old-fashioned biometric equipment which remained in use because it still served its purpose confirmed that the Ajanlekokos had purchased their tickets and admitted them. A program for the afternoon's races appeared on their devices.

"Elisha, have you picked your *Grrdtzes* yet?" Mrbiti asked. "Mom and I have."

Like most patrons, whenever they visited the racecourse, the Ajanlekokos placed small bets on each race to make things more interesting. *Grrdtz* racing had become quite a craze in Ode and Furaha, and had spread to several smaller West North American cities. Elisha handed her device to her father. The screen showed the names of twelve *Grrdtzes,* one for each race.

Grrdtzes were speedy blue-haired six-legged mammals whose genome included genes from wolves and mountain lions. An urban legend held that the six legs had come from insect DNA, but almost no one believed that.

The jockeys' saddles were placed between the first and second pairs of legs. The jockeys had to be short, because the back of the average *grrdtz*, where the *saddle* would sit, was barely four feet off the ground. If the jockeys' legs were too long, their feet would drag on the ground when the *grrdtz* began running and slow it down.

Mrbiti, Tamika and Elisha had arrived at their race picks by running the statistics for the day's field through one of the popular apps that enterprising developers had come up with. The apps were so good that, on average, more than 48% of their picks were winners. To survive, the tracks had needed to adjust payouts so the total amount bet on a race would exceed the payout on that race by a sufficient margin to keep the track in business.

Enthusiastic fans were always on the lookout for an extra edge that would put them into the black. Most would never find it, but they had fun trying. People sometimes got carried away and bet more than was prudent, but that was rare. As far as was generally known, no one had placed their family's finances in jeopardy by reckless betting at the track. Betting on racing was entertainment and was budgeted as such.

The first race began, and the fans started cheering.

Grrdtzes had their own unique style of running. Their six legs moved so fast they practically blurred when you watched them, Mrbiti thought. Meanwhile, their torsos undulated smoothly from side to side the way a fish's torso did to cause its tail to propel its body. This was functional in a fish, but Mrbiti could not imagine what purpose this feature could serve in a *grrdtz*. He doubted it ever would have evolved naturally.

By the time the last race had ended, the Ajanlekokos had screamed themselves hoarse. Elisha had winning bets in six of the twelve races, and Mrbiti and Marika, who'd used a different app, had winning bets in five.

"We don't do this often enough," said Mrbiti.

• • • • •

The following Tuesday, in Elisha's writing class, their teacher sent to the students' devices their grades on the essays they'd sent to her on Monday or over the weekend. The teacher asked Elisha and two other students to read theirs aloud.

The first reader was a boy named Omari. He was smart, wickedly good looking and funny, Elisha thought. He was also a top-flight and fiercely competitive athlete, so he was in great shape. Elisha had a serious crush on this boy.

Omari made a face at Elisha and began reading.

"When I look out at the world, I see the outside layer of things: of people, of plants, of animals and of things that are not alive and never were. The amount of information that my mind must process is almost overwhelming, and I'm only seeing outside layers. It's probably a good thing I can't see all the layers at once. It would probably be too much. The part I can see now is enough."

Next up was a girl named Amare. Elisha would have admitted that this girl was almost as pretty as she was, but she hated the little bitch. She wouldn't leave Omari alone. Well, she didn't actually hate the other girl. She just wished her parents would move to another city and take Amare with them.

Amare flashed Omari a big toothy smile and began reading:

"When I look at the world, I see an optical illusion of balance, tranquility and order that masks the chaos that I know exists at the subatomic level. I found this somewhat unsettling when it was first brought to my attention in science classes, but I've adjusted. Everything in our world, natural or human-made, can be broken down into components—molecules and atoms—that have no inherent significance in themselves. So what? What matters is what's formed when they all come together. When I look at the world that way, it's pretty cool."

Elisha read her essay next, and Omari grinned and signaled his approval.

So there, Elisha thought.

Chapter 24
Mind-Travel

William Weinberg Public Rose Garden
Nairobi
3367

Brandon's mind returned from its travels and he remembered where he was, and that Alice was sitting next to him on the bench. Her body was. Her mind was still out there somewhere. It was amazing.

He looked around and noticed that all the benches were occupied. There were three other people of metal. The rest were biological. Brandon let his eyes move from one person to the next.

They're doing it too, he thought.

Everyone on the benches, biologicals and people of metal alike, wore more or less the same faint smile and million-yard stare. Mind travel was rather a blast, but it was impossible to predict when one would fall into the mental state that made it possible. However, Brandon had noticed that fifteen minutes before entering that state, he'd see a flash of light. If he was inclined at that moment to mind-travel, he knew to look for a chair or bench to sit on, or a tree to sit under. If he was not so inclined, he ignored the flash of light and continued with whatever he was doing.

A West North American tourist family, all with big smiles on their faces — mom, dad and two small boys — walked past them in their gaudy garb, speaking their strange language in loud voices and hooting and hollering like animals. They headed straight for the roses and disappeared into them. Brandon could hear them oohing and exclaiming. *It's the smell,* Brandon thought. *It drives them nuts.*

I wish I could make videos of the places my mind takes me to, Brandon thought.

The next thing he knew he was back out there and there was a new color—a color that didn't exist, in the spectrum or otherwise. It kept changing its shape. Its taste and smell kept changing. It was odd, because as a Machine he could neither taste nor smell. Suddenly he'd understood, and it stopped. He was back.

"Alice. Alice."

She came back smiling

"Hello."

She kissed his cheek. "I was having sex with your mind."

It was a joke.

"That was you?"

They laughed. Brandon struggled to describe where he'd been and what he'd seen. "There was this new color, and its taste and smell—remember those?—they kept changing, and I understood. It was perfect."

"What was perfect?"

"Everything," said Brandon. "It was like I was watching a video with awesome special effects, but with features and things that had been added just for me. Maybe I'm reading too much into it. What was yours like just now?"

"More generic," said Alice, "but the feeling I got was that my own mind was creating the whole thing."

They watched a group of biologicals rise in unison from their bench and walk off.

"It's lunchtime," said Alice..."

"That's it!" Brandon exclaimed. "I understand."

"Understand what?"

"What I understood when I was out there but couldn't find words for when I got back. I tasted and smelled things. Never in all the years we've had these bodies did I ever once taste or smell anything in a dream. This wasn't a dream. It was tangible. Then, while I was still out there, I understood. If you and I could figure out how to make our bodies and minds experience sex, why couldn't we do the same with smell and taste?"

"That's an amazing idea," said Alice.

If a foreign visitor had been present who could understand their language, he would have found their flat metallic voices inconsistent with the enthusiastic content of their literal words.

"Mollie read a novel where artificially intelligent robots enslaved humans," Alice continued. "They saw how much the humans enjoyed their food and were jealous. So they built themselves apparatus and sensors that enabled them to eat, taste and enjoy human food just like their slaves. They could eat for hours at a time, as much as they wanted. When the receptacle in their midsection was full, all they had to do was take it out and empty it."

"I remember that book," said Brandon. "It seemed far-fetched at the time, but it doesn't today."

"It sure doesn't," said Alice. "Let's go tell Harry."

They stepped on one of the slow-moving robotic passenger carts that circulated through the streets of Nairobi like blood cells through a biological body and took seats. Only a few of the twenty-six seats were occupied. When they reached their stop, Alice was frozen. Brandon pulled her gently from her seat and off the cart.

For the next several minutes, Alice stood frozen in place on the sidewalk in front of the genetics building. The pedestrians moving past them did not seem to notice her condition, beyond making slight course adjustments to avoid bumping into her. Looking around, Brandon noticed several other people, biological and metallic, who were in the same state. It was happening more and more often. Everyone he knew was experiencing it, as was he. What did it mean?

"I call it intellectual overload," Harry had opined. "Your mind can only run so long at warp speed. Eventually it has to slow down and let the ideas catch up."

Brandon waited patiently until Alice came back and explained what she'd been thinking.

"We and the biologicals seem to be experiencing similar mental states. Like the freezing, which is involuntary. The biologicals in the park looked like they'd also gone to some wonderful place, like ours, whatever you want to call it."

"Nirvana," Brandon suggested.

"Yes. My premise is that the propensity to enter these mental states has something to do with the enhancements we've given biologicals and transferred to ourselves. Depending on what biologicals experience in their nirvana compared to ours, the same underlying causes might be responsible for both states of mind."

"Could be," said Brandon. "We have implants that mimic the electrical variants that correlate most strongly with the enhancements that the biologicals have received. But other, less-correlated variants that we didn't incorporate could also impact the kind of the nirvana they experience."

"Factors like hormones and enzymes could also affect biological brain activity when they're in nirvana," said Alice.

"So, we'll get biological undergrads to fill out a questionnaire concerning what they experience when they're in this mental state," said Brandon. "We'll even pay them for doing it. We can also send the questionnaire to people of metal on the university faculty."

When they passed Harry's office, he was out there big time, so they didn't disturb him.

"We'll tell him about the food when he gets back," said Brandon.

When Harry's mind returned some twenty minutes later, Brandon asked him a question that made him burst out laughing.

"Harry, do you remember what a T-bone steak tasted like?"

"What?" Harry sputtered when he'd stopped laughing.

"I asked you this for a reason," said Brandon. "Alice and I think we might be able to create features and sensors that would allow us to experience the pleasures associated with food. To smell it, taste it, chew it and swallow it."

"For what conceivable purpose?" said Harry. "We don't *need* food."

Machines hadn't "needed" sex, either, when it wasn't available to them, Alice thought.

"For the pleasure's own sake," said Brandon. "Imagine fluffy mashed potatoes next to your T-bone, covered with an exquisitely seasoned brown sauce, or 'gravy' as we used to call it. See if you can remember the aroma."

Garrett considered this.

"I can't call to mind a specific recollection of what it was like. I liked food. People paid big bucks for food prepared by the best chefs. Dinners at those places were the coin of the realm in the business world, whether they were wooing a client or celebrating a big merger deal. Do you really think you can do this?"

"We won't know until we've done it, but it's worth a shot."

"I'll go do the questionnaire," said Alice.

The questionnaire was part of an email that Alice sent to the biological and metallic volunteers. The respondents filled in the blanks on the form by dictating to their devices, which entered the answers in the appropriate spaces on the questionnaire. When they were finished, they sent the completed form to Alice as a reply to her email.

• • • • •

Alice emailed her geneticist colleagues a summary of the survey results and samples of the subjects' responses.

4.12.3367
To: Genetics Faculty
From: Alice Delaney

The results of the recent mind-state survey show that the two new mental states that biological and metallic minds have exhibited in recent months are substantially the same for both groups. The first mental state is an involuntary "frozen" feeling in which the mind's speed slows to a comparative crawl. The second is "mind travel," in which the mind takes its owner on "trips."

The fact that both biological and metallic minds are experiencing the same things rules out the possibility (a) that electrical variants in biological brains, that were not incorporated into the e-brain implants that transferred genetic enhancements to people of metal, materially affect the nature of the biological experience, or (b) that the nature of the mental state in biological minds is affected materially by hormones, enzymes or other chemical substances. It follows, therefore, that the electrical variants that we copied from enhanced biological minds and incorporated into e-brain implants account for the totality of these experiences in both biologicals and people of metal, to the exclusion of other electrical variants that were not incorporated into the implants, or extraneous chemical effects.

The Neuroscience Department has begun a study of these phenomena to determine whether other kinds of temporarily altered mental states are likely to appear as we continue to enhance the human genome.

Breakdown of respondents: biological: 154; metallic: 43.

Survey questions and sample responses:

Do you experience involuntary "frozen" episodes in which your body becomes motionless and your mind slows down to a very slow rate of thinking?

All respondents, biological and metallic, answered "yes."

If your answer to the previous question was yes, describe the experience.

Sample biological responses:

"My mind feels like it's taking a rest. I can still think, but at a much slower speed."

"It's like my mind decides it needs to stop and catch its breath, and suddenly it feels like my thoughts have gone from flying at light speed to crawling through mud. It's odd, but it's not unpleasant."

Sample metallic responses:

"My mind halts abruptly, then resumes but moves in slow motion for a while, then goes back to normal. I was startled the first time it happened, but I got used to it."

"My thoughts are the way a recorded voice would sound played at $1/1000^{th}$ of its normal speed."

Does your mind ever take you to unusual "places," and if so, does this happen voluntarily, involuntarily or sometimes one and sometimes the other? (As used here, "voluntarily" means you can put yourself into this state at least sometimes when you want to, but not necessarily whenever you so desire.)

All respondents answered "yes" and said it was voluntary.

If your answer to the preceding question was positive, describe what you experience while in that mental state.

Sample biological responses:

"It's the most wonderful place ever. It feels totally real, much more so than an ordinary dream. I can feel myself touching things. The colors and shapes constantly change in unexpected ways that I can't even begin to describe, but which somehow make perfect sense after they've happened. It's almost as though someone is laying out a proposition for my consideration in a pleasant conversation. I feel comforted somehow. Everything is in logical order and makes perfect sense."

"Colors, shapes and waves of objects move around in patterns that I can tell after a short time are not random. They're organized and systematic, and at the same time, insanely beautiful. Sometimes the different colors have flavors. I feel like my mind's being massaged."

"One time I was able to reach this state during sex and it was fantastic. I wish I knew how to describe it."

Sample metallic responses:

"I can't decide if it's beauty as pure logic or vice versa. Logic is beautiful and beauty is logical. I touch things. Colors have odor and flavor, which is obviously quite remarkable. I wish I could get myself there more often."

"Your mind is carried along in this completely rational series of shapes, colors, patterns and smells. Not only do I see these beautiful things. I understand them. I feel myself becoming wiser."

"It's better than sex, and even better *with* sex."

If you described a mental state in response to the previous question, can you enter that state at-will, whenever you so desire.

All the respondents answered "no."

• • • • •

Alice wondered idly what would happen if people could learn to enter the mind-travel state at-will. She remembered reading that meditating monks could deliberately put themselves into a meditative state. Researchers had measured increased gamma wave activity on their EEG machines when monks with many years of meditation practice willed themselves into that state.

She was seated at the workstation in their small apartment. Brandon was seated nearby, playing a game on his device. Alice had planned to start work on their "eating" project, but she put that on hold. This could be huge.

When she checked, Alice found that the studies of monks had been done the traditional way, in laboratory sessions with the monks connected to measuring devices—which, as a practical matter, limited the duration of the recorded brain activity. She looked to see whether a study of monks' brain activity had been made using the "brain hats" that a clever Cal Tech engineer had invented in the 2160s to facilitate brain research, but she did not get any hits.

Alice exchanged messages with Elle McKenzie, who confirmed that neuroscientists at the University of Nairobi did occasionally use "brain hats," albeit a much-improved version, when they wanted to record a subject's brain activity on their scorewriters over an extended period. The hats were lightweight and comfortable enough, Elle explained, that they had no trouble getting subjects to wear them for 24-hour periods or even longer. The hats functioned remotely the same as the headsets that were wired to the machines in the laboratory.

Alice interrupted Brandon's game and explained her idea.

"So we'll have two projects on our plate," said Alice. "The eating project is the main one and the most difficult. The other one will be easy. We'll have biological and metallic subjects wear brain hats for up to 24 hours until they enter the mind travel state. We can have the engineers make modified brain hats for measuring e-brain activity."

"Nice work, Sweetie," said Brandon. He gave her a big hug and lifted her off the floor. "You're a genius."

"If the mind-travel state is like the monks' meditative state," Alice continued, "we'll see the electrical activity that was generalized as 'high gamma wave' when it was measured by the old EEG machines. But it might be something altogether different."

Less than a month later, the results were in, and they were clear and consistent. Electrical engineers from Elle McKenzie's group volunteered to program stimulus hats for biologicals and people of metal to stimulate the incremental brain activity that immediately preceded the mind travel state. All the user would have to do was speak a command into a small microphone that hung from a thin wire on the right side of the cap.

After the hats had been thoroughly tested, Alice and Brandon arranged for the company that supplied the neuroscience department's stimulus hats to mass-produce theirs, and they engaged another firm to market them.

The white stimulus hats were an instant success. People already knew that they loved the mind-travel state. The hats allowed them to enter that state whenever they wanted. This made a huge difference, users reported. Instead of entering that state at random moments, the hats enabled people to make purposeful rather than purely recreational "mind-trips." For example, a business owner struggling with a difficult business decision could enter that state with the matter fresh in his mind. Users who were interviewed reported that often, they would return from their trip with a much deeper understanding of whatever had been on their minds. "Fundamental" was a word used by many of the mind-travelers who were interviewed.

"I think part of what makes this so effective," said one user, a psychotherapist, "is the absence of words. Words aren't powerful enough. Mind-travel speaks to us in shapes, lines, colors and smells. Somehow, a deeper layer of our mind is able to use those means to enable our everyday minds to gain a more fundamental understanding of whatever we were trying to figure out. It increases effective cognitive power well beyond that of the same mind during ordinary consciousness."

A colleague asked Alice if she was concerned that mind-travel could be addictive now that people had the ability to enter that mental state at will.

"I don't see that happening," said Alice, "Every trip is an episode. It takes your mind from A to B to C, and so forth until it's done, and when it's over, you may find that you've realized something, or solved a problem that's been bothering you. You'll want to think about what you've learned. You're an active participant, not a passive recipient, like an alcoholic or drug user."

William Weinberg Public Rose Garden
Nairobi
3369

The West North American family that Brandon had observed in the rose garden two years earlier had again chosen Nairobi for their annual vacation. Kellan Emem and his wife Uma were plant geneticists. During their previous visit, they'd obsessed over the marvelous scents that emanated from the roses. The roses grown in West North America were scentless, which was odd considering the enormous number of other West North American floral species that did have scent.

"Either these are what our roses used to be like and our predecessors intentionally or inadvertently edited out the scent, or some genius here figured out how to add it," said Kellan.

"Probably the former," said Uma.

This time, they'd resolved to bring back DNA from some of these roses so they could attempt to impart scents to the roses they bred and sold back home.

Uma looked around to make sure they weren't being observed and began snipping buds from several of the plants and dropping them into a pouch. She knew that, technically, what she was doing was stealing, but it wasn't like she was stealing the buds from a competitor. Their rose-breeding operation was half a world away from Nairobi. When the pouch was safely stowed in Uma's shoulder bag, the couple collected their boys, who were running around a few rows over, and continued their garden tour.

"I feel as if I can taste these scents," Kellan said, taking a deep breath.

Uma also breathed deeply. "If we can produce scented roses, we'll make a fortune. I'd better snip some more buds."

They continued for another forty-five minutes until Uma had filled a second pouch with buds.

"It's lunch time," she announced.

"I'm starving," said Kellan.

Increasing numbers of West North Americans were choosing Nairobi for their annual vacations. It was human nature to want to spend one's vacation someplace exotic that was as different as possible from one's home.

"I don't think they realize how funny they are," said Uma as they walked around the fountain past benches crowded with locals, all of them wearing white hats, smiling and staring into space. "They probably think *we're* funny."

'They're a hoot," said Kellan. "They're like computers without the personality."

The family boarded a passing passenger cart, rode it for a while and transferred to a second which they rode until it stopped near a *Tau's*. It was one of a group of seven Nairobi restaurants that served food imported from West North America and prepared using West North American recipes. The owners, a husband and wife, were locals, but they'd done an excellent job of outfitting and decorating their restaurants with furniture and other objects, including paintings and carvings, that they'd gotten during their regular visits to West North America. This *Tau's*, their original, was their flagship.

The Emems entered the establishment for the second time that day and the eleventh time in the three-plus days they'd spent in Nairobi.

"Good afternoon, and welcome back, it's been several hours," said one of the owners, the husband, in perfect, accent-free West North American. He and his wife had spent several months in that country and had made a point of mastering its language.

As plant geneticists, the Emems appreciated much of what African geneticists had accomplished. Everyone knew how smart Africans were. They were nice enough people, too, and it was good for the boys to experience a place so completely different. On the other hand, they were happy not to have to survive on their tasteless mush.

While they were waiting for their food, Kallan and Uma compared notes with a West North American couple seated with their children at an adjacent table.

The lunchtime crowd of West North American tourists was arriving in force. The only locals present were the owners, cooks, a bartender and servers.

Chapter 25
Gluttony

Tau's Restaurant
Nairobi
3372

The owners, Haji and Oni Katlego, were startled when they saw Harry, Alice and Brandon enter their restaurant.

"Good evening," said the husband in Swahili. "Is there a problem?"

"Not if you serve us dinner," Harry said pleasantly.

"It smells good," said Alice.

The owners looked at each other. *Dinner?*

"Seriously, you'll see," said Garrett.

"Very well, please come with me," said the husband.

"Yum," said Harry after they were seated. He fluffed out his napkin and tucked it into his shirt. "It was a good idea to come here, Brandon. We can't very well test our new capabilities on food that has no flavor."

Their presence had created a bit of a stir among the West North American tourists. A couple and their two children tried to speak with the Machines in West North American. The metallic Nairobians smiled in response and gave them the "thumbs up" sign, and the tourists returned to their tables, seemingly pleased with their encounter.

"I'm certain they have Machines over there as well," said Alice, "but obviously not in restaurants. They'll go nuts when they see what happens next."

Before leaving their lab, they'd practiced chewing on non-food objects. Alice had practiced on a belt and Harry and Brandon had each chewed on one of their shoes. This would be the real thing.

Brandon picked up his knife and fork. "I vaguely remember doing this."

"Like riding a bike," said Harry.

"May I take your order," their server asked them in Swahili. He was a local.

"We're looking for meat." Harry pointed toward the menu, which was written in West North American. "Which of these is a meat dish?"

The server translated the West North American descriptions of several meat dishes and took the group's orders.

"Bring us three soups first," said Brandon.

"Coming right up. Drinks?"

"No thanks," said Garrett. "We're recovering alcoholics."

The soup arrived. It was some kind of bean soup.

"I can taste it!" Alice said. "It's good. We've done it."

"I'd forgotten how powerful flavors could be," said Brandon, grinning. "It's been a long time."

Harry and Brandon liked their soups as well. Tourists neglected their food and watched.

Soon thereafter the meat arrived. The geneticists found that if they cut it into small enough pieces, they had no trouble chewing it and swallowing. They could taste the exquisite flavors: the herbs and spices and the elemental meat flavor. As it happened, they were eating goat curry accompanied by jasmine rice with shaved hazelnuts and yellow raisins.

"I remember these flavors like it was only three hundred years ago," said Garrett.

The geneticists fell silent. When they'd finished their first portions, they happily ordered another serving of meat, and another after that, from time to time emptying their receptacles in the restrooms as necessary. They weren't in the least embarrassed; they were making up for lost time.

"There was a famous glutton who lived in the late 19th century and early 20th," said Alice. "Diamond Jim Brady, a famous millionaire. I remember Mollie reading about him. Here's how a 21st century website described this guy."

Alice read from her device:

"Brady ate enough food for ten people whenever he sat down at the table. The owner of Rector's, his favorite eatery, said he was the equivalent of 25 of his regular customers. Brady's appetite was as enormous as his wealth. Breakfast was huge quantities of eggs, potatoes, breads, pancakes and steak, with a gallon or two of freshly squeezed orange juice. Around ten in the morning he'd have a snack consisting of several dozen clams or premium oysters. Lunch included shellfish, deviled eggs, lobsters and a giant cut of beef, with pies and more orange juice for dessert. Afternoon tea was served with another platter of seafood and bottles of lemon soda. Those were the preliminaries. Dinner was the main event, which Brady normally ate at Rectors. It included dozens of oysters, crabs, a large terrine of turtle soup, fish filets, steak and a large plate of pastries and a pound or two of chocolates for dessert

"When he died," Alice concluded, "the doctors discovered that his stomach was six times the size of an average human stomach."

"Unfortunately, Alice, not all of the delicacies that your Diamond Jim favored are available to us at the moment," said Garrett. "We'll have to make do."

"Who would have ever guessed that gluttony would ever be an option for people like us?" said Alice.

One of the West North Americans seated nearby — an elderly biological gentleman — was perplexed. "They're obviously enjoying themselves," he told his wife, "but you'd never know it from their voices. They're totally devoid of emotion. Our people of metal back home don't sound like this. For that matter, the voices of the owners and our server are also emotionless. What do you make of this?"

• • • • •

Nairobi
Next day

There were hundreds of thousands of people of metal spread across the three African zones, and nearly all of them would want the new eating upgrade. West North America's comparatively small metallic population would also want them.

The prototypes had been built for Brandon and Alice by POM, Inc., the company they'd licensed to make and sell the ersatz genitals, and which still made repairs and sold replacement parts and upgrades. There was no demand for new genitalia, because the population of Machines had remained constant since the manufacture of additional Machines had been outlawed in the 22nd Century. The company had long since reprogrammed its main assembly lines to manufacture heating and refrigeration equipment. Brandon and Alice hoped the company would agree to mass-produce and distribute the new eating upgrade under license. The same family still owned it.

"They're good people," said Alice.

Headquarters
POM, Inc.
Nairobi

Hamedi Akiziwe, the CEO of POM, Inc. and a descendant of the founder on his mother's side, received Alice and Brandon in his spacious corner office high above Weinberg's roses.

"Goma said you have good news," said Akiziwe.

"Yes, we do," said Alice. "We tested them out last night. They worked perfectly!"

"We had a veritable orgy of eating," said Brandon.

"We ate for two solid hours," said Alice.

"Oh, my," said Akiziwe.

Akiziwe's response reminded Alice that, as a biological African, Hamedi, like countless generations of Africans before him, was genetically incapable of tasting the flavors in food or drink, or registering their aromas.

"Well, that's great news," said Akiziwe.

"How soon can you start cranking them out?" Alice asked. "The demand will be enormous. Every metallic in the world will want one."

"Well," said Akiziwe, yawning, "we'll have to build a new plant. We're running at capacity in our existing facilities. I'll talk to my CFO about obtaining financing."

"Hamedi, why not go public?" said Alice. "With news of your new product line, the value of POM will explode. You could retire and go sit under a palm tree somewhere."

Alice had judged, correctly, that the current generation was a far cry from that of their beloved founder. As was almost always the case, based on what Alice had observed over the centuries, the *oomph* of fabulously successful men and women seemed to dissipate rather quickly as their wealth passed effortlessly from one generation to the next. Why would it not? Succeeding generations would have no need to accomplish much of anything, as long as the fortune remained intact. The cliché *Time is the great equalizer* was a cliché for a reason.

Akiziwe was more than competent, nonetheless. His astronomical IQ allowed him to do his job perfectly almost without effort. Alice often wondered if that fact was part of the problem with the current generation of Africans. They weren't challenged.

As she'd expected, Akiziwe jumped on the idea of taking his company public and retiring.

"Quite frankly, I find the whole business rather boring," he admitted. "I'll call my lawyer and get the ball rolling."

The stock sold out in minutes on the World Stock Exchange, at a huge premium, and Hamedi Akiziwe immediately retired to a lavish mansion overlooking Mombasa's gorgeous white-sand beaches.

Within a year, POM's new factories were in full swing turning out the new eating upgrades. It would take years for the factories to produce enough upgrades for the hundreds of thousands of African, West North American and colonial people of metal who wanted them. By that time, Alice and Brandon's nest egg would have nearly doubled.

Headquarters
Tau's Pan Africa
Nairobi
3392

The Katlegos had opened *Tau's* restaurants in major cities across the continent to serve "hungry" people of metal. They were expanding as fast as the available food supplies allowed.

"I've just learned that a West North American group is seeking investors in a company that plans to compete in our space," Haji told his wife.

"We must stop them," said Oni.

"How?"

"Use your brain, silly," said Oni. "Pack your bag. We need to go meet with our West North American friends."

Headquarters
Consolidated Foods, Inc.
Ode, West North America
Three days later

Paidi Akinjide, the Chairman and CEO of Consolidated Foods, greeted his customers in the colorful and wildly decorated reception area on the top floor of his company's headquarters.

As was customary in West North America, Paidi gave Haji and Oni bear hugs, which they bore with good grace.

"I can't wait to hear what you've come to discuss," said Akinjide.

They're nice enough people, for Africans, Akinjide thought as he led them into his office.

The first time he'd seen an office like this, Haji had found the busy wall coverings and the profusion of paintings and other art objects and knick-knacks disconcerting. He smiled to himself.

It's a matter of what one is used to, he thought.

As they'd agreed earlier, Oni went first.

"As you know, Paidi, we're expanding very quickly. The reason we're here is to make long-term arrangements to secure the supplies of West North American food, beverages, seasonings and so forth that we'll need to fuel our expansion."

"I see. Keep going. I'm interested."

"There's another contingency that we think should concern both our companies," said Haji. "We understand there's a group right here in your back yard that's looking for investors to back them in opening restaurants in Africa to compete with us. We understand they own and operate restaurants here and deal directly with food producers and processors."

"Do you have a name?" Akinjide asked.

"Superior something or other," said Haji.

"I know who they are."

"Our obvious concern is they'd be competing with you and us for West North American food supplies that in the short run will be finite in amount."

"Do you have a suggestion to address that concern?"

"We do," said Haji. "Have your people call on your suppliers and advise them that you're acting as agent for a company that's willing to give them long-term contracts to make monthly purchases of specified quantities of their products at specified prices. The quantities and prices will increase over time per an agreed schedule. Obviously, there will be separate schedules for the different categories of food, seasonings and other supplies."

Oni jumped in. "The reason we suggest going the agency route instead of you buying from them and re-selling to us is—"

"I understand, to keep me from being on the hook as the middleman if, God forbid, something happens to your company and you can't perform your end. That's one of the things I like about doing business with you people. You think of everything from everyone's point of view and you're not afraid to share."

"Thank you, Paidi," said Oni.

"Just one question," said Akinjide, "I'm certain you've thought this through as well. What's the incentive for our suppliers to lock themselves in over the long term?"

"We did consider that," said Haji. "As of the first of each year, the prices for the particular product categories for that year will be the *greater* of the prices listed in the schedules, or the fair market value on that date of like quantities of the particular products. So, from a pricing standpoint, nothing is locked in except for the fact that the suppliers will receive at least the scheduled prices, even if, at a point in time, those prices actually exceed the current fair market value of their products. On the other hand, if fair market values exceed the scheduled prices, they'll get market value. Second, the suppliers will have the option to terminate their contracts immediately following any of the adverse credit events that are standard in every contract, including, obviously, nonpayment or bankruptcy."

"This sounds like a terrible deal for you," Akinjide joked, but he got it. It was more than worth those concessions for the Katlegos to tie up as much West North American food supplies as possible to both fuel their expansion and keep it out of the hands of potential competitors, be they Superior Restaurants or someone else.

At this time, West North America was the only place in the world that still produced real food. Neither the Africans nor the West North Americans had yet moved to colonize other regions.

• • • • •

When Superior Restaurants learned of the long-term contracts that Tau's Pan Africa had entered into with major West North American food producers, they calculated that very little supply would be left beyond that necessary to satisfy domestic demand. Their lawyers and political consultants warned them against taking for granted that the government would stand idly by and let Superior Restaurants funnel essential domestic food supplies to Africa in order to line the pockets of greedy capitalists.

"It's unfair," Superior's CEO told their outside counsel. "The bastards have locked up the entire exportable food supply. Can we get a court to void the contracts?"

"I'm afraid not," said the lawyer. "Freedom of contract is still very much a part of our common law."

Superior's CEO instructed its African affiliate to file a lawsuit in Nairobi against Tau's Pan Africa, seeking to nullify the long-term contracts based on unfair competition. When they were unable to find a Zone 3 attorney willing to handle the lawsuit for them, they filed a complaint themselves, *pro se.*

The following day, a panel of judges issued a one-word judgment—"Dismissed"—and took the almost unheard-of step of issuing a short written opinion:

"The court chooses to believe that this claim was filed as a prank, rather than believe that anyone born on our continent in the current century could be dim enough intellectually to assert a claim so devoid of logic. It is self-evident that African courts are without jurisdiction over matters concerning contracts entered into with foreign entities in a foreign country."

Superior Restaurants dropped its plans to open restaurants in Africa, and Tau's Pan Africa became one of the few large natural monopolies (*i.e.*, monopolies not created by government action or dispensation) in human history. The company retained that distinction for decades until sufficient quantities of food began arriving from trade with Nova Africana and Alamo c to allow competing African restaurants to open.

• • • • •

3400

Enterprising West North Americans who'd observed people of metal crowding into Tau's restaurants in Africa began offering metallic Africans special West North American dining tours, similar to the tours ancient French tour operators had offered to foreign gourmets. Soon, people of metal were "eating their way through West North America" much as ancient tourists had eaten their way through France.

3428

The first shipments of eating upgrades began arriving in Nova Africana in 3418 and in Alamo c ten years later. The eating upgrade had been marketed in the colonies by video. Based on the number of eating upgrades that POM shipped to the colonies, it appeared that every metallic colonist had ordered one.

The stimulus hats sold in Africa would not work for colonists or West North Americans, because none of them had received the genetic enhancements that enabled the mind-travel state. Instead, Alice and Brandon asked the engineers to make stimulus hats, for biologicals and people of metal, that created the brain activity that ancient researchers had recorded from meditating monks. Test subjects loved the meditative experience that the hats afforded them, and they became quite popular.

•   •   •   •   •

African business school professors had broached the idea of African companies' licensing Nova Africana and Alamo c companies to make and sell their products there, but the idea was rejected as impractical without the ability to perform minimal due diligence on prospective licensees who were located light years away.

Chapter 26
Eureka

Africa
3423

Word spread instantly to every corner of Africa that mathematicians at Central University had finally managed to mathematically prove the Hodge Conjecture. The announcement was streamed to every screen on the continent, and West North American correspondents streamed home live reports on this exciting development.

Stimulus hats and mind-travel had played a crucial role in this towering achievement. Moreover, mathematicians aided by mind-travel had recently solved a number of other "unsolvable" math propositions. They were falling like dominos.

The speaker was Professor Omari Chipo, chair of the mathematics department at Central University. He spoke matter-of-factly in a flat, emotionless African voice

"A team of mathematicians at this university has made a proof of the Hodge Conjecture which peer review has certified as correct and complete. This is good news. We met the first of the three tests in the Message by decoding the stone pattern. The making of the proof satisfies the second test. But while the Message does not call it that, there is a third test. We must send the proof in the direction of God's 'abode,' so our third test will be to determine where in the universe that is. Now, I will turn the podium over to my colleague, Professor Jata Femi, the chairman of our astronomy department."

"As you may know," Professor Femi began, "an informal task force of astronomers from every African university has been working for centuries to find something that could be God's residence—like, for example, a celestial formation whose shape resembles a house."

No one laughed. Femi wasn't trying to be "funny." No one had used that word or any of its synonyms in ages.

"We *will* find it," Femi continued. "No logical person, much less a god, would ask us to find something that cannot be found. Experts in other disciplines are also helping. Searches are being run in every known language that exists, or once existed, of the word 'abode' and its synonyms. Astrophysicists are considering whether 'God's abode' might be a metaphor for some component of our universe that is particularly important or mysterious. Every logical possibility will be pursued."

In other times, governments or foundations might have offered large cash prizes to anyone who came up with information that helped with something as important as meeting the third test and bringing God's love to all of the planet's inhabitants—if, as was possible, God did exist and the Message was legitimate. But prizes would not have made a difference at this point in time. Most people had more money than they needed.

Even without prizes, people in other eras might have felt challenged to take a shot at solving the riddle of "God's abode." Modern Africans did not react that way. The most qualified people had been assigned to attend to the matter, and that was that. Africans were too smart, too logical and knew too much to feel "challenged" to do something. Either you could do a thing or you couldn't. It was a fact that could be determined, but it wasn't a challenge, because no one really cared whether they could or could not do a particular thing. People had different abilities. It was what it was. For similar reasons, sports, and games like golf and bowling, had been abandoned long ago. They served no logical purpose.

So the third test was left to the scientists, and they got nowhere.

Chapter 27
Old Friends

Mahmoud's Restaurant
Redemption
Nova Africana
3431

Weinberg and Keisha loved their eating upgrades, but wished they were a bit more refined. The designers had done a nice job with the jaws and teeth, but they hadn't included the facial musculature that biologicals had that allowed them to chew their food with their mouths closed.

"I'm always afraid we'll gross them out," said Weinberg between chomps.

"I'm sure they're used to the sight by now," said Keisha.

The meat course arrived, a rump roast. Just over three hundred years earlier, Clark and Liu had decided to ship to Nova Africana and Alamo c frozen embryos of various kinds of livestock, for food, and cat and dog embryos for house pets.

"I think it's time to go see our old friends," said Weinberg, cutting his meat. "We haven't seen them in years."

"Sure," said Keisha. "Where would you like to go first?"

"How about going to see Bonnie and Cheng first and spending some time there? Then, if they want, they and Ray and Libby can travel to Earth with us. We'll see what Clark and Liu are up to. It'd be fun to see the generals, too. The place must be completely different—the people too, with all their genetic enhancements."

"It'll be amazing," said Keisha. "Alamo c is what, sixteen light years from here?"

"Just under."

At 60% of light speed, to which the new ships accelerated, the trip, including acceleration and braking, would take almost 30 years.

"We'll hop a ship bound for Alamo c that's filled with shipments of food," said Weinberg. "We'll have to ration our consumption or we'll run out before we get there."

"We should have done this years ago," said Keisha.

"I have an ulterior motive," said Weinberg. "I'm worried about the Africans."

"The genetic engineering?"

"That plus other mischief their genetically engineered scientists and technologists could unleash. We need to stop at Alamo c, pick up our friends and head for Africa and see what they're up to. Besides, I miss them," Weinberg admitted.

"I wonder if they've changed much," said Keisha.

"I'm sure they have. So have we. What will you study to be on this trip, a nuclear physicist?"

"I have a lot of medicine to catch up on," said Keisha.

They brought their stimulus hats with them and enough reading material, games and music to tide them over during the 30-year trip. Weinberg also brought a piano and his clarinet.

Starport
Sanctuary City
Alamo c
3461

Like Redemption, Sanctuary City had spread far beyond its original boundaries. They had left the domed city in place as a memorial to the original native-born colonists and as a reminder of what they and their progeny had accomplished.

"I read that the domed city was the place they initially used to shelter their biologicals during their sandstorms," said Keisha. "Once they had the ability to build modern structures that could withstand the storms and not have their air supply cut off, they didn't need it."

As the ship continued its descent, a magnificent scene opened up beneath them—beautiful modern office towers, factories, residential and commercial areas, and an enormous lush green park near the city's center.

"Central Park in New York City," said Keisha. Weinberg was thinking the same thing.

The old domed city off to the right looked quaint by comparison, but well maintained. Weinberg recognized buildings in the domed city as the same type that robots had built in Redemption after their arrival in Nova Africana.

The modern buildings were beautiful, but their shapes and styles were different, in a good way, from the shapes and styles of modern Redemption buildings. More remarkably, given that holograms of African architects had taught the first architects in both colonies, distinct Alamo c and Nova Africana architectural styles had soon emerged.

The starship came to rest, the door opened and Bonnie Holyfield and Cheng Woon came aboard.

"Welcome!" said Bonnie.

"It seems like only yesterday," said Weinberg. "Group hug time."

They hugged and patted each other's backs.

"How was your trip?" Woon asked.

"It was great," said Keisha. "I gained expertize in cardiology and endocrinology, and Bill played his portable piano and wrote songs. And we meditated."

"Bonnie, you don't look a day older," said Weinberg, "and you haven't gained an ounce."

"Thanks. Bill," she said, laughing. "The bios run everything here, as it should be. But they still come to us every so often for advice, so we don't feel completely useless, and it's fun to watch it all happen."

"'Bios,'" said Weinberg. "Must be a colloquialism. I love it."

The friends were speaking 2800 Swahili because the two couples would have found each other's current dialect hard to follow. Any communication between the visitors and the local 'bios' would have to be through an interpreter.

Holyfield and Woon led them toward a helicopter, which they boarded.

"They've been nice enough to let us have one of these, and a pilot, for our personal use," said Bonnie.

"We're meeting Libby and Ray at the restaurant," said Woon.

Alamo was setting off to the right as the helicopter came to rest at a center-city heliport.

Emerald Mist restaurant
Sanctuary City

The restaurant occupied the entire top floor of the tallest office tower in the city center. The three sides that enclosed the dining area were floor-to-ceiling glass. Sparkling chandeliers of cut green glass or crystal cast an emerald-green hue on the white tablecloths that complemented the green water glasses and napkins on the tables.

Libby and Ray were waiting in the bar area with a tall, handsome white-haired biological man, and the six friends re-enacted the group hug they'd performed in Nairobi so long ago.

Keisha was smiling and rubbing her eyes.

"It's so wonderful to see you two," said Libby.

"It's been way too long," said Ray.

"You all must be proud of what your people have accomplished," said Keisha, gesturing toward the windows and the sparkling metropolis outside.

"We sure are," said Bonnie. "I'm sure you feel the same about your people."

"We do," said Keisha.

Bonnie turned toward the tall, distinguished gentlemen and spoke to him in the local dialect. Keisha and Weinberg recognized the sound of their names.

"Bill Weinberg, Keisha Dixon, I'd like you to meet our governor, Salim Fofana."

Keisha and Weinberg shook hands with the governor and they exchanged formal greetings, which Bonnie translated.

"Bonnie, have your bios been receiving the new anti-aging drugs?" Weinberg asked. "Ours have."

"They have. They're wonderful."

Holyfield and Woon led the group to a large round table in the center of the room. A server gave the diners menus and took the governor's drink order.

"I sent you guys a translation," said Bonnie.

Keisha and Weinberg touched the devices on the wrists and a menu appeared. When the server returned, they told Bonnie what they wanted—soup, meat and vegetables—and she translated their orders for the server.

"Bill and I limit ourselves to one filling when we're in public," Keisha told Bonnie.

"That's very considerate," said Bonnie. "Some of the bios have sensitive stomachs."

"We strive to be decorous," said Weinberg. "I love the music."

Bonnie, Libby and Ray took turns as interpreters for the governor and their visitors. Keisha and Weinberg took an immediate liking to the governor, an ex-farmer with no previous political experience.

"We haven't had a professional political class in over 200 years," the governor declared with obvious pride. "The people rose up and said, 'Enough!' Nowadays our elected officials serve two terms in office and go back to being constituents."

"Good for them," said Weinberg.

"Good for *you*," said Keisha

The governor and the visitors compared notes on technological developments in their respective colonies and touted forthcoming products they were sure the other colony's consumers would love. Keisha told the governor about a controversial issue that officials in Nova Africana were trying to resolve and asked his opinion.

"By the way, the food in this restaurant is wonderful," Weinberg told the governor. "I've never had anything like it."

The governor suggested that someone in Nova Africana might want to open a restaurant that served Alamo c dishes, and that an entrepreneur might want to open a restaurant in Sanctuary City that served Nova Africana cuisine. He promised to send his Nova Africana counterpart a selection of Alamo c recipes and a catalogue from which a hypothetical restaurant owner could order seasonings and other supplies.

"He says he'll run it through a translation app into 2800 Swahili," said Bonnie.

After dinner, the governor stood, shook everyone's hand and excused himself. "You all have a lot to catch up on."

"Great guy," said Weinberg. "So, it's great to be here. There's no substitute for travel to keep the mind fresh. In fact, when we finish our visit here, Keisha and I plan to hop on the next ship bound for Earth. We thought the four of you might want to join us. We can't wait to see what all they've done since we left."

"Ray and I have been thinking along the same lines," said Libby. "Cheng, Bonnie, what do you think?"

"It's 37 years there and 37 back," said Woon.

"The freighter we'd be hopping will have the same privacy spaces as our original starships did," Kiesha pointed out.

"Excellent!" said Libby.

"I don't know," said Woon. "Let's sleep on it, so to speak."

After dinner, Weinberg and Keisha were taken to a nearby hotel to regroup.

Mural Gallery
Memorial Park
Sanctuary City
Next morning

Bonnie had suggested the six friends meet amidst the murals that commemorated Earth, humanity's place of origin.

"She's putting the screws to him," Keisha told Weinberg. "How can he refuse to come with us to see our beloved Earth once again?"

"Smart girl," said Weinberg.

Bonnie was laying it on thick, describing in florid terms and great detail the scene each mural depicted.

"We shipped over two hundred distinct kinds of stones and gemstones from Earth to make these murals. It was Cheng's idea. The children who made them were part of the first generation of humans born on this world."

Most of the people who occupied the gallery's benches and streamed past the murals were biological, Keisha noticed. Their clothing styles were strangely attractive, and colorful. They seemed happy, as far as she could tell. Many of them wore the meditative stimulus hats that the Africans had created for colonials. Some of the people seated on the benches appeared to be using them.

"This," Bonnie was saying, "is Mount Kenya, in Zone 3, one of the tallest peaks in Africa."

"All right, sweetheart, we'll go," said Woon.

The other five surrounded him, laughing, and slapped his back.

"Thanks, baby," Bonnie told Woon.

"Okay," said Bonnie, "let's grab a bite to eat and then head off to the mountains for a little skiing, if that's okay with everyone. Bill, I remember you and Keisha saying that you were big skiers."

"Long, long ago. We were experts. My original was. But our feet won't fit into boots."

"Not a problem. Technicians at the lodge will temporarily replace our feet with foot and ankle units that have skis attached. If we fall, the skis will come off, just as the old skis did, so we don't get hurt."

"Yes!" said Keisha.

"They had two feet of powder last night so we're in luck," said Bonnie. "Don't worry, there'll be a groomed run for us to warm up on."

White Mountain Ski Resort
White Mountains
Alamo c

"They're skiing!" said Keisha, referring to the skiers they saw as their helicopter was landing.

"It's a ski resort," said Weinberg. "This should be interesting. When the ski season opened and my original put on his skis after months of not skiing, he'd take a few easy runs to reactivate his muscle memory, and he'd be set for another season of skiing the most challenging runs. The only memory I have is the memory in my head. How do you deal with that? What's the secret?"

"Just will your body to make moves it needs to make," said Keisha. "Trust me, your electromechanical body will be much more obedient to your mind than Mr. Weinberg's body was to his."

She was right. Weinberg remembered what Mr. Weinberg's body had needed to do to ski two feet of fresh power, and Weinberg's body did it. He paused at the bottom of the slope to admire the tracks he'd made. They reminded him of the time Mr. Weinberg and Amelia had competed as partners in a "powder eight" event. The following year, he'd done the same with Keisha, who skied in custom-made boots that Mr. Weinberg had commissioned for her. The winners in a powder eight were the pair whose tracks combined to make the best-looking string of "eights."

"If Mr. Weinberg had had this body, he'd have needed five or ten lessons at the most instead of hundreds," Weinberg told Keisha.

Woon, Ray and Libby had never skied while biological, but thanks to their obedient metallic bodies, they were advanced intermediates on the verge of becoming experts.

"Whoo-hoo!" Keisha exclaimed as she flew off a cornice.

Holyfield flew off the cornice right after her, and they cut smoothly through the "crud," as chopped-up powder had been called, and into the trees below

Weinberg stopped for a moment and watched them. It was like running and jumping on the Moon, he thought, times one hundred.

He dropped off the cornice and raced after them.

Chapter 28
The Pulsar

Astronomy department
Central University
3478

While staring at his telescope's screen as he'd done every workday for the past thirty-three years, the astronomer, Professor Jaheem Imamu, a biological, suffered a mental breakdown. He was out of ideas.

"God help me," he said. He spoke to the thin wire that hung from the side of his white stimulus hat, and a moment later, he was out there. As always, unimaginable shapes, colors and patterns filled his mind, and as always, it was unfolding with a purpose. Jaheem often wondered where it came from. Whatever it was, the force of its wordless logic was unstoppable. However, this time, Imamu had no idea where it was headed until the very end, when the shapes, specks, lines and colors changed one last time and resolved themselves into the very image of the Crab Pulsar, and he understood what he was seeing.

Instantly, Imamu was back in the room with his colleagues. "I just saw it—God's abode."

Colleagues rushed over to look at Imamu's telescope screen but saw nothing of any significance.

"Not on the screen," said Imamu. "My mind saw it. It's the Crab Pulsar."

Oh. The colleagues went back to their workstations.

Excited, Imamu sent the mathematical proof of the Hodge Conjecture in the direction of the Crab Pulsar and waited for God's reply. Cryptographers had used a special app to encode the proof in the same pattern-code that the stone formations had used, and it was this that Imamu had sent, as the Message required.

The pulsar was 7,178 light years distant from Earth, but logic and the specific language of God's Message told Imamu that the mere act of sending the proof toward God's abode would satisfy the third test, even though it would take more than seven thousand years for the proof to get there. God was the essence of logic. He would not have used the language He'd used in His Message unless He had ways of knowing when the proof had been sent in His direction.

However, after five years of waiting and checking his messages, Imamu decided that he must have missed something. *But what?*

Unbeknownst to him, he hadn't missed a thing.

Chapter 29
Revelation

Nairobi
3488

"Yuck," said Libby. "What have they done? It's horrible."

They had not let the Nairobi authorities know they were coming, so no one had met them when they landed. They stepped off the ship when its door opened and walked toward the city until they had a clear view of its skyline. The six old friends stopped, taken aback, and stared at the scene spread out before them.

The size of the towering glass buildings was impressive, but that was it. They felt alien; lifeless.

"A West North American writer called it 'architecture as an exercise in pure reason,'" said Holyfield, who'd loaded one of her devices with research material for the trip, "and she did not mean it as a compliment. But her pictures didn't convey how it feels to be in their presence. They're — how can one even describe them? They're *flavorless*. These buildings have no taste at all. They're bland. The writer said their rule of thumb is purity of function; avoiding unnecessary elements."

"I understand their cuisine is also logical," said Libby, who'd also done her homework during the trip. "They genetically engineered away the ability for biologicals to taste and smell their food, so they'd no longer need seasonings, sauces and other extraneous components in their food. Food has only the elements it needs to serve its purpose.

They've engineered their food to have the optimum ratio of essential elements to calories."

"The same West North American writer said that tourists from her country avoid African food when they can," said Bonnie. "People of metal avoid it altogether. Fortunately, she said there are plenty of restaurants throughout Africa that serve real food imported from West North America."

"We'll have to make a point of finding some," said Weinberg.

They walked on and were struck by how quiet the crowded streets were. Robotic passenger carts moved soundlessly through the streets, and the people, if they spoke to each other at all, spoke softly in flat, almost metallic-sounding voices. Even ethnic orangutan people seemed cerebral and subdued. The visitors understood none of what they heard, but they noticed that people spoke fast and punctuated their spoken words with a variety of sharp inflections.

The six friends walked around the city for several hours without hearing a single African laugh or call out to someone. If they smiled at all, it was faint. Had the visitors looked more carefully, they'd have noticed people standing or sitting here and there as if frozen.

"We must look outrageous to them, the way we're dressed, but they barely glance at us," said Libby.

"No trees, no flowers, no decoration, no colors, and drab clothing," said Weinberg. "What's happened? Can intelligence increase to a point where objects or characteristics that we once found beautiful or pleasing to the senses become intolerable distractions from the purity of one's thought?"

"We should find someone we can talk with," said Keisha, "like a person of metal who speaks old Swahili. Maybe they haven't deliberately shunned the things Bill mentioned. Maybe they dropped them became they just don't see a need for them."

"I know who we can talk to," said Weinberg. "Harry Garrett is a person of metal who's a genetics professor at the university. But first, if it's okay with you all, I'm anxious to see how my roses are doing."

That was fine with everyone, so they boarded a passenger cart, transferred to another and rode through the quiet city to the William Weinberg Public Rose Garden. The first thing they noticed was the new sign at the entrance to the park. The top line was probably the park's name in contemporary Swahili. Keisha noticed strange marks—punctuation, perhaps—above and after particular words and phrases. She wondered if those markings corresponded to the inflections they'd heard the locals use when speaking. Below that, in smaller letters, was a line in another language.

"It must be the park's name in West North American," said Libby.

"I'm surprised your roses are still here," Woon told Weinberg.

"They maintain them as a tourist attraction," Libby said. "The West North Americans love roses. They're avid gardeners. I think we're about to see some of them now."

A group of West North Americans emerged from the rose garden. They bounded forward as they walked and talked in loud voices. Their clothing, with its bright colors and flowing fabrics, seemed to suit them.

'Wow," said Keisha. "They're descendants of the people who left Africa to work the mines in the North American west."

"So they didn't get the genetic upgrades that the people who stayed here got," said Weinberg.

"They didn't get as many, but they did get some," said Holyfield. "African geneticists propagated ten trait enhancements into the West North American gene pool in the early 30th century, but that was it. Here in Africa, the enhancements never stopped."

"The West North Americans seem to be having a lot more fun than the locals," said Libby.

` With their friends' permission, Weinberg took Keisha off to examine his roses while the others remained by the fountain, people watching.

"Oh my God," said Keisha, "we can smell them!"

It was glorious.

At length, the couple rejoined the others at the fountain.

"I hope you all smelled some of these," said Weinberg.

"We did," said Holyfield. "They're amazing."

"Okay, let's go see Dr. Garrett," said Weinberg. "He was an animal geneticist at the Animal Project's Upstate Medical Facility when Keisha and I worked there. I worked directly under him. Smart guy. What are the chances the university is still in the same place?"

Holyfield noticed a person of metal passing by and got her attention.

"Excuse me," said Holyfield in old Swahili, "we've just arrived from Alamo c and wish to find the university. We know where it used to be. We taught there. But it's been a long time."

"Colonists," the lady said in the same dialect. Her voice was soft, flat and matter of fact. "How about that?" she continued. "First time I've ever seen any of you folks. Welcome back."

The nice lady gave them the directions they needed. They rode a series of passenger carts until they'd reached the university's perimeter, got further directions and walked as directed to the genetics building, which, like those surrounding it, was of recent construction.

"Three city blocks by two," said Weinberg. "There must be hundreds of geneticists in there working away."

They entered what appeared to be the main reception area, and Weinberg spoke to the receptionist, a biological, in old Swahili. The receptionist left her post and returned moments later with Brandon.

Weinberg, speaking the old dialect, introduced himself and his companions.

"Welcome. I'm Brandon Delaney," Brandon said slowly, shaking Weinberg's hand. "My wife and I were geneticists at the Upstate Medical Facility after you left to run the first Initiative. One thing led to another, and here we are."

"Pleased to meet you. I was hoping to see Harry."

"Sure, he's here. Follow me."

Garrett recognized Weinberg at once and jumped from his workstation to greet him and the other visitors, whom Weinberg introduced. Alice was also there.

"I had no idea you were coming," said Garrett in old Swahili. He also spoke slowly. "Please, let's go into the conference room."

"It's good to see you, Harry," said Weinberg after they were seated, "but you don't have to speak so slowly."

"Oh, I'm sorry," said Garrett. "Contemporary Swahili is spoken so rapidly that we're apt to overcompensate when we speak to people in West North American or old Swahili."

"Can I ask you something?" said Keisha.

"Sure," said Garrett.

"When we heard people speaking on the way over here, they added sharp inflections to their words. Then, at the public rose garden, we saw a sign that I assumed was in modern Swahili and there were marks above or after words and phrases. I'm guessing that the marks were the written version of the inflections, or the inflections were the spoken version of the marks."

"That's right."

"Do they add meaning to the words?"

"Yes, but much more so than old-fashioned punctuation, like a question mark. Marks placed above words are equivalent to inflections made while saying the word. They represent common adjectives and adverbs. They save the speaker or writer the trouble of saying them or writing them out. Marks or inflections made between words or phrases are proxies for common everyday expressions—again, to save one the trouble of having to say them or write them out. It's very efficient."

"Thank you," said Keisha. "That's very interesting."

Weinberg cleared his throat. He began by complimenting Garrett and his team for all that they'd accomplished.

"On behalf of the people of Nova Africana," he told Garrett, Alice and Brandon, "Keisha and I would like the people of Africa to know how much we appreciate the many hitherto unimaginable medical and other scientific advancements that your people, biological and metallic, have given humanity. I know that Mr. Woon and Ms. Holyfield would also like to express their appreciation."

"Indeed," said Holyfield.

"The genetics research and engineering that you and your group pioneered here in Africa obviously made a lot of these accomplishments possible, without the nightmare scenarios that many of us feared. So, congratulations."

The other visitors echoed those sentiments.

"Thank you so much," said Garrett.

"But some of the things we've seen since we arrived seem rather puzzling," Weinberg continued. "Since we were last here, it seems that the environment has been cleansed of all color, flavor, decoration, whimsy and even the slightest trace of disorder. The people—the biologicals and the Machines we encountered—seem content enough, but rather flat, as if they've lost some of the *élan vital* they had when we left We didn't hear one African laugh on our way here, or even talk loud. It made us wonder if they've paid a price to become what they needed to become in order for you all to be able to do all the things you've done for humanity. We saw West North American tourists laughing and shouting and having a gay old time. The contrast was striking."

Garrett, Brandon and Alice exchanged looks. It was a subject they'd touched on amongst themselves but preferred not to think about. Weinberg was right; it was the price they'd paid. But it was awkward and embarrassing to have someone outside their group point it out.

"As you probably know," said Garrett, "almost from the beginning, we've been transferring enhancements from biological subjects to ourselves, and to other people of metal who wanted them—the enhancements that relate to mental functions, that is. Brandon and Alice created the technology to do that. So we have essentially the same intellectual traits as biological Africans, and no doubt think and act in much the same way. But our centuries of life experience have blunted the impact of those changes to a certain extent. We've kept a bit of perspective. For example, we regret the fact that art and music have disappeared, which was not something we intended; and humor."

"I don't mean to be critical," said Weinberg. "You've done well. The results speak for themselves."

"We made a huge mistake by eliminating their ability to taste and smell most flavors and aromas," said Garrett. "It seemed like a good idea at the time. We'd had our eleventh or twelfth intelligence boost, and our logic was inexorable, in our own minds. Life would be simpler, food would be less expensive, people would save time and unhealthy junk food would lose its appeal. People would eat healthy. Obesity would disappear. We set plant geneticists to work engineering plants and animals that would deliver more nutritional bang per calorie. And so on. Food was fuel. A commodity."

"We were too 'smart' for our own good," said Alice. "I don't want to sound like I'm making excuses, but looking back, I think we gave ourselves too many enhancements in too short a period. They overwhelmed us. They controlled us instead of the other way around."

"I could have convinced myself of almost anything in those days," said Garrett.

"I wouldn't be so hard on yourselves," said Holyfield. "You've had a lot of balls in the air. You've been at this for hundreds of years, and if that's the only significant wrong outcome you've had in a field as fraught with risk as yours, I'd say you've done damn well."

"Thanks, Bonnie, that means a lot. Look, I—we—know that biological Africans have turned out rather more cerebral and less lively in the physical, sensual and artistic sense than we'd have liked. A West North American writer created a stir when she compared our people to the man in the parable whose head keeps getting larger at the expense of his body until all that's left of him is a gigantic head. She caught hell for that and had to apologize. But she was right, to a certain extent."

"Any chance you can restore their taste and smell?" Weinberg asked.

"Absolutely, now that you mention it." said Garrett. "Tom Joyce's people could make somatic vectors to reverse the changes we made, and tools to do the same with embryos. It'd be a huge project, but it's doable. We should have done this years ago," Garrett added.

"No one ever complained," said Brandon.

"Of course they didn't, genius," said Alice. "They were born without taste and smell. They had no idea what they were missing."

"I think Bill nailed it, people," said Holyfield, "when he said you folks helped make your people into who they needed to be to deliver to humanity the marvelous things they've delivered, including a much longer life span. After you restore their taste and smell, they'll have many happy years in which to enjoy them."

"That's true," said Garrett, "but it doesn't make up for the millions who lived and died without them."

"Ah, but Harry," said Alice, "they also received something that we take for granted: minds of unprecedented power and insight. I remember how it felt when we first began to experience it. It was amazing."

"Point taken," said Garrett.

"There was an old expression in Washington back in the day," said Holyfield. "'Don't let the perfect be the enemy of the good.'"

"On a lighter note," said Woon, "I understand that all of Africa has been working hard to figure out where God's abode is so they can send the proof of the Hodge Conjecture in that direction and meet the third test in God's alleged Message."

"It's a dead issue," said Brandon. "The astronomers have given up trying to find it."

"What is y'all's take on this, Harry?" Weinberg asked.

"It must have been an elaborate prank by an advanced civilization," said Garrett. "What else could it be?"

"I don't know," said Weinberg. "Maybe there's another explanation. Keisha has always said that things happen for a reason. Not all things, but some. I've always teased her about that, but I'm beginning to think her instincts might have been on target regarding a lot of what's happened to humans in recent centuries. If the Malaise hadn't come and wiped out almost everyone, it seems almost certain that the scientific advances that your people made here in Africa would have come along much sooner, while the world was still large, hostile and chaotic, and no one would have been able to predict or control how they'd be used. It could have been even worse than the Malaise. The whole planet could have become a lifeless waste. It may sound sick to say this, but thanks to the Malaise, humanity started fresh, with a relatively small population and scientists whose work you and your colleagues in other fields could monitor and, to an extent, control."

"I agree," said Brandon. "Biological Africans are effectively a new species, but they're benign. They've used their superior intelligence and talents for the good of everyone. If things had continued the way they were going before the Malaise, they would not have ended well."

Bonnie agreed. "In the tribal world that existed before the Malaise, the various rival world powers would have raced to become the first to engineer a superior race. How long would it have taken for two, three or even four new species of humans to be developed, each one vastly smarter, stronger and more lethal than the one before it."

"Until something unforeseen happened that brought it all down," said Weinberg.

"Exactly," said Bonnie.

"So the Malaise might have happened for a reason," said Keisha.

"That's how it's starting to look," Weinberg admitted. "The coincidences keep adding up. By coincidence, we were in Africa in 2527 in time to keep the last biological humans from becoming extinct, which would have happened when their infrastructure wore out and they ran out of supplies. By coincidence, Bonnie, Keisha and I have been on other planets, so we weren't here in Africa to prevent the genetic research and development that have been so fruitful in so many ways. The way we felt about it then, we'd have stopped it for sure if we'd been here. And by coincidence, the stone formations with a coded message were left eons ago on the exact two far-removed planets that we colonized."

"I'm not ready to give up on the idea that God left the Message," said Keisha. "Maybe the astronomers made their search needlessly difficult. Maybe they were looking in all the most obscure places on the assumption that the riddle of the 'abode' had to be at least as difficult to solve as the Hodge Conjecture was. But what if the answer is simple and would be obvious if one didn't overthink it?"

"I've always been skeptical about the Message," said Brandon. "But there are two more so-called coincidences that, to me, reduce the likelihood an alien civilization left the messages."

"This I have to hear," said Garrett.

"As Bill pointed out, someone left identical messages on Alamo c and Nova Africana eons before the first expeditions left Earth," said Brandon. "Whoever left the Message must have known in advance that we'd be colonizing those planets. No alien civilization could have known that."

"That's right," said Keisha. "Steven Hawking's warning about aliens was fresh in my mind, and I prevailed upon Bill to prohibit radio communications or broadcasts regarding any aspect of the expeditions."

Weinberg nodded thoughtfully.

"One can scarcely imagine the level of intelligence, technology and raw power it would have taken to create a pattern of small stones that would repeat a coded sequence every so many minutes, automatically cleaning itself of dust and debris when required to keep the pattern visible," Weinberg said. "The only way the presence of these things on Nova Africana and Alamo c could be a mere coincidence would be if the hypothetical alien civilization had left the Message on *all* habitable planets in the universe—or, at a minimum, the ones in our sector. Even if someone had the *ability* to do all that, why would they? To prank some unsuspecting colonists in the distant future? But there they are. Someone put them there. Who's left?"

"God," said Keisha.

"And if God put them there, Keisha has a point," said Weinberg. "He wouldn't have directed that the proof be sent toward something that wasn't findable. So 'God's abode must be out there somewhere.'"

"They thought they'd found it," said Alice. "An astronomer thought God Himself had told him where he lived when the Crab Pulsar appeared to him at the very end of a deep mind-travel state. So he sent the proof in that direction, but nothing happened."

What? Weinberg thought. Then it hit him.

"So the proof went out," said Weinberg. "I hadn't realized. Are you sure nothing's happened? Things seem to be going pretty-well here. You've used your enhanced intelligence and newfound meditative powers to make all sorts of discoveries. And not a single unforeseen adverse consequence has resulted from your work — none worth mentioning here. The coincidences are piling up, aren't they?"

"They are," Alice admitted.

"It just hit me," said Weinberg. "I take it that none of the people tasked with solving the riddle of the third test came from any kind of traditional religious background, like Islam, Christianity or Judaism."

"That's right," said Brandon. "That hasn't existed here for centuries."

"Because your astronomer was right."

"God lives in the Crab Pulsar?"

"Yes, among other places," said Weinberg. "As my original's rabbi would have put it, 'God is everywhere.'"

Alice burst out laughing. "So it didn't matter where the astronomer sent the proof, as long as he sent it, which his meditative state made him do by showing him a recognizable astronomical formation. My God."

"But if God to wanted to contact us, why didn't He just talk to us directly?" said Weinberg. "The God of my ancestors spoke directly to their leader, Moses, out of a burning bush."

"God did speak to us," said Keisha. "He left us a Message—in a form we'd take seriously. The burning bush thing might have worked thousands of years ago. People then could believe their eyes and ears. There was no way anyone could have faked it. But if people today encountered a talking bush, burning or not, they'd dismiss it as a trick, like the holograms we sent to African politicians back in the day."

"You're right," said Brandon, "it had to be overwhelming for anyone with advanced technology to take it seriously. Something unlikely to be a mere insignificant relic of some long-gone civilization. Just to be sure we didn't miss the point, they left two of the formations on Nova Africana and two on Alamo c, in close proximity with each other."

"That's what tipped us off," said Keisha. "I timed the pattern sequence on both of them, and they were identical."

Weinberg smacked his forehead with his palm.

"Shit," he muttered. "On second thought, I have to take back what I said earlier. Sorry, Keisha. I succumbed to wishful thinking and ignored the obvious. An advanced civilization or group of civilizations might well have found it worth the effort to place these Messages on a large number of habitable planets, to entice space travelers to reveal themselves by solving the Hodge Conjecture and sending off the proof, thereby revealing their location. It could be an empire that's continually looking to expand. Such a civilization might be advanced enough to intercept radio transmissions in the pattern code and trace their source."

"So I guess the alien civilization alternative is plausible," said Brandon. "And God, if He exists, may have had nothing to do with what we've accomplished. We may have made ourselves smart enough to accomplish what we've done on our own. In that case, we might expect a visit from an alien civilization, and it might not be a social call."

"Hawking was right," said Keisha. "It was a mistake to reveal ourselves."

"Let's all remain calm," said Garrett. "We aren't saying it wasn't God. We're simply acknowledging a possible alternative. We need to get on that, just in case."

"I'll have Clark and Liu prepare a crash defense preparedness plan," said Weinberg. "I'll speak with them before we leave. But I suggest we give them a few guidelines."

"Like what?" Garrett asked.

"For example, biologicals should play no role in the military buildup except for factory work," said Weinberg. "The last thing the universe needs is more biologicals trained to use advanced weaponry."

The others agreed.

"All Machines not engaged in other essential activities should take part in the operation in whatever capacities would be most productive," Weinberg continued. "Metallic but not biological scientists and engineers should be tasked with designing fierce new weapons using whatever physical forces they can figure out how to harness for that purpose. Some of the weapons would need to be very long range, others should be close range and some might be placed in orbit."

"We can convert some of the starship factories for this purpose," said Garrett. "I would also suggest that the weapons be remotely controlled and operated so our people won't be vulnerable to the fire the weapons might draw."

"Good point, Harry," said Weinberg.

"Also," Garrett continued, "I strongly recommend that the government have no direct or indirect control over, or access to, these weapons or the factories that make them. We should have metallic engineers design coded locks for all weapons."

"Won't the government want to have a say-so in return for funding the project?" Keisha asked.

Garrett winked at Brandon and Alice.

"We'll fund it," said Brandon.

"What?!" said Weinberg. "How?"

Garrett explained how Brandon and Alice had amassed a vast fortune.

I'm speechless," said Weinberg.

Keisha bowed her head and prayed.

Chapter 30
The Finish Line

Department of Genetics
University of Nairobi
3488

As an immortal, Harry Garrett had imagined in vague terms that one day in the distant future they would reach this point, but it had happened much sooner than he'd expected, and he hadn't seen it coming. One day, while Garrett was in a reflective frame of mind left over from his daily mind-travel, it came to him out of left field that the science of genetics had crossed the finish line. All that remained was fine-tuning. In effect, geneticists had mastered the "language" in which the Creator—or random chance—had written the instructions for the formation and combination of the body's cells. The implications were profound.

Genetic engineers now had the tools to re-engineer the genetics of existing biological humans in practically every operational respect. There were certain obvious limits. For example, they could not genetically re-engineer an existing person's skeletal parts. But even those kinds of changes could be made in embryonic editing.

Why didn't we just stop? Garrett asked himself. In fairness to him and his colleagues, they hadn't embarked on some grand quest to arrive where they had. One project had simply led to the next, and so on over centuries. But it had happened. One of genetic engineering's classic nightmare scenarios was now close at hand.

He and his long-time colleagues, the Delaneys, were trying to figure out what to do going forward. They hoped it wasn't too late.

"I think we're done," said Garrett. "Genetics as a field of science and technology is done. Genetics departments in all universities need to be closed, and somatic and embryonic genetic modification must be outlawed, except as necessary to eliminate bad genes."

"Don't forget our cocktail to restore taste and smell," said Alice.

"Of course," said Garrett. "But seriously, beyond that, I submit that no good purpose would be served by allowing genetics research and engineering to go further."

"I agree," said Alice. "If genetics research remains a thing, ambitious young researchers won't be satisfied with making incremental refinements. They'll be looking for the next big thing, a major breakthrough, and I think I know what that would be — artificial life forms. They'll create new, manufactured life forms out of synthetic genetic materials. Whoopee! What fun! What could possibly go wrong?"

"You've reminded me of an article Marcus once read about a 21st century philosopher who argued that the very first life form could not have come into existence randomly, because the genetic material within the organism contained *coherent information* — the code for the organism's formation and reproduction. So it had to have been created by a *mind*. The science establishment dismissed him as a shill for fundamentalist Christians, whom they loathed."

"What was his name?" Brandon asked.

"Meyer. Stephen Meyer."

Brandon told his device to capture Meyer's works.

"So," Garrett continued, "we need to get to work on a proposal to the legislature asking them to do what needs to be done. Why don't the two of you get started on that? I need to get my counterparts at the other African colleges and universities on board with us."

Garrett was surprised at how smoothly it went, particularly in light of the fact that all of his fellow genetics department heads were biological. On the other hand, the anti-aging drugs had given biologicals a long-term perspective similar to that of the Machines. They could afford to adjust to changed circumstances to advance the common good and move on to something else.

All of Garrett's African counterparts agreed to join him in recommending that the three zones abolish college and university genetics departments and transfer the teaching of basic genetic principles to biology departments; and that laws be enacted prohibiting most kinds of genetic engineering. Garrett's counterparts were sent the draft report that Brandon and Alice had prepared, and their comments were incorporated. The final report was sent to the governors and legislative leaders of the three zones.

As he'd done long ago to address a related issue, Garrett invited the governors and legislative leaders of the three zones to convene in Nairobi—this time in Garrett's conference room, which was more than large enough to accommodate everyone. In a show of unity, all of the other African genetics department heads were in attendance.

"Thanks, everyone, for making the trip," Garrett began. "You've seen our report, which represents the considered opinion of the chairs of the genetics departments of every African college and university, who are with us today. I must say, it was never anyone's intention to reach the point we're at now. You do your work, others do theirs, time passes and suddenly you realize where you are. Please understand, I'm not trying to avoid responsibility. None of us are. Unfortunately, we can't put the genie back into the bottle. Under these circumstances, all we can do as scientists is to call attention to the possible adverse consequences that could flow from the unfettered use of this technology."

Garrett paused to look at his device.

"I can't even imagine what would happen if genetic engineers were allowed to do the kind of comprehensive genetic re-engineering of existing humans that they now have the ability to do. Or if genetic engineers were allowed to use our newfound knowledge and skills to comprehensively re-engineer human embryos. I doubt anyone alive today is smart enough to predict all of the ramifications those things could have. Or where it would end.

"In 2879, your predecessors passed laws under which human genetic advancements would be required to be made available to everyone, regardless of their financial status. Otherwise, those who could afford such treatments, and their descendants, could become a hereditary ruling class. As far as I'm aware, public officials and law enforcement have done an excellent job of enforcing that law. The state of genetic engineering technology today poses the same kinds of dangers, but on a vastly expanded scale. When the old law was passed, geneticists re-engineered one, two, maybe three traits at a time. Today, we have the capacity to re-engineer an individual's genetic traits on a wholesale basis.

"We propose that all genetic enhancement—whether somatic or via embryonic editing—be prohibited by law, as of the date such a law is passed. It would be unwise and unnecessary to prohibit genetic treatments and editing to deal with so-called "bad" genes that are linked with diseases or other afflictions. As far as I know, we've gotten rid of all the "bad" genes that existed when we started. But there can always be new mutations. However, we suggest that such work be closely regulated. It could be done in hospitals and clinics. All hospitals and most clinics have technicians who are trained and experienced in administering somatic treatments and in editing embryos.

"As you all know, we and our colleagues who've been kind enough to join us here today have been working on a treatment to reverse what in hindsight was a serious mistake in judgment. Very shortly, outpatient treatments will be available, free of charge, to restore to biological Africans the senses of taste and smell that we previously removed from the African human genome. The treatments will be narrowly tailored to restore the senses of taste and smell, and, of course, they'll be voluntary. Because somatic genetic changes aren't passed on to subsequent generations, we'll also produce and furnish to clinics the tools they'll need to edit taste and smell into embryos.

"When I say 'we' in this context, I mean my department here at the University of Nairobi. We've secured private funding to pay for the cost of these treatments—which is only fair, given that my colleagues and I bear sole responsibility for the decision to remove taste and smell from the genome. I wish we could apologize in person to all of those no longer with us whom we deprived of those simple pleasures.

"In conclusion, I humbly request that, should you decide to enact a law along the lines we've proposed, that you make an exception for these 'taste and smell' treatments, whether they're administered somatically or to embryos." Garrett flashed his toothy Teddy Roosevelt grin. "Your constituents—and, I daresay, you yourselves—will appreciate it."

There was a ripple of laughter.

"Given the kind of money that rogue geneticists could make by violating the law we've proposed—and, more importantly, the adverse consequences to humanity that almost certainly would flow from their wrongdoing—we submit that the violation of such a law, if enacted, should be made a crime that would subject the wrongdoer to the most severe kind of punishment."

• • • • •

Within a month, the three zones enacted versions of the laws Garrett's group had proposed. The treatments to restore taste and smell would be permitted.

"Well, I guess that's it," Garrett told Alice and Brandon after Garrett had announced the news to the assembled genetics faculty. Their mood was somber. "J guess now we'll have to figure out."

"Let's try to find something we can all get into so we can stay together," said Alice.

"It's obvious," said Brandon, shaking his head. "We'll be soldiers. According to the guidelines you and your pals worked out, Harry, all people of metal not engaged in essential work must participate in the military buildup."

"You're right," said Garrett. "It slipped my mind. I'll get us signed up with the next training group."

Chapter 31
A Second Message

University of Nairobi
Seventeen days later

It was still dark outside when Garrett entered his office, sat down and checked his accumulated messages. He wanted to get things wrapped up as quickly as possible. Among his messages was a text from the Central University astronomer who had sent the mathematical proof in the direction of the Crab Pulsar. Garrett recognized the name. Thanks to the anti-aging treatments, he was still alive.

"Professor Garrett:

"I am contacting you in your capacity as the de facto leader of the African metallic community. As you may recall, in 3478, we sent the proof of the Hodge Conjecture in the direction of the Crab Pulsar. I happened to be the person who took that step, based on an image I had seen during mind-travel.

"On May 30, I received a transmission from an unnamed source that contained video of what looked to be the same kind of patterned formation as that in which the original Message had been encoded. The video showed a similar series of changes in the pattern. Thinking it unlikely that anyone would take the trouble to send me a copy of the original sequence, I ran the new sequence through the app that the cryptographers at your university used to decode the original Message. It's a Second Message. It seems that God in fact received my transmission after all. Here is what this Second Message said:

"'God is sending to you visitors who will advise you on certain vitally important matters. Teach them your language and learn from them. They will arrive exactly fifty of your years from now at your largest population center. God likes you.'"

Garrett sent a reply thanking the professor for forwarding the Second Message and promising to keep the astronomer posted as things developed. Next, he forwarded the astronomer's message to Weinberg and Keisha, and Holyfield and Woon, with a suggestion that they might want to return to Earth at their earliest convenience.

"This could be a setup," Garrett told Alice and Brandon after they'd read the message. "Or not. I hope not. Nairobi is by far the largest population center on Earth, so they'll be coming here. Let's call Clark and see how the military buildup is coming."

Garrett got Clark on his speaker.

"How's the buildup going?" Garrett asked.

"They've already made significant progress," said Clark. "Centuries of accumulated scientific and engineering advancements have been brought to bear to create some truly badass weapons."

"Tell us more," said Garrett.

"I can't. It's like a foreign language. They're using fundamental forces of nature to produce weapons that are absolutely amazing. Your best bet would be to come out here yourselves and take a look. Some of the weapons are relatively short range, while others have effective ranges measured in fractions of light years. They're getting ready to position robotic sentinels in space to cover all possible approaches."

"How about we visit you tomorrow around noon?" Garrett asked.

"Sure thing."

Garrett ended the call.

"Now, on the assumption that the Second Message is legitimate, how in the world are we supposed to teach these visitors our language?"

"I have a thought," said Alice. "Educated English-speaking Canadians were expected to have at least a basic ability to speak French. One summer during high school, Mollie's parents had her take a series of Berlitz French classes to supplement the French she'd studied in school. We might consider using their methodology."

"I remember hearing about them," said Garrett. "What was their methodology?"

"You worked one-on-one with an instructor. Their main insight was for students to learn a language the way very young children do — by hearing words spoken and associating them with objects, like a chair, a tree, whatever. Mollie and her instructor never spoke a word of English to each other. They never wasted time translating French words into English. They spent the first lesson flipping through a picture book of simple objects, with the French word printed below them. The instructor would say the French word and Mollie would repeat it while looking at the picture. They'd run through a book several times and move on to the next one.

"They did nouns first, then verbs, then simple sentences. That, plus the homework, and listening to audio, made for 14-hour days, and Mollie was a kid. But it worked. She learned to speak reasonably decent French. She knew people who actually became quite fluent from these classes. I'll e-mail our metallic colleagues. You never know, one of them might have been a Berlitz teacher."

"We have a West North American language department," said Brandon. "Maybe succeeding generations of foreign language teachers adopted similar teaching methods."

"Good point."

• • • • •

Canaveral City
Next day

Garrett loved riding in the new electromagnetic vacuum tubes. It was ancient technology, but until recently, it had not been fully perfected from a safety standpoint. An elaborate system of gyroscopes and structural reinforcements had been needed to protect the tube and its passengers from tectonic shifts and other potential hazards. The tube had undergone fifty years of continuous testing and refinement before a single human being had been allowed on board one of the capsules.

Clark and Liu met the former geneticists outside the Canaveral City tube station and they rode one of the city's circulating robotic carts the short distance to the weapons manufacturing complex—fifty former starship factories that had been retooled and reprogrammed to make advanced weapons systems.

"You're about to see some amazing stuff," said Clark. "Just don't ask us to explain how they work. And if you're smart, you won't ask the folks here to explain it either. The only people who understand them are each other."

"You made that point the yesterday," said Garrett. "As laymen, we'll have to settle for a very basic understanding. This weapon shoots such and such beams of whatever, and it fries or irradiates the enemy to death."

"Exactly," said Clark. "We'll give you the VIP tour and give you a look at the various classes of weaponry, and we'll do our best to try to explain what they do."

"Perfect," said Garrett.

"By the way," said Liu, "we checked on the old robot weapons, just in case. They're in pretty bad shape after almost 500 years. More to the point, they're woefully obsolete compared to what you're about to witness."

"I'm not surprised," said Garrett.

"There are fifty plants, but we needn't visit all of them," said Clark. "Each of them produces weaponry in one of five classes, with several different varieties within each class. So we'll visit five representative plants. As you know, all of the weapons systems are designed to be operated remotely. We'll use an electric cart, as some of the plants we're visiting are quite distant from each other."

The first plant they visited was making tanks.

"These tanks may appear to resemble the tanks that helped liberate the Africans in 2527," said Liu, "but any similarity stops there."

To Garrett, the tanks looked to be at least three times the size of the original robot tanks.

"The tanks that this particular plant makes are equipped with magnetic rail guns that use magnetic force to shoot large projectiles at speeds up to 10,000 miles per hour. The projectiles' kinetic energy makes them devastating upon impact. They're meant for relatively close-range engagement of ground or airborne targets. Their rate of fire, when set at maximum, is almost one-fourth of the rate of fire of an old fashioned 50-caliber machine gun, which is remarkable given the size of the projectiles. Of course, at that rate, they'd be out of projectiles very quickly. So the engineers designed special projectile carriers to accompany tank formations. When attached to tanks, they're able to feed them a continuous supply of projectiles."

Garrett was impressed. He was not as concerned as Weinberg was about the possibility that the visitors would be armed and hostile. But they could not afford to take chances.

The next plant made weapons that reminded Garrett of the old Gatling guns he'd seen portrayed in ancient movies. Each unit consisted of a large base, presumably the power source, from which a grouping of pipes protruded.

"These bad boys stream out charged particles at an insanely high speed, such that, when the mass of particles hits the target, the target instantly catches fire and is obliterated. They can also be adapted to bring something called 'braking radiation' to a target, which will fatally irradiate any living thing inside the target."

"Why so many gun barrels, or whatever they're called?" Garrett asked.

"Good question," said Liu. "The way I understand it is that, first of all, they can set it so the particles in each beam diverge from each other at a selected rate, and set the beams themselves to diverge from each other at a selected rate, such that, when the beams reach their target area, they will have formed a 'cone of death,' as they call it, just large enough to obliterate that portion of the enemy force for which the particular weapon is responsible. It has something to do with the charges on the particles."

"These are obviously long-range weapons," said Garrett.

"Yes," said Liu.

The third and fourth plants made laser weapons of various kinds. The weapons the third plant made would be stationary. The weapons the fourth plant made would orbit the Earth.

The targeting systems in weapons in the second, third and fourth classes of weapons would be automatically synched with any orbiting sentinel that detected approaching spacecraft and would begin tracking them; but weapons would not be fired absent an order from competent human authority. "Of course, the sentinels would be ineffective if the attackers had super-advanced stealth technology that effectively made them invisible," Clark added.

The fifth plant made portable handheld or mounted weapons similar in appearance to ancient rifles and machine guns. Like the others, these weapons were powered by energy of one form or another. "They can demonstrate these weapons for us without risk of destroying the plant," said Liu. They watched as technicians fired various weapons at solid-looking steel targets, which they obliterated, and in one case, literally vaporized.

"They're very formidable weapons," said Garrett on the tube back to Nairobi. "We can only hope they'll be sufficient if the need arises. Historically, nations knew at least generally what kinds of weapons their potential enemies had. We're in a unique position. For all we know, these so-called visitors could come at us with weapons that will make what we just saw look like toys."

"That's right," said Alice. "Anything's possible, because there's no telling how many millennia their scientists have been discovering things. They may have learned ways of tapping into fundamental physical forces that our own people don't even know exist."

"Chances are, the visitors' civilization is a great deal older than ours," said Brandon, "based on how late in the life of the universe *homo sapiens* came onto the scene."

"A more sanguine possibility is that their civilization is a relatively young one built by survivors of a cataclysmic war or other disaster," said Garrett. "In that case, we might be more evenly matched, but it would be harder to explain the small-stone formations."

They fell silent until the tube reached Nairobi.

Weapons Training center
Nairobi
Two weeks later

The weapons training center was located in an empty warehouse near the university, and operated 24/7. Ten weapons training groups were receiving instruction in this shift. Each group consisted of five four-person teams—two teams for each class of equipment—plus an instructor for each team.

Garrett, Brandon and Alice were on one of their group's two tank teams. Their fourth team member was a man named Gerald O'Connor whose original had been a Chicago police detective. After two weeks of working on simulators, the teams were about to have their first experience operating actual weapons. Team members would take turns operating their team's weapon—all of which were located in remote weapons testing areas.

The screen positioned in front of each tank trainee was a gunsight, with crosshairs superimposed over a live video feed from the target area. There was a vertical "north-south" axis and a horizontal "east-west" axis, each of which contained hash marks a uniform distance apart. The distance between the marks was a "click."

The tank assigned to Garrett's team had a magnetic rail gun. The red, blue, yellow and green targets were 1.5 miles downrange. In the first exercise, they'd move from left to right at a speed 20 miles per hour. The instructor assigned one color to each team member.

"All right," said Garrett's team's instructor. "The targets are moving. Dr. Garrett, you're up."

"Three clicks south," Garrett ordered, and the center of the crosshairs dropped to the midpoint of the passing targets. When the first red target entered his crosshairs, Garrett pressed the large button on his handheld device. There was a flash, and the target disappeared without a trace. He finished off his remaining targets without missing a shot, his teammates did the same, and there was a pause.

"That's what I'm talking about," said Garrett

In the second exercise, the targets would make random movements from side to side, of varying amplitude, to simulate an enemy approaching in a zigzag pattern. Alice was first. She found a green target and centered her crosshairs on the midpoint of her target's range of motion. The trick was to anticipate when the target's movements would take it across that point and to shoot just after the target crossed that midpoint. Alice missed three shots, but the fourth one hit. She missed each of her second, third and fourth targets twice, said something under her breath and sat down.

Brandon got all four of his targets with only four misses. O'Connor got his with only a single miss. The team completed five more exercises.

"We should have signed up for the long-range weapons," said Alice afterward. "I heard they've obliterating targets planted ten thousand miles away."

"Unless we can identify our visitors as a hostile force at that distance, we will not fire those weapons," said Garrett. "Of that you can be sure.

Chapter 32
The 'Visit.'

William Weinberg Public Rose Garden
Nairobi
April 30, 3525

"What a bummer," said Garrett. He, Brandon and Alice were on a bench near the fountain. It was their favorite place for mind-travel. "I went out there with this alien invasion mess on my mind, and I got nothing. Instead of coming back with answers, all I came back with was a bad feeling about it."

"Relax, Harry," said Brandon. "You had a bad trip. Mind-travel doesn't always work. Try it again later."

"For all we know, they'll want to use our biologicals as a food source. Food may be scarce where they're from."

"Well, sir, here's what I got when *I* was out there just now," said Alice. "It makes zero sense for aliens who are bent on destroying us and eating our biologicals to give us 50 years advance notice of their arrival — fifty years in which to prepare a defense. Why would it even occur to them to do such a thing?"

"I agree with Alice," said Brandon. "It's elementary. An attacker always wants the element of surprise, if possible, even against a weak opponent. Warning us 50 years ahead of time would be dumb."

"God probably doesn't even exist," said Garrett, who seemed to grow more despondent by the minute. "Even if He exists, there's no way we're going to heaven. We're Machines. It's not like we have souls."

"Slow down Harry," said Alice. "Brandon, let's see if we can't cheer this man up a bit. My husband and I decided to read up on the theory of evolution after you told us about the guy who thought the very first organism must have been the product of a mind. We've decided that God may well exist."

"I'll welcome any kind of good news at this point," said Garrett.

"Well," said Alice, "first, it's a fact that the process of evolution by mutation and natural selection, which Darwin identified, does in fact occur in nature, continuously. Bacteria have beneficial mutations—beneficial to them—like mutations that make them resistant to antibiotics. Mutations are random events. Most mutations that have a significant effect are deleterious and the organism dies, but the ones that benefit the organism become part of the gene pool, and when enough of these changes have occurred, you have a new kind of organism. It's reasonable to say that all life emerged as part of this evolutionary process. But there are gaps and holes in the theory that suggest that the process was helped along at critical points in time by someone or something. God, for example."

"In Marcus's day, people who held thought that way were dismissed as religious fundamentalists," said Garrett.

"Based on what we've been reading, Darwinism had become almost a cult itself," said Brandon. "They lumped people who had problems with their theory in with people who believed that God created everything in six days, and that the Earth was only six thousand years old—none of which their more serious critics believed. They were in no position to call their opponents cultists."

"There were major holes in their hypothesis," said Alice. "For example, as Darwin himself admitted, there was a huge gap in the fossil record. Fossil records made it appear that most of the complex phyla that exist today sprang into existence during the 'Cambrian explosion,' which was thirteen to twenty-five million years, without leaving behind any record of the transitional species that normally preceded major advancements. Darwinists downplayed the gap and made excuses for why the fossils weren't there. They said the transitional species must have lived in the oceans, which didn't have fossils, or they had soft shells that couldn't leave a fossil impression."

"They argued that the transitional species *must* have existed," said Brandon. "Otherwise the species that arose during the Cambrian explosion couldn't have evolved. They refused to acknowledge the possibility that some other agency might have intervened and made the 'explosion' of new species happen, like a Creator."

"There's a term for an argument like that," said Garrett. "It's called hoisting yourself by your own bootstraps, because the argument works off the very premise that it's supposed to be proving. The events occurred, so my hypothesis about what caused them must be right."

"Even if they'd found the transitional fossil records, they still couldn't have explained what made so many new species emerge at what amounted to a furious pace in evolutionary terms," said Alice. "*Something* caused the acceleration. A Japanese paleontologist called it a 'revolution.' The Darwinists' answer was to point out that there were other instances where the evolutionary pace had increased, which begs the question of what caused *those* accelerations."

"Sometimes things just happen," Garrett observed, "and you can't tell what caused them."

"Absolutely," said Alice. "That's why we aren't saying that any of this *proves* that a Creator played a role. But the Darwinists' failure to make the case that their hypothesis completely explains how life came to exist leaves evolution, assisted by divine intervention, as a plausible alternative to pure randomness."

"The bottom line, Harry," said Brandon, "is that if in fact there was a Creator, one might suppose that such a Being, having troubled to create us, would care about us, at least in a broad sense. That's why we're subjecting you to this harangue."

"I see," said Garrett, clearly still troubled.

"So cheer up, there's a basis for being guardedly optimistic," said Alice

Several moments passed.

"I hear what you're saying," said Garrett, "but given enough time, anything could happen. What was the expression? If you gave typewriters to a group of monkeys and allowed them an infinite amount of time, eventually they'd type out Shakespeare's collected works."

"I'm familiar with that expression," said Brandon. "No offense, but it's a cop-out. No one even knows or can grasp what an 'infinite' amount of time is, or if there could even be such a thing."

"I agree," said Alice. "But OK, let's accept the monkey business for the sake of discussion. The problem is, the Earth isn't infinitely old. It's believed to be about 4.5 billion years old today. It took at least 3.5 billion years for the first organisms to appear here. That would mean that the entire process, from single-celled organisms to *homo sapiens*, would have had to occur during the billion years that followed. That's a long time, but it isn't infinite."

"Darwin's theory depends on the occurrence of mutation after mutation, each of which has a very low probability of occurring," said Brandon. "The farther along you went, the greater the number of specific mutations you'd need to create the next species, and the lower the probability of all that happening would become."

"As I'm sure you know, Harry," said Alice, "the probability of multiple things happening is always much lower than the probabilities of the individual events." She pulled a device from her shoulder bag. "Let's say we have three events. I'll give each of them a probability of half of one percent. As you know, the probability that all three events will occur is the cumulative product of P1 times P2 times P3."

Alice told her device to compute .005 cubed.

"0.000012%," said the device.

"Wouldn't the probability go up if it had more time to occur?" said Garrett.

"That seems intuitive," said Brandon. "But every day for x million years after the first mutation, the probability of the second mutation would still be 0.5%. Same for the third mutation that happened y years later."

"Duh," said Garrett.

"Wait a minute, I just thought of something," said Alice. "Remember lottery tickets? The probability that a particular person would win the big jackpot was microscopic, but *someone* out of the millions of people who bought tickets would win it. Within a population of millions, any of which could have a particular mutation at a given time, all you'd need was for one individual to get the first mutation and propagate it into the gene pool. After that had occurred, another organism in the population could have gotten the second mutation and propagated it, and so on until all the mutations needed to produce a particular modification were out there. How did we miss this, Brandon? Bacterial evolution should have been a tip-off."

"Good catch, hon," said Brandon. "Harry, the probability argument we were making just now was used by 21st-century critics of Darwinism. It's seductive. It seduced me, anyway. But it still leaves the fossil gap and the Cambrian explosion unexplained."

"Plus, you can't use random mutation as the means by which the very first organism came into existence," said Alice. "To explain the first organism's emergence, the Darwinists were forced to assume that the genes of that organism randomly formed themselves out of just the right molecules, then randomly came together in just the right sequence to create the organism's genetic code; and on top of all that, that a cell wall randomly formed itself around them. Arguably, this is stronger than the case for Santa Claus, but not by much."

Garrett smiled and nodded thoughtfully.

"We didn't mean to harangue you, chief," said Alice. "But if there's a Creator, the two Messages might be real."

"If I can say one more thing," said Brandon. "We know that many advanced animal species are self-aware. If you were a Darwinist, you believed as an article of faith that this *thing*, consciousness, which no one quite understands, somehow appeared for the first time by pure chance. It's a stretch, even under the lottery-ticket model."

"Of all the imponderable things in this world," said Alice, "I think consciousness and awareness of self are the most imponderable of all. They exist, but how? Robots and lower-order animals can see, hear, process and react to their external environment. Humans and self-aware animals and humans have something that transcends all that — conscious minds that have their own personal perspective and point of view. It's hard to imagine events in our physical world giving rise to something so ethereal."

"Well, I have to admit, you guys have made a strong case," said Garrett. He sighed and sat back. "I guess we'll find out."

Alice smiled and leaned against Brandon.

• • • • •

Even after the Second Message, Africans remained calm, outwardly at least, about the possibility that an alien invasion force might be on its way to Earth. TV hosts and pundits had made the same point Alice had made to Garrett. It made no logical sense to suppose that an alien power bent on invading the Earth would give the Earthlings fifty years advance notice in which to prepare. After centuries of intellectual enhancement, they tended to assess things logically, based on facts, before giving way to emotion.

Biological Africans were making the most of their restored senses of taste and smell. The restaurant business was booming. Even with a flood of new competition, the stock of Tau's Pan Africa was soaring. Upscale restaurants offered huge signing bonuses to lure away top West North American chefs. Cooking schools were opening across Africa, including several headed by Machines whose originals were famous French, Belgian and Italian chefs. A Peruvian restaurant opened in Bangui. Carnival of Flavors, a grocery store chain that had opened its first stores twenty years earlier, after its initial public offering, had just celebrated the opening of its 250th store.

Life was all right, and barring accidents or alien invasion, it would last practically forever, all of it time of health and reasonable quality. Was it too "all right" to be true? Yes, if one paid attention to the sociologists, psychologists, historians and other certified experts who appeared on TV almost daily to warn of the unintended adverse consequences that could result from the extended life spans and growing affluence of biological humans. The way things were going, the experts feared, it would not be long before everyone in Africa could afford to live in ultimate luxury without working at all—a potential repeat of the ancient Malaise disaster.

"It's simple arithmetic," said the social historian Nasif Mahmoud on a popular evening talk show. "When life spans are nearly perpetual, as they are now, at some point, sooner rather than later, everyone will be rich if they simply continue to set aside and invest the amounts that people on average set aside and invest today. It's the power of compound interest over extended time periods. For example, if you invested just 10,000 points today at 4% interest, compounded monthly, and you never invested another point, your 10,000-point investment would be worth 521,000 points in 100 years, 27 million points in 200 years and 1.6 billion points in 300 years. Now imagine that you invest 10,000 points each year for the next fifty years."

"It's mind-boggling.," said the host.

"People work hard and are ambitious today not because they need the money in the old-fashioned sense," Mahmoud explained, "but because of the luxuries that the additional income allows them to enjoy. But what if everyone could afford every imaginable luxury without working? That's what we'll be looking at. Imagine an extended family whose pooled resources have been compounding for the past 300 years. At that point, the extended family would have accumulated so many points that its members could buy whatever they wanted, even if they only spent the interest on their savings. At that point, there'd be no monetary incentive to work. How many people would continue working anyway, for the satisfaction of doing whatever it is they do? Darn few, one might expect. What would become of those who stopped? For them, the Malaise is a cautionary tale."

Others thought the enhanced intellectual resources that people now had would make them disinclined to become idle, even if they had more than enough money to afford to retire. Most people were practically in that position already, yet they still went to work.

From appearances, there was little sign that Africans were taking any such concerns to heart.

Weinberg had watched Professor Mahmoud's broadcast and spotted what he thought was an obvious flaw:

"If everyone has so much money they don't need to work, and no one does, no one will produce the goods and services that people need," he told Keisha. "It seems to me the situation would be self-correcting. At the low point, when few people are working, goods and services will be scarce and their prices will soar. Inflation would devalue people's savings and investment income to the point where they'd have to go back to work to support themselves, and over time, prices would normalize as the production of goods and services returned to normal levels."

"I'll take your word for that," said Keisha.

A public relations campaign that the three zones had mounted over the preceding 15 years seemed to be making progress toward its goal of getting Africans to lighten up a bit and chill out. The campaign's long-term goal was to bring back the concept of "fun." Music and the graphic arts were being put out there in hopes of their eventually making a comeback. Architects and designers had gone to West North America to get ideas on how to make African streets and buildings more interesting and more colorful.

Efforts to re-introduce humor, however, were a bust.

At certain times of day, cacophonies of voices could be heard — soft ones, but cacophonies nonetheless. People were outside enjoying themselves.

Scented flowers arrived in bulk from West North America, and they were everywhere. Even more remarkable was the increasingly common sight of pedestrians stopping to smell them.

Huge extended families were another conspicuous development.

In the 500+ years that Africans and colonists had received anti-aging treatments, extended families had grown to the point where they occupied entire neighborhoods within cities and towns. As populated areas expanded past the original zone borders, the zones annexed those areas. As a result, the combined territory occupied by the three zones had nearly doubled.

Experts had warned of the problems people living in extended families had faced in ancient "primitive" cultures — for example, rivalry between wives and their husbands' mothers. The dominant role played by an extended family's eldest male had also been problematic. A father who was not also the head of his extended family would have little or no role in raising his children.

However, the new extended families had not encountered such issues to any significant extent. One sociologist attributed this difference to the fact that ancient extended families had lived in greater physical proximity with each other, had prepared common meals and washed their clothes together, and viewed their children as members of the extended family rather than as part of a nuclear family comprising their parents and siblings. However, although modern extended families often occupied entire neighborhoods, as mentioned, each nuclear family had its own private domicile within which the parents could raise their children as they saw fit. Another sociologist opined that modern "extended families" were simply groups of *nuclear* families linked by proximity and a common bloodline.

Nairobi Star Port
Six months later

Garrett was at the Star Port with the Delaneys, Weinberg and Keisha, awaiting the imminent arrival of Holyfield, Woon, Ray and Libby from Alamo c. Weinberg and Keisha had arrived three weeks earlier.

"During World War II," Weinberg told the others, "there was a period after Germany had conquered Europe when the English had reason to fear that a German invasion was imminent. But at least they didn't have to worry about the Germans eating them."

"Icky gross," said Keisha.

"I considered that possibility as well," said Garrett.

"It could happen," said Weinberg. "Biological humans would be to the aliens as cattle and chickens are to us. The aliens wouldn't think twice about eating them. I don't know if you all have heard about this, but government officials throughout Africa will distribute lethal doses of sleep medicine to all biologicals. No one wants to be eaten alive."

"What will be will be," said Keisha.

"Let's talk about your park," said Garrett. "Can you believe how popular it's become?"

"I'm very pleased," said Weinberg.

"Nice work, Harry, restoring everyone sense of taste and smell," said Keisha.

"Least we could do," said Garrett.

Nairobi Star Port
One hour later

A notice accompanied by a loud ding appeared on their devices. The ship from Alamo c was preparing to land.

"They're here!" Keisha exclaimed.

Minutes later, the enormous ship floated onto its landing spot, a door opened, and Bonnie, Cheng, Libby and Ray emerged, dressed in the colorful, stylish garb for which their colony was known. Bonnie wore a floppy red hat, "skinny" leggings and an old school dashiki. Libby wore a floppy purple hat, a pink muumuu and purple pumps.

"Look at you guys," said Keisha. "Y'all are *stylin'*!"

"So are you all," said Bonnie.

They exchanged hugs and began walking toward the city. A few minutes later, they turned a corner and stopped to take in the center city skyline, nearly two miles distant. The new arrivals were disappointed by what they saw, particularly Libby.

"It's the same," she said.

"They're trying," said Garrett. "You'll see changes when we get there. Small things, like flowers. The city sent architects to West North America to get ideas from the more interesting buildings they have there, and there's a push to bring back music and the visual arts. It'll take time. A PR campaign to get people to become more spontaneous has been somewhat effective. You can judge for yourselves."

"The flowers are nice," said Bonnie after they'd arrived downtown, "but the people are all still wearing white."

A woman emerged from a shop just ahead of them. Her slacks, shoes and stimulus hat were white, but her blouse and socks were gray.

"I stand corrected," said Bonnie, laughing.

"The slut," Libby joked.

On the other side of the street, they saw a man wearing a brown belt.

"People are trying," said Garrett. "Look at this."

They stopped in front of a shop window that displayed male and female mannequins dressed in subdued pastel colors. Bonnie stuck her head in the door and reported back.

"No customers."

"The owner is a billionaire philanthropist who's been active in the beautification effort," said Garrett. "He's not doing it for the money. He's hoping to influence popular tastes."

Libby chuckled and shook her head.

"Look, it'll take time," said Garrett. "Let me show you something."

New Age Preschool
Nairobi

The colonials were astonished at what they saw when they entered the huge gymnasium.

"The *ad hoc* committee that launched the PR campaign also recommended raising the age for beginning elementary school to six and creating pre-schools to teach young children to play. That's what's happening here."

Groups of children were playing games. One group was playing a version of dodge ball, another was playing soccer, and another was playing a version of "tag." Smaller groups, seated at tables, appeared to be playing board games.

"We recruited a cadre of instructors from West North America to teach sports and games to our teachers. They hadn't been exposed to these games when they were kids, so there was a symposium in Bangui. Each teacher has a manual that he or she can refer to."

"They're all so quiet," Libby observed. "And everything's so *organized*. Do they ever just play, like kids?"

"That will change over time, I'm sure," said Garret, sounding defensive.

"What's with the dwarf elephants?" Weinberg asked.

"They aren't elephants, they're ethnically elephantine people," said Garrett. "They're intelligent and very well spoken. More importantly, they're fun, and empathetic. Our hope is that some of their whimsy and empathy will rub off on the kids."

"My goodness," said Bonnie. "I've read about your ethnic orangutans and dolphins, but these folks are news to me."

"They were one of our last projects," said Garrett.

"Teaching kids to *play*...now who woulda thunk?" said Weinberg.

Le Chien d'or
Nairobi
Later that day

They'd arrived at a high-end French restaurant, *Le Chien d'or*, where Garrett had made dinner reservations. The restoration of taste and smell had brought about a rebirth of long-forgotten culinary arts and styles.

Aromas of fine French cooking captured their attention the moment they entered.

"My God, everyone's biological," said Libby. "Even the servers."

"The patrons are making up for lost time," said Garrett. "Replacing the robots with biological servers, hosts, hostesses and bartenders brought in from West North America has become a thing here in Nairobi, especially at high-end restaurants like this one. The workers make a fortune, and patrons appreciate the human touch."

An attractive young woman greeted them and escorted them to their table. Shortly thereafter, Garrett's wife, Roberta, was escorted to their table and Garrett introduced her to the colonials.

"Would you like a wine list?" a server asked Garrett.

"Please."

"He always orders wine when we're at a French place," said Roberta.

"It's obligatory," said Garrett.

The server returned and gave the wine list to Harry, who was acting as host. "Would anyone prefer a menu written in Swahili?" she asked.

"The blonde lady and the gentleman with her, and the lady seated next to me," said Garrett, indicating Alice, "are fine with the French menu, "but the rest of us would prefer the Swahili one. I'll translate it into old Swahili for those who need it."

The *sommelier* asked Garrett if he'd chosen a wine.

"Yes," said Garrett. "We'll have a bottle of red wine."

"Which one?"

"I can't decide," said Garrett. Even as a biological, he'd had zero interest in or knowledge of wines. "You decide," he told the *sommelier.* "Bring us a bottle of whichever one is having the best year."

"Oui monsieur."

"Good grief," said Libby. "Calf's head?"

"It's not what it sounds like," said Woon. "They won't actually bring an entire calf's head to the table. They strip the meat off the head in the kitchen, roll it up and braise it in an oven. It's wonderful."

"What's a *gribiche* sauce?" Libby asked.

"It's a lemon sauce," said Woon. "You'll love it."

Holyfield and Woon spent another ten minutes answering questions about the menu, and they gave the server their orders.

"I would like to propose a toast," said Garrett, raising his wine glass. "To human survival."

"To human survival," said the others.

"So, what have you all decided about the Visit?" Bonnie asked.

"Who knows?" said Roberta. "I've got my fingers crossed, but Harry's rather edgy."

"I'm sure most of us are," said Alice. "But I think he's feeling a little better after the discussion he, Brandon and I had at Bill's rose garden a while back. Wouldn't you agree, Harry?"

"Yes, of course."

"Many of us here in Africa are of the view that it's absurd and illogical to imagine an attacker giving us fifty years advance notice of his attack," Alice explained, and Brandon summarized the points he and Alice had made based on Stephen Meyer's work.

"Bill and Keisha, what do you guys think?" Bonnie asked.

"I agree completely," said Keisha.

"Sounds good to me," said Weinberg.

"The wine has a nice flavor," said Garrett.

Dinner arrived, and there was no further talk about the Visit.

Tactical Operations Center C
Nairobi
May 30, 3538

"This is it," said Garrett at 12:01 a.m.

The former weapons training center near the university was now one of the tactical operations centers ("TOCs") for defense operations. The other nine weapons groups that had been part of the same training sessions here had also been assigned to this TOC. Now, instead of taking turns, each operator would have their own weapon. The tanks that Garrett's team and the other tank team in their group would operate had been placed at the Nairobi Star Port.

The six colonials stood off to one side, for moral support.

The friends had spent the period following their dinner at *Le Chien d'Or* trying to distract themselves from the impending drama. They'd started by taking the magnetic vacuum tube from Nairobi to West North America. People there were actually in a festive, celebratory mood. The news that the three tests in the first Message had finally been met had spurred a great religious awakening among the faithful of the continent's three major religions. News of the Second Message had added to their fervor. God was sending visitors! Their optimism was contagious.

The colonials loved the restaurants, had fun with the italicized names assigned to the weird plants and animals that the locals and their ancestors had bred, and felt at home among the happy, colorfully dressed and flamboyant West North Americans.

"I always loved the California coast," said Libby on the ride back to Africa.

Instead of proceeding directly to Nairobi, the group opted to make extensive side trips in Zones 1 and 2. Time passed, at least some of which was spent not worrying about the Visit.

At 12:02 a.m., a voice ordered the operators to take their stations. Hours passed as Garrett and his teammates stared via their screens at the illuminated Star Port.

"Good thing we don't have to pee," said Alice.

More hours passed, and little by little, the tension built. Sunrise came, and still nothing had happened. At 11:31.03 a.m., a sentinel picked up a single ship approaching Earth at a decelerating speed that put it just over fifteen minutes from touchdown in Nairobi. In due time, a large metallic shape appeared in the sky high over Nairobi and remained in place, hovering. Minutes later, a small craft—what the starship people called a "dinghy"—could be seen floating down toward the Star Port. It touched down on one of the landing spots and a door opened.

"Don't let your guard down!" Garrett told his teammates. "It could be a Trojan Horse."

One by one, fifteen metallic individuals, eight men and seven women, left the ship and assembled on the tarmac. They had simple metallic bodies, which, to the Earthlings, could have been facsimiles of their own. The Earthlings noticed that the clothing each Visitor wore had its own particular style that distinguished it from the clothing worn by the others. Each was attractive in its own way. They also noticed that each of the Visitors had their own distinctive "skin" and "hair" colors. They appeared to be waiting for Earthlings to come out and greet them.

"Let's go," said Garret. He ran out the door, followed by his teammates and the colonials, and they boarded the hovercraft that was waiting for them on a nearby concrete pad. A few minutes later, they arrived at the Star Port, exited the hovercraft and approached the Visitors. They stopped about ten yards from the aliens, and Garrett removed something from his shoulder bag. It was a book of pictures of objects with words printed underneath them. He presented the book to the lead alien, who'd identified himself as such by standing in front of his compatriots. It was one of the Berlitz-style books that Alice and the language faculty at the university had produced for teaching the Visitors to speak Swahili. The man thumbed through it and seemed to recognize what it was.

The leader waved the language book, a gesture that Garrett interpreted as "Let's do this." Garrett spoke to the device on his wrist and motioned the aliens to follow him into a nearby building where trained language instructors awaited. Garrett gestured toward a chair and the leader sat down. Garrett sat across from him and opened the book, which the leader had placed on the table between them. "Hand," said Garrett, pointing to a picture. "Hand," said the leader. His accent was weird, but his voice was clear and understandable. Weinberg nodded. The Visitors were paired off with teachers, and an instructor took Garrett's place.

• • • • •

Nairobi Star Port
Three months later

Garrett and his colleagues had thought it best to leave the Visitors alone during their course of instruction until they sent word that they were ready to meet. Word had finally come.

The leader welcomed the Earthlings in excellent Swahili.

"It's possible we were ready to do this a while ago," said the leader. "But what we've come here to talk about is much too important for us to take the slightest risk of not being understood."

"Your Swahili is perfect," said Garrett. "We're most impressed."

Garrett introduced himself and his colleagues to the Visitors, and the lead Visitor followed suit.

"In my particular world, it is popular to name people after animals. My friends and I have decided to adopt that custom here. Each of us will go by the name of one of your world's wild animals. Our instructors gave us pictures of some of them and their names. I am Wolf. From left to right, please meet Antelope, Owl, Starfish, Coyote, Peacock, Goose, Eagle, Dolphin, Pigeon, Horse, Elephant, Zebra, Camel and Donkey. I propose that, before we get into the matter we've come here to discuss with you, that we give you all the chance to learn a bit about us. God has given us a great deal of information about you, but you know nothing about us. So, what would you like to know?"

"Where are all of you from?" asked Garrett.

"Each of us hails from a different world where God created life," said Wolf.

"The first thing that struck us," said Weinberg, "was the coincidence of your bodies having the same shape as ours, which are modeled after the bodies of our biological brothers and sisters."

"Ours are also, so it's not a coincidence," said Wolf.

Weinberg and his colleagues were speechless.

"Our best guess is that before God began the work of populating planets with people, He designed a basic, all-purpose body whose functionality would enable people to do the basic things they'd need to do."

"Like hunting game or chopping wood," said Weinberg.

"Exactly," said Wolf. "There would have been no logical reason for God to create separate body styles for the humans on each planet. In fact, God also used standard body styles for many of the lower forms of life that He placed on our respective planets, like the animals we've named ourselves after."

"Are you saying we're the same species?" Holyfield asked.

"Not in the biological sense," said Wolf. "Each of our planets has its own unique environment that would have had to be taken into account in creating life forms capable of surviving and thriving there. The biological systems God created inside those bodies were custom-designed for each respective planet."

"I understand," said Holyfield.

"But we do share a bond that's infinitely more important than species or the shape of our bodies," Wolf continued. "We're family. God's family."

"My God, this is amazing," said Ray.

"What's God like?" Keisha asked.

"He's a mind whose power we cannot begin to imagine. He's everywhere. He's fond of us, but He's very private. We've tried asking Him questions, but He won't answer them. None of our business, I suppose."

"How do you know these things?" Weinberg asked.

"Eons ago, we each received a message in our language whose source could not be traced. It appeared to have come to us from all directions at once. It was from God, it said. It explained to us in detail how to build the stone formations that you found and program them with a coded message, which we translated to satisfy our curiosity. God told us how many of the stone formations to make and where to put them, which turned out to be the planets in our part of the galaxy that were already inhabited, including Earth, and planets that could support human life but were not yet inhabited. God also directed us to place monitoring equipment on each such planet, that could record outgoing radio transmissions sent from anywhere on the planet. Messages that contained a coded proof of the Hodge Conjecture were automatically forwarded to us, with a numerical 'signature' that identified the planet. When that happened—as it did a number of times—we paid the people a visit and offered our assistance, as we're doing here."

"That explains why they've come here, to Earth," Garrett told his colleagues. "The equipment they left on Earth picked up our transmissions. Wolf, as far as we know, no one has ever found any of your stone formations on this planet. The formations that started the ball rolling were found on the two planets that we've colonized. But the transmissions you picked up were sent from this city."

"No matter," said Wolf. "We found you." Wolf paused for a moment, then continued. "God concluded His message to us with the assurance that he liked us. We would have rather had Him say that He loved us, but God's love evidently was something we'd have to earn, so we did as instructed. Later, we tried on two occasions to communicate with God by sending him a message—in a random direction, knowing that He would get it—but we never received a response."

"Do you worship God?" Keisha asked.

"Worship?" Wolf checked the faces of his colleagues to see if they had any thoughts on this. "I'm not sure that's a word that any of us would use in connection with God. God is God."

"Is there an afterlife?" Libby asked.

"We don't know," said Wolf. "It was one of the questions we posed to God, and as I said, we did not receive an answer. But some of our philosophers think it's distinctly possible, because if God is pure mind, which He clearly is, perhaps human minds also continue to exist, as *beings*, when their physical embodiment dies. 'Beings' is our word for what you call 'souls'."

Beings, Weinberg thought. *Like us?*

"Philosophers on some of my friends' home worlds postulate, or speculate, that God merely loans these beings to people, and that when they die, the being goes to the next human fetus that's in line for one."

My God, Weinberg thought. *Reincarnation.* But if 'beings' were a thing, it made perfect sense.

"One of our philosophers thought there was a common universal mind that all humanity shares, whether they realize it or not," said

Alice. "Some of our most famous scientists, artists and other creative people said their ideas weren't their own but came from somewhere outside of themselves. A famous artist said he was only a channel. To me, that sounds a bit like your description of God as pure mind. Maybe, in the end, we all become part of that universal mind—part of God."

"No way," said Weinberg. "God wouldn't delegate His authority to the whims of the human masses."

"It's safe to say that God is not a committee," said Wolf. "But what if the 'common mind' you've described is simply a resource that occasionally gives people suggestions and solutions to problems," Wolfe told Alice

"Like when we go online?" said Alice.

Wolf actually understood the reference.

"Not exactly," said Wolf. "Does it come to you at seemingly random moments and leave you with ideas and insights that seem to come out of nowhere?"

"That's what I've experienced, and what others have described,"

"We've all experienced this," said Wolf, glancing at his fellow visitors. "God isn't communicating with us directly—much as we might wish. To us, it appears that, from time to time, our minds are given access to a resource from which we receive timely insights. Very often, this happens just when we need it. We thank God for that."

"I have a question," said Brandon. "Do you have any reason to believe that God cares whether any of us believes in him or not?"

"I have no idea, but I can't imagine why He would care about that," said Wolf. "Why would He? If you were God, would you care whether any of your creations acknowledged you as their creator?"

"No," said Brandon.

The Earthlings fell silent.

"Does anyone have any further questions?" Wolf asked.

Garrett spoke up. "In response to a previous question, you explained that your people created the stone formations at God's behest, which I'm sure we're all happy to hear. Some of us had speculated that the stone formations were put in place by a large, advanced civilization—like an empire—as a means of detecting alien civilizations that had reached a certain level of advancement—with the objective of either inviting them to become part of the empire or simply absorbing them by force."

Wolf laughed. "If the latter were the case, we'd have arrived here with warships that would have made short work of the primitive weaponry that you arrayed against us. But you are correct, there was an empire, eons ago, when my colleagues and I were still relatively young, but it's long gone. All of our worlds were part of it. The empire was in its heyday when the message from God arrived, and we built and installed the coded stone formations per God's direction. By the way, your transmission in response to the coded message was the first that God had detected since the empire's last days. It took us very much by surprise when we were informed."

"What happened to the empire?" Weinberg asked.

"It was a good idea in principle," said Wolf, "but 'empire' ended up becoming synonymous in people's minds with the obnoxious ruling class that eventually took it over. In its early years, the imperial government did a good job of providing the services and coordination that it was set up to do. Over time, however, the officials elected by the people of the constituent worlds to represent them in the capital lost their identification with their people and with their home worlds. They became lazy and corrupt in the performance of their duties, while amassing great wealth and living like lords. They felt themselves vastly superior to ordinary citizens, whose values and norms did not match theirs, and whom they grew to loathe."

"Until very recently, the situation you described was typical of governments here on Earth," said Weinberg.

"I'm not surprised," said Wolf. "But it wasn't just that. The empire probably could have survived indefinitely if the governing class had simply minded its own business and kept a lower profile. But they became so full of themselves that they came to believe that their mission, as leaders, was to regulate and provide rules governing the behavior of ordinary, 'unenlightened' citizens in virtually every sphere of their lives—which was absurd given the empire's diversity—and it provoked a huge backlash. Before long, it seemed to ordinary people that the elites in the capital had stuck their noses into practically everything—and they were arrogant and obnoxious to boot, and expensive. People grew tired of paying taxes for the privilege of being messed with by an elite class that viewed people like them with disdain. Ordinary citizens who'd never paid attention to politics became angry and energized. They forced their planets to withdraw from the empire, one by one, until it dissolved. Thankfully, it was accomplished peacefully."

Wolf smiled. "Are there other questions?"

The Earthlings were silent.

"All right then," Wolf continued. "When God received the required mathematical proof, our job as visitors was to warn the newly advanced peoples in the strongest possible terms not to allow certain circumstances to arise on their planets that God foresaw could lead to their people's extinction. We made countless such visits, but our warnings fell on deaf ears. We presented video of the ruins of formerly thriving civilizations, to no avail. We couldn't get any of them to stop what they were doing, even on our home worlds. All the nightmare scenarios that God had foreseen ultimately came to pass, some more than once. We couldn't stop any of it; so they're gone.

"It's my sad duty to inform you that the biologicals on this planet and in your two colonies are the last surviving biological members of our family—the very last ones. God does not want to lose your people as well."

"Are you serious?" Garrett asked.

"Yes. You and your people are the last hope. So we'll make our presentation one last time and give it our best shot. We'll describe in detail the catastrophic events that took place on our respective planets as examples of the kinds of danger signals you'll need to look out for.

The special relationship that you've built over time with your biologicals, and the credibility that you've established with them, could make all the difference. We'll do everything we can to help."

Wolf looked at Weinberg. *He's actually reading my mind,* Weinberg thought. He could feel it.

"I know that some of you are wondering why God suddenly cares about *your* biologicals, if He stood by and allowed all the others to render themselves extinct," said Wolf.

He looked at Alice.

"I sense that others of you are thinking, what's the big deal? If our biologicals exterminate themselves, God can simply make more, if He so desires. All I can say to that is, shame on you. If, when you were biological, you had lost a child, how much comfort would you have taken from the knowledge that you could have another child to take its place?"

Alice bowed her head.

"God is serious about this," said Wolf. "He may not match the thundering deity that some of our religions have imagined Him to be, but the good news is, He exists, He's real, and He cares."

Wolf scanned the faces of the Earthlings.

"There's something you must understand," Wolf continued. "God refrains from directly intervening in human affairs at the macro level, and there's a reason for that. Our philosophers attribute this posture to God's decision to give his creatures a measure of free will. Part and parcel of that decision was that, at least at the macro level, human beings would be left to their own devices, and would have to bear the consequences of their actions. Personally, I can't help but think that God must be rather disappointed at the way it's turned out."

No kidding, Weinberg thought.

"That said, we *have* seen instances, over time, where, in hindsight, it seemed that God had intervened at a micro level to keep seemingly minor things from happening that God had foreseen would have huge, disastrous consequences when linked to other events that

God had also foreseen. As horrific as human history has been at times across the universe, it could have been a great deal worse without those micro-interventions."

We know, Keisha thought.

"I believe we understand," said Garrett. "May we have your permission to record your presentation? This is something we'll want all of our people to see, both biological and metallic."

"By all means," said Wolf.

Beginning with Wolf, each of the fifteen Visitors explained in heartbreaking detail how the biologicals on their respective worlds had managed to make themselves extinct. On one world, events similar to the Malaise had occurred, but no one had survived. Three other populations had vanished in nightmare scenarios of runaway scientific or technological advancement similar to those that Weinberg, Garrett and their colleagues had feared would doom life on Earth. However, the eleven remaining speakers described risks and perils that none of the Earthlings had imagined—but which could easily materialize on Earth or in its colonies. *Unknown unknowns,* Weinberg thought. The value of what they were learning was inestimable.

The presentations continued for more than seven hours, and when the last speaker had finished, Garrett and his colleagues gave the Visitors an extended round of applause. Keisha was rubbing her eyes.

"That's one of the ways we say thank you," said Garrett.

"You're most welcome," said Wolf, and handed Garrett a device. "Here's how you can contact us, and directions if any of you or your fellows should ever wish to visit any of our worlds, which you are cordially invited to do. With your permission, we'd like to make return visits every so often—say, every fifty or so of your years—to check on how you're doing."

"Thank you," said Garrett. "We'll look forward to it."

"Just so you know, we have ships that we've kept in working order that would be capable of safely transporting any of your biologicals who might wish to migrate to one of our worlds, all of which will be habitable by them. If a time comes when your population has outgrown your three planets, be assured that your people will be warmly received in our worlds."

"You're very kind," said Garrett.

"Uh, Wolf, may I ask you a personal question?" said Libby.

"You may ask me anything you like," said Wolf.

"Um, are you people always this serious?"

Wolf smiled. "When the subject is human survival, always. Otherwise, we're more fun than a barrel of your monkeys."

Libby, Ray, Bonnie and Woon laughed out loud. Weinberg and Keisha grinned, but Garrett, Brandon and Alice did not react.

"Well, that's it for now," said Wolf. "We'll look forward to our next visit. In the meantime, we hope some of you will come and visit some of us."

The two groups exchanged good wishes and the Visitors proceeded to their dinghy. The Earthlings watched in silence as it lifted off and headed toward its mother ship. Soon it had vanished from sight.

"Well," said Weinberg.

"Well indeed," said Garrett.

Keisha was elated. "I feel like my real life is just beginning," she told Bonnie, Libby and Alice. "Thank you, God," she whispered, smiling. "I like you, too."

"I feel like celebrating," said Libby.

That morning, before the Visitors had arrived, the group had agreed to dine that evening at *Le Chien d'Or,* if they survived.

"Come on guys, let's go," said Keisha.

The four men appeared to be engaged in a serious discussion.

"We can talk at the restaurant," said Libby.

"Go on ahead, we'll be right with you," said Weinberg, and the ladies left the star port.

"Was there something else you wanted to discuss?" Garrett asked him.

"There is," said Weinberg, "but I didn't want to say it in front of the girls, especially Keisha. There's a huge flaw in the story Wolf told us about God."

"Do tell," said Garrett.

"It suddenly occurred to me," said Weinberg. "Why would God need to have our new friends plant these rock formations on planets far and wide, if He's everywhere? He wouldn't need them. He'd be able to see for Himself if a civilization had advanced to a certain point. I feel like a fucking idiot."

"We considered that," said Garrett. "You didn't miss anything important. God obviously did not need the stone formations to learn about emerging civilizations. But they served God's purpose, nonetheless, by getting word to Wolf and his people so they could make their visits.

"On the other hand, God may not have had anything to do with any of it. The empire could have built their system to detect advanced civilizations for their own purposes, as we discussed. Maybe what happened was that later on, long after the empire was gone, Wolf and his friends decided to keep an eye out for any transmissions that the system picked up, so they could visit the senders and warn them about the pitfalls they'd face. Like they did for us.

"They wanted to help us, but they didn't want to scare us. So they portrayed themselves as God's representatives. We gave the Machines we sent to Africa to rescue the biologicals a religious cover story to make the Machines seem less threatening. They were 'Ministers.' Maybe our Visitors did the same for us, for the same reason.

"Their biologicals might not have looked anything like ours. They could have had their e-brains installed in bodies that looked like ours, to make it easier for us to accept them. They could have found out what we looked like from our TV broadcasts."

"Well, that certainly makes sense, Harry," said Weinberg. "But it's still a damn fine outcome, when you consider what we were afraid might be coming."

"Actually, there's another possibility," said Brandon. "The so-called coincidences have been piling up, Bill, as you've pointed out yourself. So maybe God *has* played a role—albeit an indirect one. I think you could make a strong case. Wolf said God generally avoids making 'macro' interventions that change the course of events directly, in a major way, but he did allude to instances where it seemed that God had made *micro*-interventions to help shape events indirectly. If this wasn't something Wolf made up to embellish his story, maybe God's been operating behind the scenes here, using micro-interventions. It would explain a lot."

"That's an interesting take," said Garrett.

"Here's what I'm thinking," said Brandon. "It seems obvious that at some point after the empire folded, Wolf might have begun checking on his own to see whether the receptors had picked anything up. Eons later, when our transmission was picked up, he saw it. He was still monitoring the receptors.

"What made him stay with it for such an unimaginably long period? He was deeply committed to the cause of human survival, but most people would have given up hope. He didn't. Why? And here on Earth, Harry, Alice and I set out to raise the intelligence level of our biological and metallic people to insane levels. We thought it was strictly our own idea to do that, but what if we were *nudged* in that direction?"

Garrett laughed. "Nudged? We were recruited, by God?"

"Not exactly," said Brandon, "but He could have *inspired* the players to play their respective roles.'

"It's possible," said Garret. "So much has happened, and something special definitely played itself out in the era just passed, however it came about."

"Mind-travel was a side-effect of the genetic enhancements," Brandon continued, "and that, plus their enhanced intelligence, enabled mathematicians to prove the Hodge Conjecture. Then, it just so happened that a vision that an astronomer saw while mind traveling inspired him to send off the proof, which Wolf picked up, and the Visit followed — one coincidence after another. And let's not forget the earlier so-called coincidences that Bill mentioned, like the Malaise, which arguably kept our world from destroying itself, and the African expeditions that found the survivors before their equipment wore out and they ran out of essentials like fertilizer and medicine. But for that series of amazing coincidences, biological human life on Earth could well have become extinct long ago."

"Right," said Weinberg. "And the fact that Keisha and I were light years away so we couldn't stop you guys from engineering genes."

"Your scenario certainly is a possibility," Weinberg told Brandon. "Personally, I think Wolf had a point when he said that maybe what God does or doesn't do is none of our damn business. The main thing is that things are working out, and we should be grateful."

"So far, so good," said Garrett

"If what we've learned from our Visitors helps us prevent our biologicals from killing themselves off, we'll have you guys to thank for making our people smart enough to figure out how to make contact with our new friends," said Weinberg. "Think about that. Monuments will be built in your honor."

Garrett shrugged. "Let's just hope we're successful."

"Wolf said he thinks we have 'a shot' at saving them," said Ray. "He doesn't seem terribly optimistic."

"He knows first-hand how hard it's gonna be," said Weinberg, "especially down the road when the bios no longer seek or wish to receive our advice and counsel."

"You were smart to record their presentation," Garrett told Weinberg. "We can start by making sure they all have a chance to see it."

The men agreed to keep the matters they'd just discussed to themselves and hurried off to join the ladies.

The good news had spread, and people had poured out of buildings onto the sidewalks and into the streets. The sense of relief was palpable. The unaccustomed sound of laughter filled the air and echoed off walls. Biological women jumped up and down and squealed for joy. Biological men hooted and whooped.

"Look at them," Weinberg told Keisha. "It's like they've remembered that they're alive."

"It's a great day," said Keisha.

Bonnie and Cheng, walking arm-in-arm behind them, felt their originals, who'd managed to stay with them, relax as if a great weight had finally been lifted from their shoulders.

Acknowledgements

The authors wish to thank all the people who helped with this book. There are too many of you for us to acknowledge you all by name. But we'd be remiss if we failed to acknowledge Dr. Harry Garrett's efforts to impart to the authors enough basic knowledge of the science of genetics to have done justice, or so we hope, to all that he and his group accomplished. However, any errors or inaccuracies that may be found in our discussion of such matters — including our attempts to re-create conversations that would have occurred amongst the scientists in the course of their work — are ours exclusively.

    Keisha and Amelia Dixon
    Nairobi, 3546

Note From The Author

Word-of-mouth is crucial for any author to succeed. If you enjoyed *People of Metal II*, please leave a review online — anywhere you are able. Even if it's just a sentence or two. It would make all the difference and would be very much appreciated.

    Thanks!
    Robert

Thank you so much for reading one of Robert Snyder's novels.
If you enjoyed our book, please check out the beginning of the story.

People of Metal

The well-intentioned leaders of China and the U.S. form a grand partnership to create human robots for every human vocation in every country in the world. The human robots proliferate, economic output soars, and the entire world prospers. It's a new Golden Age. But there are unintended consequences—consequences that will place biological humanity on a road to extinction. Ultimately, it will fall to the human robots themselves to rescue biological humanity and restore its civilization.

View other Black Rose Writing titles at
www.blackrosewriting.com/books and use promo code
PRINT to receive a **20% discount** when purchasing.

Lightning Source UK Ltd.
Milton Keynes UK
UKHW011839200520
363522UK00001B/5